URBAN LEGENDZ

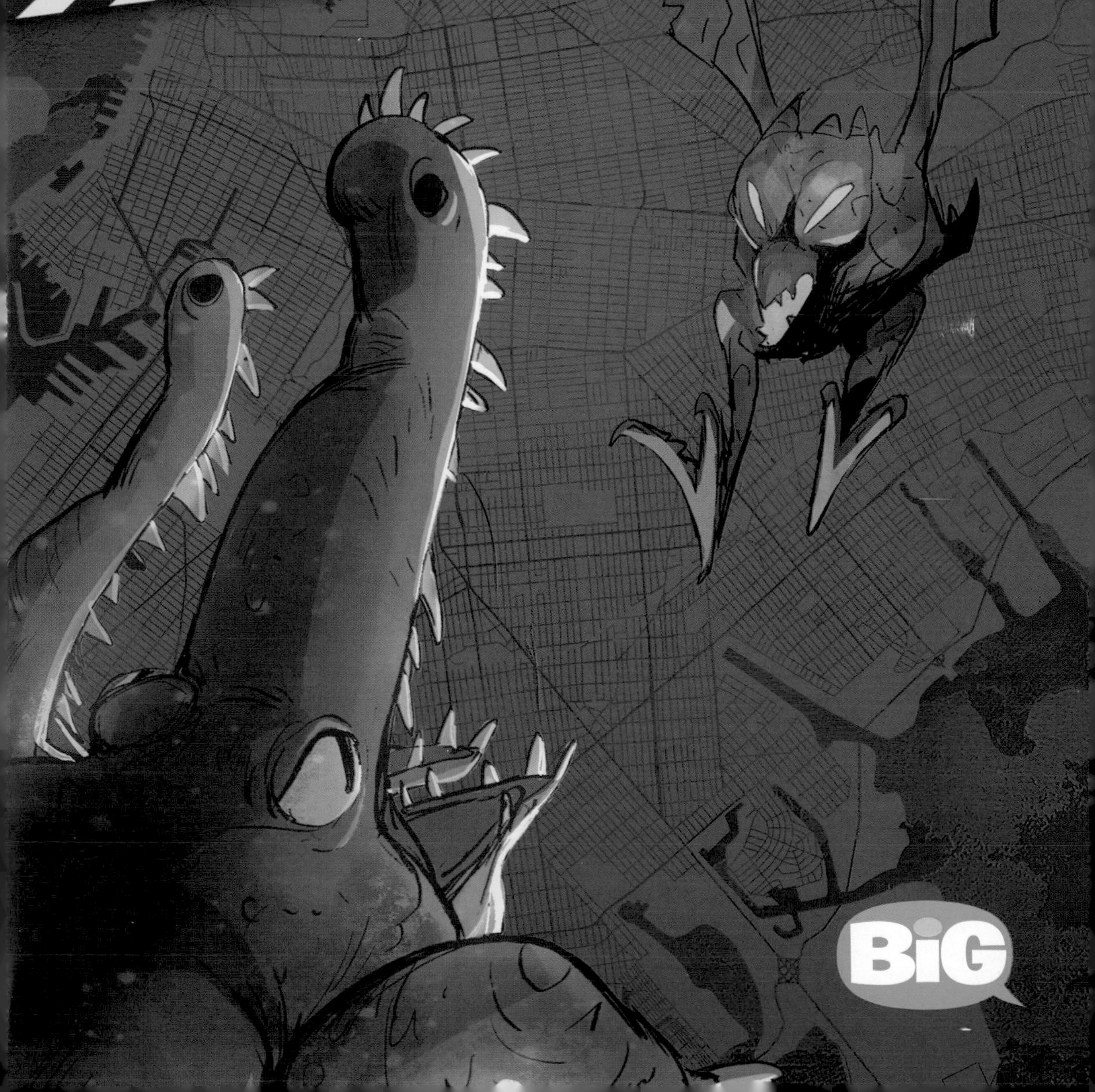
BiG

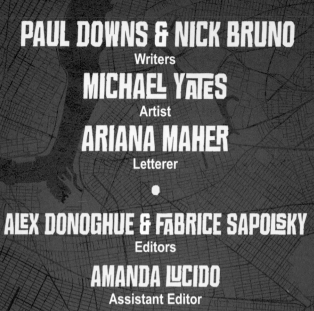

PAUL DOWNS & NICK BRUNO
Writers

MICHAEL YATES
Artist

ARIANA MAHER
Letterer

•

ALEX DONOGHUE & FABRICE SAPOLSKY
Editors

AMANDA LUCIDO
Assistant Editor

JERRY FRISSEN
Senior Art Director

FABRICE GIGER
Publisher

Rights and Licensing - licensing@humanoids.com
Press and Social Media - pr@humanoids.com

Paul Downs: *To my beautiful Jenny for supporting me (and this project) from the very beginning. To Eric and Sara for your untiring creativity. To Lisa, Jerod, Matt and Paul for your willingness to read and give notes. And to Mom, Dad, Keri, and the rest of our families and friends for your endless love and support.*

Nick Bruno: *To my children Taryn, Jake, and Jarrett! May your lives be filled with adventure, and may you always have each other to conquer it no matter how scary things may get. To my wife Allison, with you by my side, no monsters stand a chance!*

Michael Yates: *To my dad, Michael L. Yates, Sr.*

URBAN LEGENDZ. This title is a publication of Humanoids, Inc. 8033 Sunset Blvd. #628, Los Angeles, CA 90046.

Library of Congress Control Number: 2019930348

BiG is an imprint of Humanoids, Inc.

BROOKLYN, NY

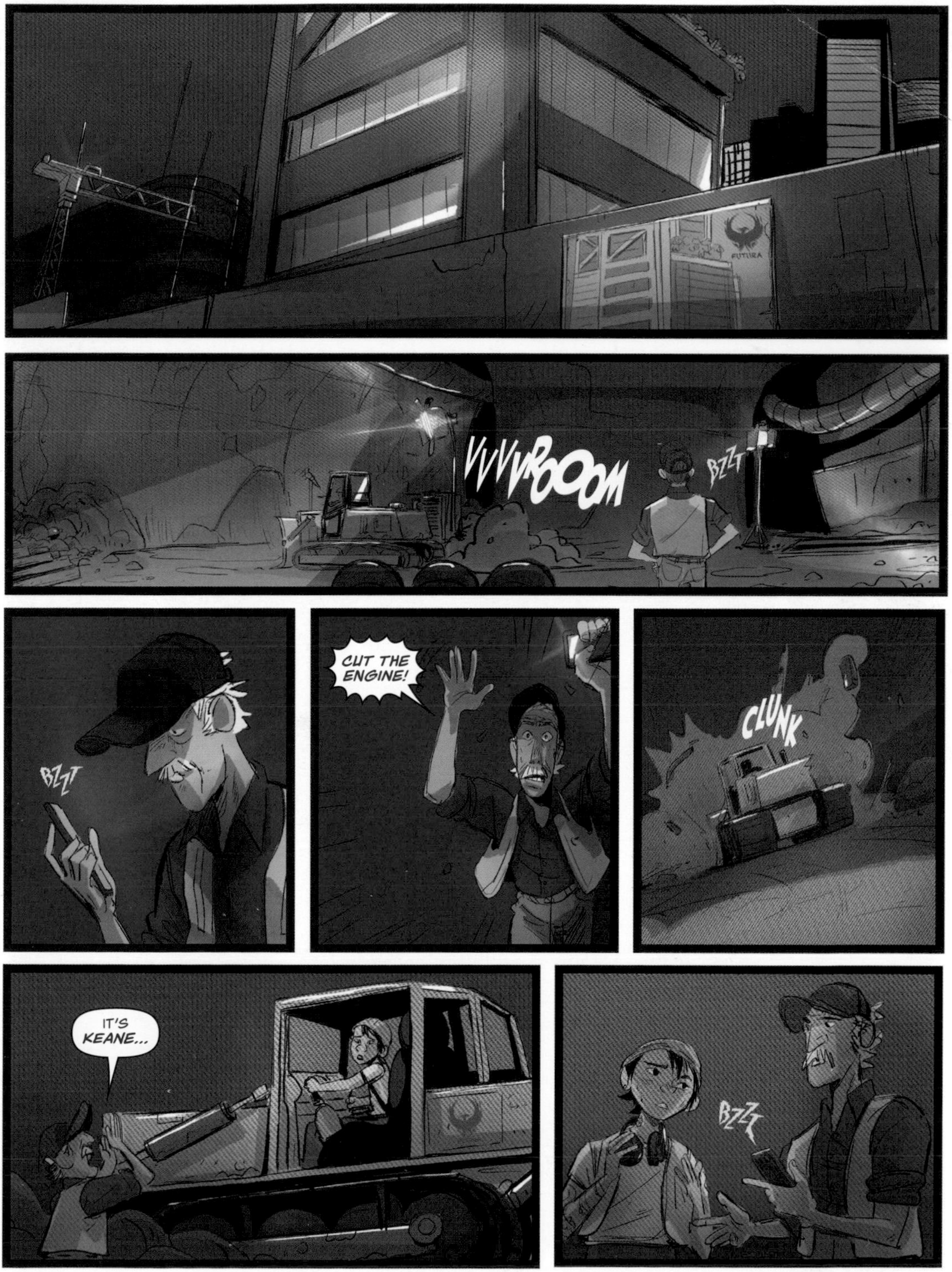
VVVVROOOM
BZZT
BZZT
CUT THE ENGINE!
CLUNK
IT'S KEANE...
BZZT

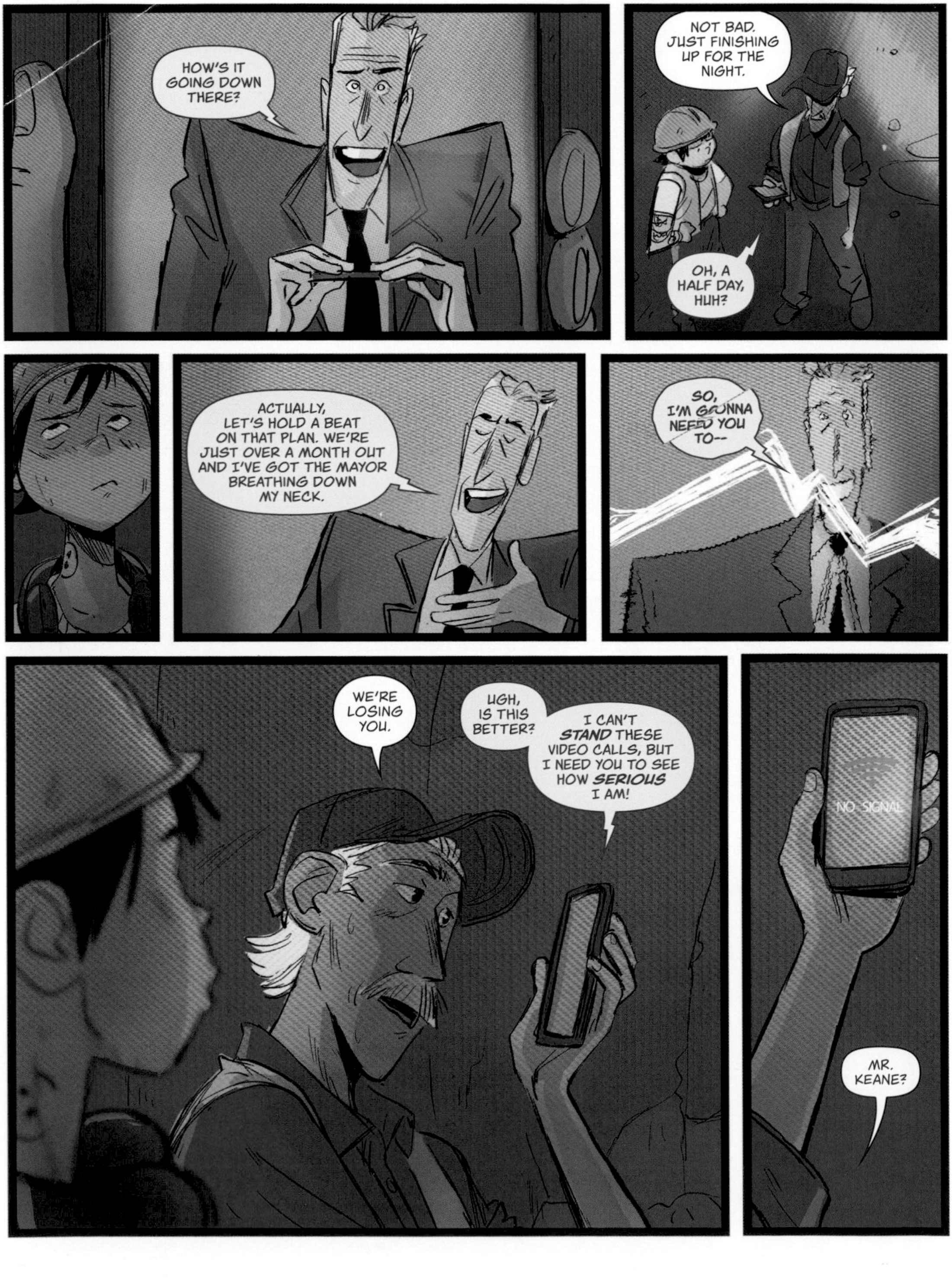
HOW'S IT GOING DOWN THERE?
NOT BAD. JUST FINISHING UP FOR THE NIGHT.
OH, A HALF DAY, HUH?
ACTUALLY, LET'S HOLD A BEAT ON THAT PLAN. WE'RE JUST OVER A MONTH OUT AND I'VE GOT THE MAYOR BREATHING DOWN MY NECK.
SO, I'M GONNA NEED YOU TO--
WE'RE LOSING YOU.
UGH, IS THIS BETTER?
I CAN'T STAND THESE VIDEO CALLS, BUT I NEED YOU TO SEE HOW SERIOUS I AM!
NO SIGNAL
MR. KEANE?

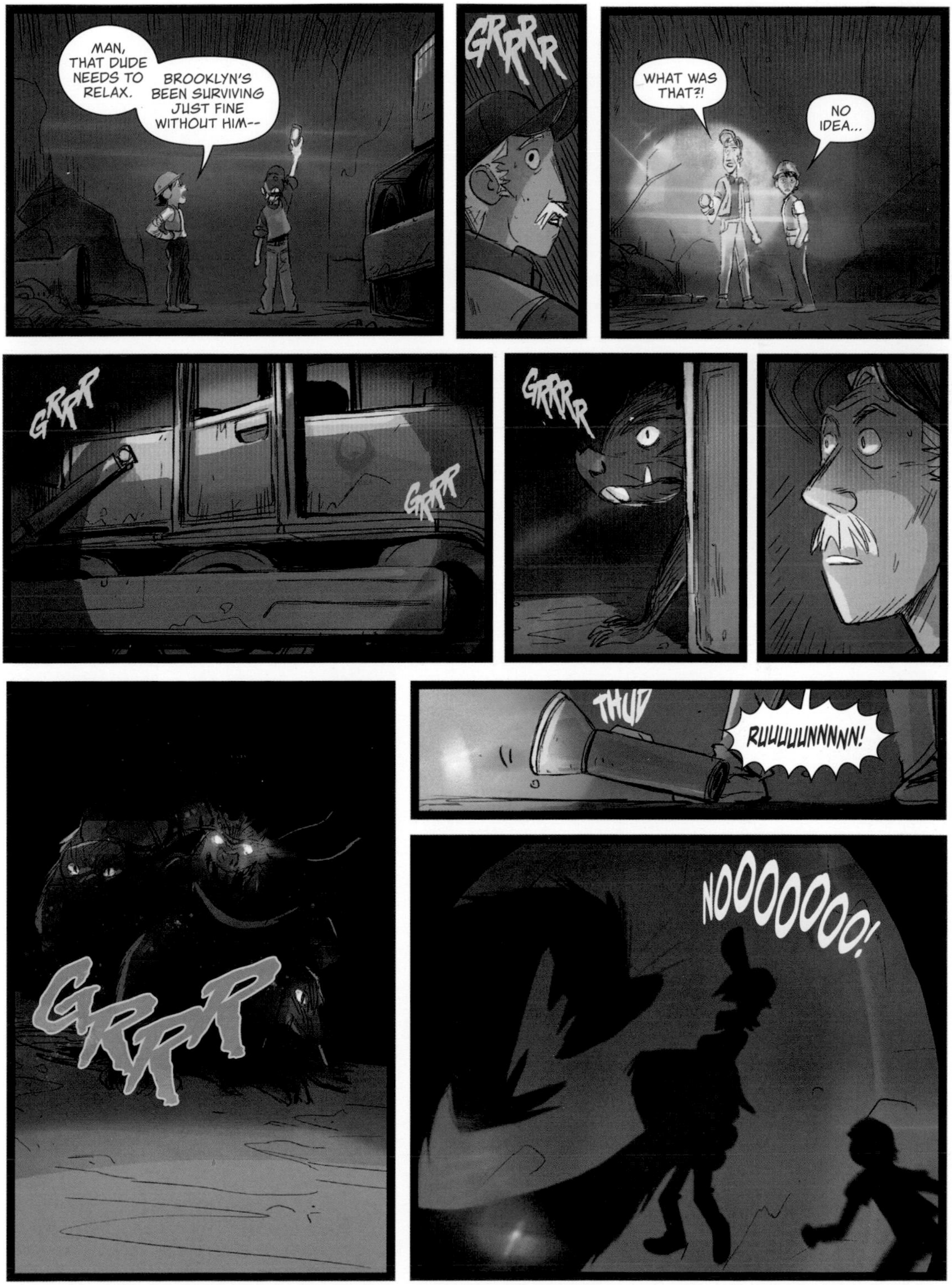
MAN, THAT DUDE NEEDS TO RELAX.
BROOKLYN'S BEEN SURVIVING JUST FINE WITHOUT HIM--
GRRRR
WHAT WAS THAT?!
NO IDEA...
GRRR
GRRR
GRRRR
GRRR
THUD
RUUUUUNNNNN!
NOOOOOOO!

ONE MONTH LATER

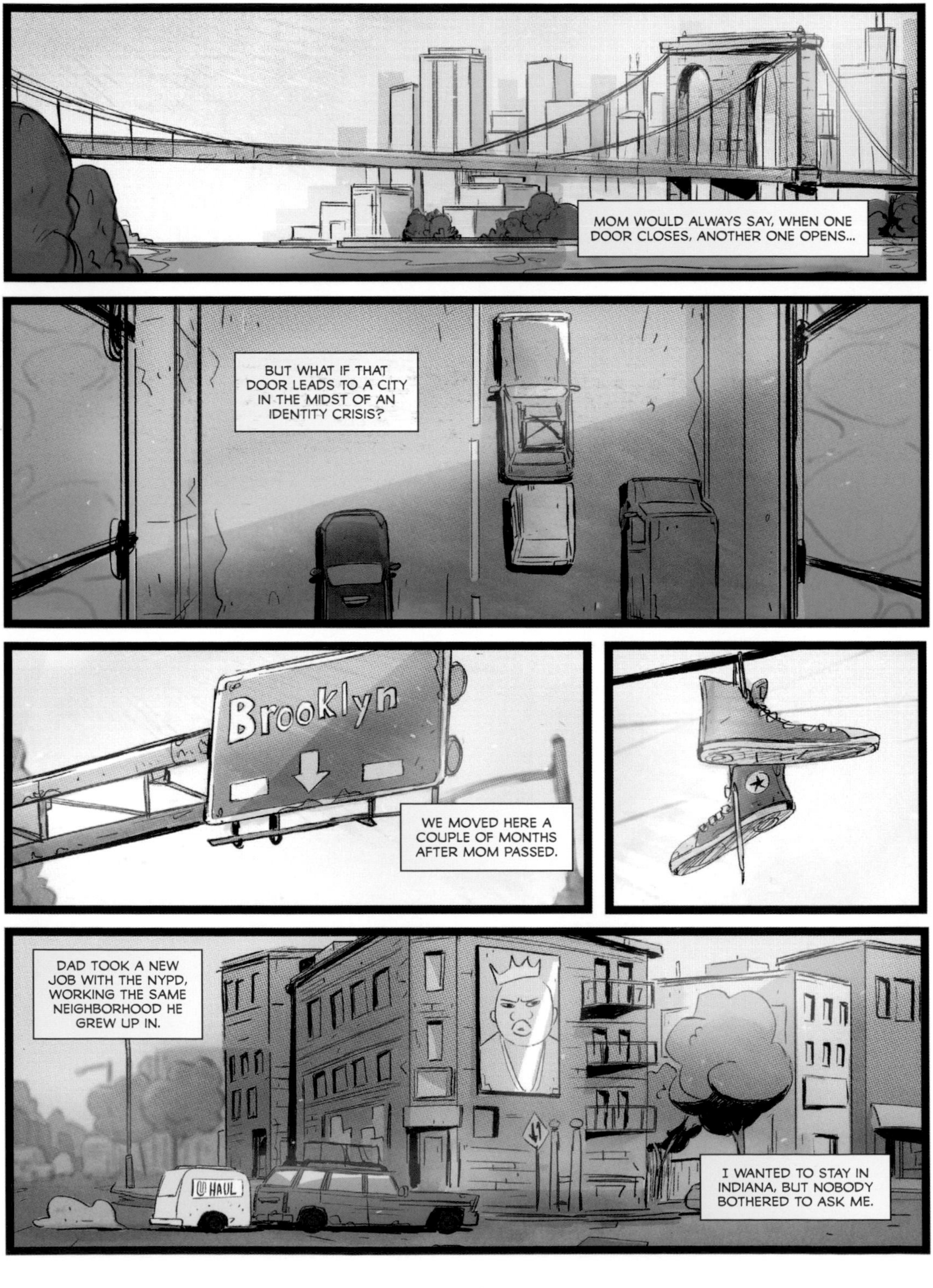
MOM WOULD ALWAYS SAY, WHEN ONE DOOR CLOSES, ANOTHER ONE OPENS...
BUT WHAT IF THAT DOOR LEADS TO A CITY IN THE MIDST OF AN IDENTITY CRISIS?
Brooklyn
WE MOVED HERE A COUPLE OF MONTHS AFTER MOM PASSED.
DAD TOOK A NEW JOB WITH THE NYPD, WORKING THE SAME NEIGHBORHOOD HE GREW UP IN.
I WANTED TO STAY IN INDIANA, BUT NOBODY BOTHERED TO ASK ME.

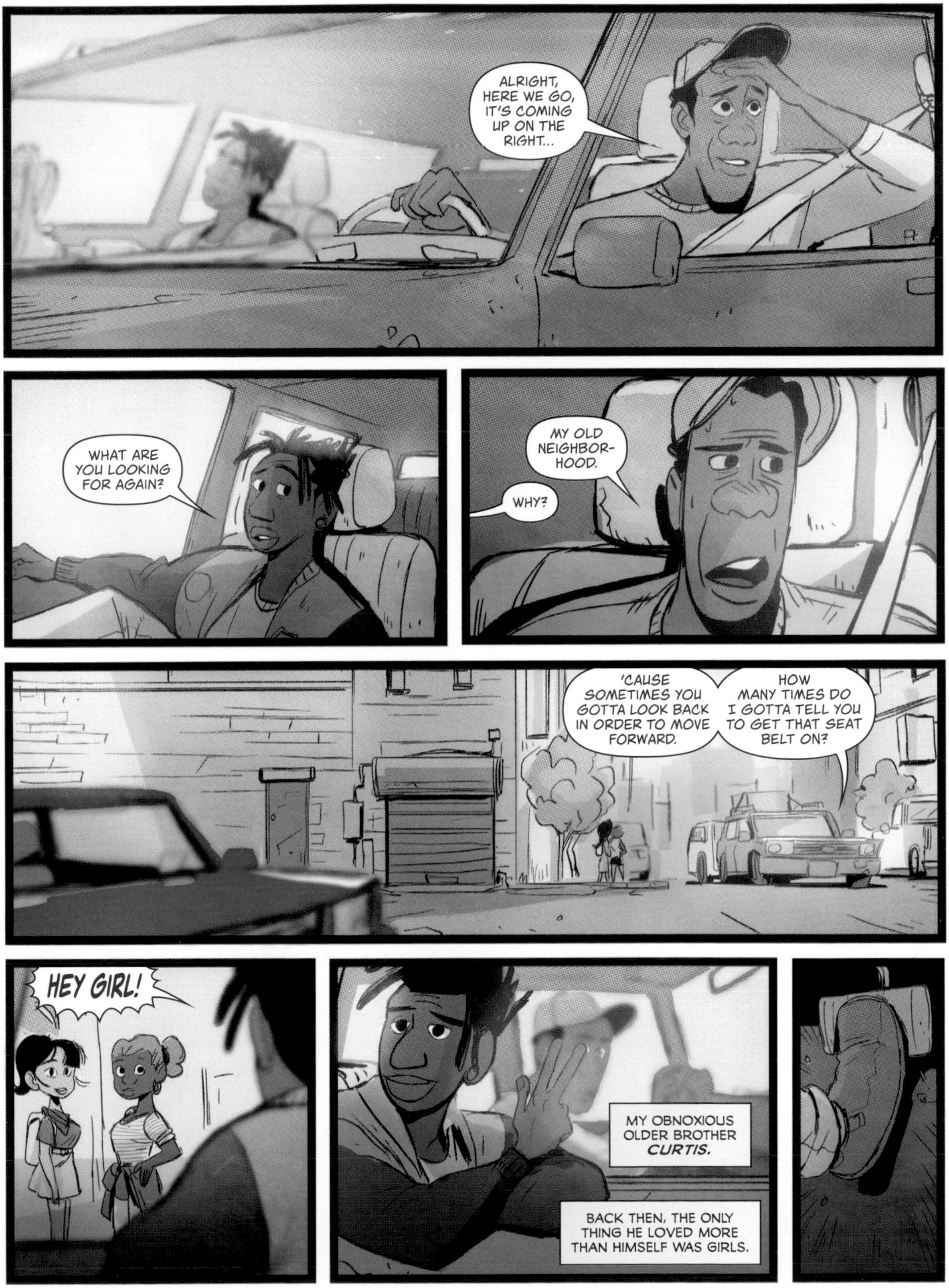

ALRIGHT, HERE WE GO, IT'S COMING UP ON THE RIGHT...
WHAT ARE YOU LOOKING FOR AGAIN?
MY OLD NEIGHBOR-HOOD.
WHY?
'CAUSE SOMETIMES YOU GOTTA LOOK BACK IN ORDER TO MOVE FORWARD.
HOW MANY TIMES DO I GOTTA TELL YOU TO GET THAT SEAT BELT ON?
HEY GIRL!
MY OBNOXIOUS OLDER BROTHER *CURTIS.*
BACK THEN, THE ONLY THING HE LOVED MORE THAN HIMSELF WAS GIRLS.

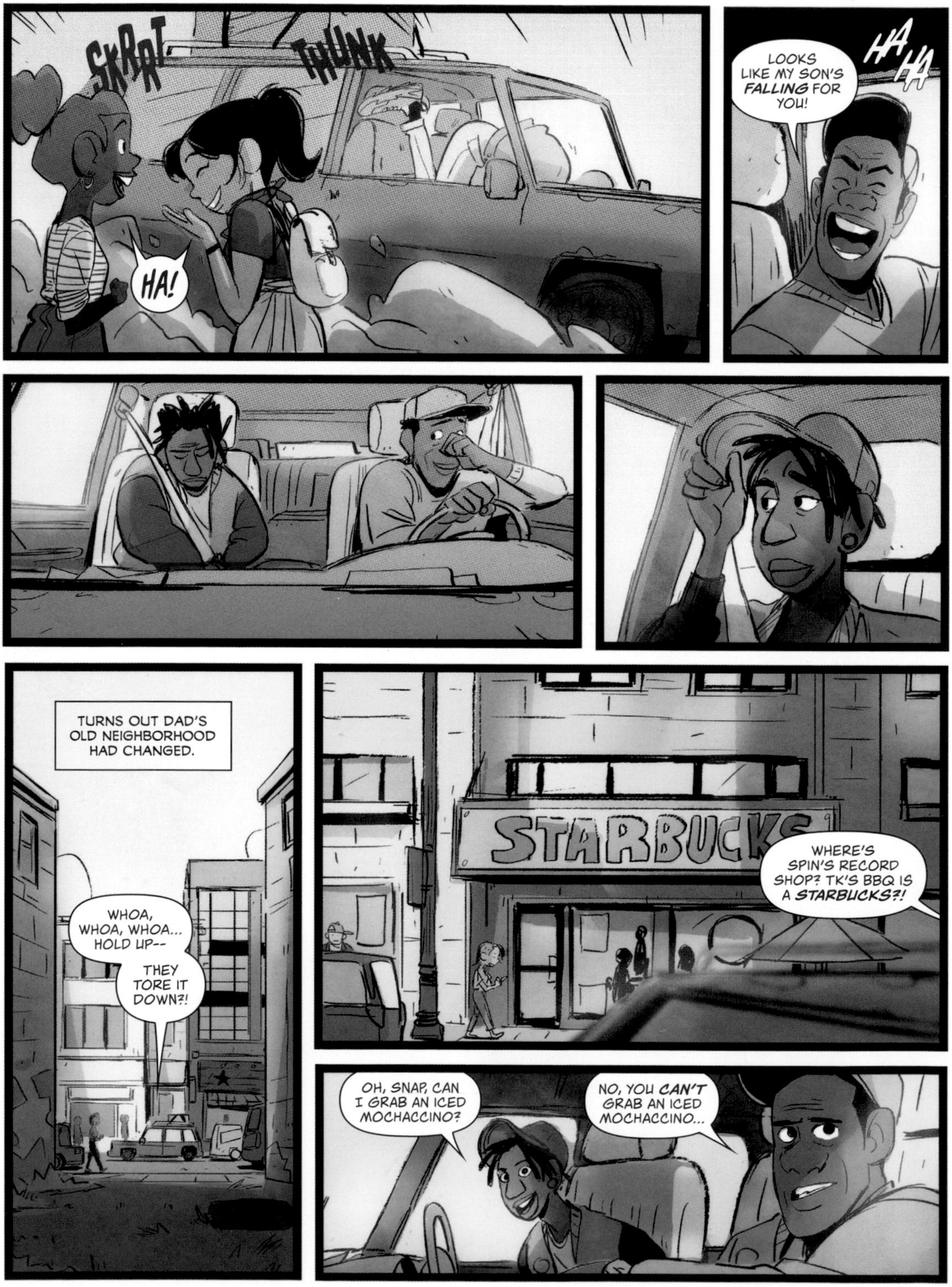
SKRRT
THUNK
HA!
HA HA
LOOKS LIKE MY SON'S ***FALLING*** FOR YOU!
TURNS OUT DAD'S OLD NEIGHBORHOOD HAD CHANGED.
WHOA, WHOA, WHOA... HOLD UP--
THEY TORE IT DOWN?!
STARBUCKS
WHERE'S SPIN'S RECORD SHOP? TK'S BBQ IS A ***STARBUCKS?!***
OH, SNAP, CAN I GRAB AN ICED MOCHACCINO?
NO, YOU ***CAN'T*** GRAB AN ICED MOCHACCINO...

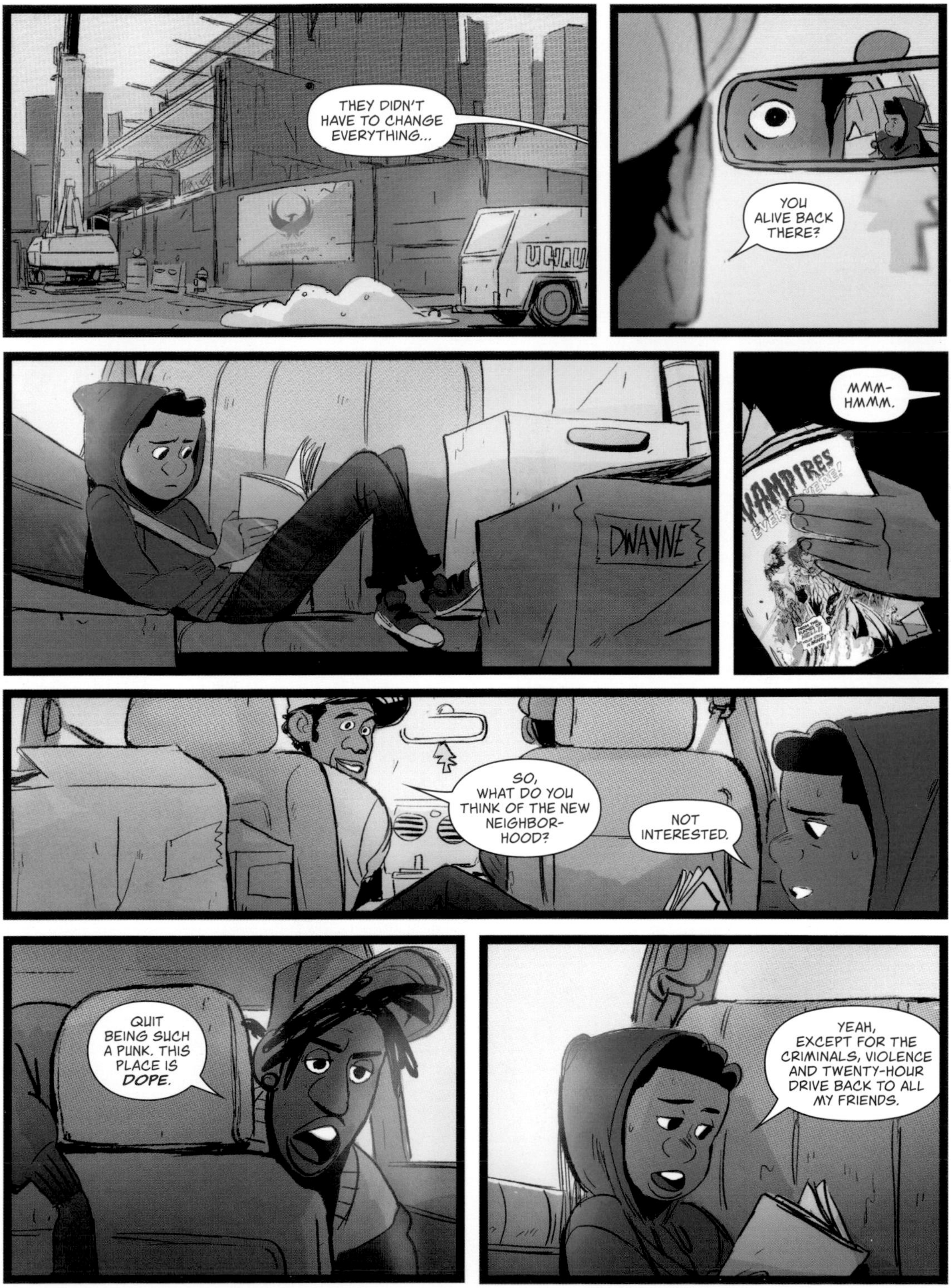
THEY DIDN'T HAVE TO CHANGE EVERYTHING...
YOU ALIVE BACK THERE?
DWAYNE
MMM-HMMM.
VAMPIRES
SO, WHAT DO YOU THINK OF THE NEW NEIGHBOR-HOOD?
NOT INTERESTED.
QUIT BEING SUCH A PUNK. THIS PLACE IS *DOPE*.
YEAH, EXCEPT FOR THE CRIMINALS, VIOLENCE AND TWENTY-HOUR DRIVE BACK TO ALL MY FRIENDS.

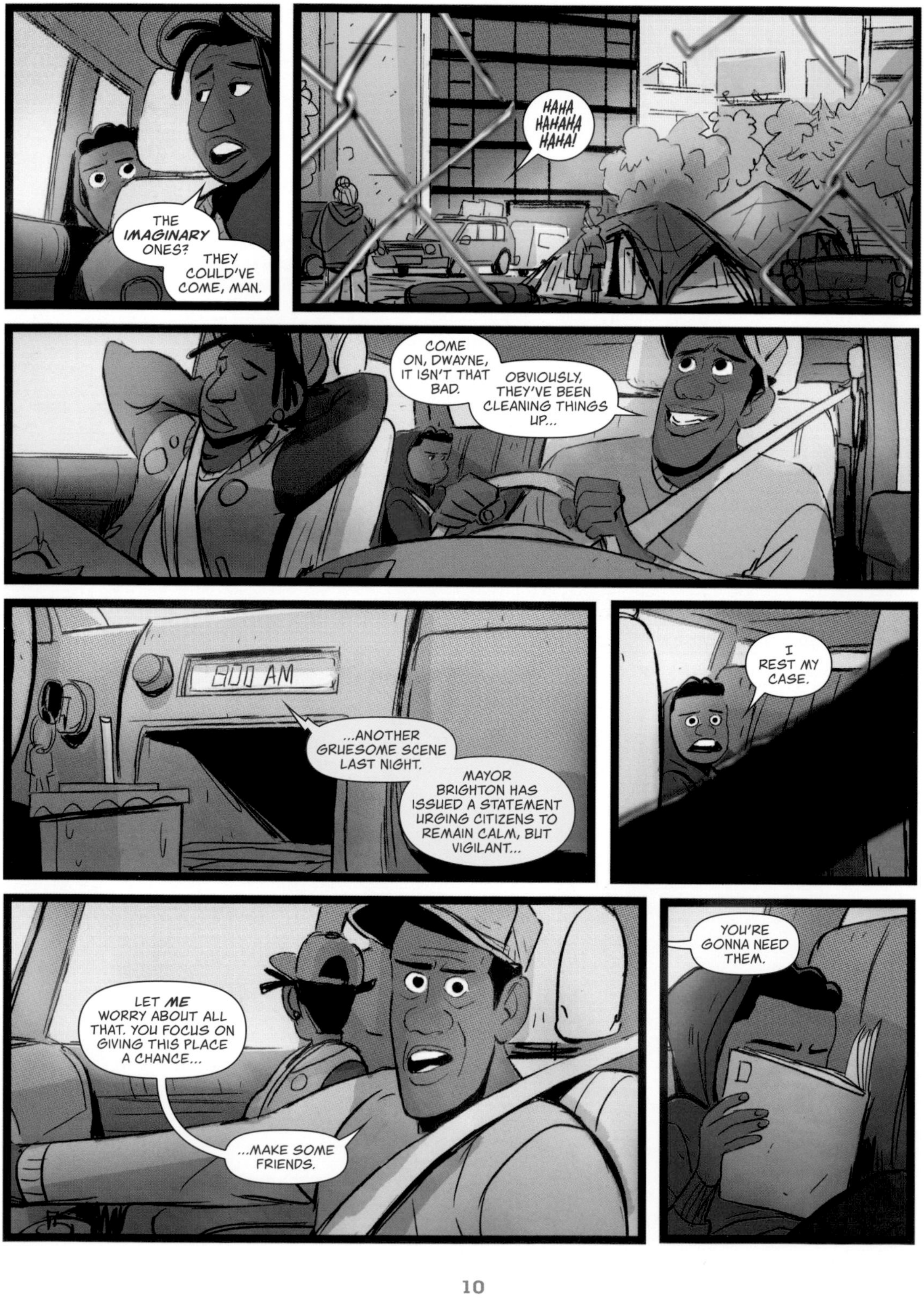
THE IMAGINARY ONES? THEY COULD'VE COME, MAN.
HAHA HAHAHA HAHA!
COME ON, DWAYNE, IT ISN'T THAT BAD.
OBVIOUSLY, THEY'VE BEEN CLEANING THINGS UP...
8:00 AM
...ANOTHER GRUESOME SCENE LAST NIGHT.
MAYOR BRIGHTON HAS ISSUED A STATEMENT URGING CITIZENS TO REMAIN CALM, BUT VIGILANT...
I REST MY CASE.
LET ME WORRY ABOUT ALL THAT. YOU FOCUS ON GIVING THIS PLACE A CHANCE...
...MAKE SOME FRIENDS.
YOU'RE GONNA NEED THEM.

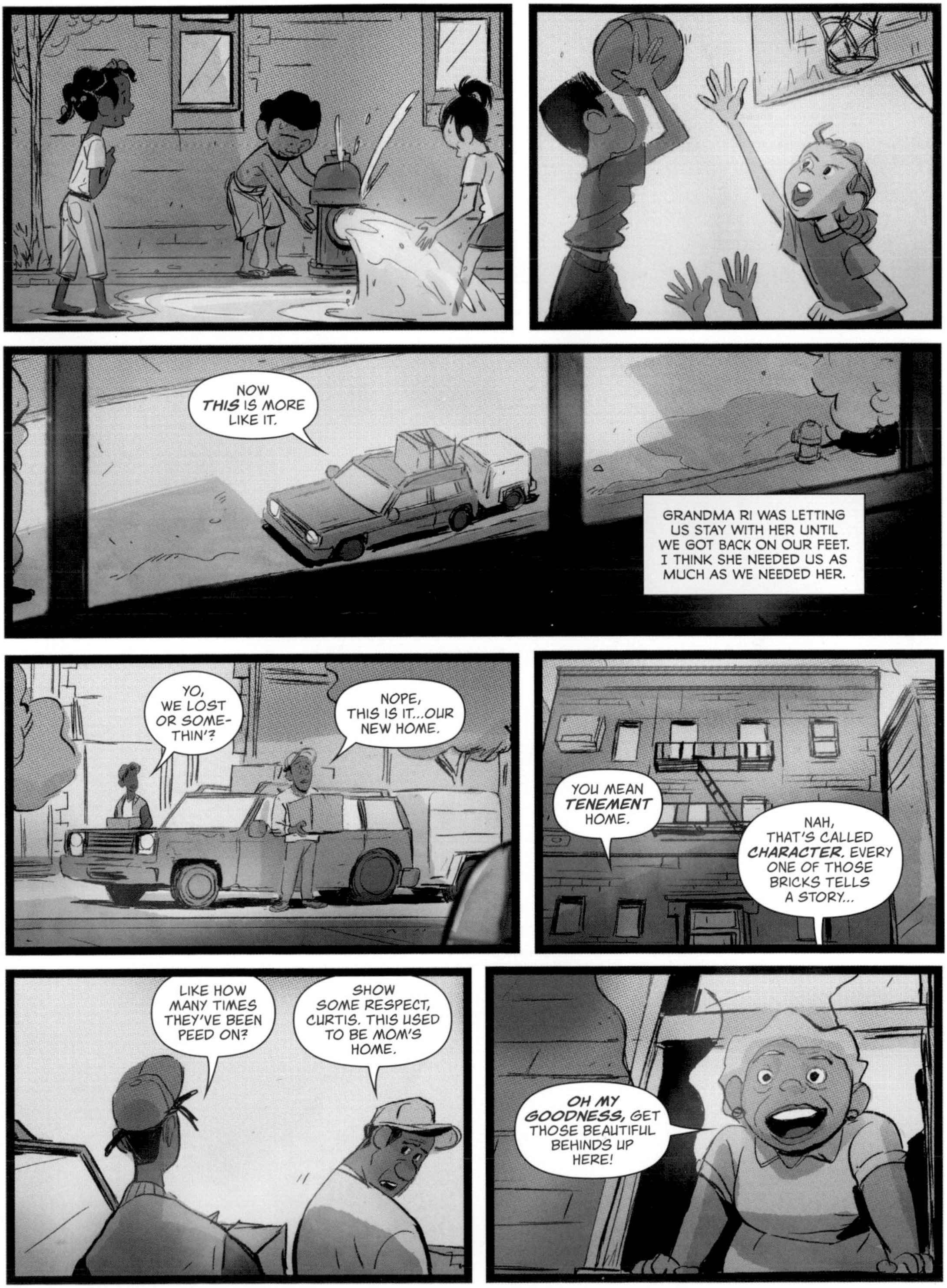
NOW THIS IS MORE LIKE IT.
GRANDMA RI WAS LETTING US STAY WITH HER UNTIL WE GOT BACK ON OUR FEET. I THINK SHE NEEDED US AS MUCH AS WE NEEDED HER.
YO, WE LOST OR SOME-THIN'?
NOPE, THIS IS IT...OUR NEW HOME.
YOU MEAN TENEMENT HOME.
NAH, THAT'S CALLED CHARACTER. EVERY ONE OF THOSE BRICKS TELLS A STORY...
LIKE HOW MANY TIMES THEY'VE BEEN PEED ON?
SHOW SOME RESPECT, CURTIS. THIS USED TO BE MOM'S HOME.
OH MY GOODNESS, GET THOSE BEAUTIFUL BEHINDS UP HERE!

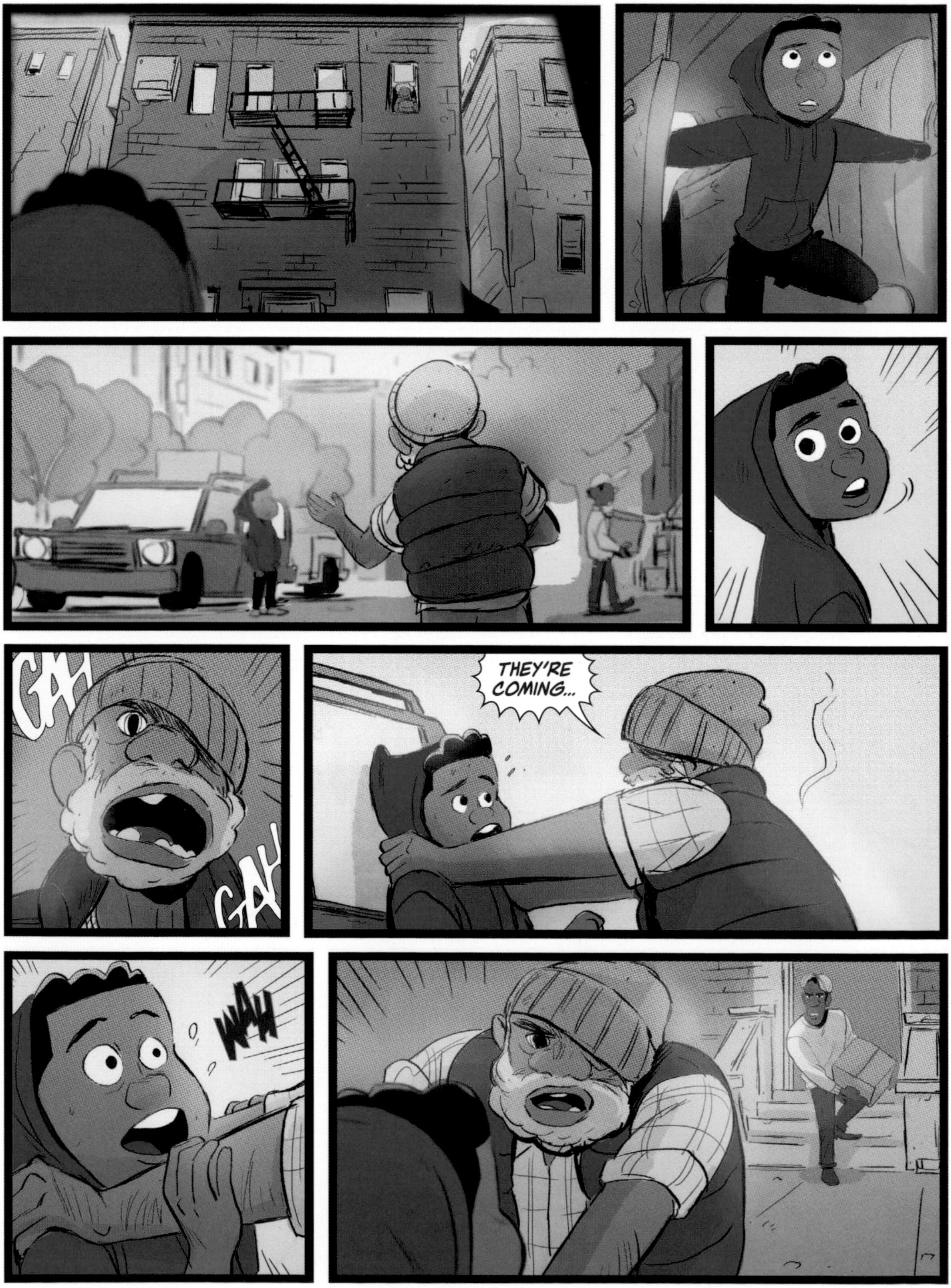
GAH
GAH
THEY'RE COMING...
WAH

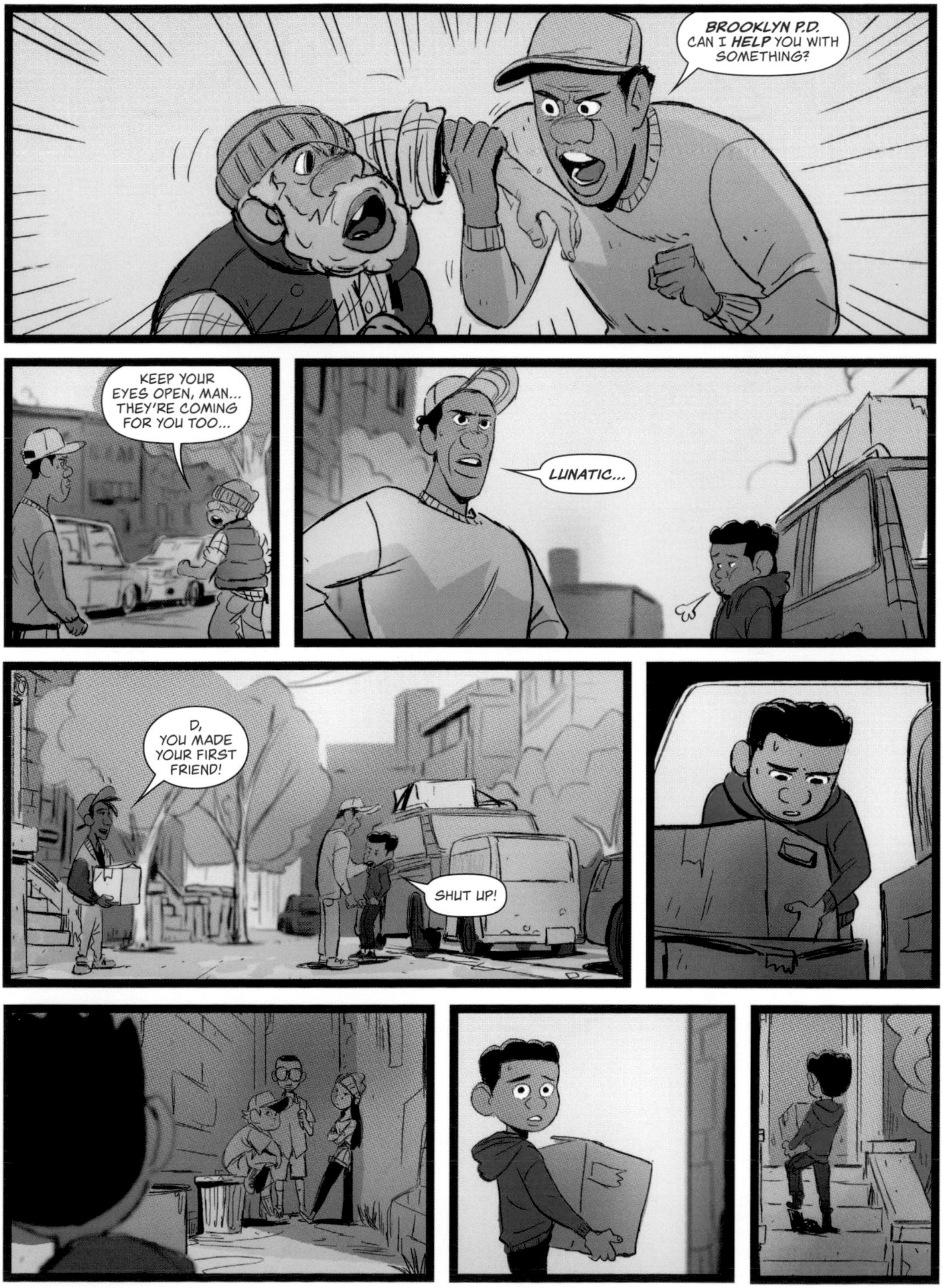
BROOKLYN P.D. CAN I HELP YOU WITH SOMETHING?
KEEP YOUR EYES OPEN, MAN... THEY'RE COMING FOR YOU TOO...
LUNATIC...
D, YOU MADE YOUR FIRST FRIEND!
SHUT UP!

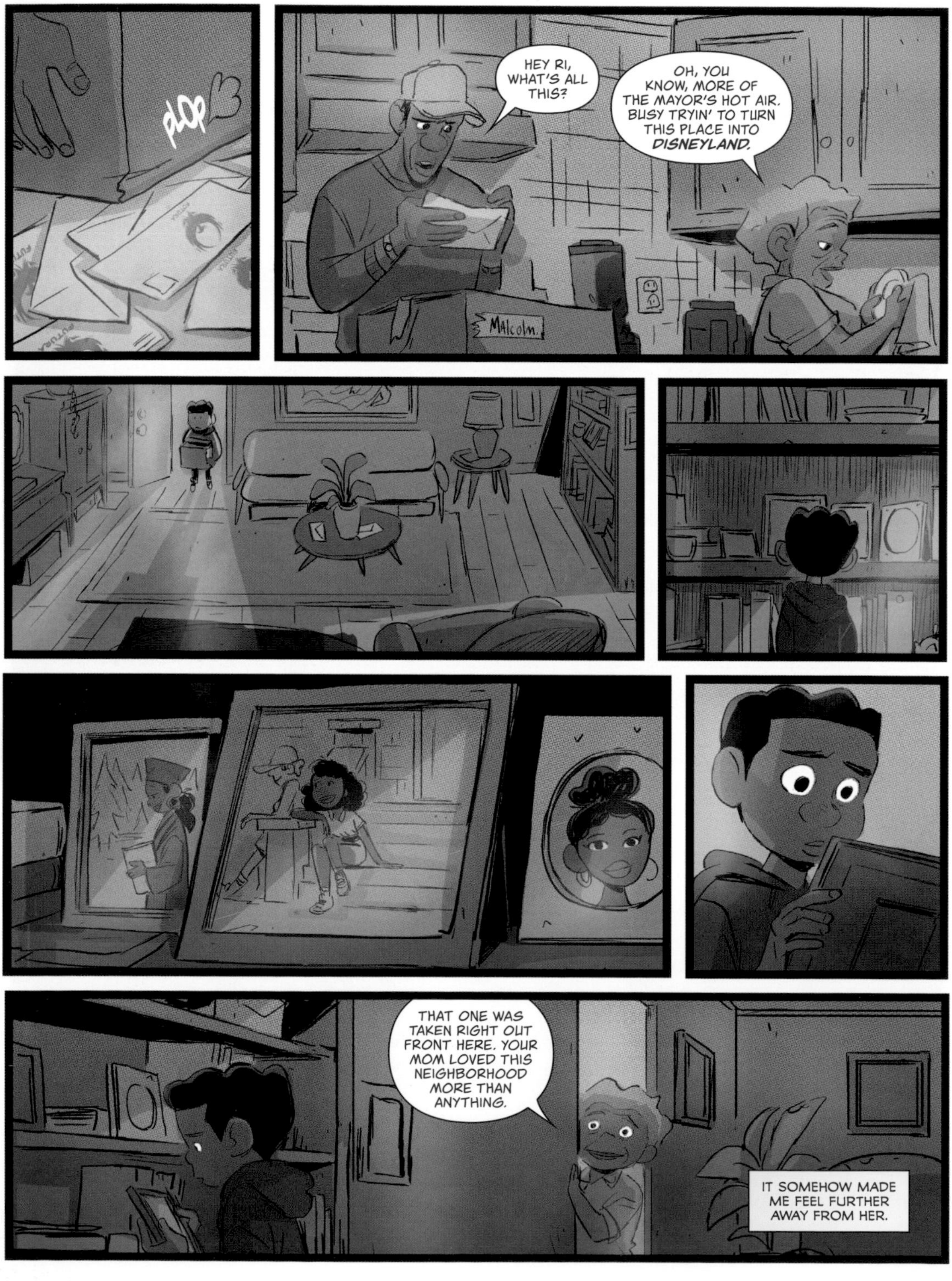
PLOP
HEY RI, WHAT'S ALL THIS?
OH, YOU KNOW, MORE OF THE MAYOR'S HOT AIR. BUSY TRYIN' TO TURN THIS PLACE INTO **DISNEYLAND.**
MALCOLM.
THAT ONE WAS TAKEN RIGHT OUT FRONT HERE. YOUR MOM LOVED THIS NEIGHBORHOOD MORE THAN ANYTHING.
IT SOMEHOW MADE ME FEEL FURTHER AWAY FROM HER.

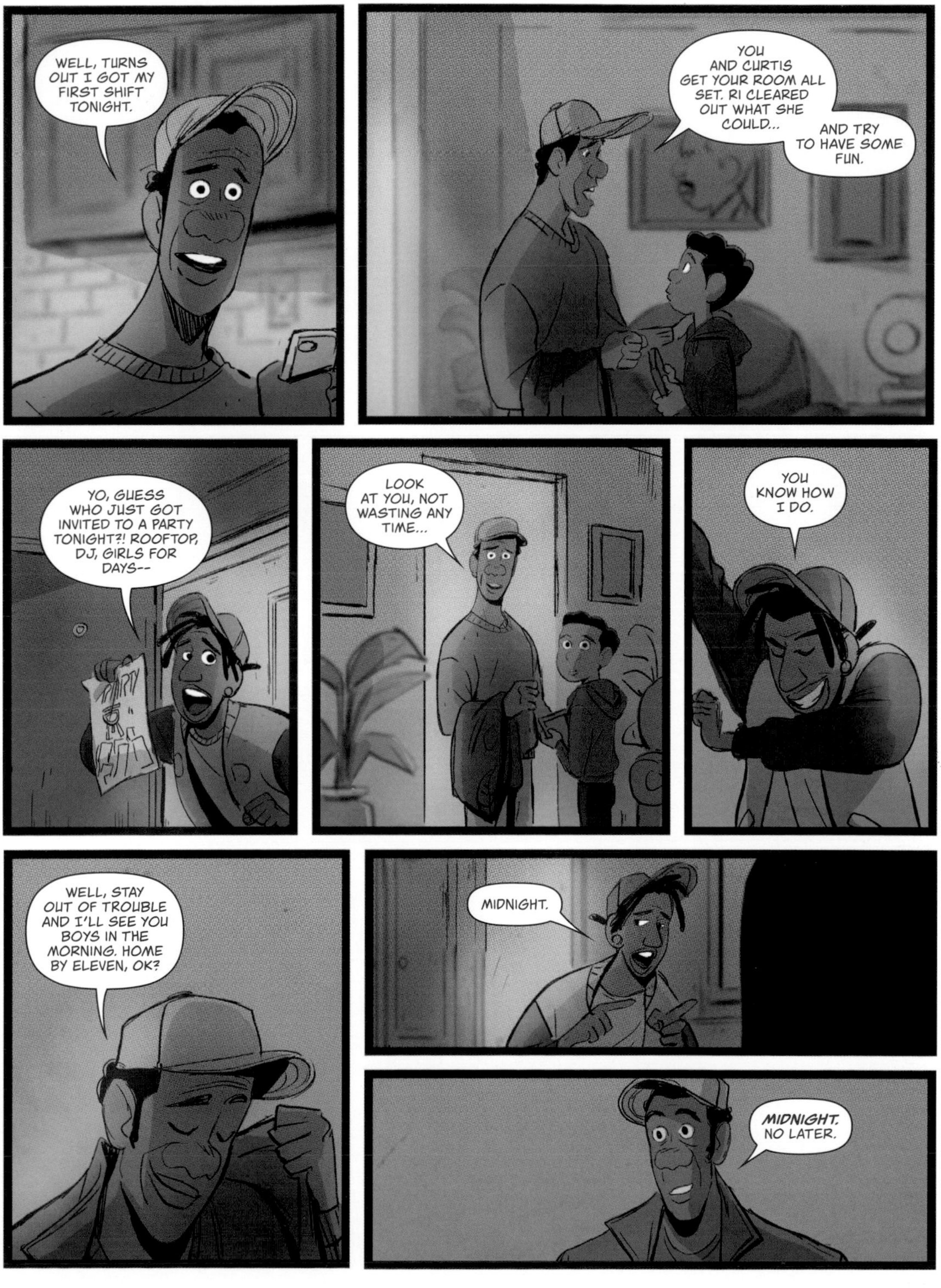
WELL, TURNS OUT I GOT MY FIRST SHIFT TONIGHT.
YOU AND CURTIS GET YOUR ROOM ALL SET. RI CLEARED OUT WHAT SHE COULD...
AND TRY TO HAVE SOME FUN.
YO, GUESS WHO JUST GOT INVITED TO A PARTY TONIGHT?! ROOFTOP, DJ, GIRLS FOR DAYS--
LOOK AT YOU, NOT WASTING ANY TIME...
YOU KNOW HOW I DO.
WELL, STAY OUT OF TROUBLE AND I'LL SEE YOU BOYS IN THE MORNING. HOME BY ELEVEN, OK?
MIDNIGHT.
MIDNIGHT. NO LATER.

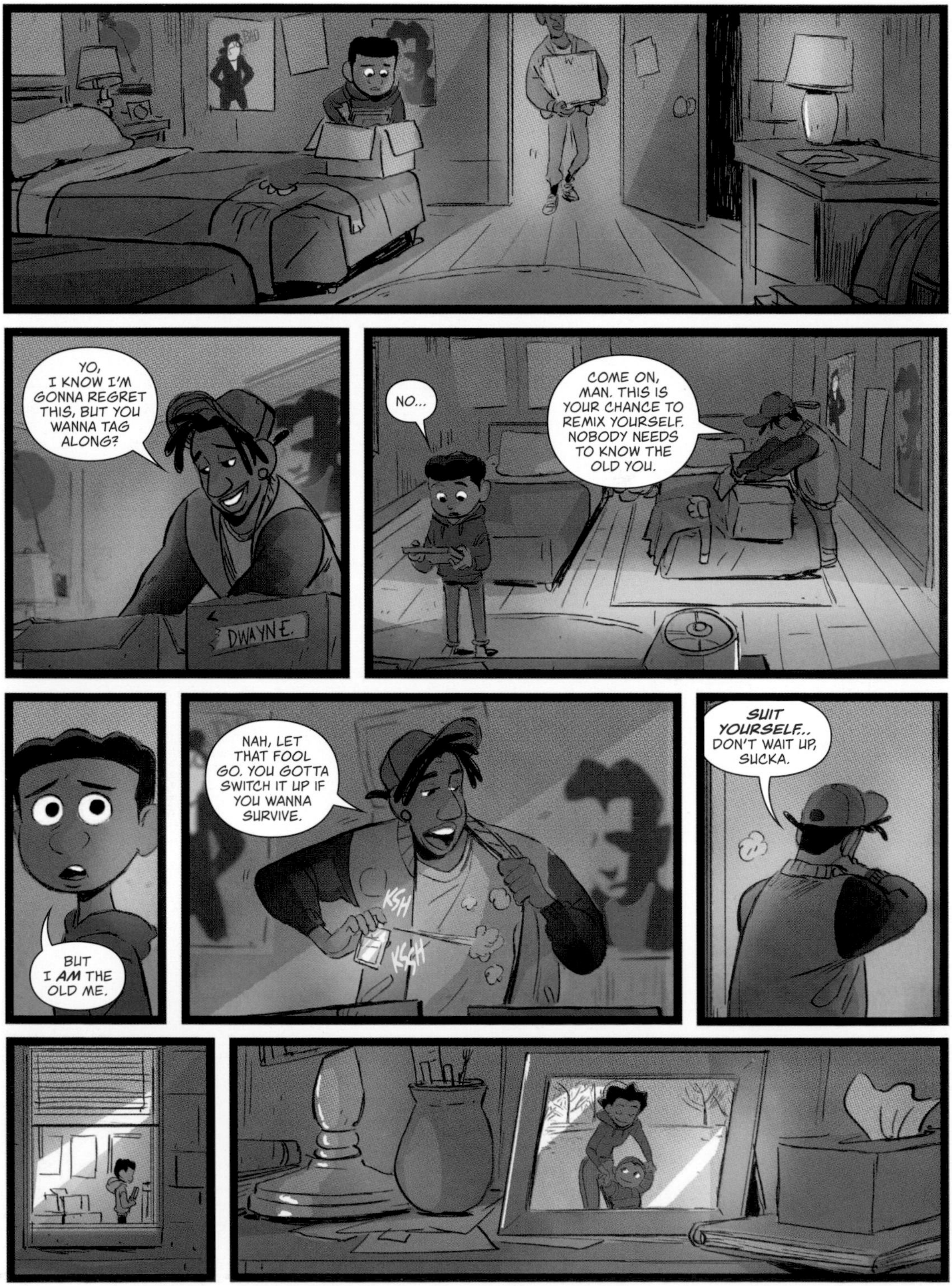
YO, I KNOW I'M GONNA REGRET THIS, BUT YOU WANNA TAG ALONG?
DWAYNE.
NO...
COME ON, MAN. THIS IS YOUR CHANCE TO REMIX YOURSELF. NOBODY NEEDS TO KNOW THE OLD YOU.
BUT I *AM* THE OLD ME.
NAH, LET THAT FOOL GO. YOU GOTTA SWITCH IT UP IF YOU WANNA SURVIVE.
KSH
KSSH
SUIT YOURSELF.. DON'T WAIT UP, SUCKA.

BROOKLYN BRIDGE PARK

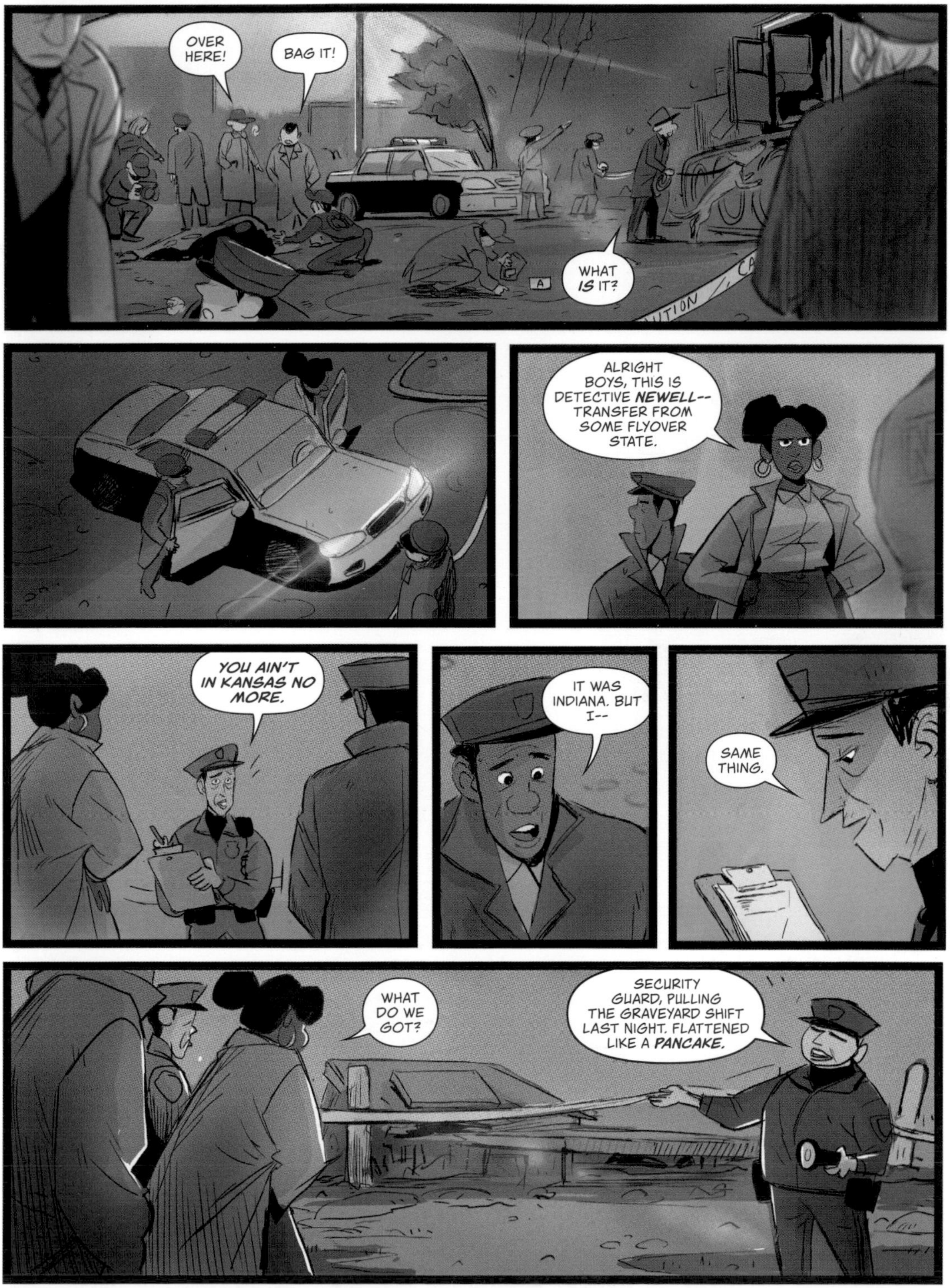

OVER HERE!
BAG IT!
WHAT *IS* IT?
ALRIGHT BOYS, THIS IS DETECTIVE *NEWELL*-- TRANSFER FROM SOME FLYOVER STATE.
YOU AIN'T IN KANSAS NO MORE.
IT WAS INDIANA. BUT I--
SAME THING.
WHAT DO WE GOT?
SECURITY GUARD, PULLING THE GRAVEYARD SHIFT LAST NIGHT. FLATTENED LIKE A *PANCAKE.*

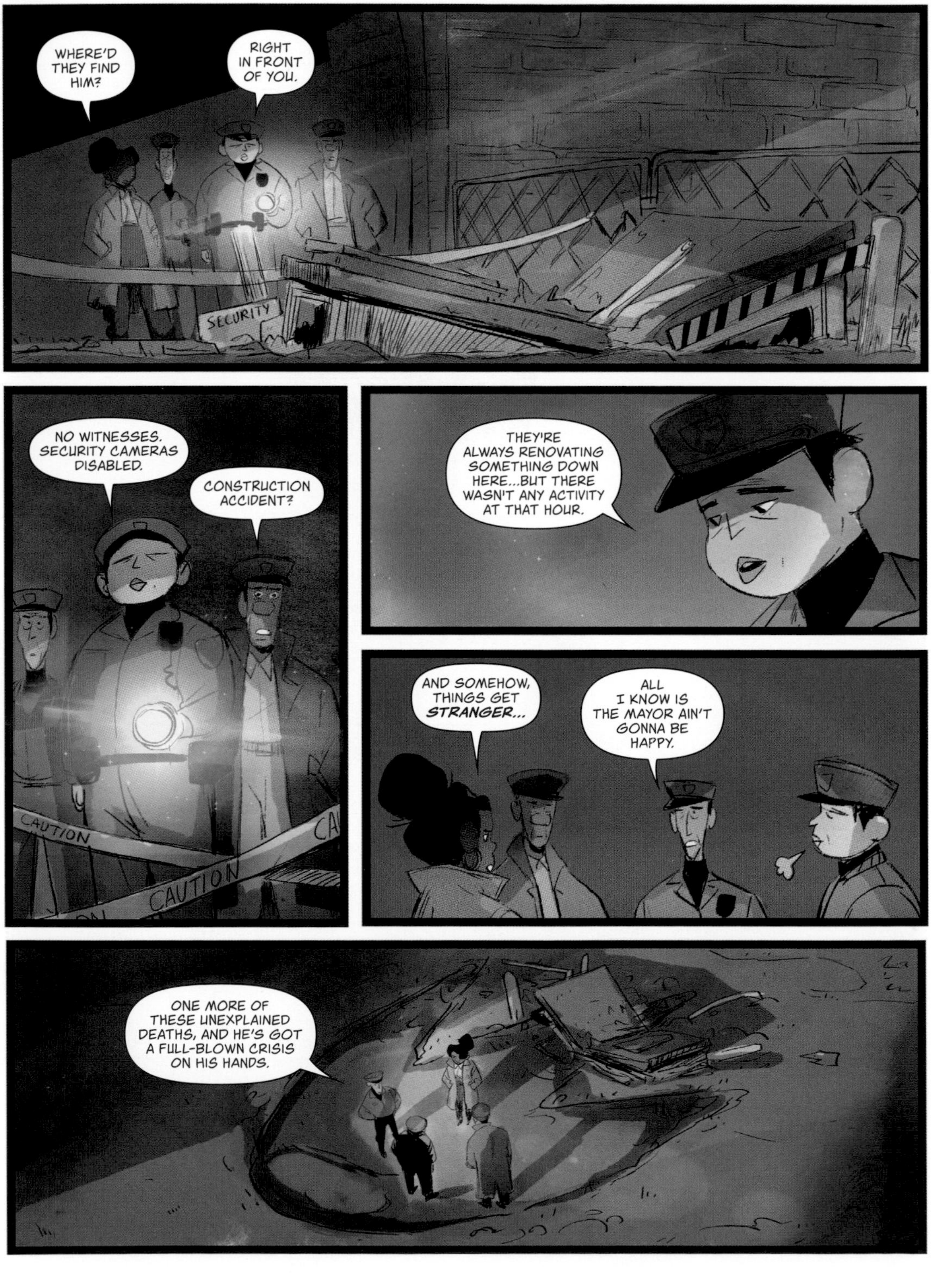
WHERE'D THEY FIND HIM?
RIGHT IN FRONT OF YOU.
SECURITY
NO WITNESSES. SECURITY CAMERAS DISABLED.
CONSTRUCTION ACCIDENT?
CAUTION
CAUTION
THEY'RE ALWAYS RENOVATING SOMETHING DOWN HERE...BUT THERE WASN'T ANY ACTIVITY AT THAT HOUR.
AND SOMEHOW, THINGS GET *STRANGER...*
ALL I KNOW IS THE MAYOR AIN'T GONNA BE HAPPY.
ONE MORE OF THESE UNEXPLAINED DEATHS, AND HE'S GOT A FULL-BLOWN CRISIS ON HIS HANDS.

MEANWHILE IN BED-STUY...

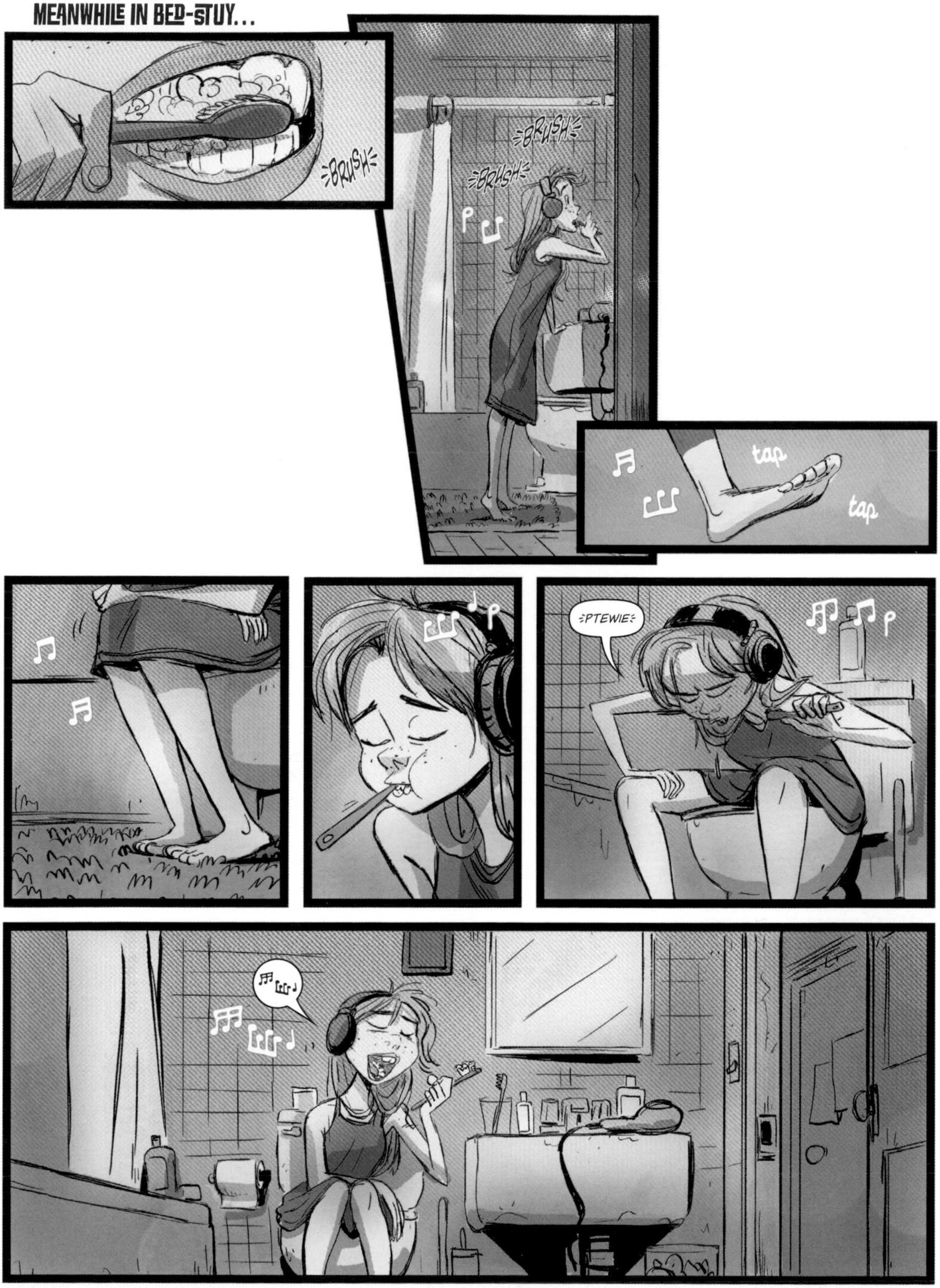
BRUSH
BRUSH
BRUSH
tap
tap
PTEWIE

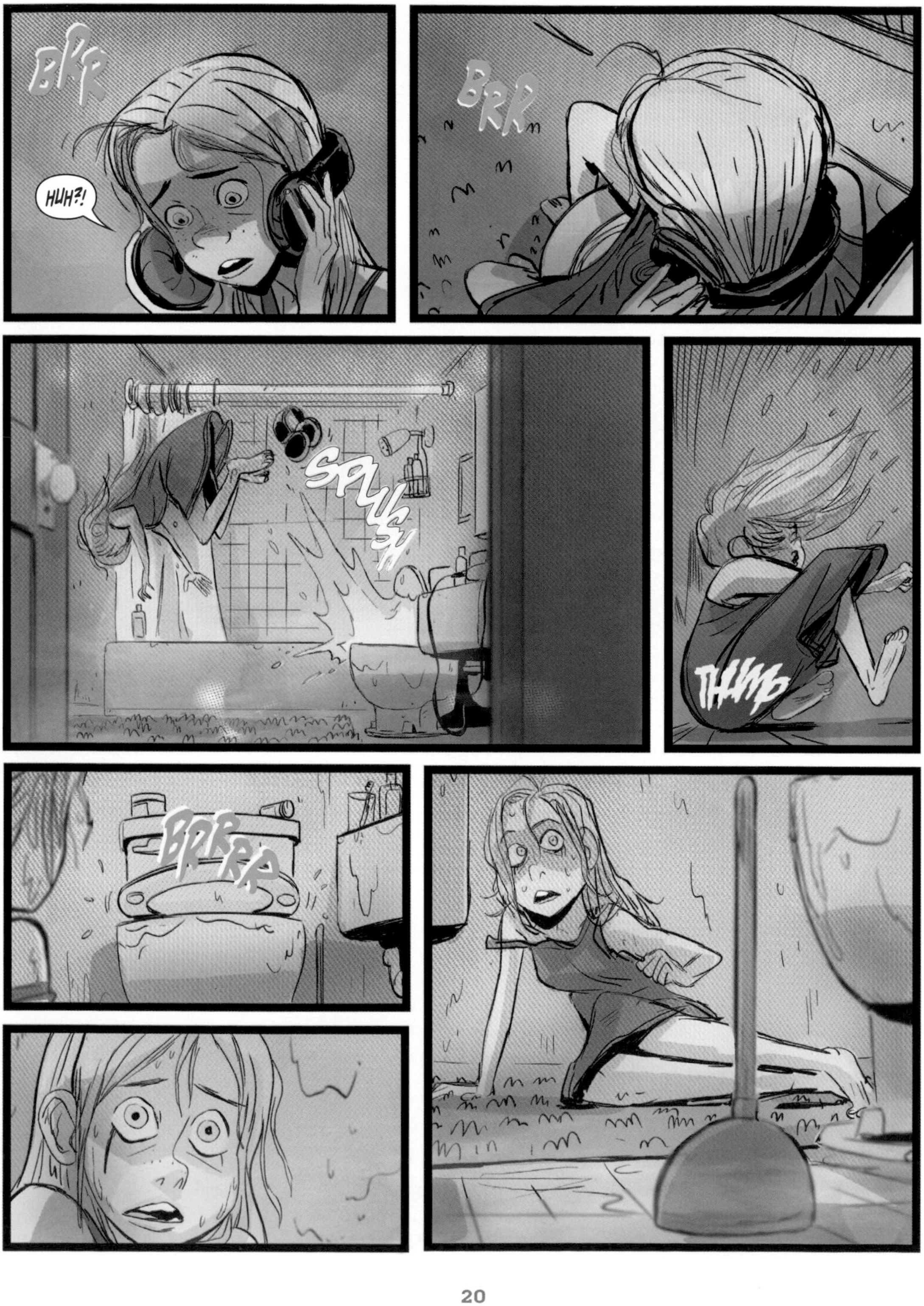
BRR
HUH?!
BRR
SPLUSH
THUMP
BRRRR

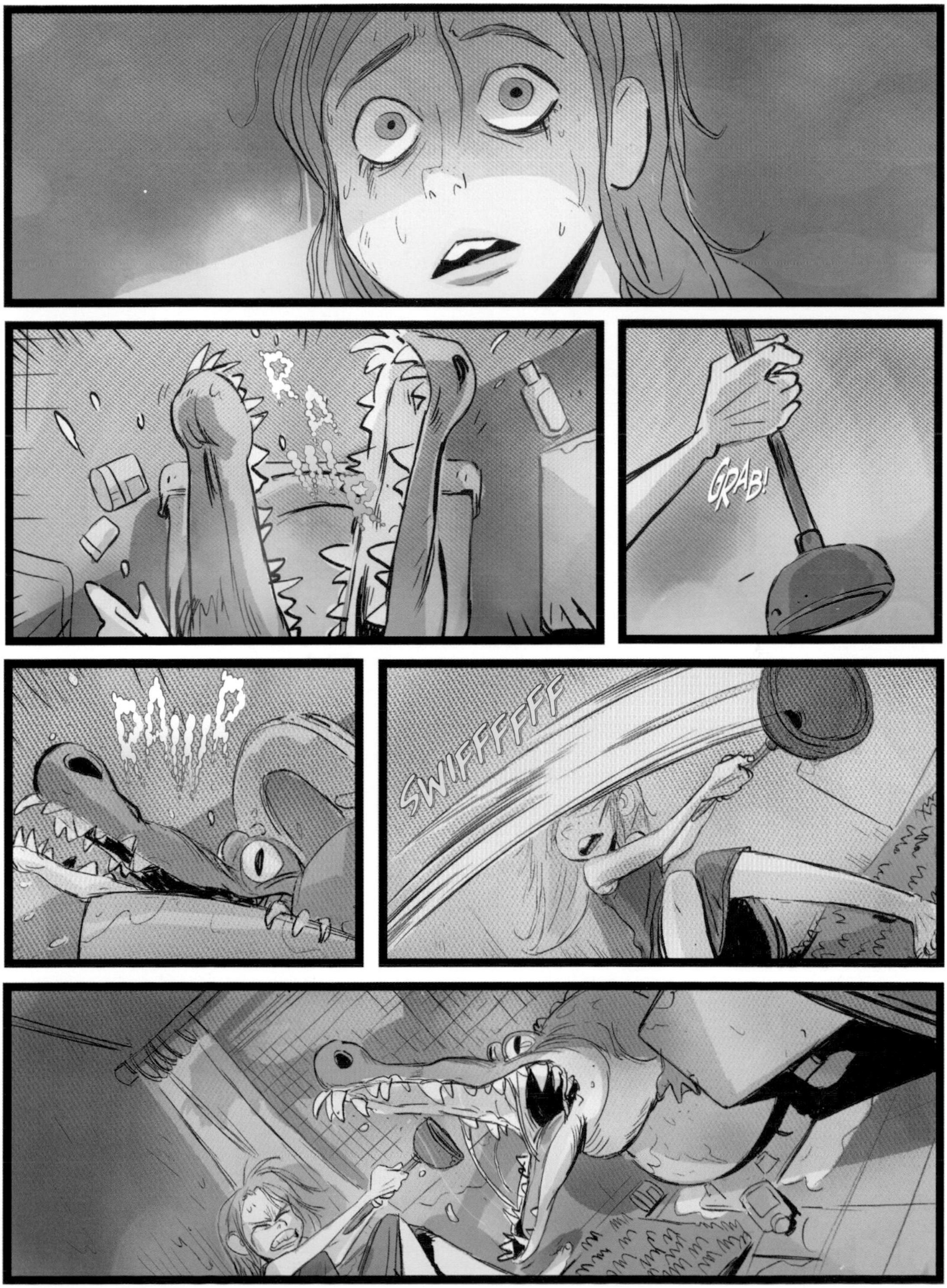
GRAB!
SWIFFFFFF

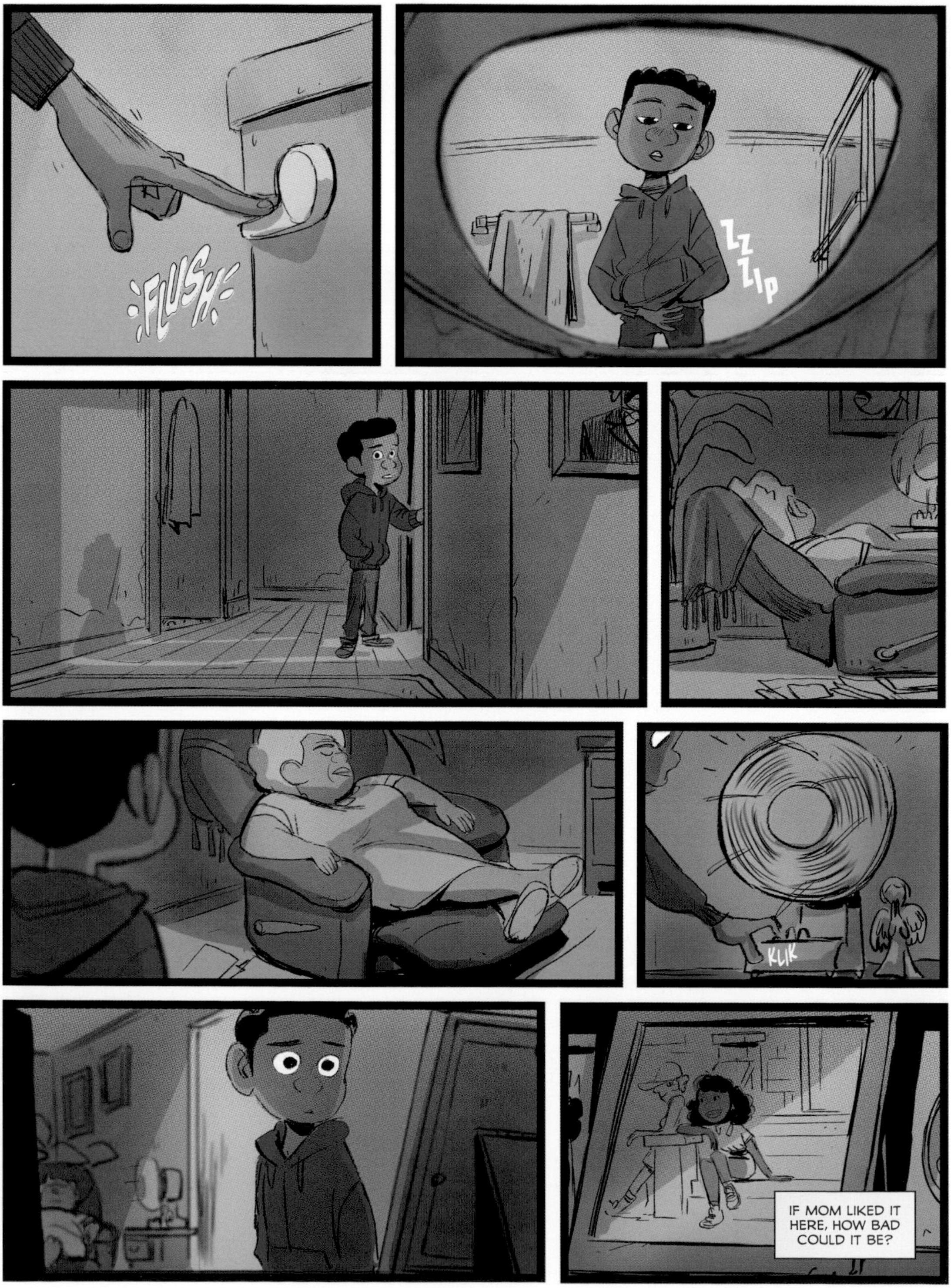
FLUSH
ZZZIP
KLIK
IF MOM LIKED IT HERE, HOW BAD COULD IT BE?

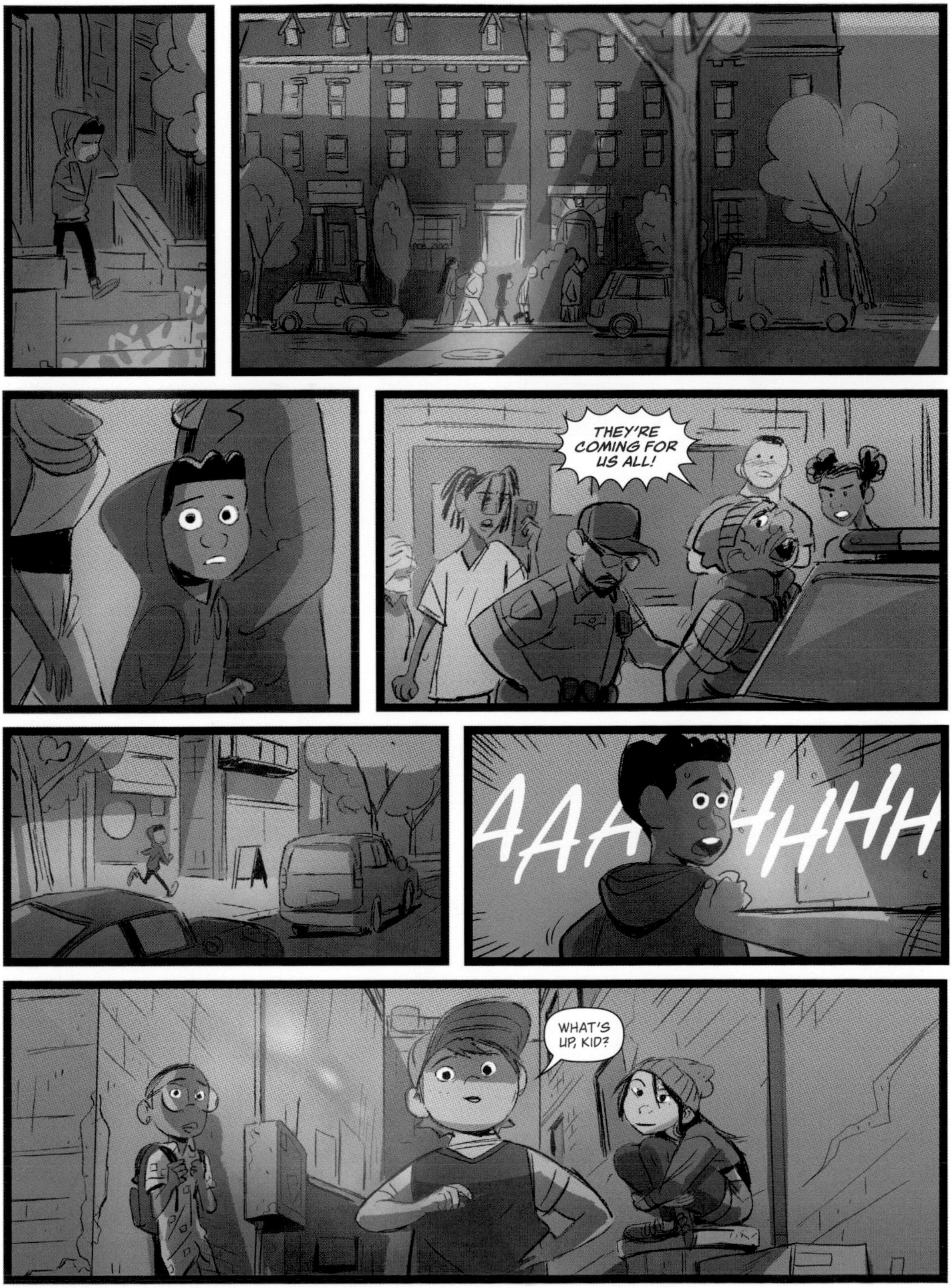
THEY'RE COMING FOR US ALL!
AAAHHHH
WHAT'S UP, KID?

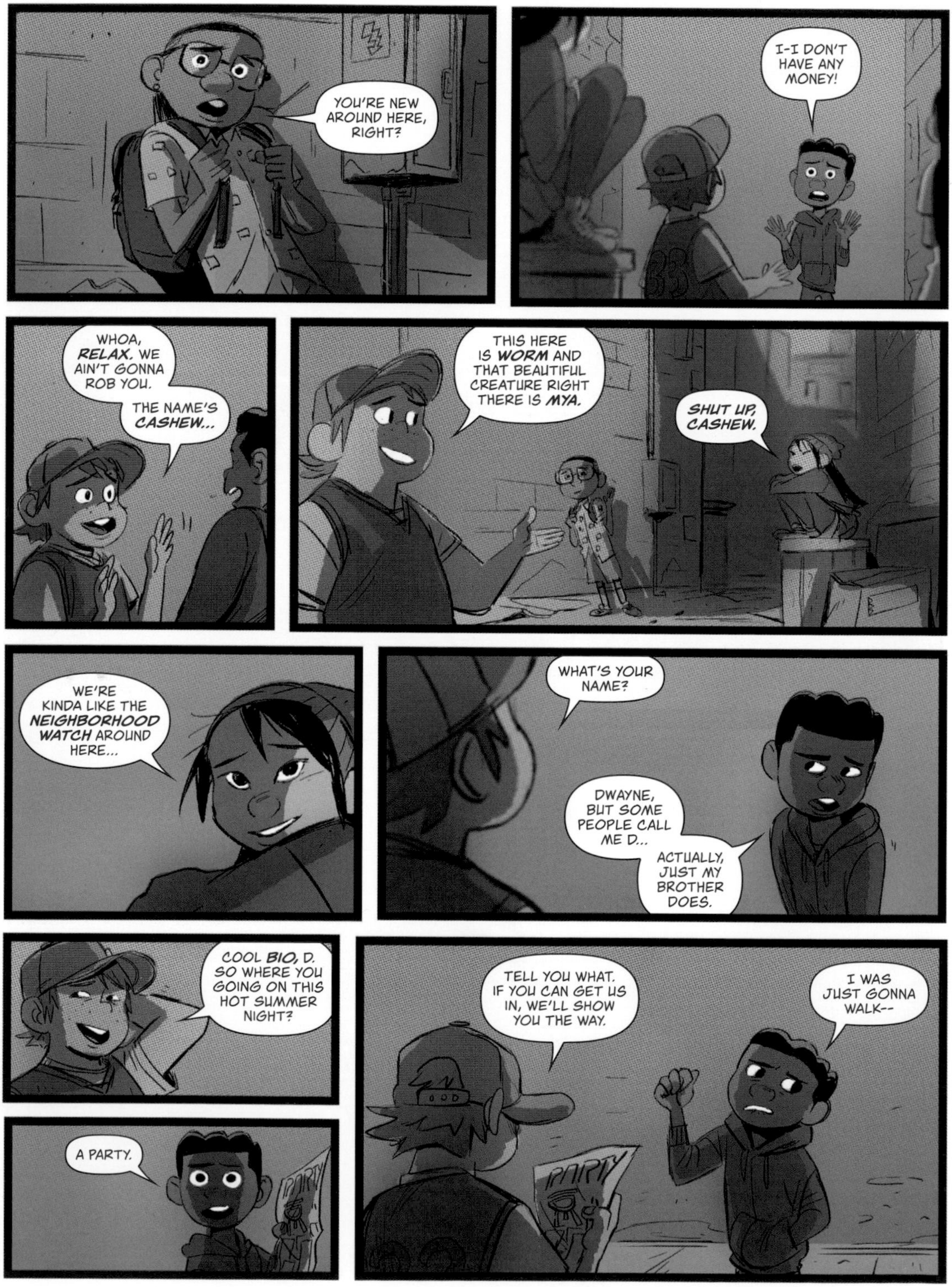
YOU'RE NEW AROUND HERE, RIGHT?
I-I DON'T HAVE ANY MONEY!
WHOA, **RELAX.** WE AIN'T GONNA ROB YOU.
THE NAME'S **CASHEW...**
THIS HERE IS **WORM** AND THAT BEAUTIFUL CREATURE RIGHT THERE IS **MYA.**
SHUT UP, CASHEW.
WE'RE KINDA LIKE THE **NEIGHBORHOOD WATCH** AROUND HERE...
WHAT'S YOUR NAME?
DWAYNE, BUT SOME PEOPLE CALL ME D...
ACTUALLY, JUST MY BROTHER DOES.
COOL **BIO,** D. SO WHERE YOU GOING ON THIS HOT SUMMER NIGHT?
A PARTY.
TELL YOU WHAT. IF YOU CAN GET US IN, WE'LL SHOW YOU THE WAY.
I WAS JUST GONNA WALK--

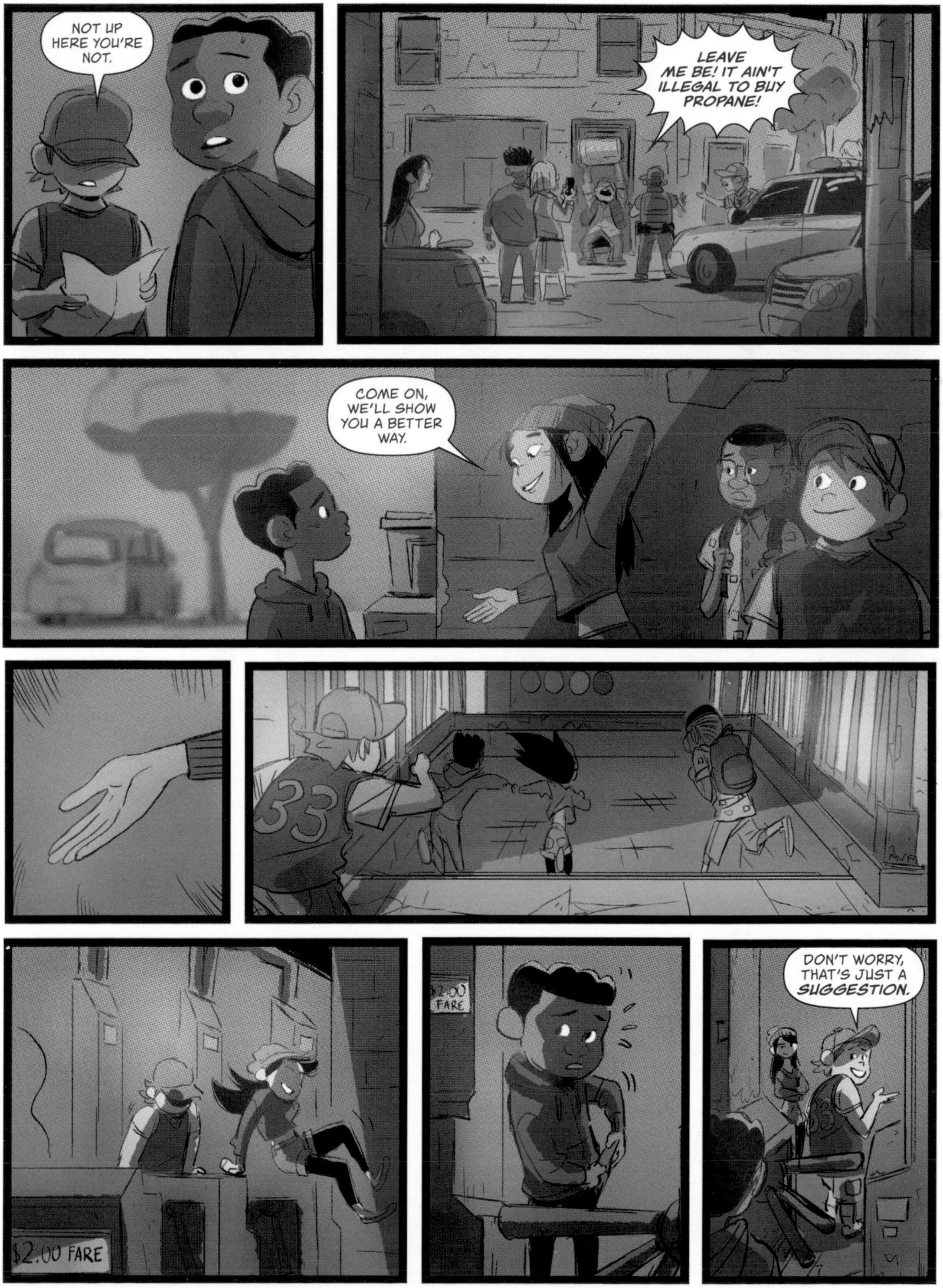
NOT UP HERE YOU'RE NOT.
LEAVE ME BE! IT AIN'T ILLEGAL TO BUY PROPANE!
COME ON, WE'LL SHOW YOU A BETTER WAY.
$2.00 FARE
$2.00 FARE
DON'T WORRY, THAT'S JUST A *SUGGESTION*.

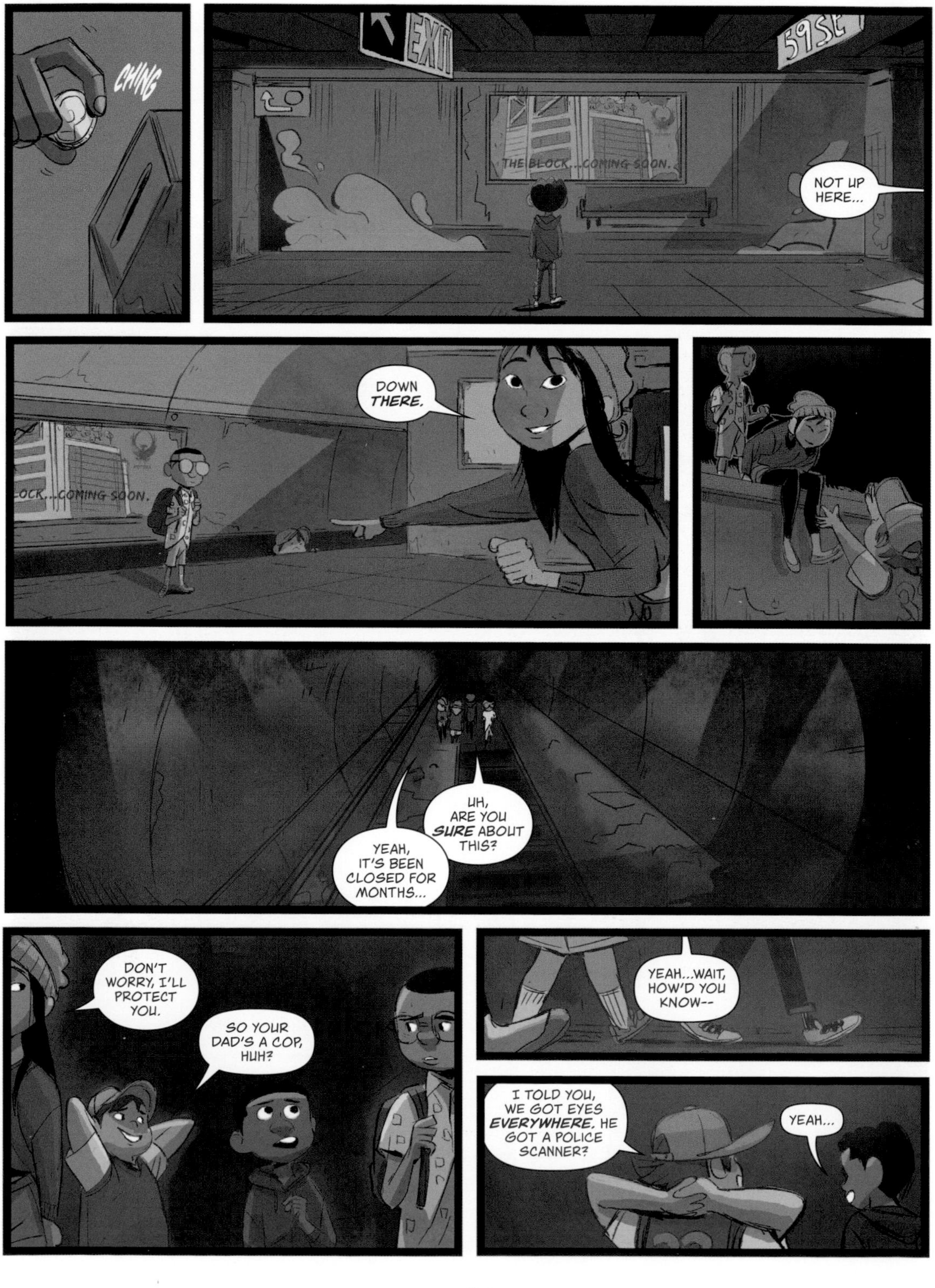
CHING
EXIT
59 St
THE BLOCK...COMING SOON.
NOT UP HERE...
DOWN THERE.
...OCK...COMING SOON.
UH, ARE YOU SURE ABOUT THIS?
YEAH, IT'S BEEN CLOSED FOR MONTHS...
DON'T WORRY, I'LL PROTECT YOU.
SO YOUR DAD'S A COP, HUH?
YEAH...WAIT, HOW'D YOU KNOW--
I TOLD YOU, WE GOT EYES EVERYWHERE. HE GOT A POLICE SCANNER?
YEAH...

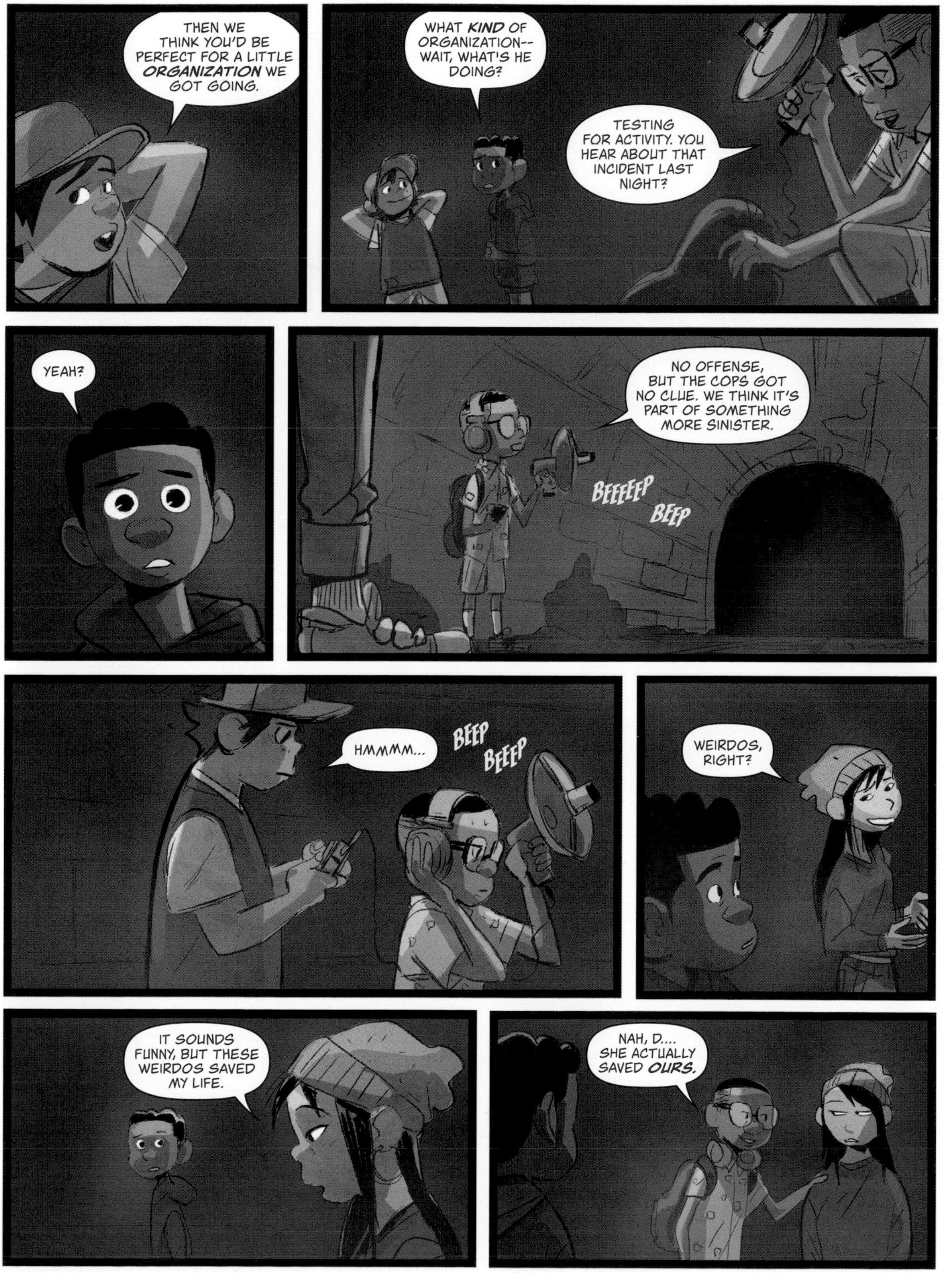
THEN WE THINK YOU'D BE PERFECT FOR A LITTLE ORGANIZATION WE GOT GOING.
WHAT KIND OF ORGANIZATION-- WAIT, WHAT'S HE DOING?
TESTING FOR ACTIVITY. YOU HEAR ABOUT THAT INCIDENT LAST NIGHT?
YEAH?
NO OFFENSE, BUT THE COPS GOT NO CLUE. WE THINK IT'S PART OF SOMETHING MORE SINISTER.
BEEEEEP
BEEP
HMMMM...
BEEP
BEEEP
WEIRDOS, RIGHT?
IT SOUNDS FUNNY, BUT THESE WEIRDOS SAVED MY LIFE.
NAH, D.... SHE ACTUALLY SAVED OURS.

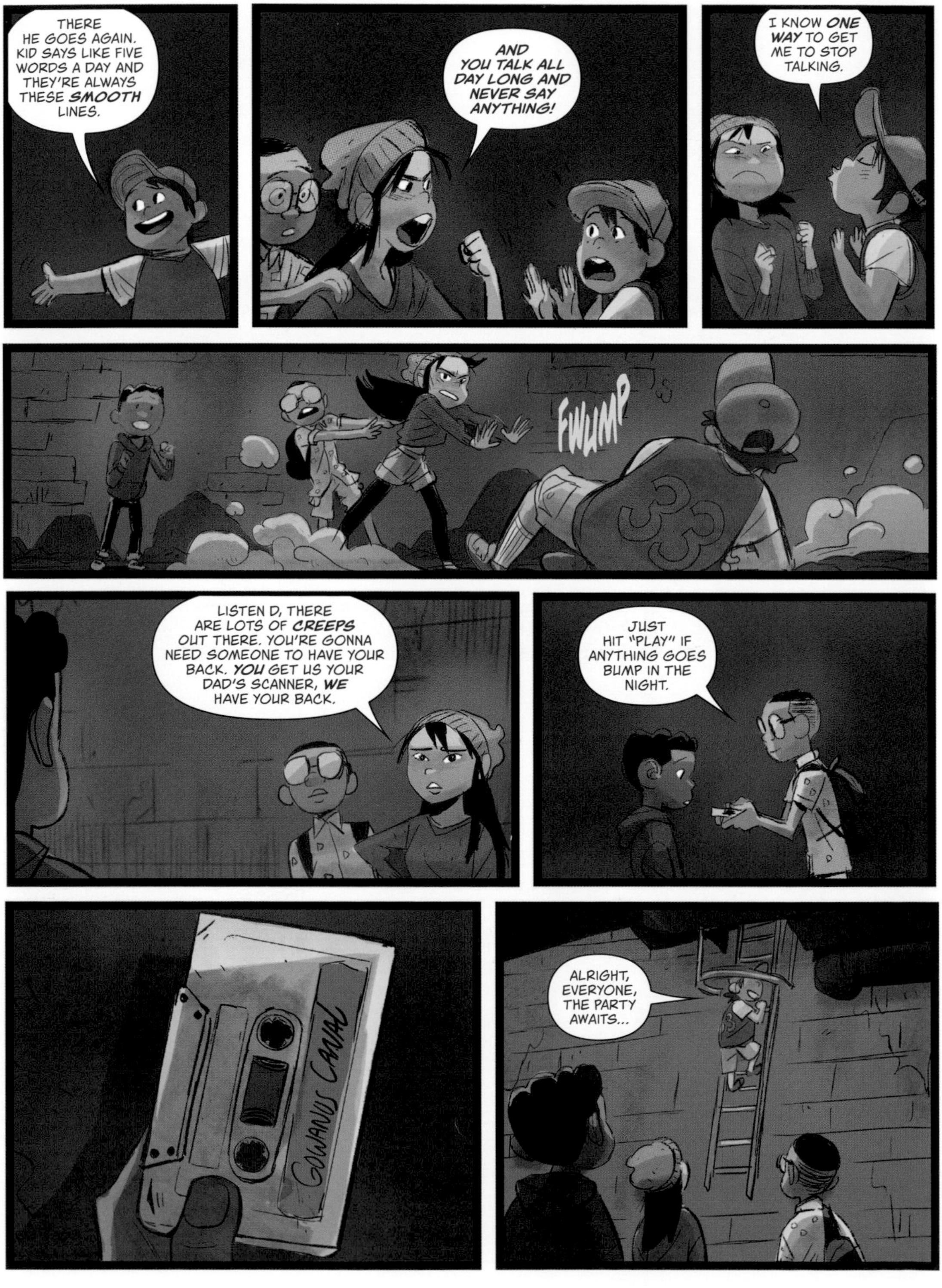
THERE HE GOES AGAIN. KID SAYS LIKE FIVE WORDS A DAY AND THEY'RE ALWAYS THESE SMOOTH LINES.
AND YOU TALK ALL DAY LONG AND NEVER SAY ANYTHING!
I KNOW ONE WAY TO GET ME TO STOP TALKING.
FWUMP
LISTEN D, THERE ARE LOTS OF CREEPS OUT THERE. YOU'RE GONNA NEED SOMEONE TO HAVE YOUR BACK. YOU GET US YOUR DAD'S SCANNER, WE HAVE YOUR BACK.
JUST HIT "PLAY" IF ANYTHING GOES BUMP IN THE NIGHT.
GOWANUS CANAL
ALRIGHT, EVERYONE, THE PARTY AWAITS...

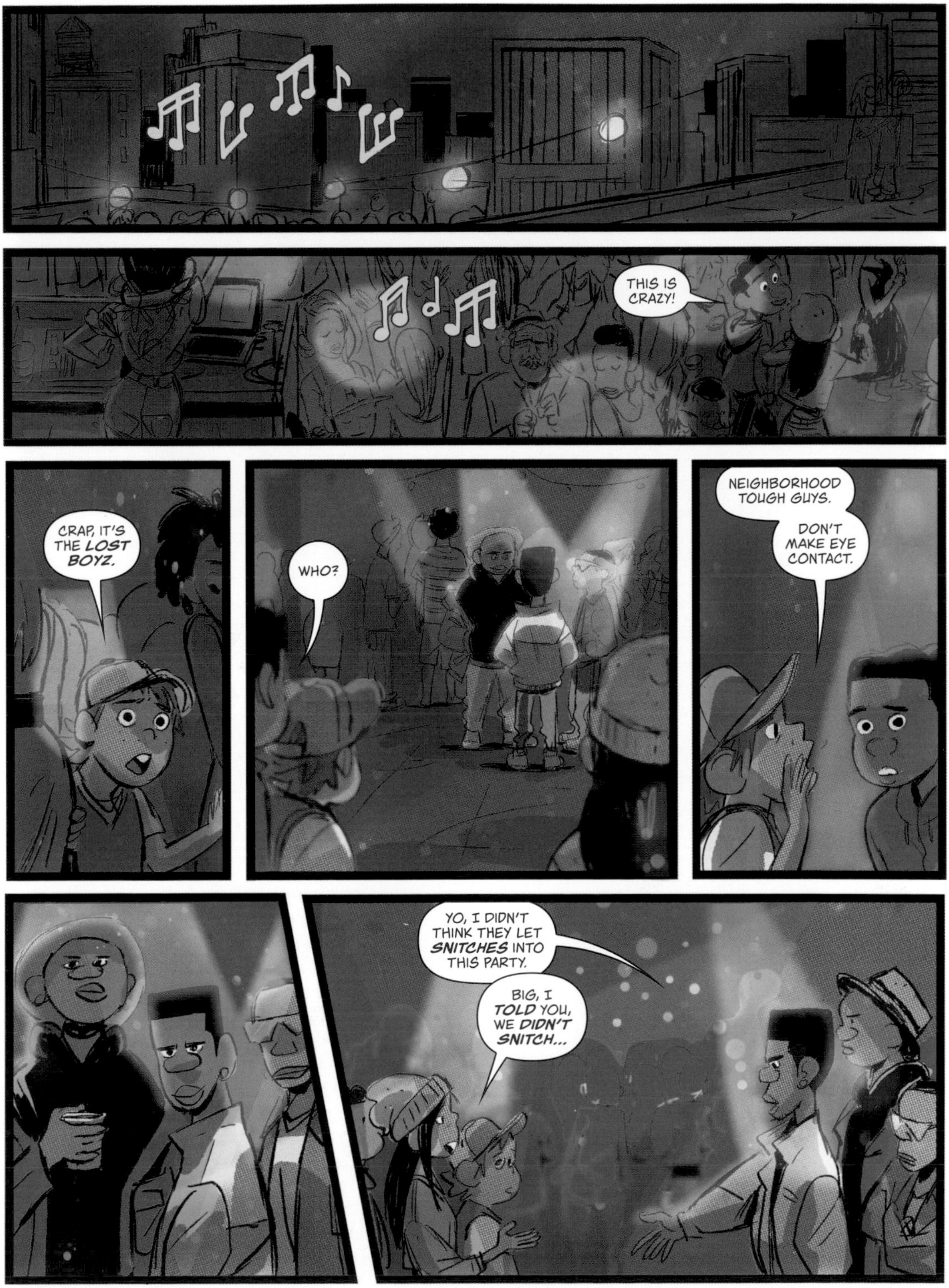
THIS IS CRAZY!
CRAP, IT'S THE LOST BOYZ.
WHO?
NEIGHBORHOOD TOUGH GUYS.
DON'T MAKE EYE CONTACT.
YO, I DIDN'T THINK THEY LET SNITCHES INTO THIS PARTY.
BIG, I TOLD YOU, WE DIDN'T SNITCH...

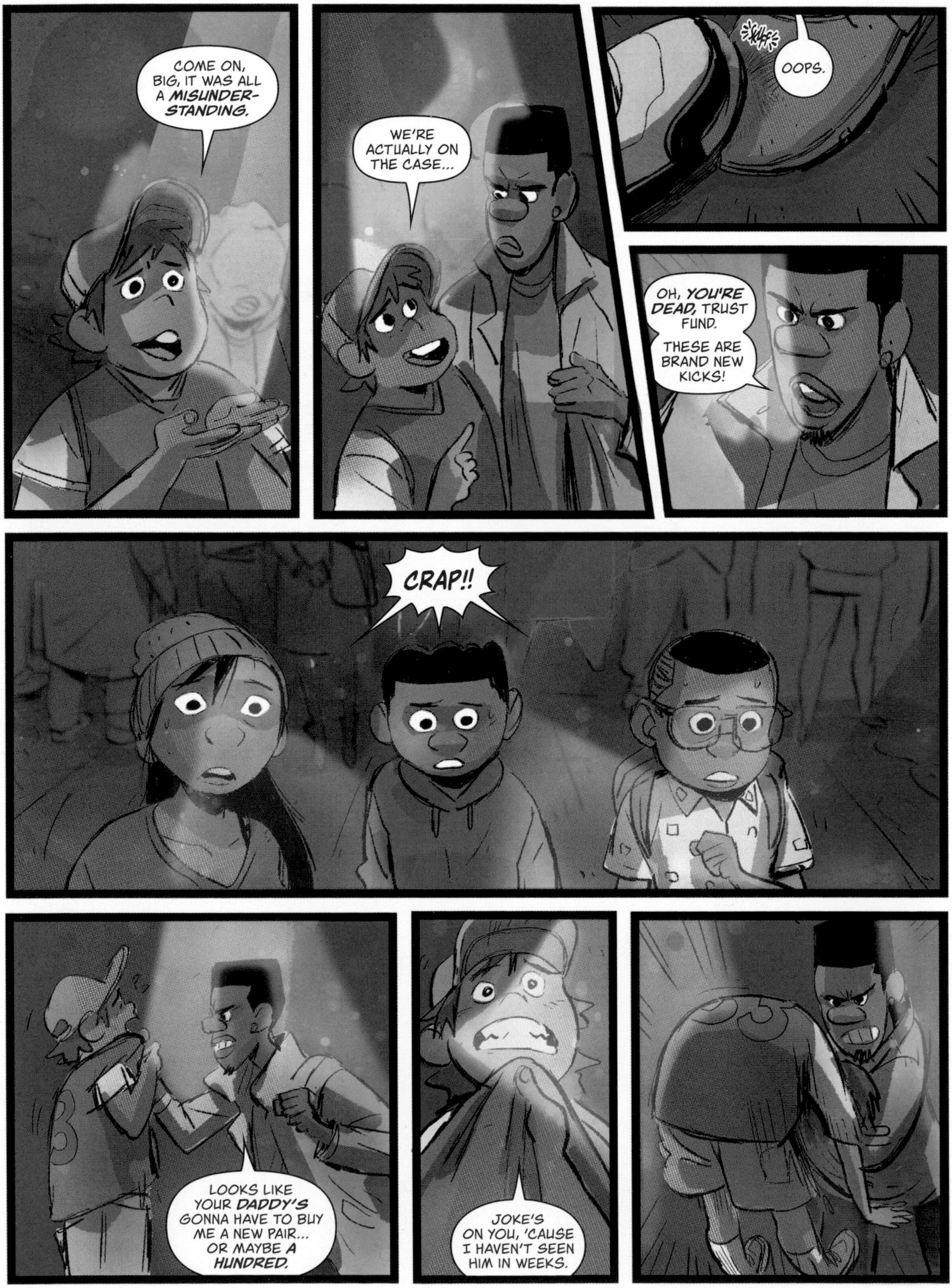
COME ON, BIG, IT WAS ALL A *MISUNDER-STANDING.*
WE'RE ACTUALLY ON THE CASE...
OOPS.
OH, *YOU'RE DEAD,* TRUST FUND.
THESE ARE BRAND NEW KICKS!
CRAP!!
LOOKS LIKE YOUR *DADDY'S* GONNA HAVE TO BUY ME A NEW PAIR... OR MAYBE *A HUNDRED.*
JOKE'S ON YOU, 'CAUSE I HAVEN'T SEEN HIM IN WEEKS.

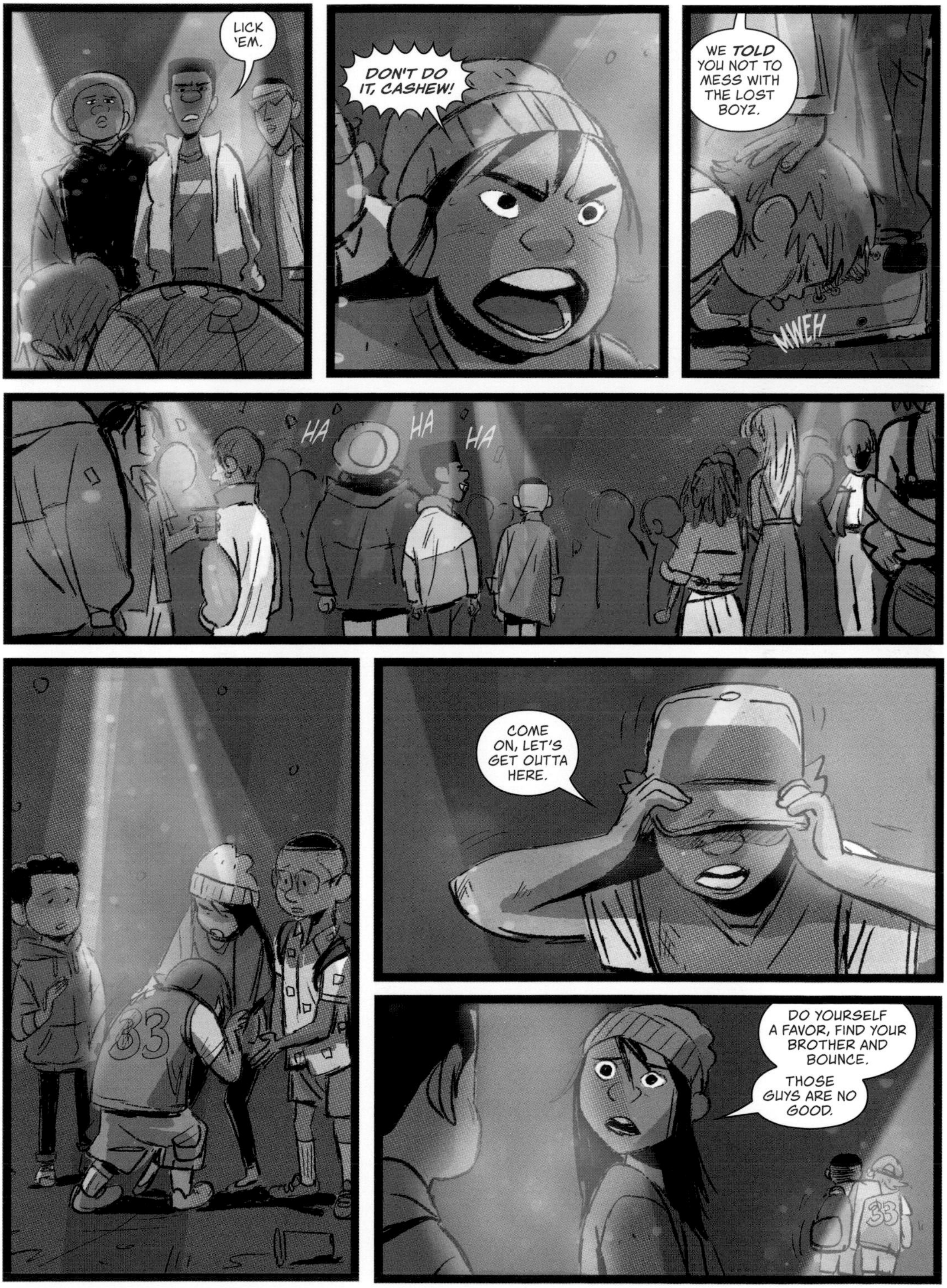
LICK 'EM.
DON'T DO IT, CASHEW!
WE TOLD YOU NOT TO MESS WITH THE LOST BOYZ.
MWEH
HA
HA
HA
COME ON, LET'S GET OUTTA HERE.
DO YOURSELF A FAVOR, FIND YOUR BROTHER AND BOUNCE.
THOSE GUYS ARE NO GOOD.

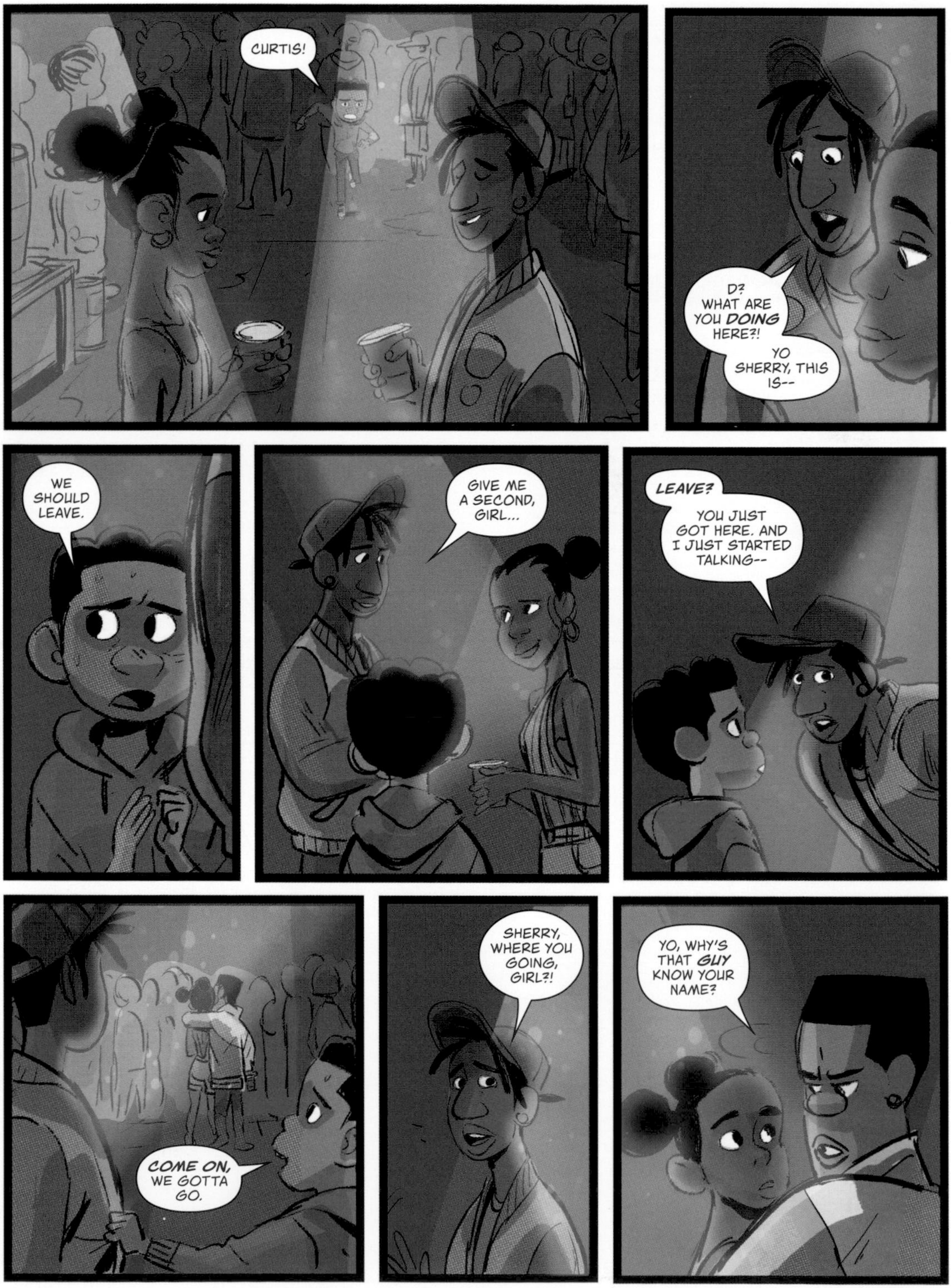
CURTIS!
D? WHAT ARE YOU DOING HERE?!
YO SHERRY, THIS IS--
WE SHOULD LEAVE.
GIVE ME A SECOND, GIRL...
LEAVE?
YOU JUST GOT HERE. AND I JUST STARTED TALKING--
COME ON, WE GOTTA GO.
SHERRY, WHERE YOU GOING, GIRL?!
YO, WHY'S THAT GUY KNOW YOUR NAME?

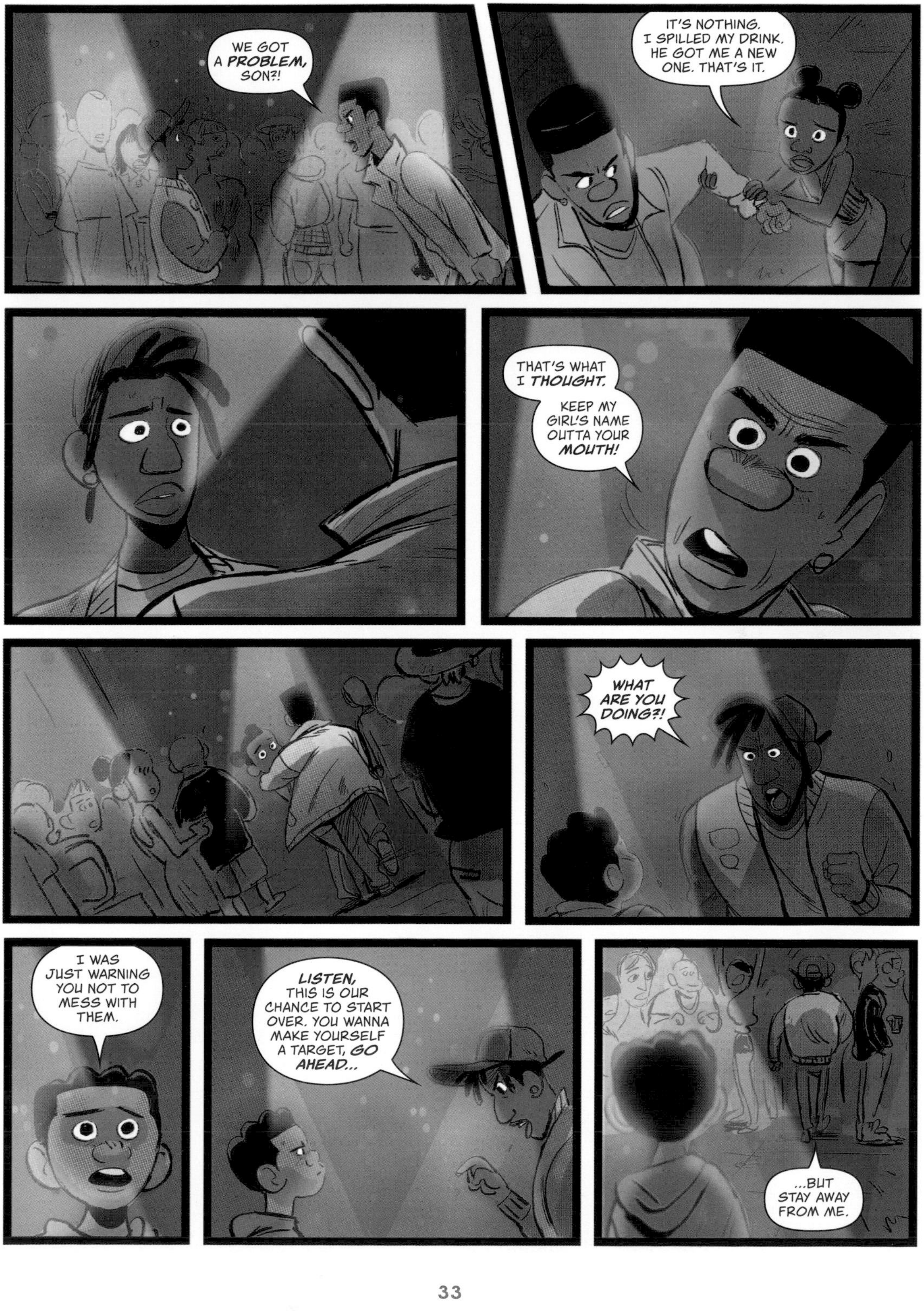

WE GOT A **PROBLEM,** SON?!
IT'S NOTHING. I SPILLED MY DRINK. HE GOT ME A NEW ONE. THAT'S IT.
THAT'S WHAT I ***THOUGHT.***
KEEP MY GIRL'S NAME OUTTA YOUR ***MOUTH!***
WHAT ARE YOU DOING?!
I WAS JUST WARNING YOU NOT TO MESS WITH THEM.
LISTEN, THIS IS OUR CHANCE TO START OVER. YOU WANNA MAKE YOURSELF A TARGET, ***GO AHEAD...***
...BUT STAY AWAY FROM ME.

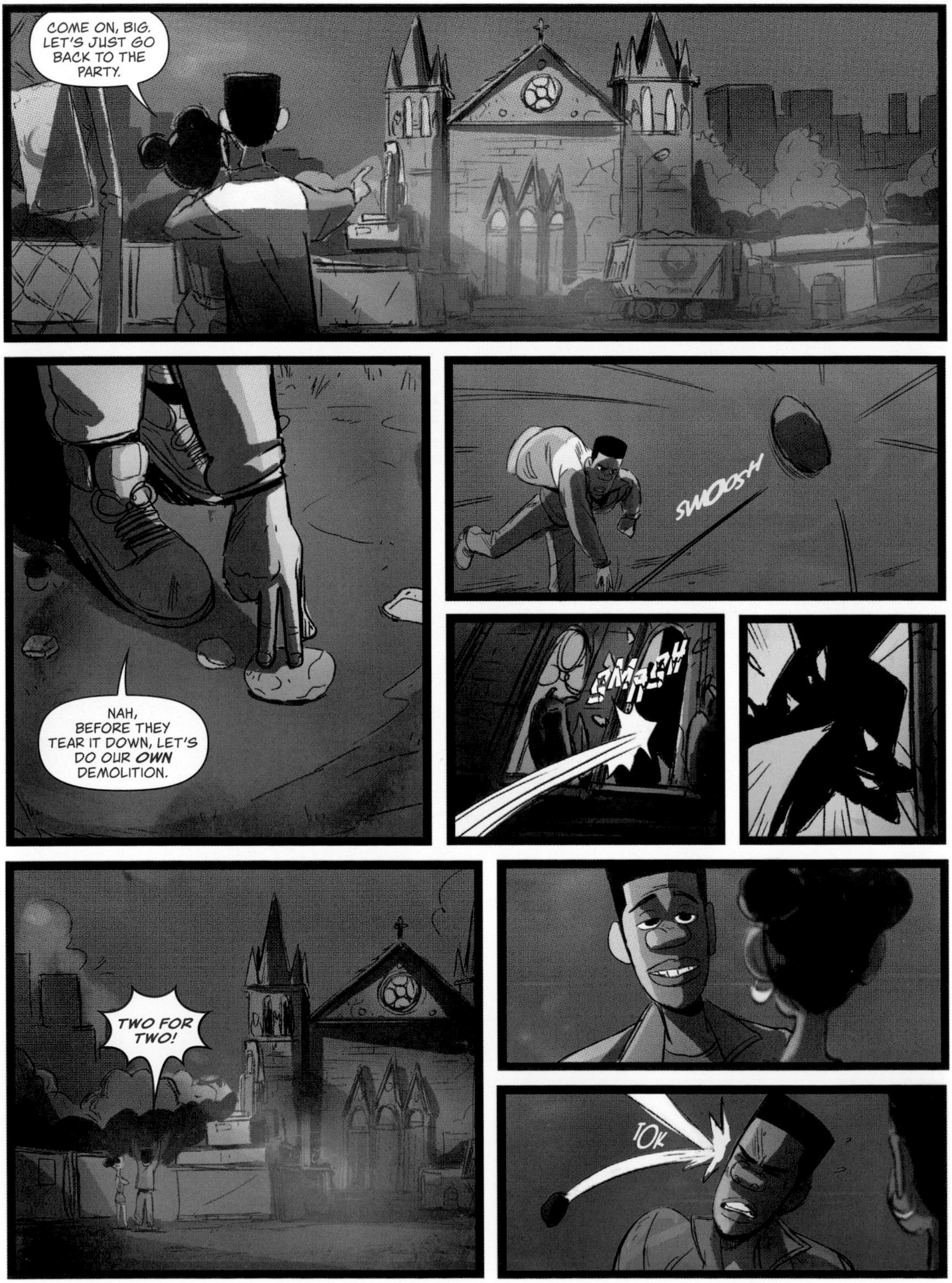
COME ON, BIG. LET'S JUST GO BACK TO THE PARTY.
NAH, BEFORE THEY TEAR IT DOWN, LET'S DO OUR **OWN** DEMOLITION.
SWOOSH
SMASH
TWO FOR TWO!
TOK

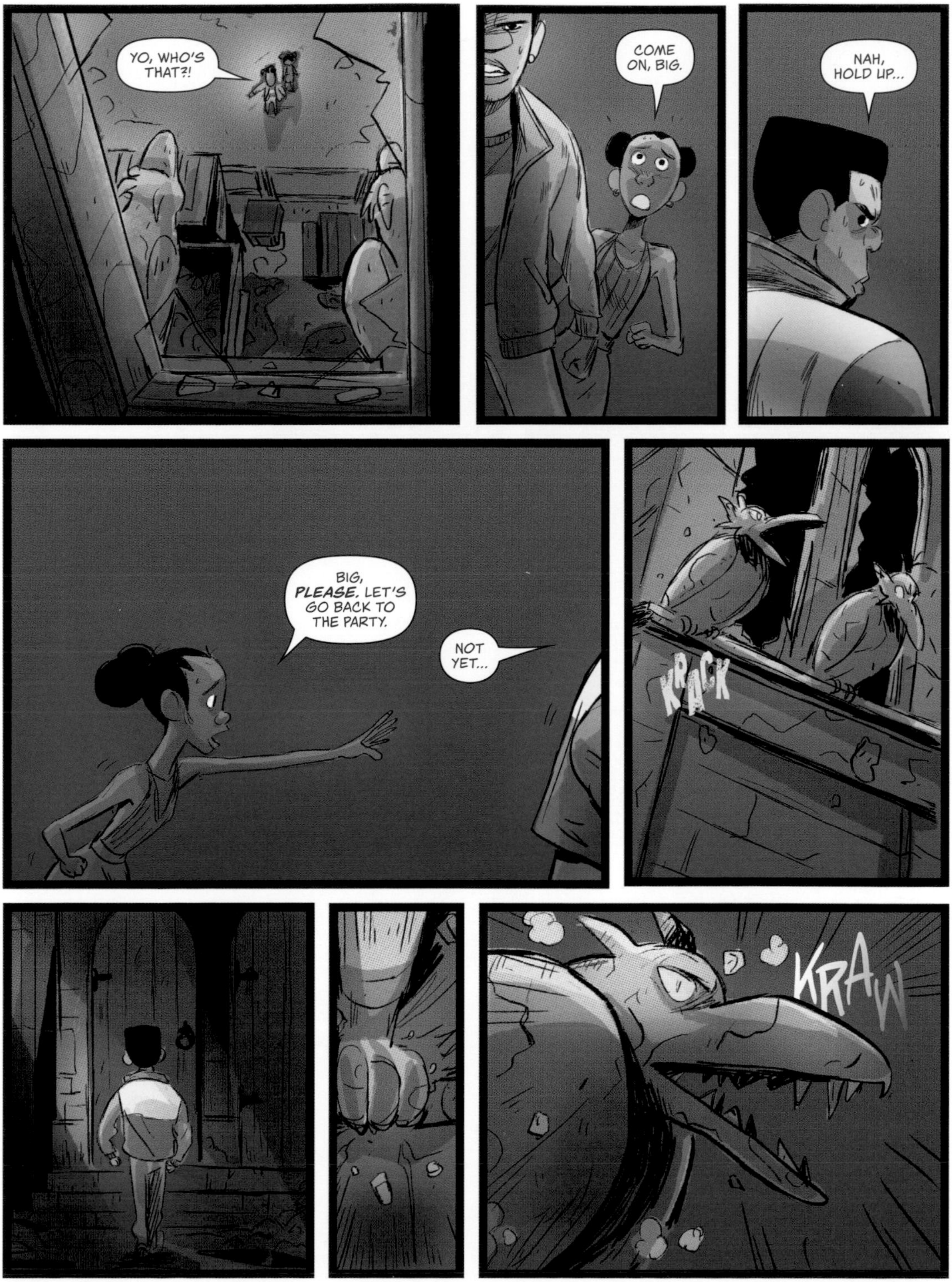
YO, WHO'S THAT?!
COME ON, BIG.
NAH, HOLD UP...
BIG, PLEASE. LET'S GO BACK TO THE PARTY.
NOT YET...
KRACK
KRAW

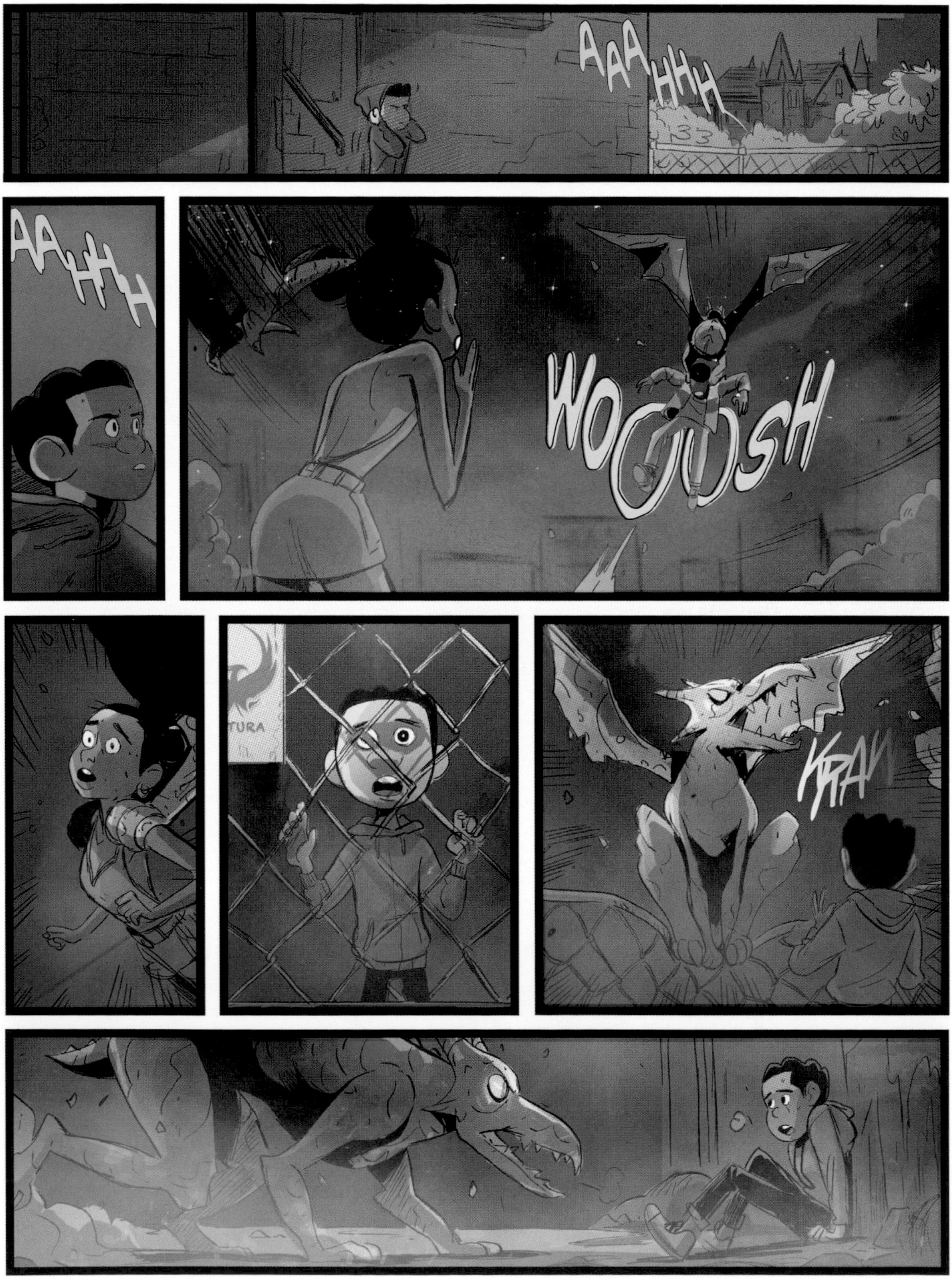
AAAHHH
AAHHH
WOOOSH
KRAK

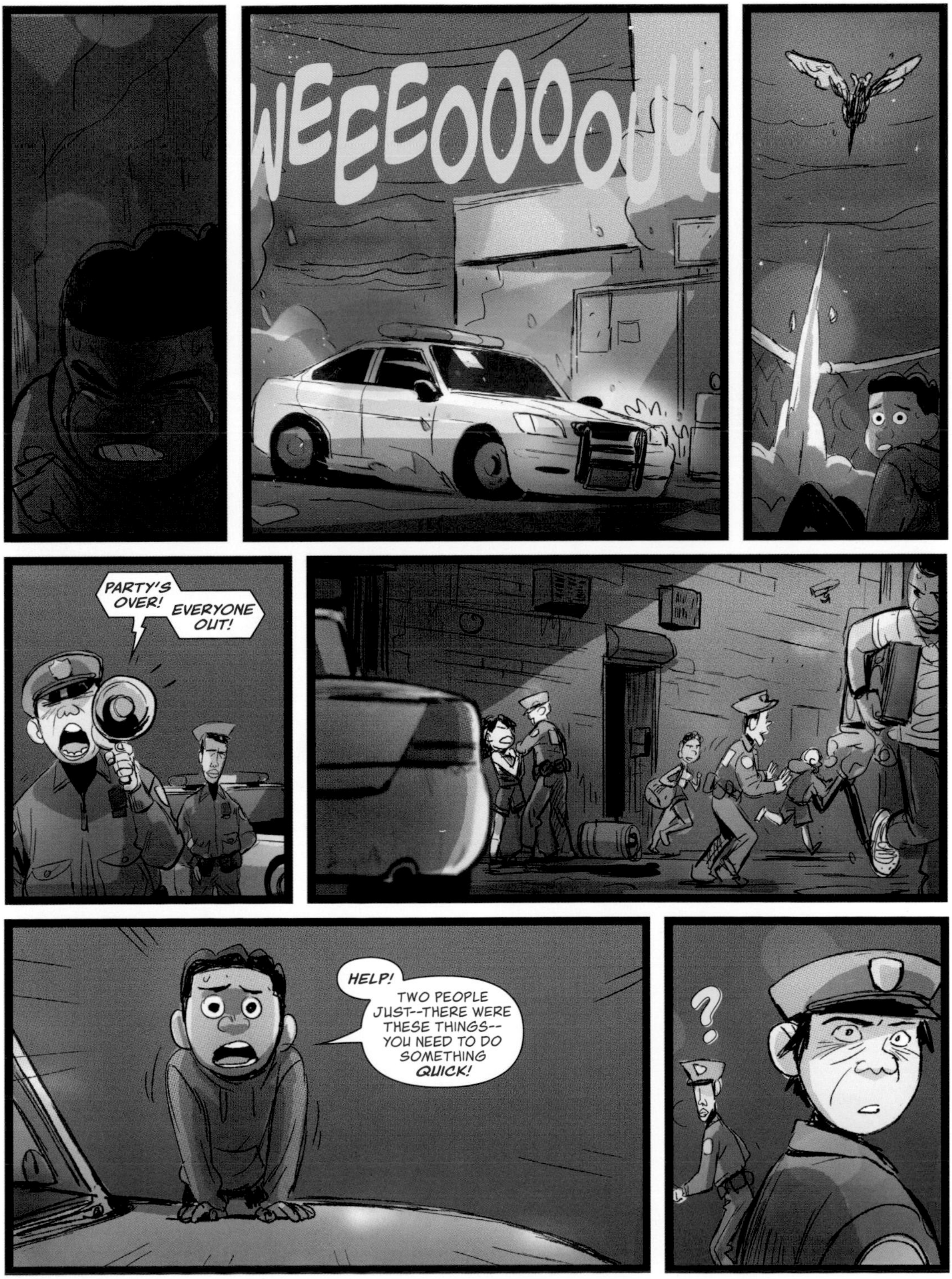
WEEEOOOOUUU
PARTY'S OVER!
EVERYONE OUT!
HELP!
TWO PEOPLE JUST--THERE WERE THESE THINGS-- YOU NEED TO DO SOMETHING QUICK!
?

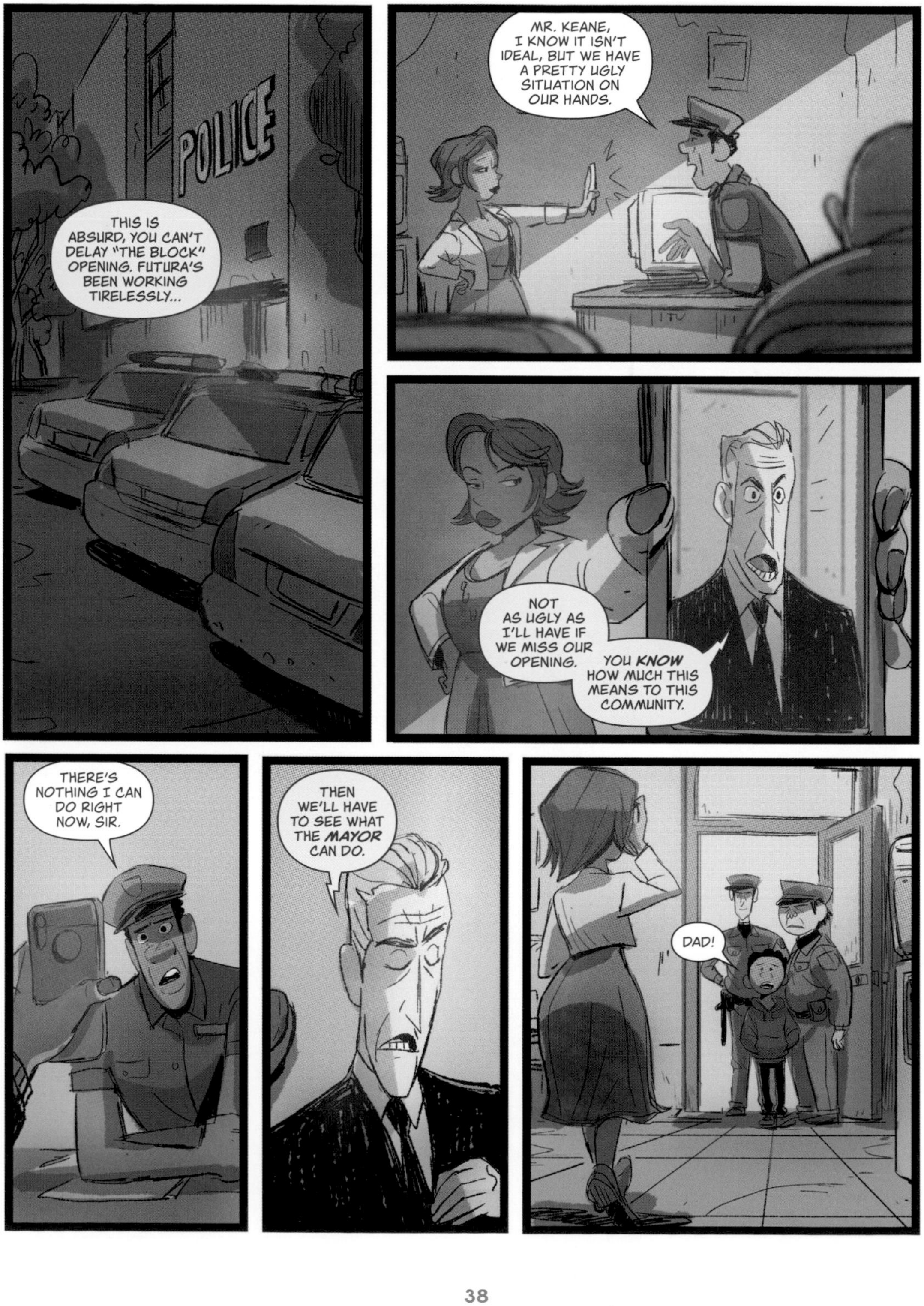
POLICE
THIS IS ABSURD, YOU CAN'T DELAY "THE BLOCK" OPENING. FUTURA'S BEEN WORKING TIRELESSLY...
MR. KEANE, I KNOW IT ISN'T IDEAL, BUT WE HAVE A PRETTY UGLY SITUATION ON OUR HANDS.
NOT AS UGLY AS I'LL HAVE IF WE MISS OUR OPENING.
YOU **KNOW** HOW MUCH THIS MEANS TO THIS COMMUNITY.
THERE'S NOTHING I CAN DO RIGHT NOW, SIR.
THEN WE'LL HAVE TO SEE WHAT THE ***MAYOR*** CAN DO.
DAD!

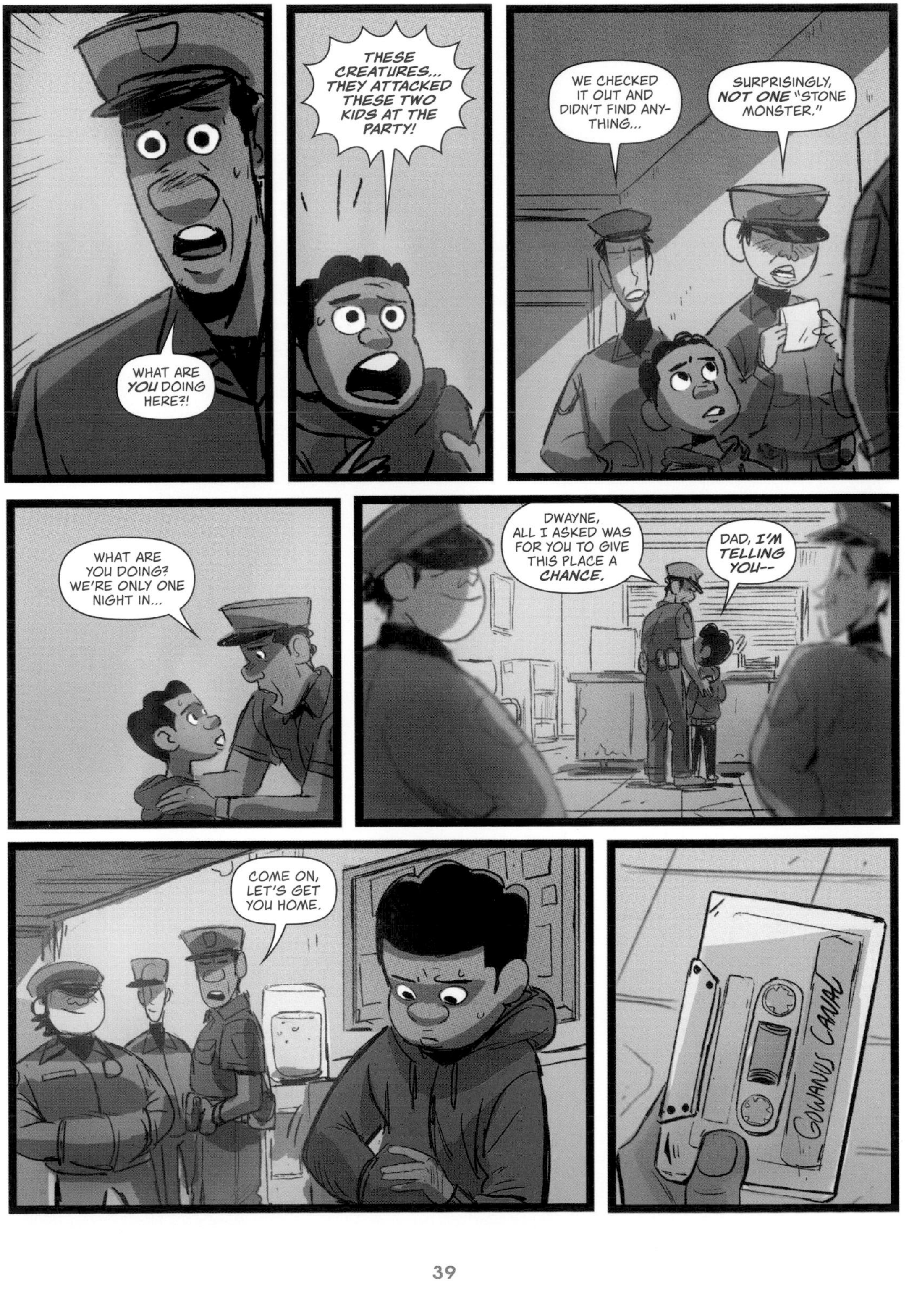
WHAT ARE YOU DOING HERE?!
THESE CREATURES... THEY ATTACKED THESE TWO KIDS AT THE PARTY!
WE CHECKED IT OUT AND DIDN'T FIND ANYTHING...
SURPRISINGLY, NOT ONE "STONE MONSTER."
WHAT ARE YOU DOING? WE'RE ONLY ONE NIGHT IN...
DWAYNE, ALL I ASKED WAS FOR YOU TO GIVE THIS PLACE A CHANCE.
DAD, I'M TELLING YOU--
COME ON, LET'S GET YOU HOME.
GOWANUS CANAL

GOWANUS CANAL

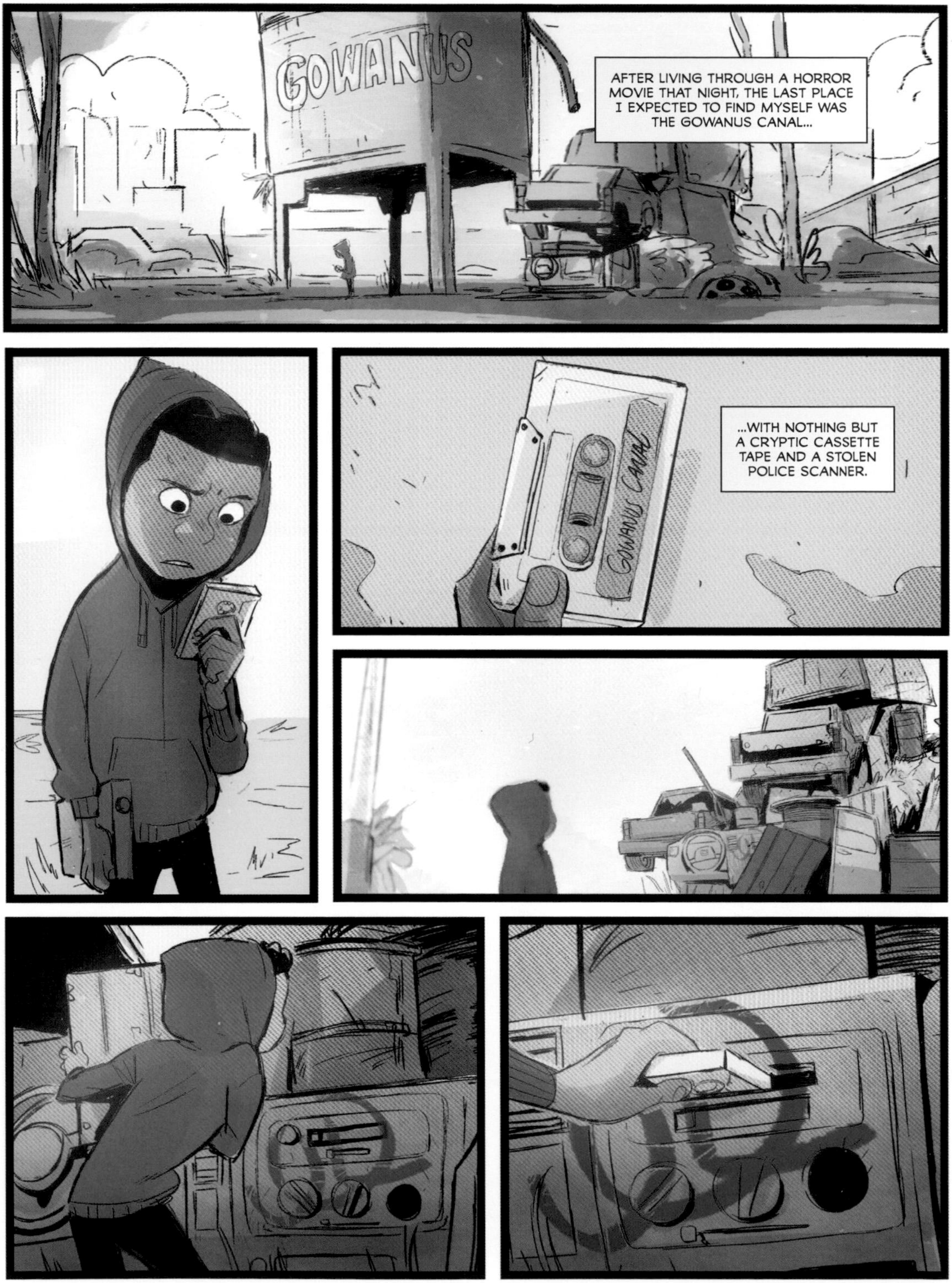
GOWANUS
AFTER LIVING THROUGH A HORROR MOVIE THAT NIGHT, THE LAST PLACE I EXPECTED TO FIND MYSELF WAS THE GOWANUS CANAL...
GOWANUS CANAL
...WITH NOTHING BUT A CRYPTIC CASSETTE TAPE AND A STOLEN POLICE SCANNER.

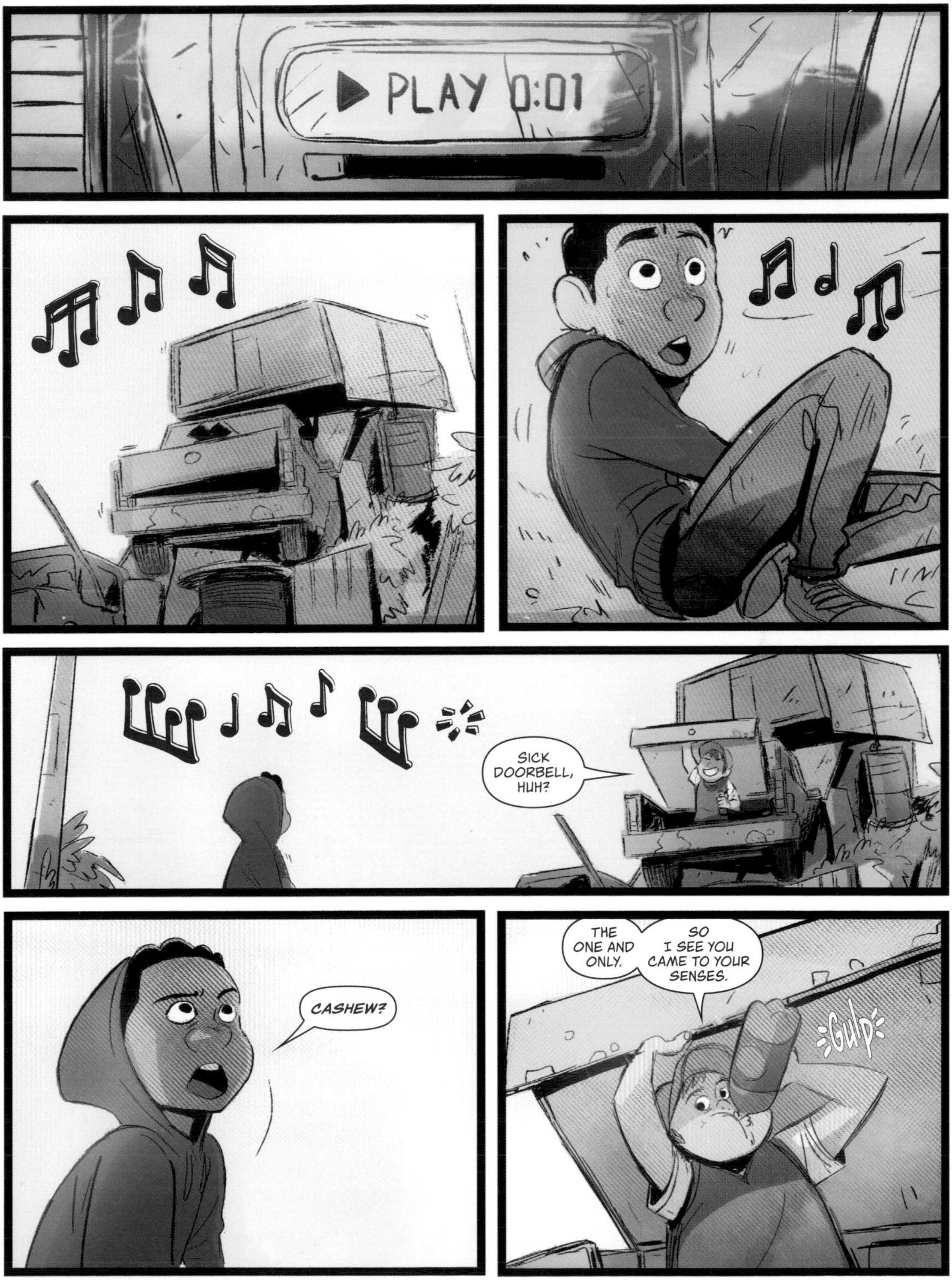
PLAY 0:01
SICK DOORBELL, HUH?
CASHEW?
THE ONE AND ONLY.
SO I SEE YOU CAME TO YOUR SENSES.
Gulp

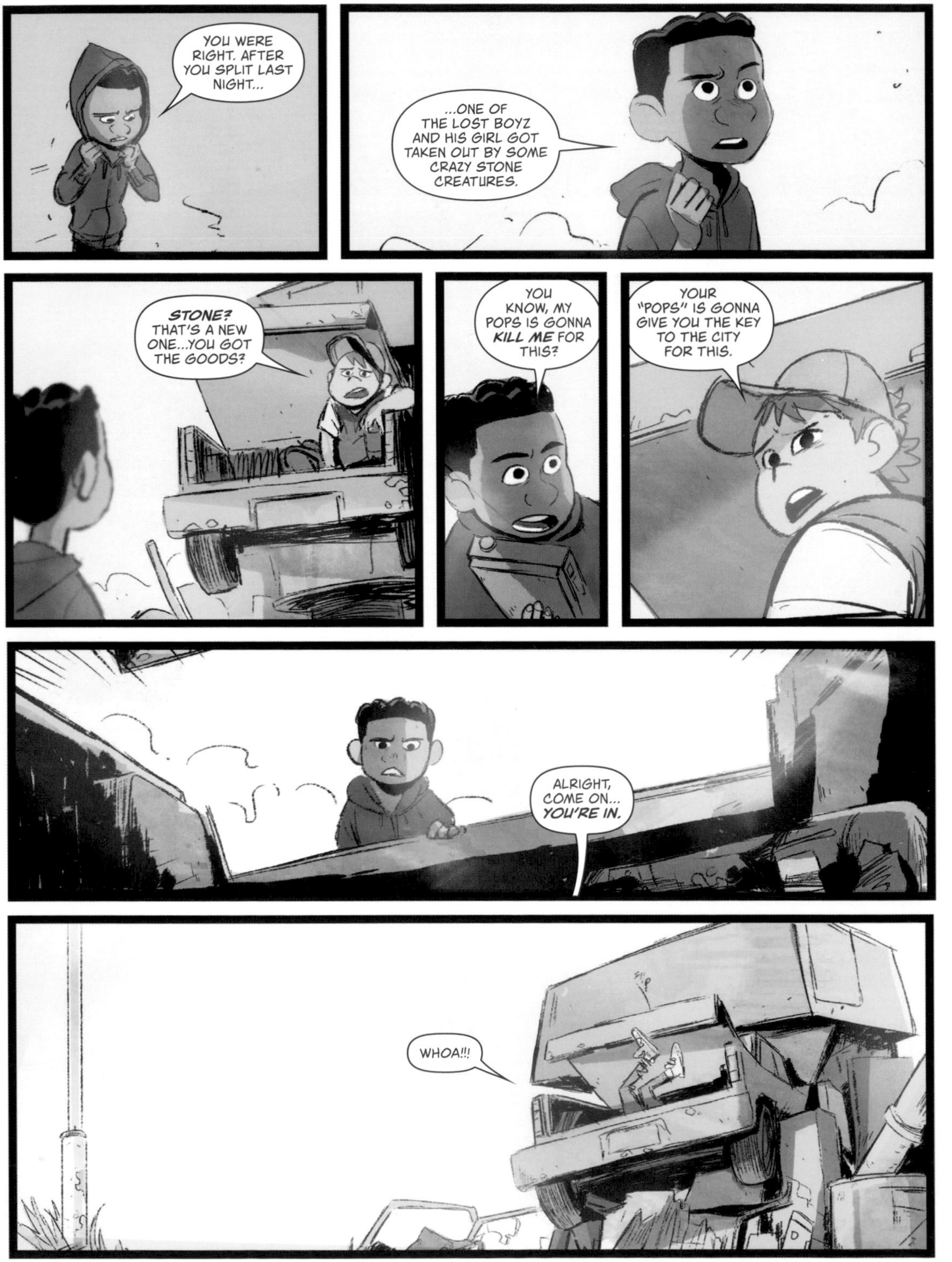
YOU WERE RIGHT. AFTER YOU SPLIT LAST NIGHT...
...ONE OF THE LOST BOYZ AND HIS GIRL GOT TAKEN OUT BY SOME CRAZY STONE CREATURES.
STONE? THAT'S A NEW ONE...YOU GOT THE GOODS?
YOU KNOW, MY POPS IS GONNA KILL ME FOR THIS?
YOUR "POPS" IS GONNA GIVE YOU THE KEY TO THE CITY FOR THIS.
ALRIGHT, COME ON... YOU'RE IN.
WHOA!!!

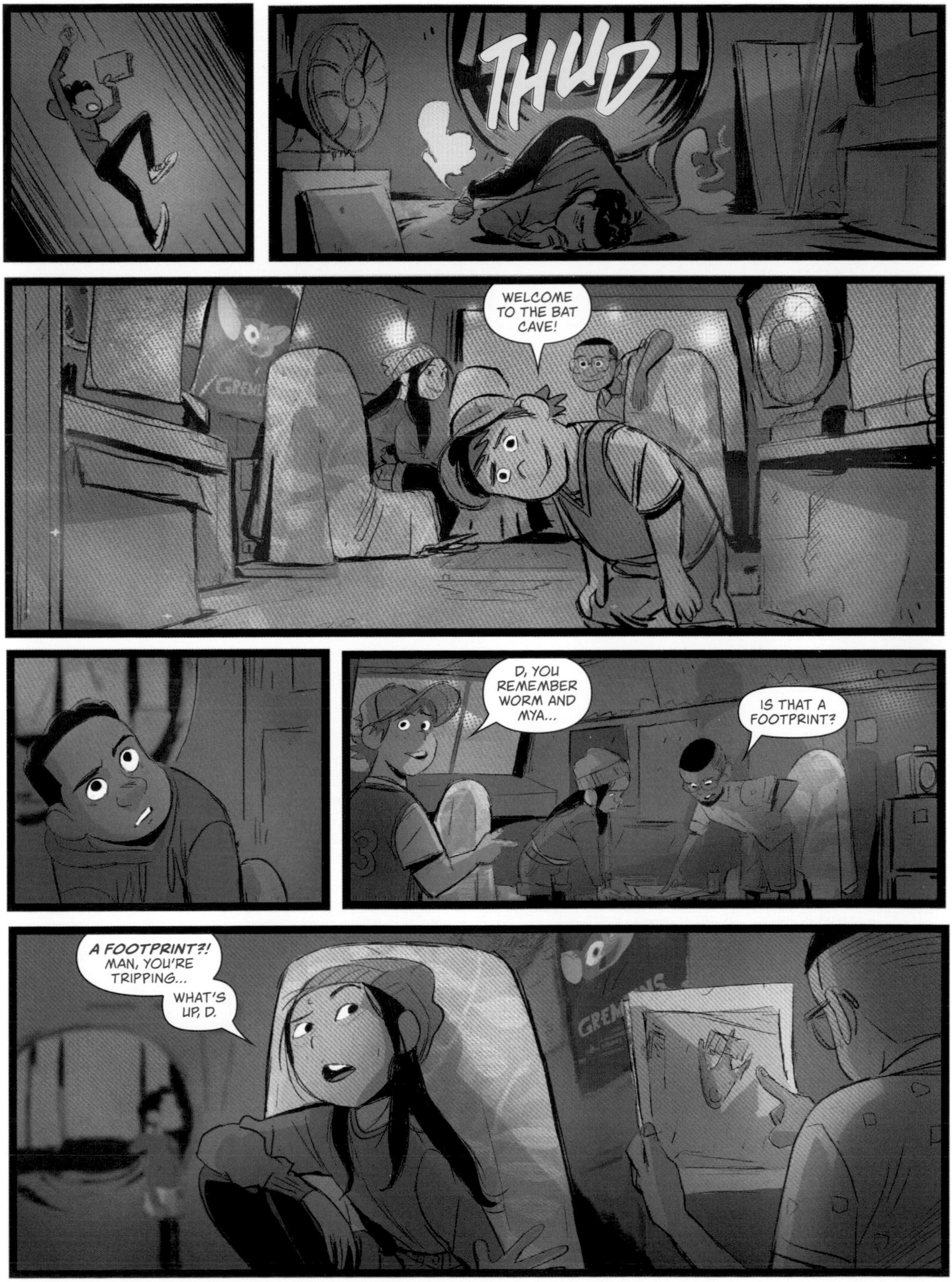
THUD
WELCOME TO THE BAT CAVE!
D, YOU REMEMBER WORM AND MYA...
IS THAT A FOOTPRINT?
A FOOTPRINT?! MAN, YOU'RE TRIPPING...
WHAT'S UP, D.

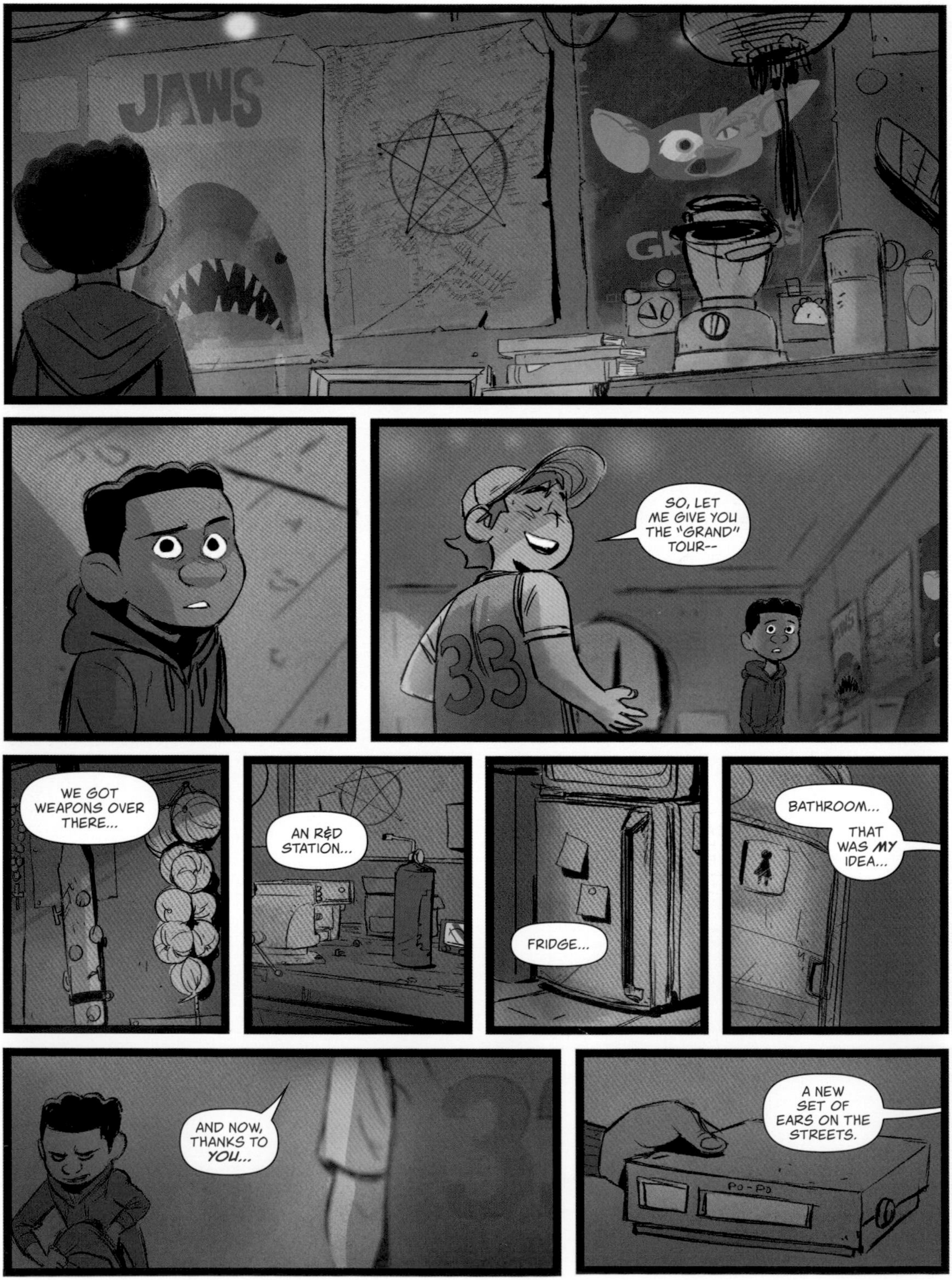
JAWS
SO, LET ME GIVE YOU THE "GRAND" TOUR--
WE GOT WEAPONS OVER THERE...
AN R&D STATION...
FRIDGE...
BATHROOM...
THAT WAS MY IDEA...
AND NOW, THANKS TO YOU...
A NEW SET OF EARS ON THE STREETS.
PO-PO

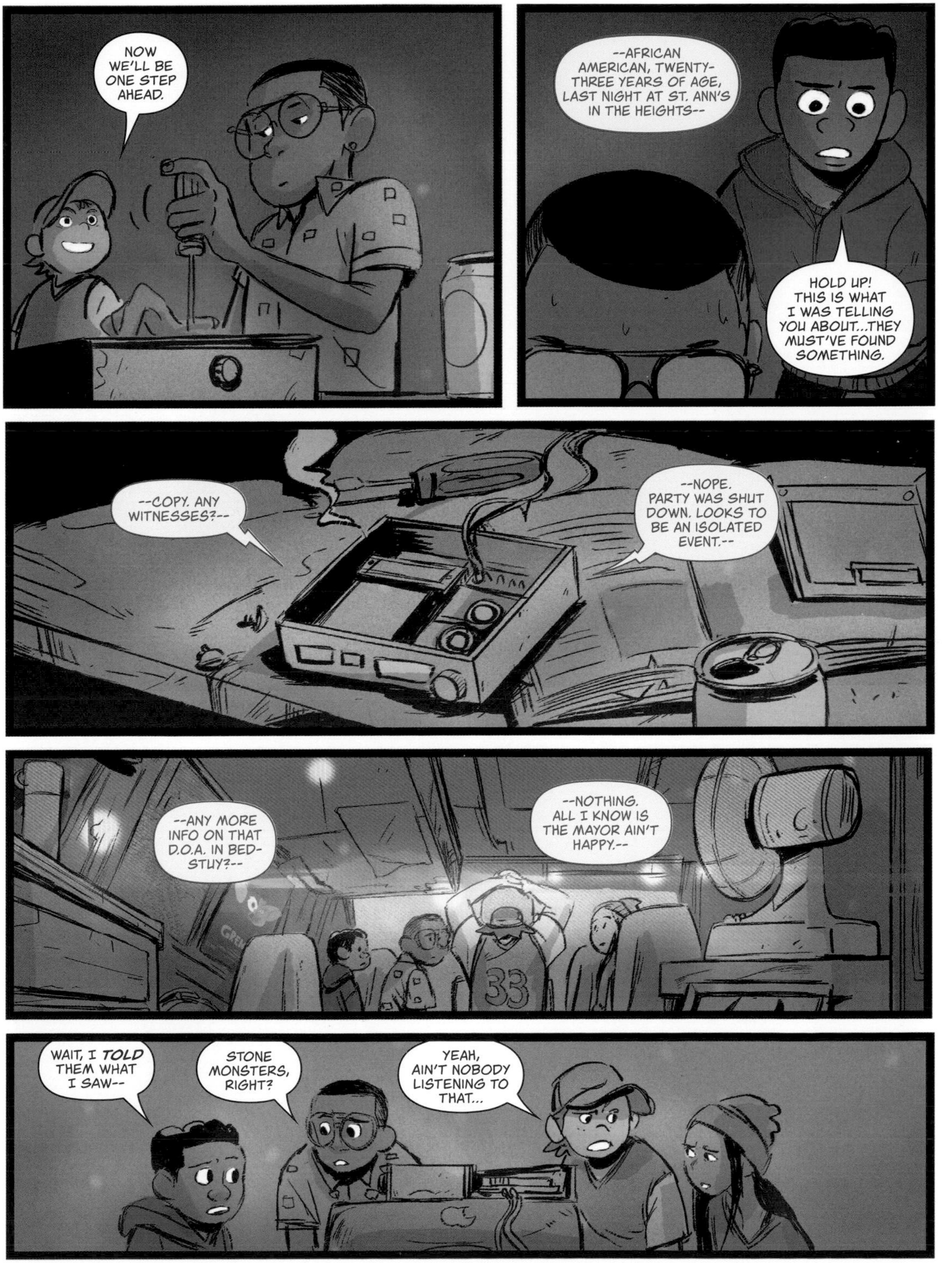
NOW WE'LL BE ONE STEP AHEAD.
--AFRICAN AMERICAN, TWENTY-THREE YEARS OF AGE, LAST NIGHT AT ST. ANN'S IN THE HEIGHTS--
HOLD UP! THIS IS WHAT I WAS TELLING YOU ABOUT...THEY MUST'VE FOUND SOMETHING.
--COPY. ANY WITNESSES?--
--NOPE. PARTY WAS SHUT DOWN. LOOKS TO BE AN ISOLATED EVENT.--
--ANY MORE INFO ON THAT D.O.A. IN BED-STUY?--
--NOTHING. ALL I KNOW IS THE MAYOR AIN'T HAPPY.--
33
WAIT, I *TOLD* THEM WHAT I SAW--
STONE MONSTERS, RIGHT?
YEAH, AIN'T NOBODY LISTENING TO THAT...

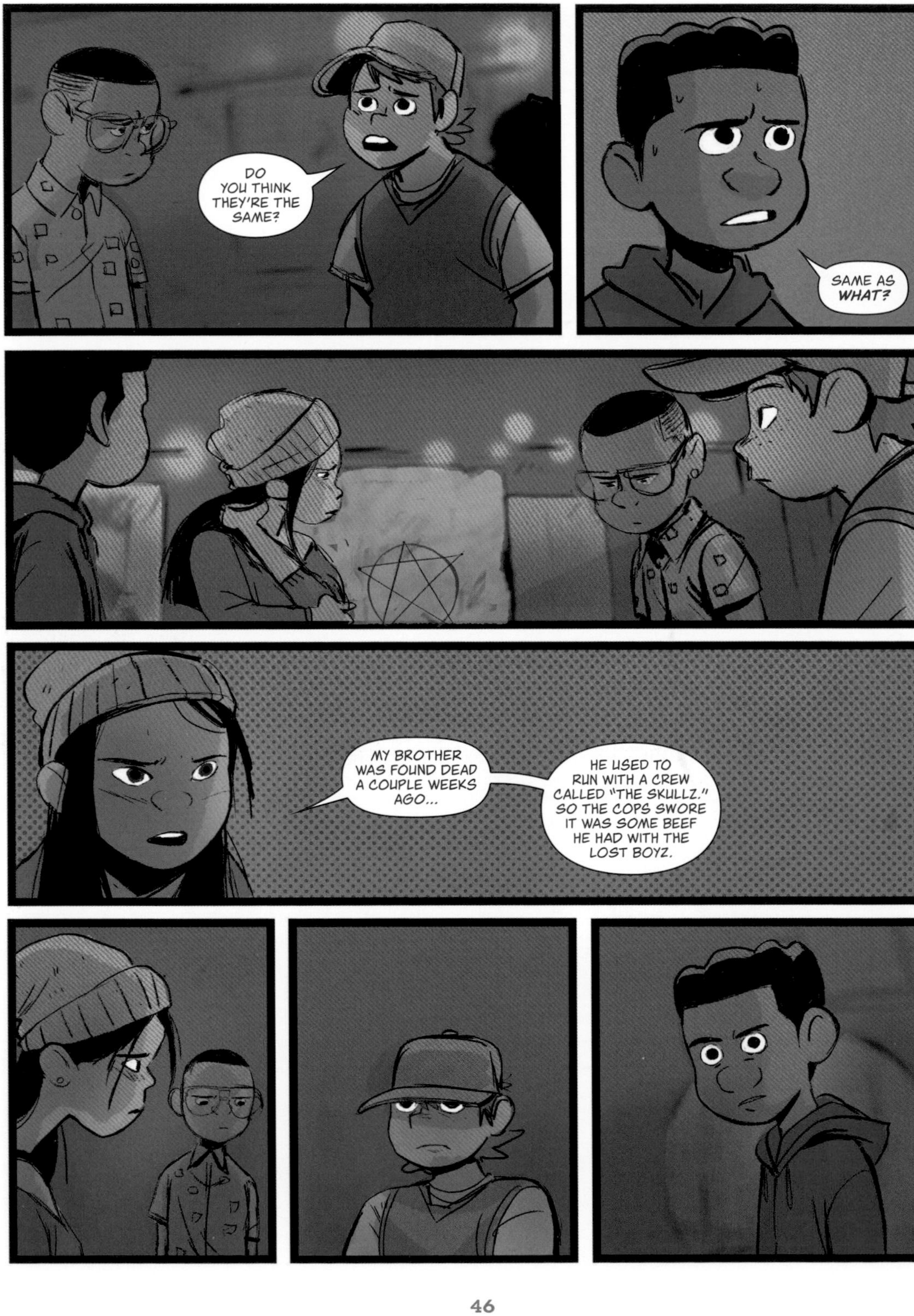
DO YOU THINK THEY'RE THE SAME?
SAME AS WHAT?
MY BROTHER WAS FOUND DEAD A COUPLE WEEKS AGO...
HE USED TO RUN WITH A CREW CALLED "THE SKULLZ." SO THE COPS SWORE IT WAS SOME BEEF HE HAD WITH THE LOST BOYZ.

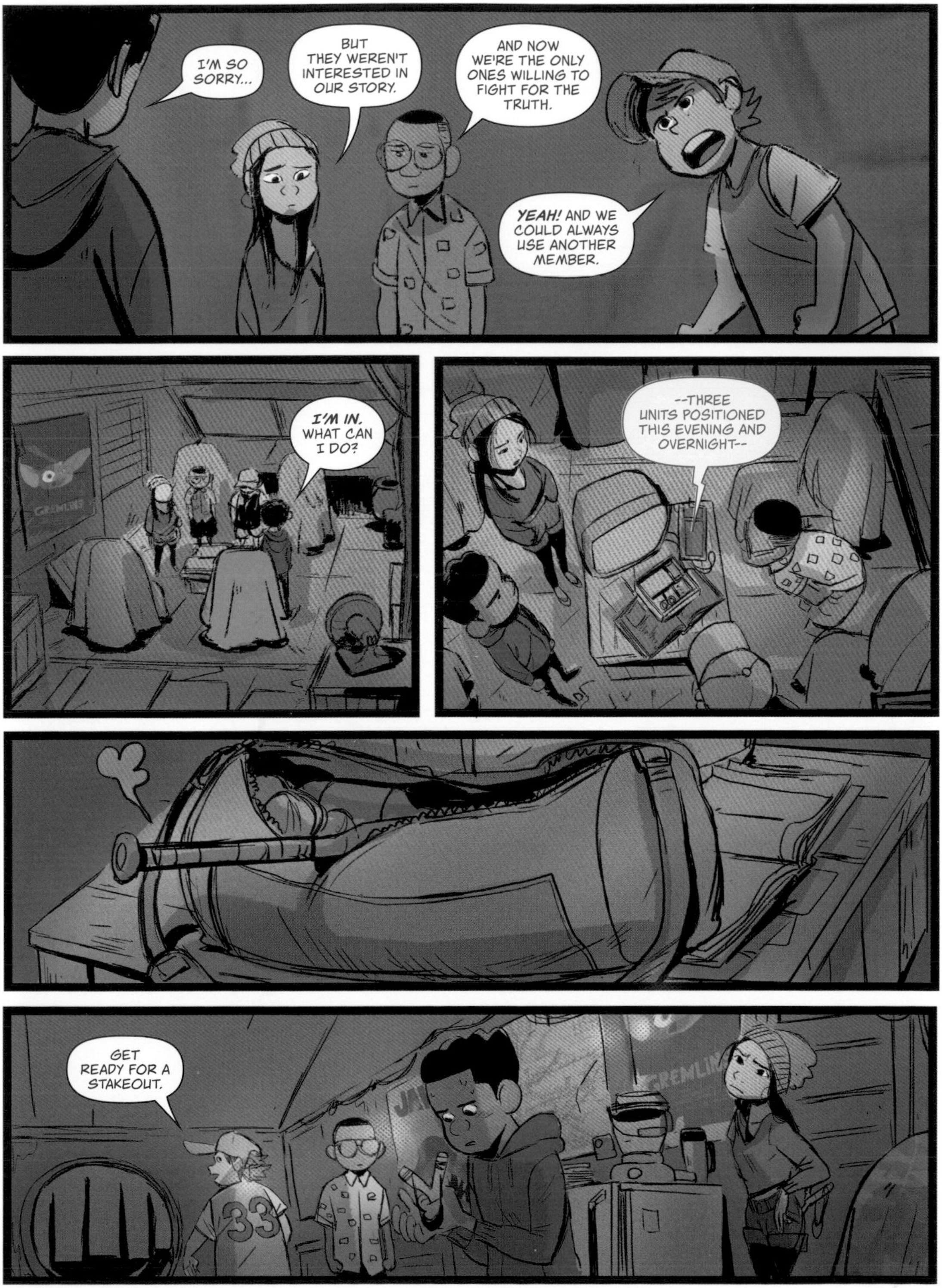
I'M SO SORRY...
BUT THEY WEREN'T INTERESTED IN OUR STORY.
AND NOW WE'RE THE ONLY ONES WILLING TO FIGHT FOR THE TRUTH.
YEAH! AND WE COULD ALWAYS USE ANOTHER MEMBER.
I'M IN. WHAT CAN I DO?
--THREE UNITS POSITIONED THIS EVENING AND OVERNIGHT--
GET READY FOR A STAKEOUT.

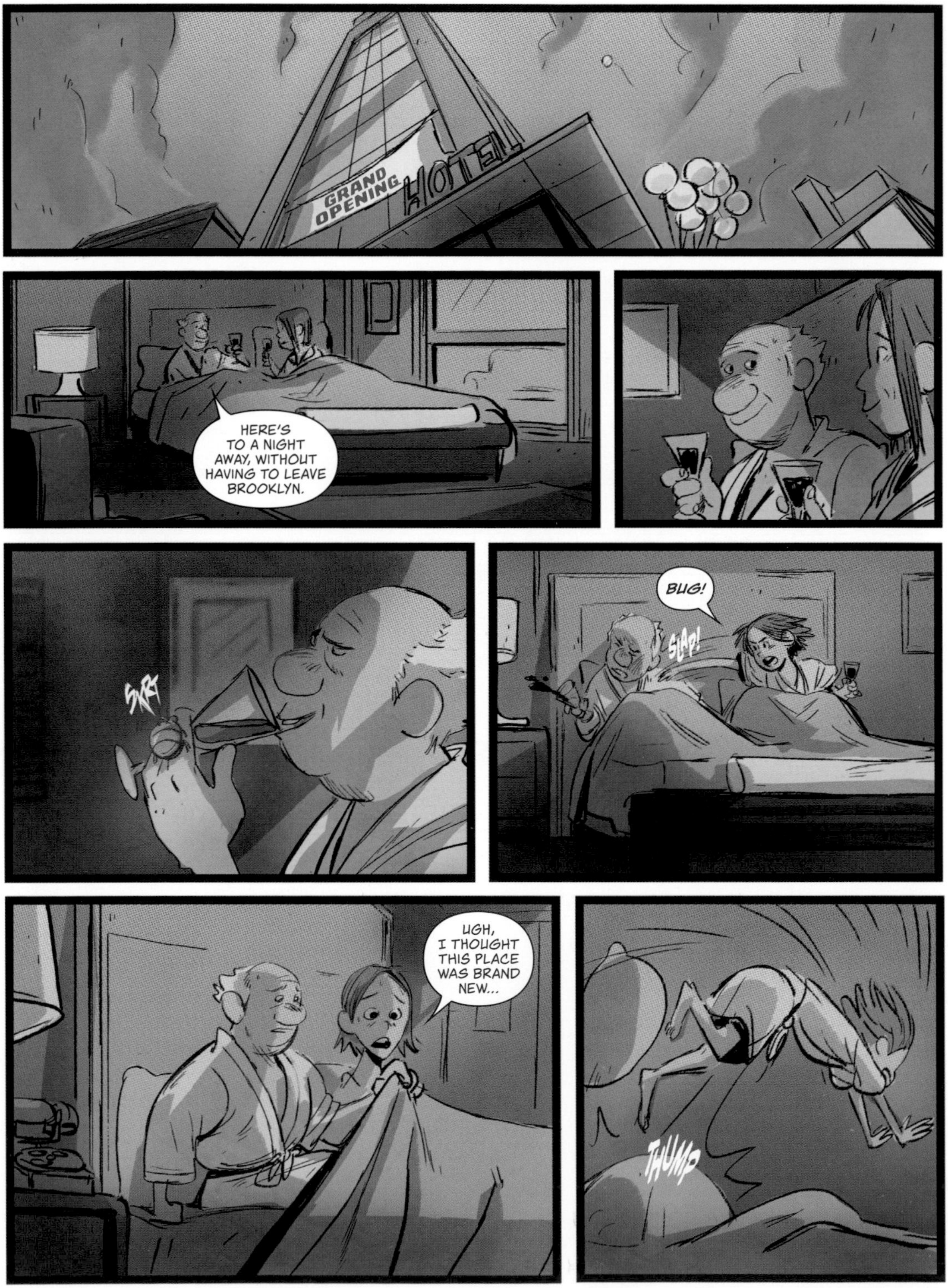
GRAND OPENING
HOTEL
HERE'S TO A NIGHT AWAY, WITHOUT HAVING TO LEAVE BROOKLYN.
BUG!
SLAP!
UGH, I THOUGHT THIS PLACE WAS BRAND NEW...
THUMP

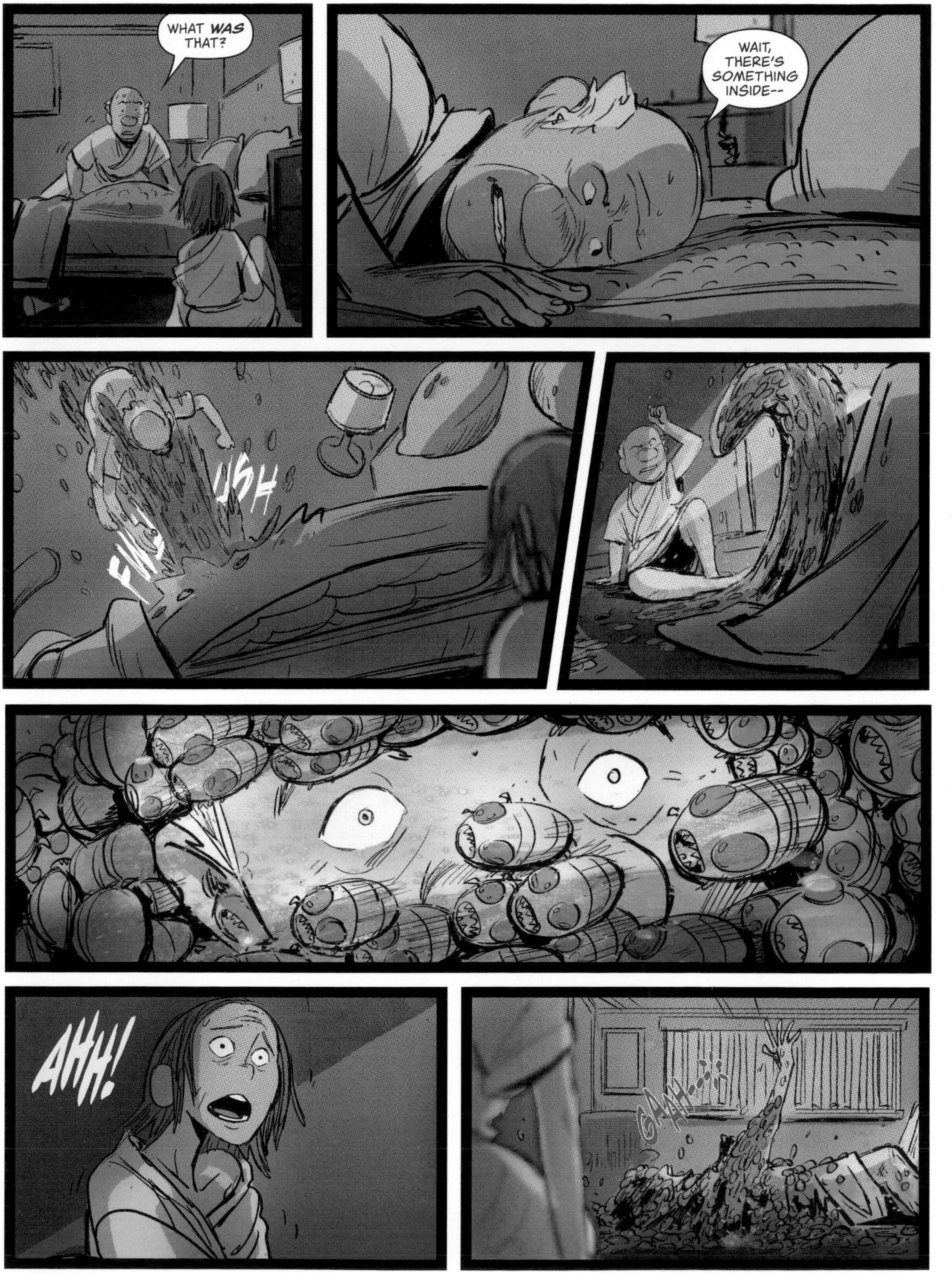
WHAT **WAS** THAT?
WAIT, THERE'S SOMETHING INSIDE--
USH
AHH!
GAAH...

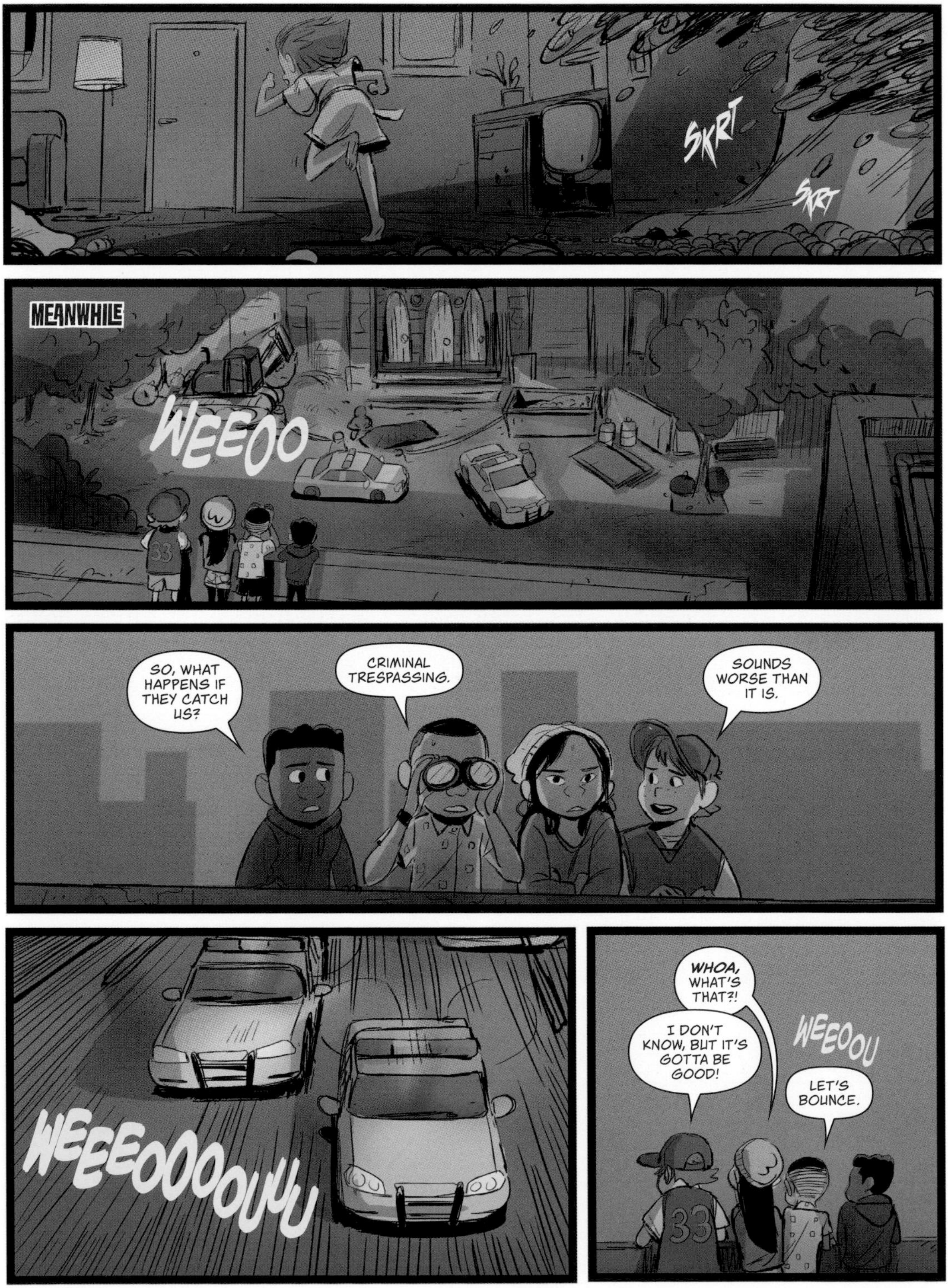
SKRT
SKRT
MEANWHILE
WEEOO
SO, WHAT HAPPENS IF THEY CATCH US?
CRIMINAL TRESPASSING.
SOUNDS WORSE THAN IT IS.
WEEEOOOOUUU
WHOA, WHAT'S THAT?!
I DON'T KNOW, BUT IT'S GOTTA BE GOOD!
WEEOOU
LET'S BOUNCE.

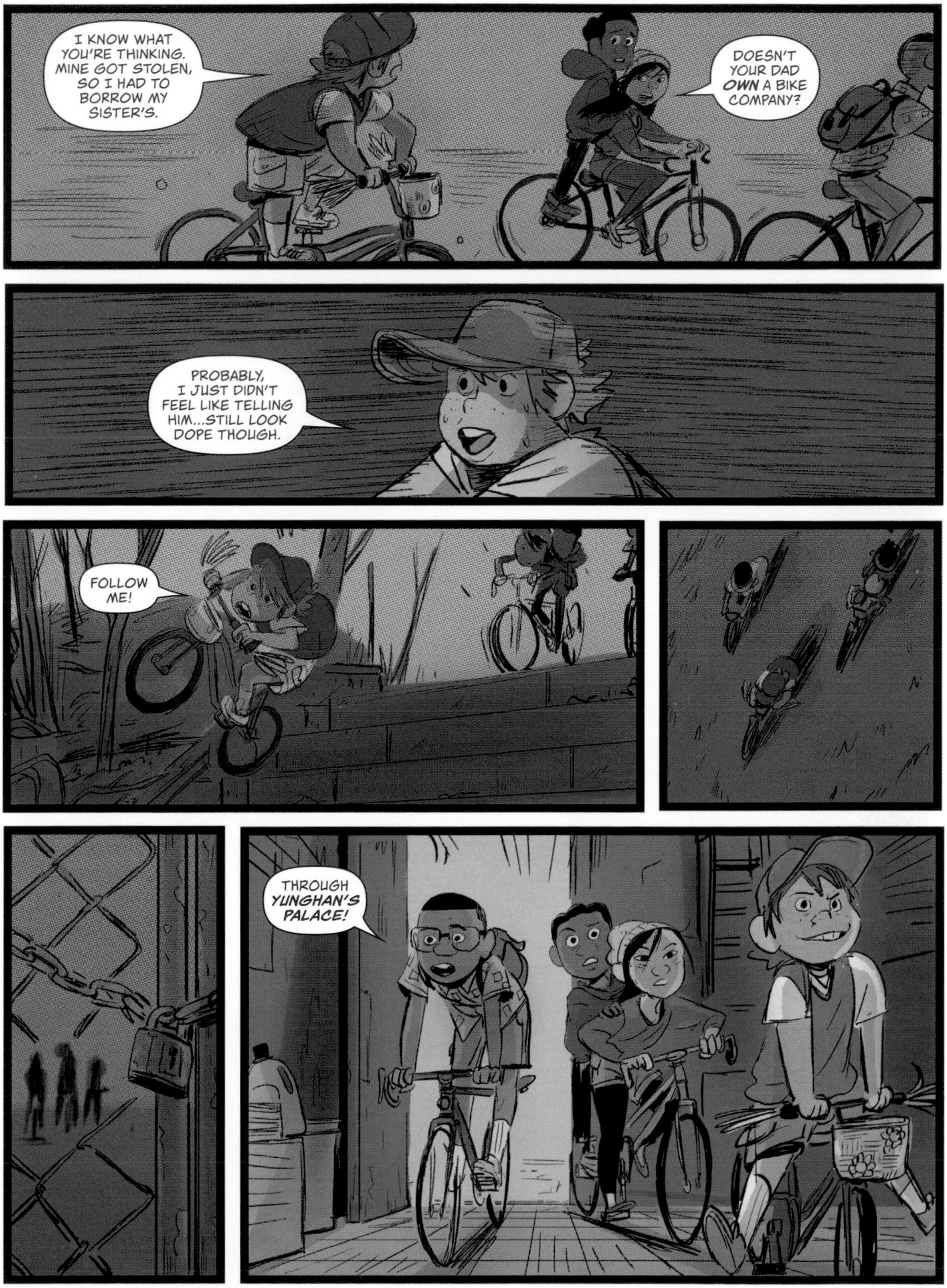
I KNOW WHAT YOU'RE THINKING. MINE GOT STOLEN, SO I HAD TO BORROW MY SISTER'S.
DOESN'T YOUR DAD OWN A BIKE COMPANY?
PROBABLY, I JUST DIDN'T FEEL LIKE TELLING HIM...STILL LOOK DOPE THOUGH.
FOLLOW ME!
THROUGH YUNGHAN'S PALACE!

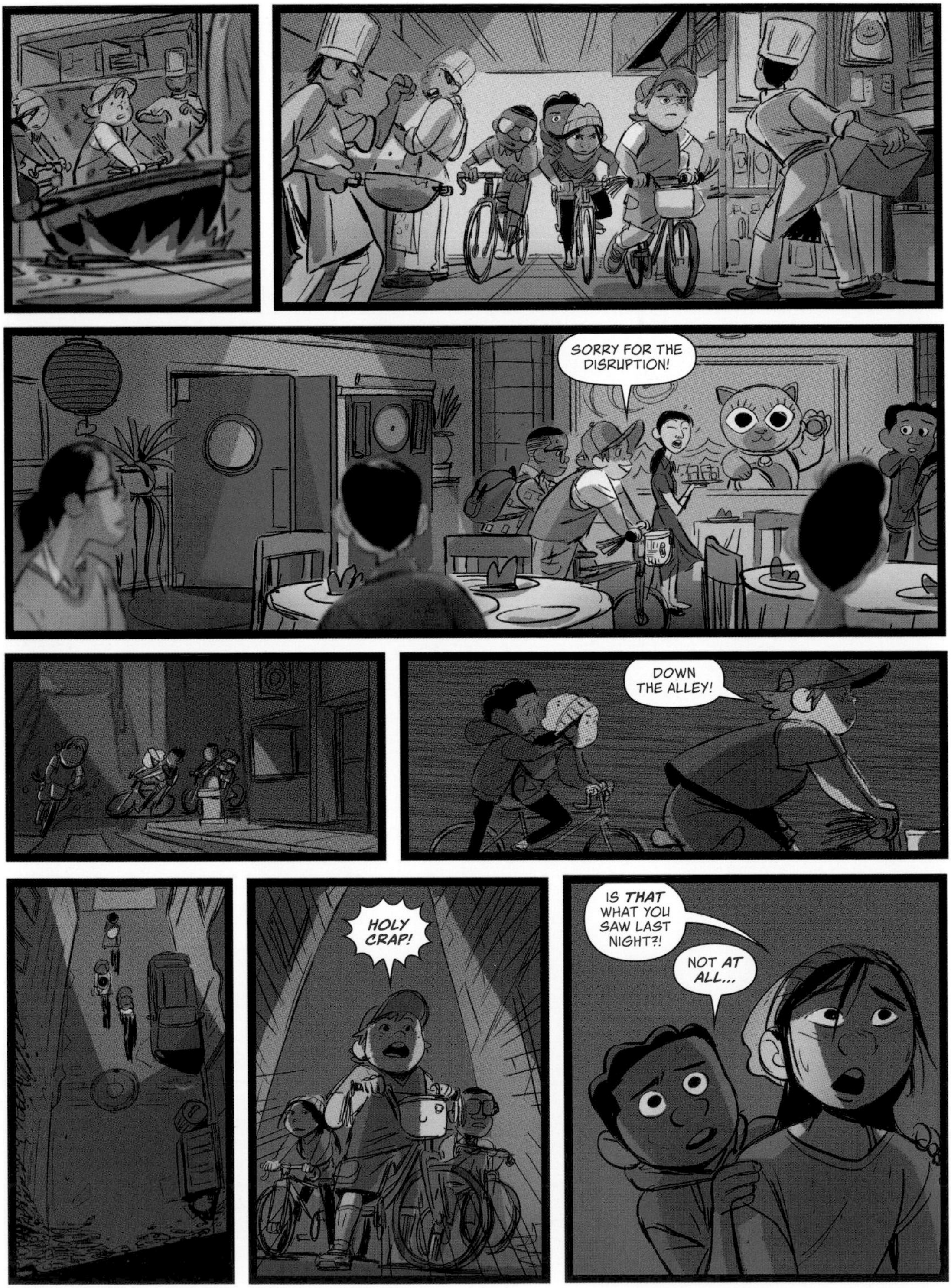
SORRY FOR THE DISRUPTION!
DOWN THE ALLEY!
HOLY CRAP!
IS THAT WHAT YOU SAW LAST NIGHT?!
NOT AT ALL...

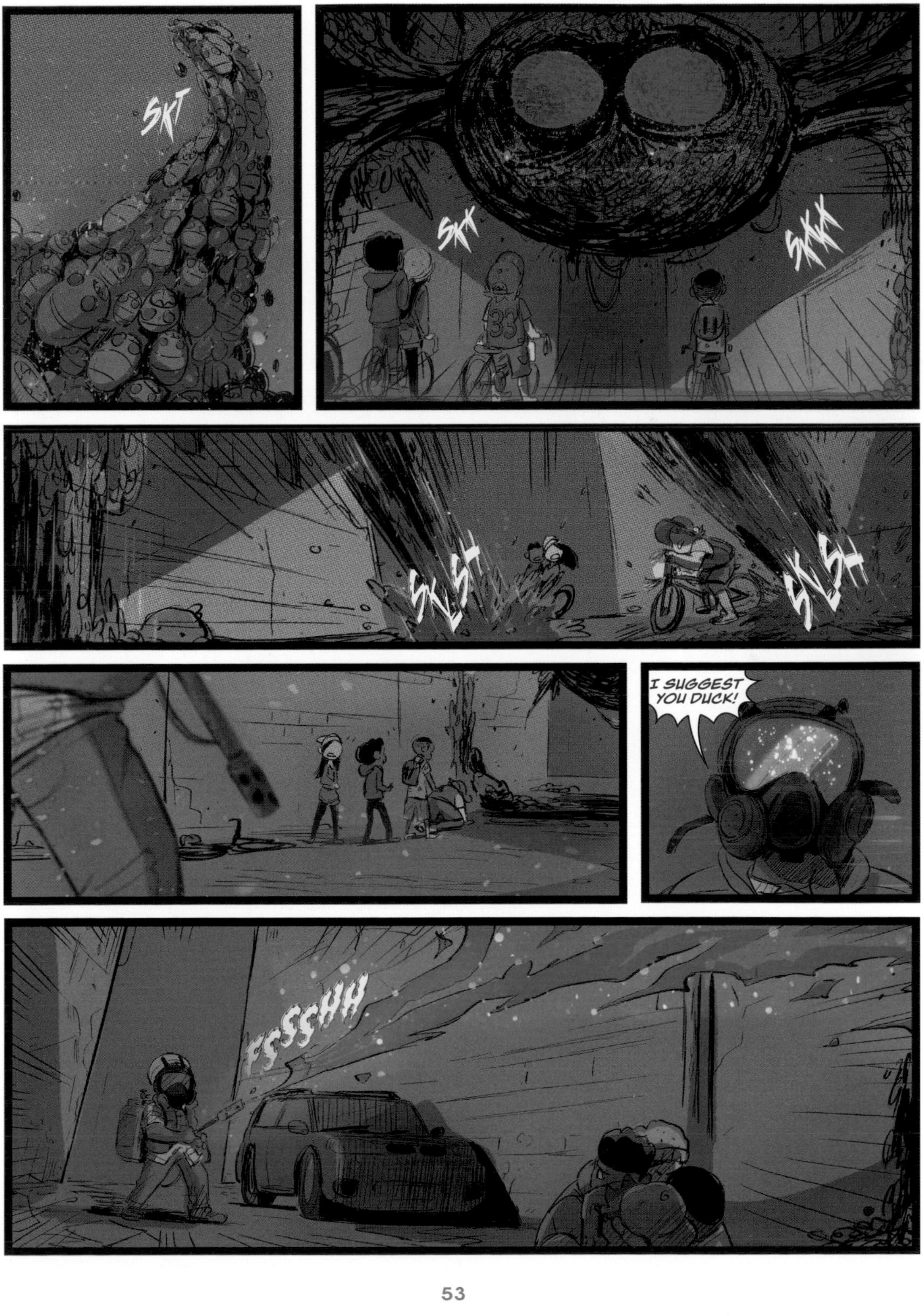
SKT
SKK
SKKK
SKSH
SKSH
I SUGGEST YOU DUCK!
FSSSHH

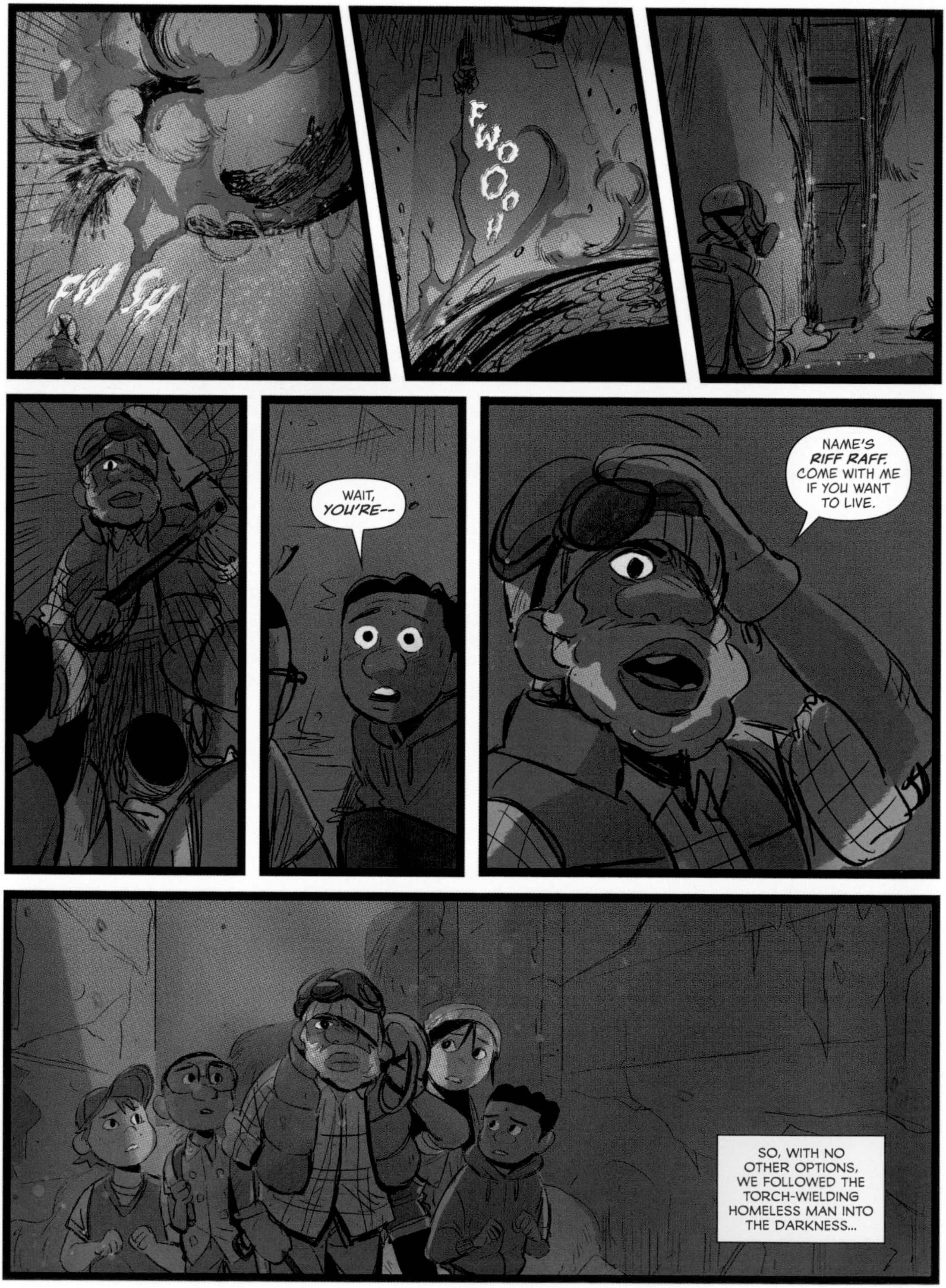
FWSH
FWOOOH
WAIT, YOU'RE--
NAME'S RIFF RAFF. COME WITH ME IF YOU WANT TO LIVE.
SO, WITH NO OTHER OPTIONS, WE FOLLOWED THE TORCH-WIELDING HOMELESS MAN INTO THE DARKNESS...

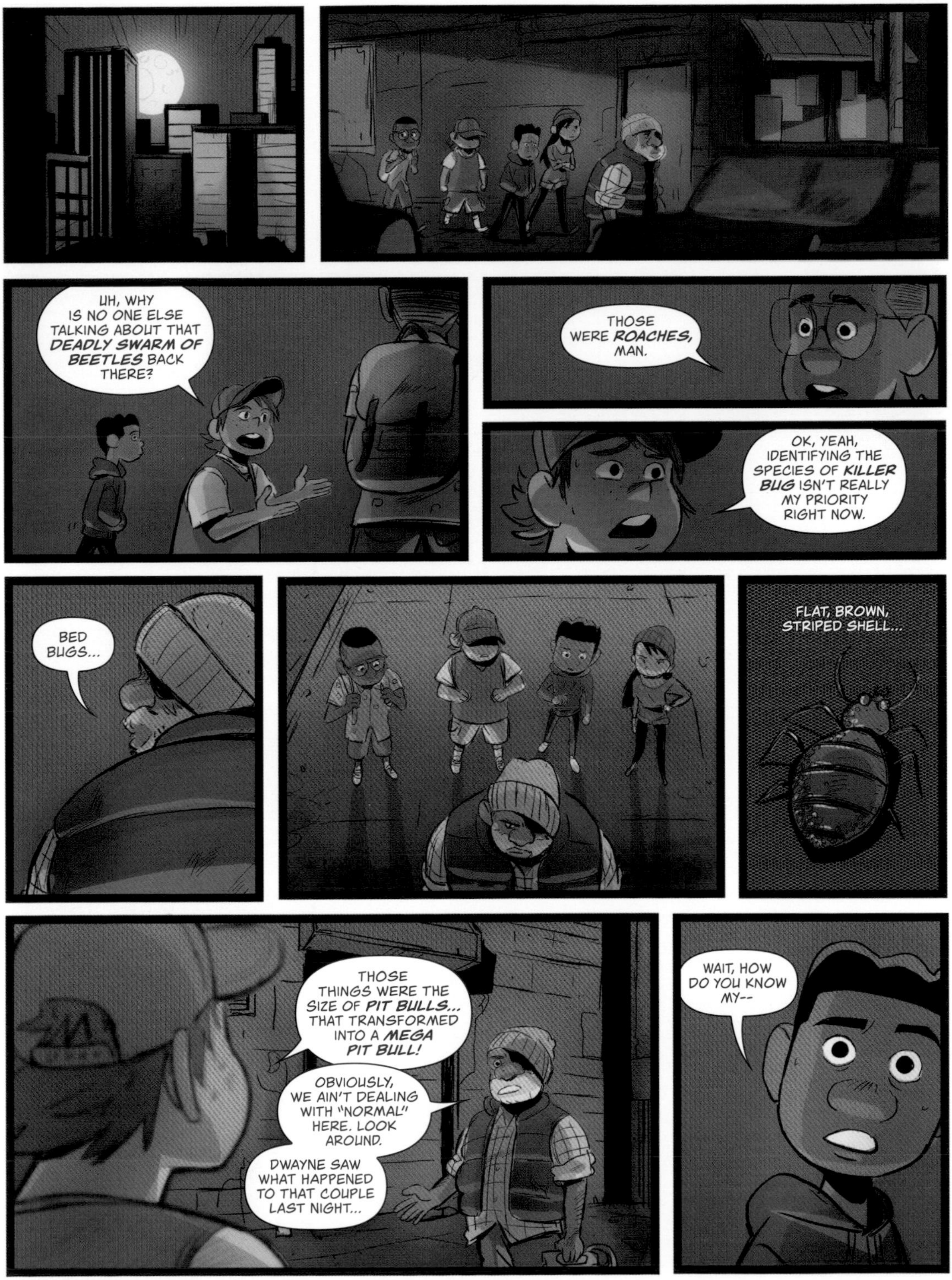
UH, WHY IS NO ONE ELSE TALKING ABOUT THAT DEADLY SWARM OF BEETLES BACK THERE?
THOSE WERE ROACHES, MAN.
OK, YEAH, IDENTIFYING THE SPECIES OF KILLER BUG ISN'T REALLY MY PRIORITY RIGHT NOW.
BED BUGS...
FLAT, BROWN, STRIPED SHELL...
THOSE THINGS WERE THE SIZE OF PIT BULLS... THAT TRANSFORMED INTO A MEGA PIT BULL!
OBVIOUSLY, WE AIN'T DEALING WITH "NORMAL" HERE. LOOK AROUND.
DWAYNE SAW WHAT HAPPENED TO THAT COUPLE LAST NIGHT...
WAIT, HOW DO YOU KNOW MY--

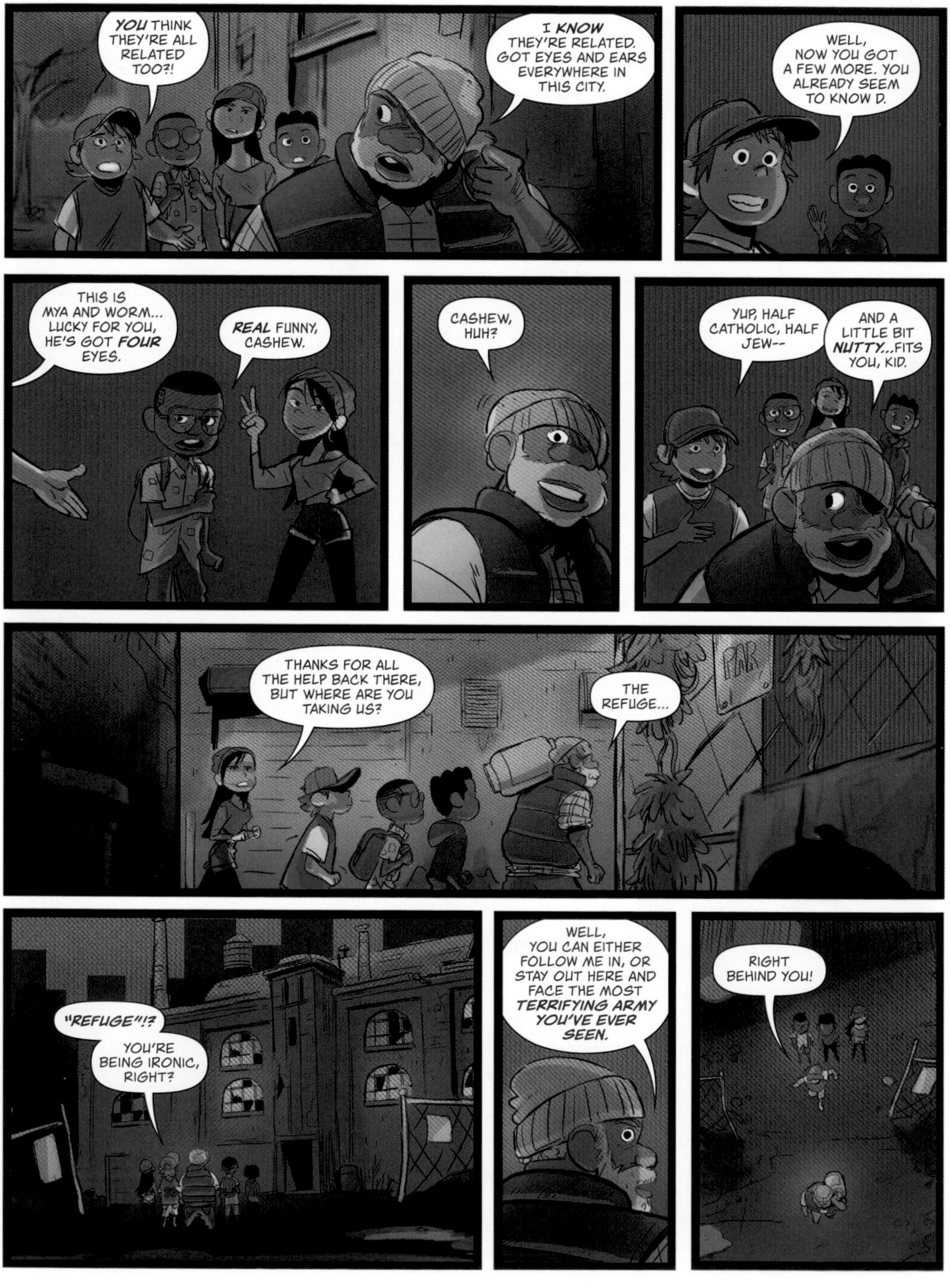
YOU THINK THEY'RE ALL RELATED TOO?!
I KNOW THEY'RE RELATED. GOT EYES AND EARS EVERYWHERE IN THIS CITY.
WELL, NOW YOU GOT A FEW MORE. YOU ALREADY SEEM TO KNOW D.
THIS IS MYA AND WORM... LUCKY FOR YOU, HE'S GOT FOUR EYES.
REAL FUNNY, CASHEW.
CASHEW, HUH?
YUP, HALF CATHOLIC, HALF JEW--
AND A LITTLE BIT NUTTY...FITS YOU, KID.
THANKS FOR ALL THE HELP BACK THERE, BUT WHERE ARE YOU TAKING US?
THE REFUGE...
"REFUGE"!?
YOU'RE BEING IRONIC, RIGHT?
WELL, YOU CAN EITHER FOLLOW ME IN, OR STAY OUT HERE AND FACE THE MOST TERRIFYING ARMY YOU'VE EVER SEEN.
RIGHT BEHIND YOU!

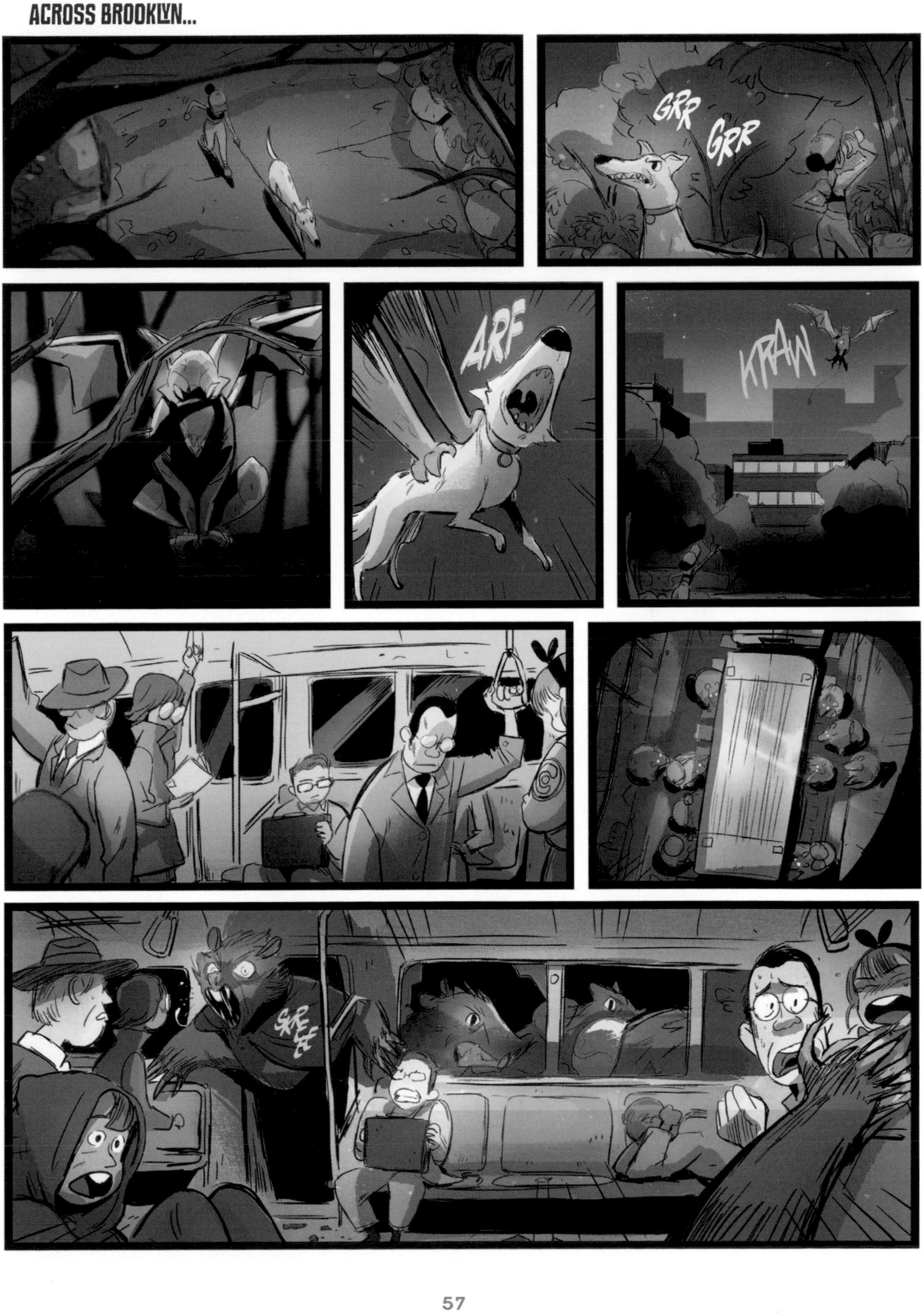
ACROSS BROOKLYN...
GRR
GRR
ARF
KRAW
SKREEE

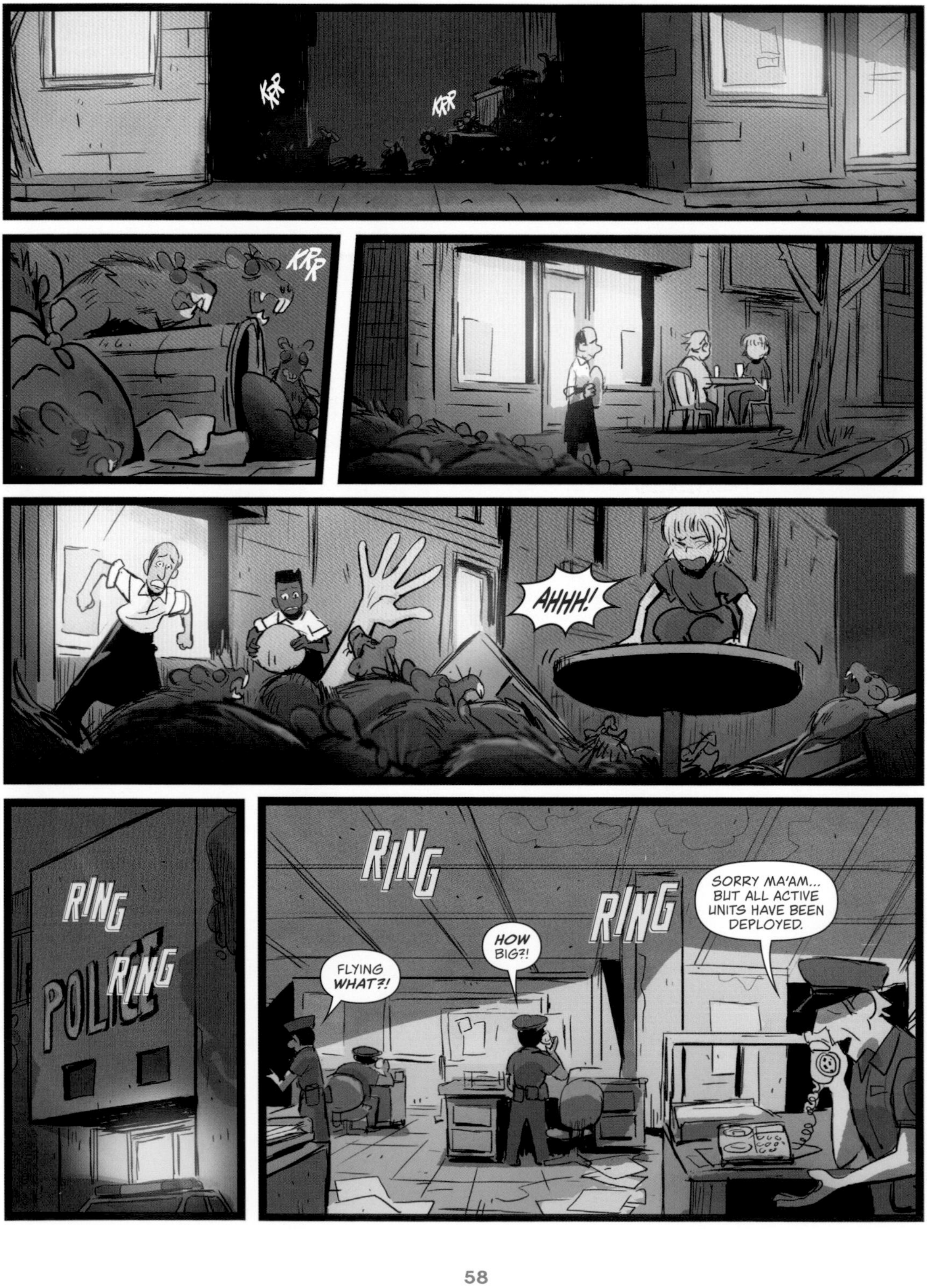
KRR
KRR
KRR
AHHH!
RING
RING
POLICE
RING
RING
FLYING WHAT?!
HOW BIG?!
SORRY MA'AM... BUT ALL ACTIVE UNITS HAVE BEEN DEPLOYED.

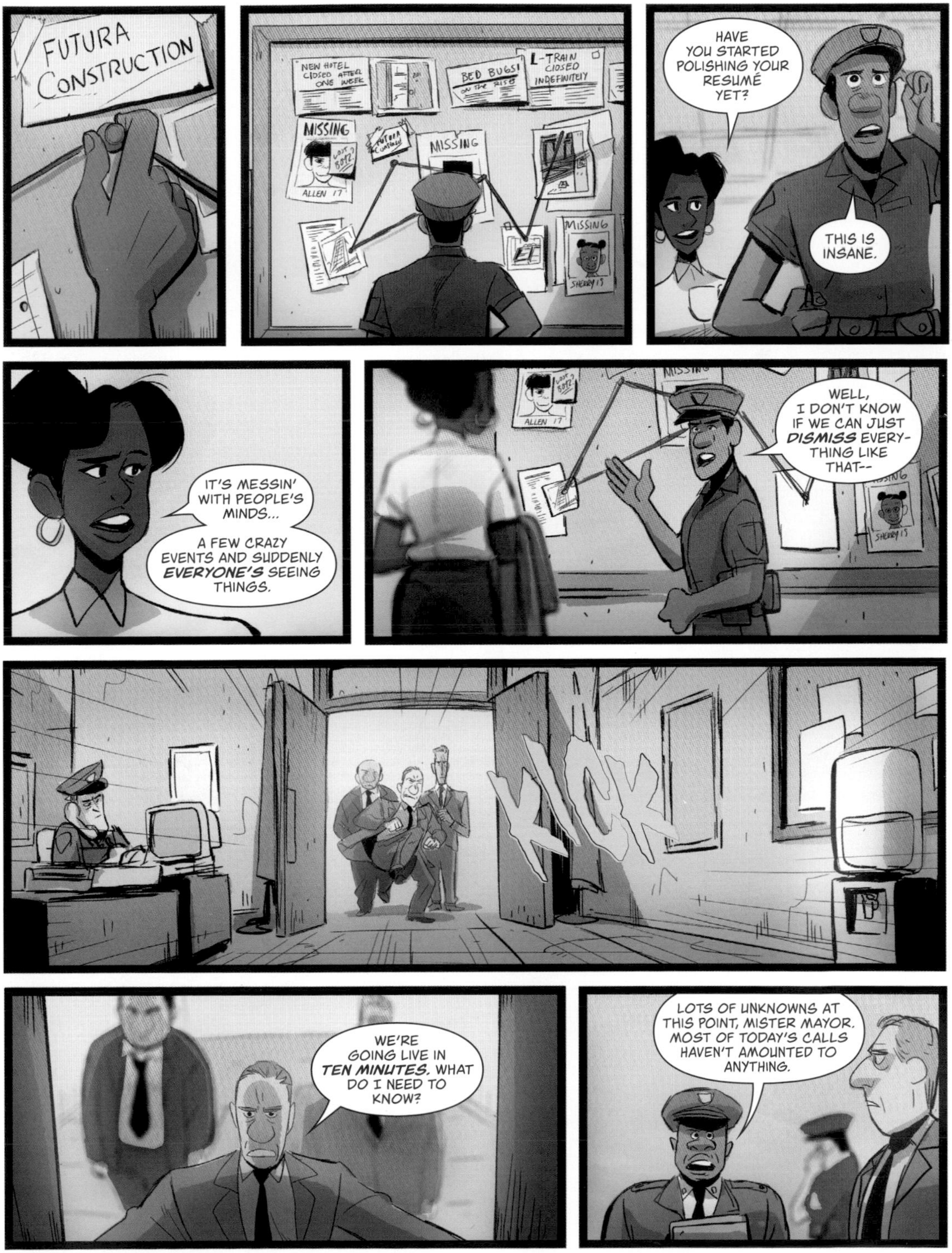
FUTURA CONSTRUCTION
NEW HOTEL CLOSED AFTER ONE WEEK
BED BUGS! ON THE RISE
L-TRAIN CLOSED INDEFINITELY
MISSING
ALLEN 17
MISSING
MISSING
SHERRY 15
HAVE YOU STARTED POLISHING YOUR RESUMÉ YET?
THIS IS INSANE.
IT'S MESSIN' WITH PEOPLE'S MINDS...
A FEW CRAZY EVENTS AND SUDDENLY EVERYONE'S SEEING THINGS.
WELL, I DON'T KNOW IF WE CAN JUST DISMISS EVERYTHING LIKE THAT--
KICK
WE'RE GOING LIVE IN TEN MINUTES. WHAT DO I NEED TO KNOW?
LOTS OF UNKNOWNS AT THIS POINT, MISTER MAYOR. MOST OF TODAY'S CALLS HAVEN'T AMOUNTED TO ANYTHING.

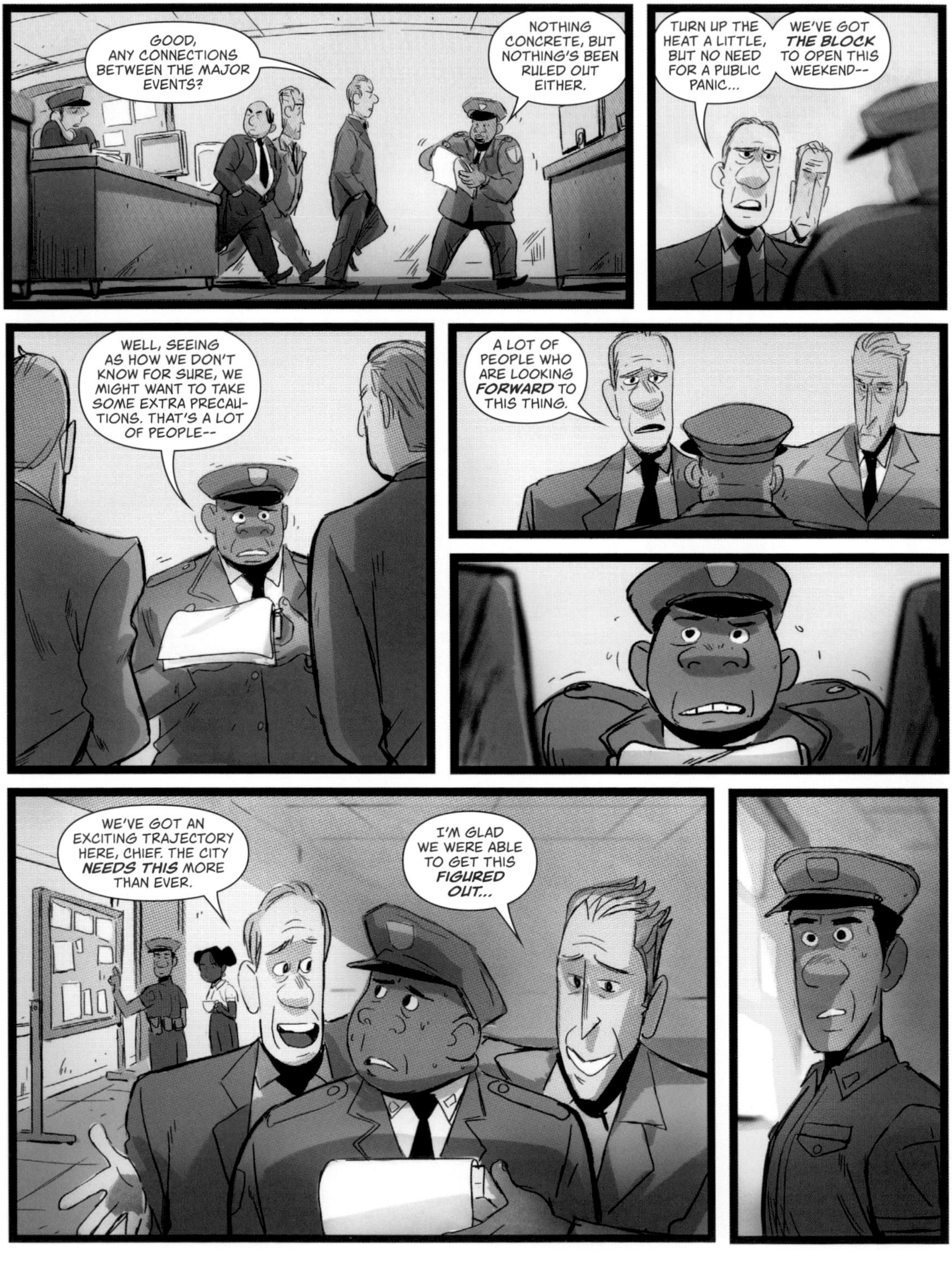
GOOD, ANY CONNECTIONS BETWEEN THE MAJOR EVENTS?
NOTHING CONCRETE, BUT NOTHING'S BEEN RULED OUT EITHER.
TURN UP THE HEAT A LITTLE, BUT NO NEED FOR A PUBLIC PANIC...
WE'VE GOT THE BLOCK TO OPEN THIS WEEKEND--
WELL, SEEING AS HOW WE DON'T KNOW FOR SURE, WE MIGHT WANT TO TAKE SOME EXTRA PRECAUTIONS. THAT'S A LOT OF PEOPLE--
A LOT OF PEOPLE WHO ARE LOOKING FORWARD TO THIS THING.
WE'VE GOT AN EXCITING TRAJECTORY HERE, CHIEF. THE CITY NEEDS THIS MORE THAN EVER.
I'M GLAD WE WERE ABLE TO GET THIS FIGURED OUT...

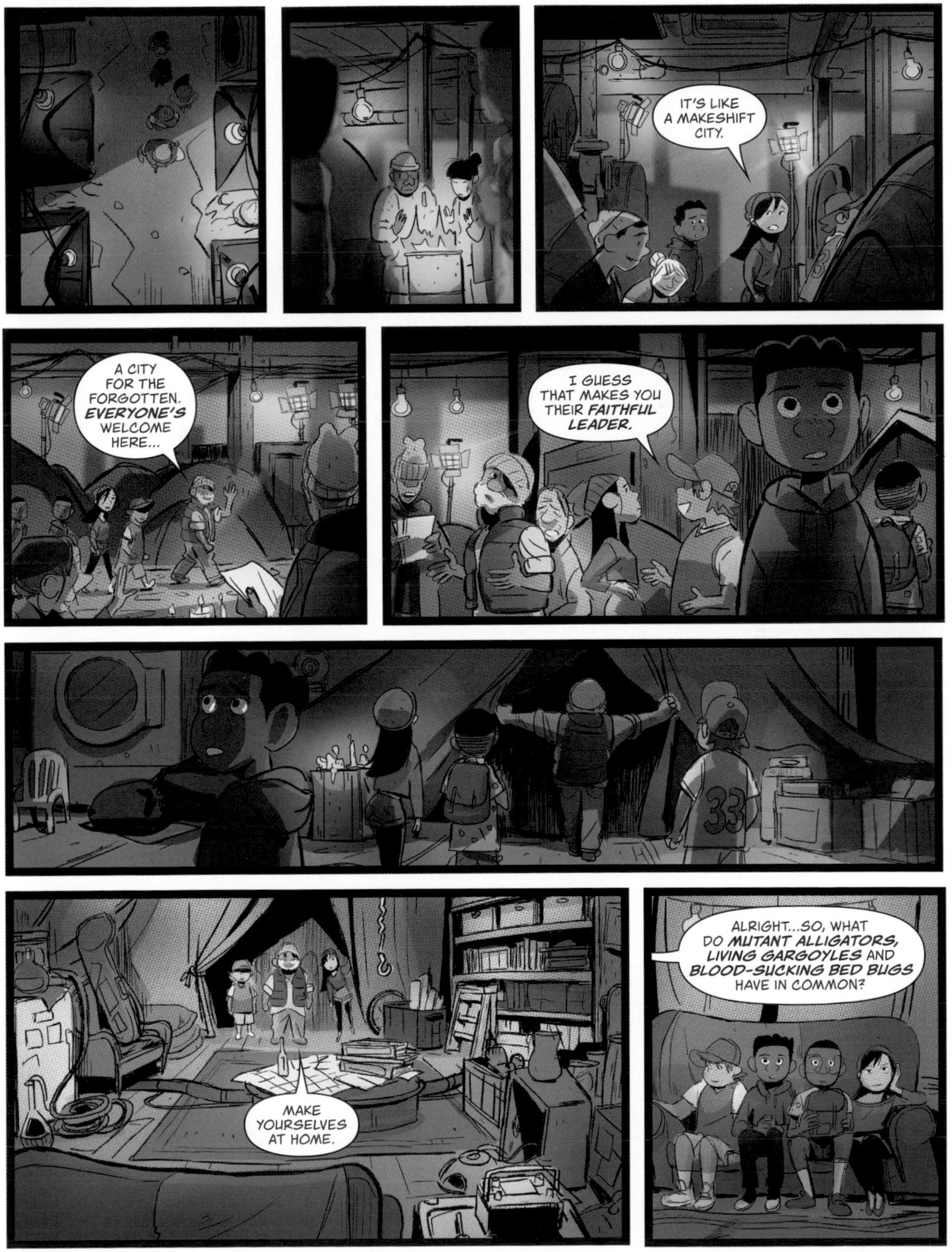
IT'S LIKE A MAKESHIFT CITY.
A CITY FOR THE FORGOTTEN. EVERYONE'S WELCOME HERE...
I GUESS THAT MAKES YOU THEIR FAITHFUL LEADER.
MAKE YOURSELVES AT HOME.
ALRIGHT...SO, WHAT DO MUTANT ALLIGATORS, LIVING GARGOYLES AND BLOOD-SUCKING BED BUGS HAVE IN COMMON?

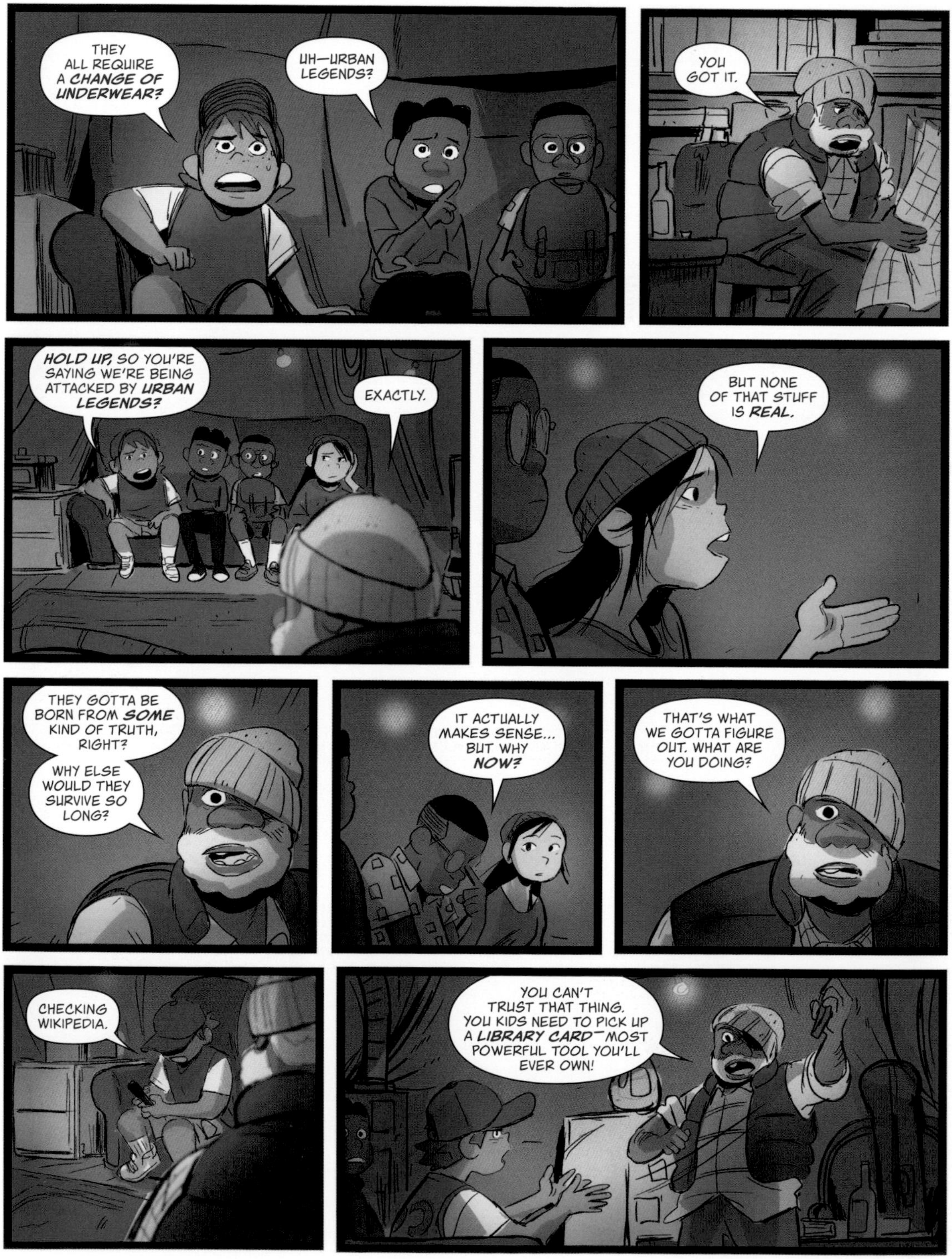
THEY ALL REQUIRE A CHANGE OF UNDERWEAR?
UH—URBAN LEGENDS?
YOU GOT IT.
HOLD UP, SO YOU'RE SAYING WE'RE BEING ATTACKED BY URBAN LEGENDS?
EXACTLY.
BUT NONE OF THAT STUFF IS REAL.
THEY GOTTA BE BORN FROM SOME KIND OF TRUTH, RIGHT?
WHY ELSE WOULD THEY SURVIVE SO LONG?
IT ACTUALLY MAKES SENSE... BUT WHY NOW?
THAT'S WHAT WE GOTTA FIGURE OUT. WHAT ARE YOU DOING?
CHECKING WIKIPEDIA.
YOU CAN'T TRUST THAT THING. YOU KIDS NEED TO PICK UP A LIBRARY CARD—MOST POWERFUL TOOL YOU'LL EVER OWN!

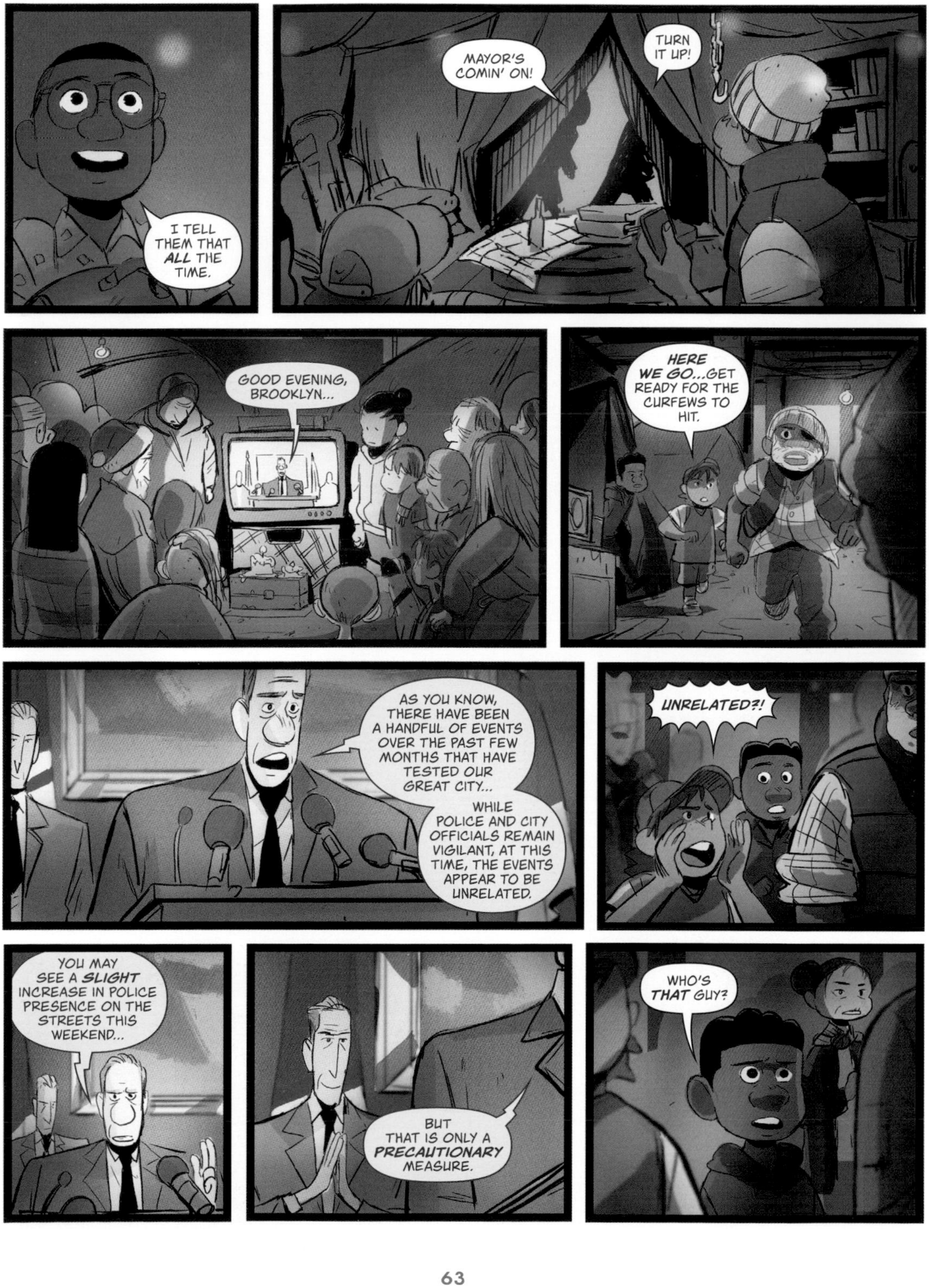

I TELL THEM THAT ALL THE TIME.
MAYOR'S COMIN' ON!
TURN IT UP!
GOOD EVENING, BROOKLYN...
HERE WE GO...GET READY FOR THE CURFEWS TO HIT.
AS YOU KNOW, THERE HAVE BEEN A HANDFUL OF EVENTS OVER THE PAST FEW MONTHS THAT HAVE TESTED OUR GREAT CITY...
WHILE POLICE AND CITY OFFICIALS REMAIN VIGILANT, AT THIS TIME, THE EVENTS APPEAR TO BE UNRELATED.
UNRELATED?!
YOU MAY SEE A SLIGHT INCREASE IN POLICE PRESENCE ON THE STREETS THIS WEEKEND...
BUT THAT IS ONLY A PRECAUTIONARY MEASURE.
WHO'S THAT GUY?

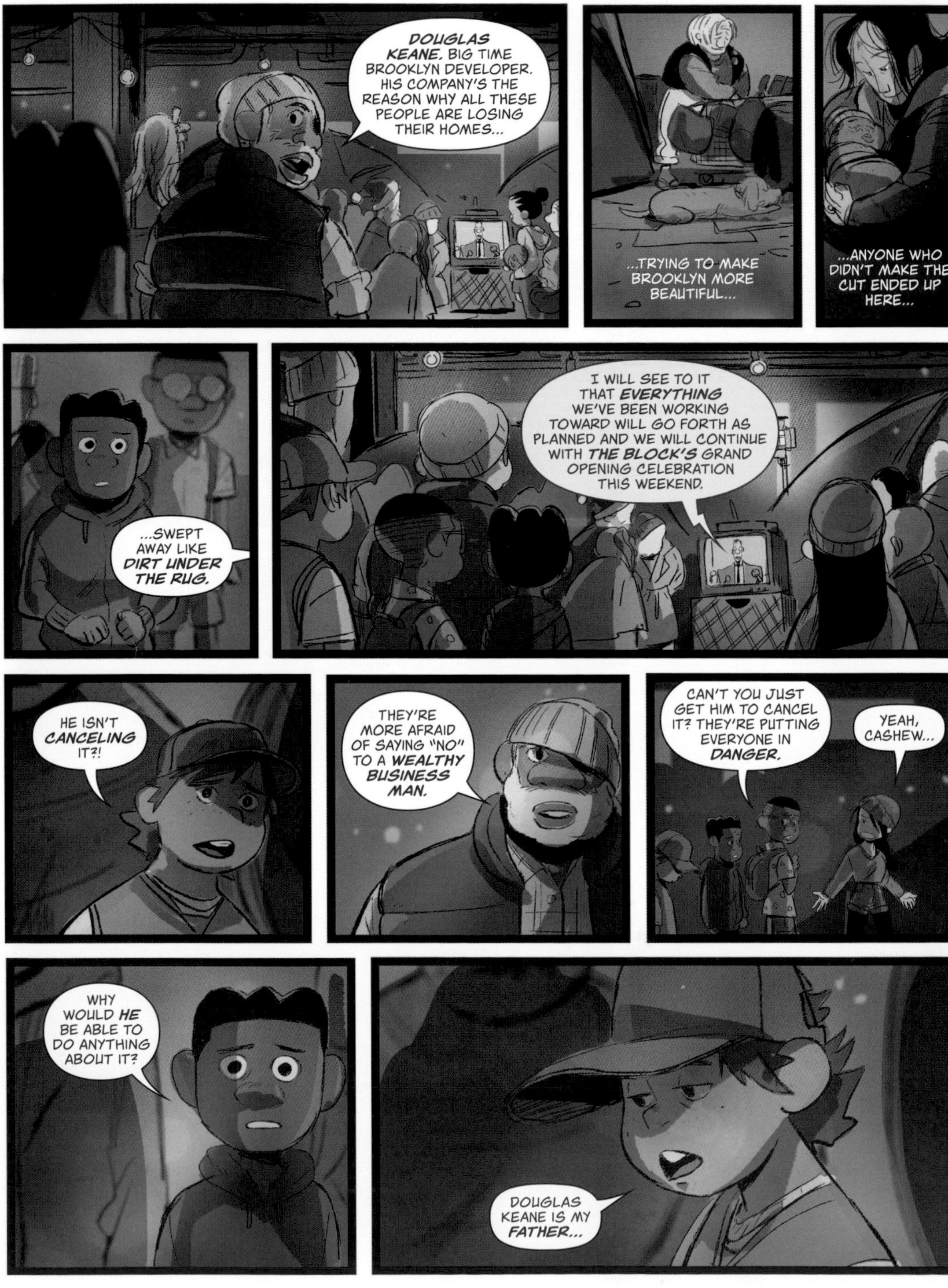
DOUGLAS KEANE. BIG TIME BROOKLYN DEVELOPER. HIS COMPANY'S THE REASON WHY ALL THESE PEOPLE ARE LOSING THEIR HOMES...
...TRYING TO MAKE BROOKLYN MORE BEAUTIFUL...
...ANYONE WHO DIDN'T MAKE THE CUT ENDED UP HERE...
...SWEPT AWAY LIKE DIRT UNDER THE RUG.
I WILL SEE TO IT THAT EVERYTHING WE'VE BEEN WORKING TOWARD WILL GO FORTH AS PLANNED AND WE WILL CONTINUE WITH THE BLOCK'S GRAND OPENING CELEBRATION THIS WEEKEND.
HE ISN'T CANCELING IT?!
THEY'RE MORE AFRAID OF SAYING "NO" TO A WEALTHY BUSINESS MAN.
CAN'T YOU JUST GET HIM TO CANCEL IT? THEY'RE PUTTING EVERYONE IN DANGER.
YEAH, CASHEW...
WHY WOULD HE BE ABLE TO DO ANYTHING ABOUT IT?
DOUGLAS KEANE IS MY FATHER...

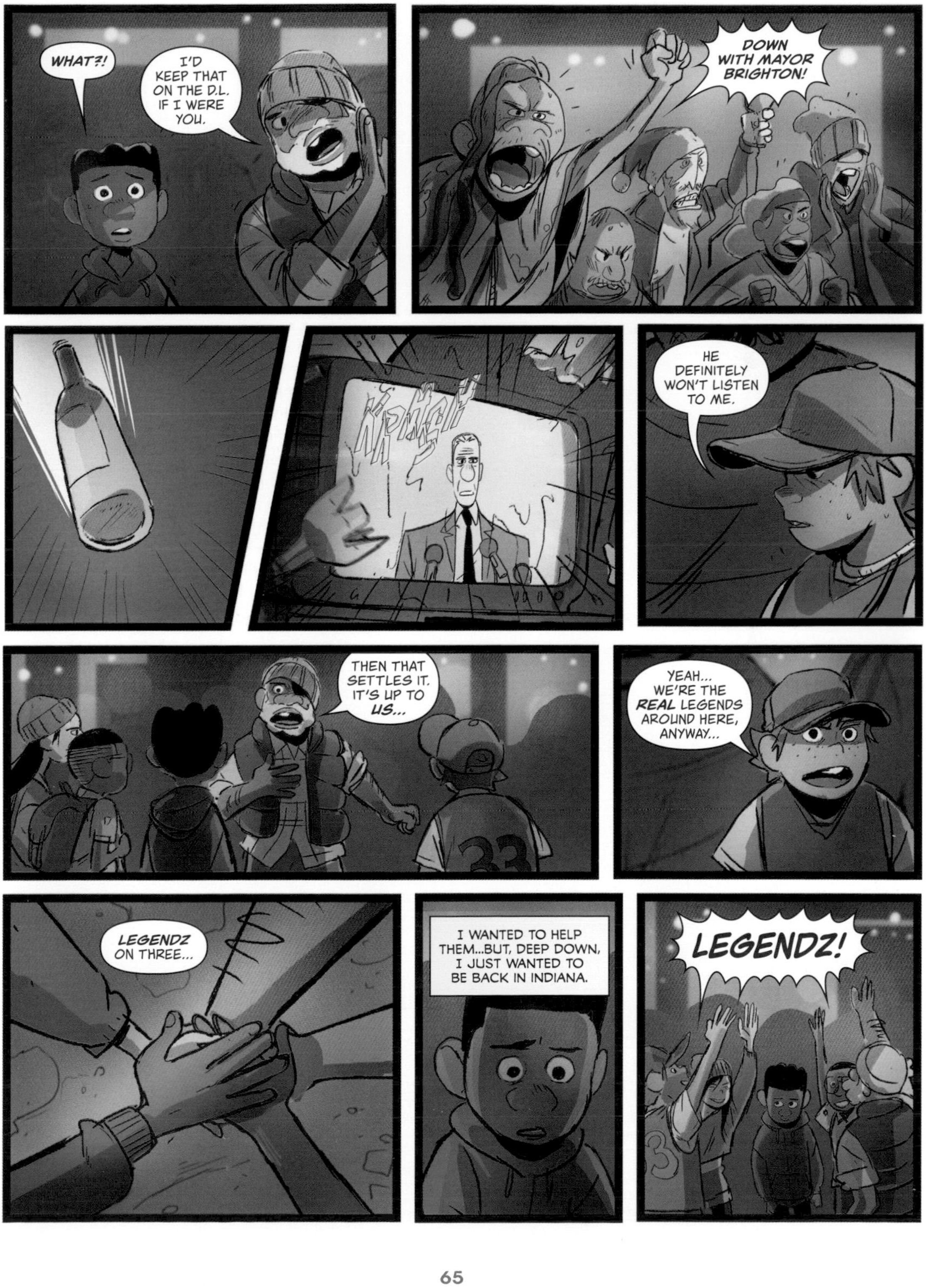
WHAT?!
I'D KEEP THAT ON THE D.L. IF I WERE YOU.
DOWN WITH MAYOR BRIGHTON!
HE DEFINITELY WON'T LISTEN TO ME.
THEN THAT SETTLES IT. IT'S UP TO US...
YEAH... WE'RE THE REAL LEGENDS AROUND HERE, ANYWAY...
LEGENDZ ON THREE...
I WANTED TO HELP THEM...BUT, DEEP DOWN, I JUST WANTED TO BE BACK IN INDIANA.
LEGENDZ!

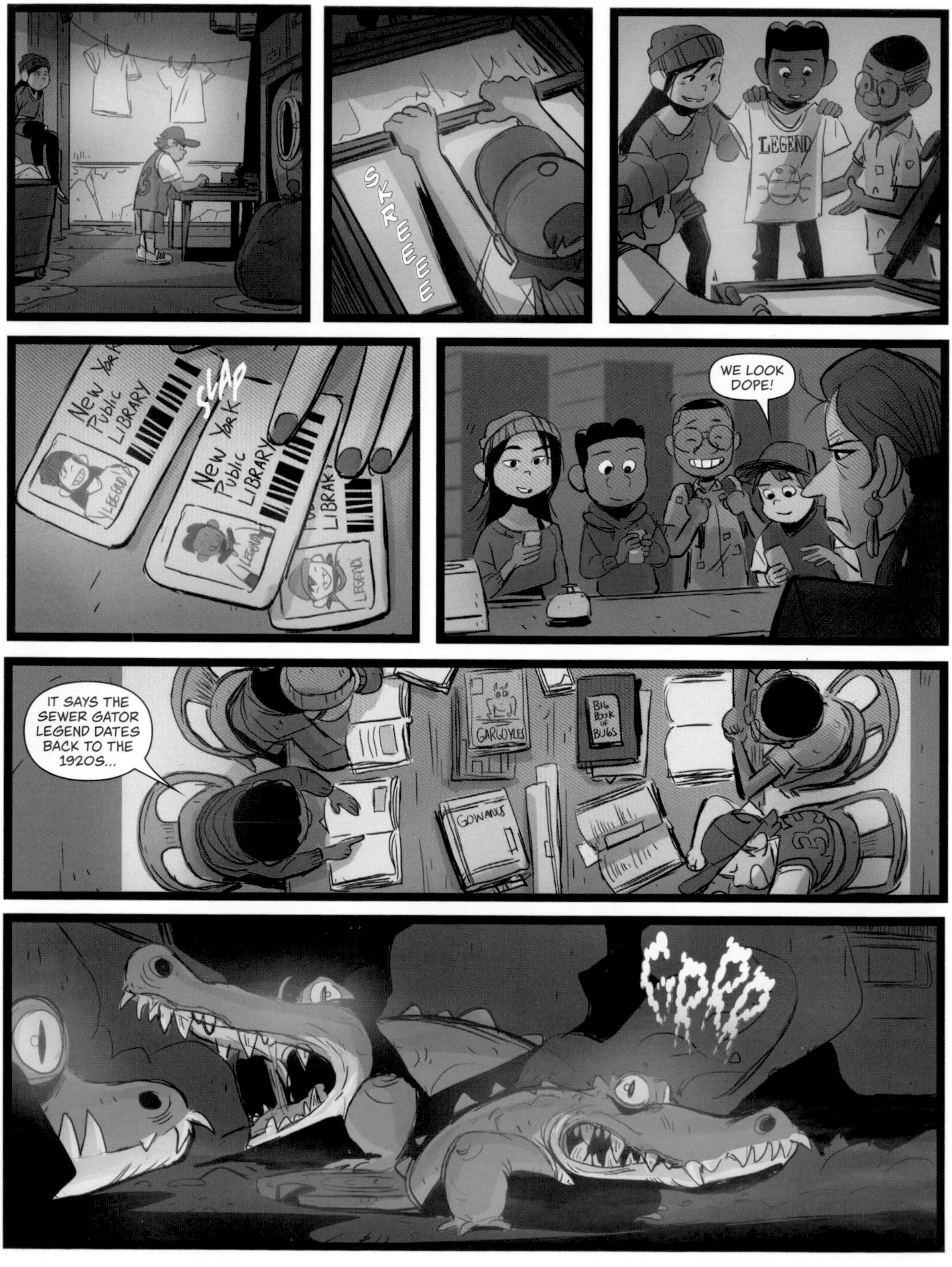
SKREEEE
LEGEND
New York Public LIBRARY
SLAP
New York Public LIBRARY
LEGEND
WE LOOK DOPE!
IT SAYS THE SEWER GATOR LEGEND DATES BACK TO THE 1920S...
GARGOYLES
BIG BOOK OF BUGS
GOWANUS
GRRR

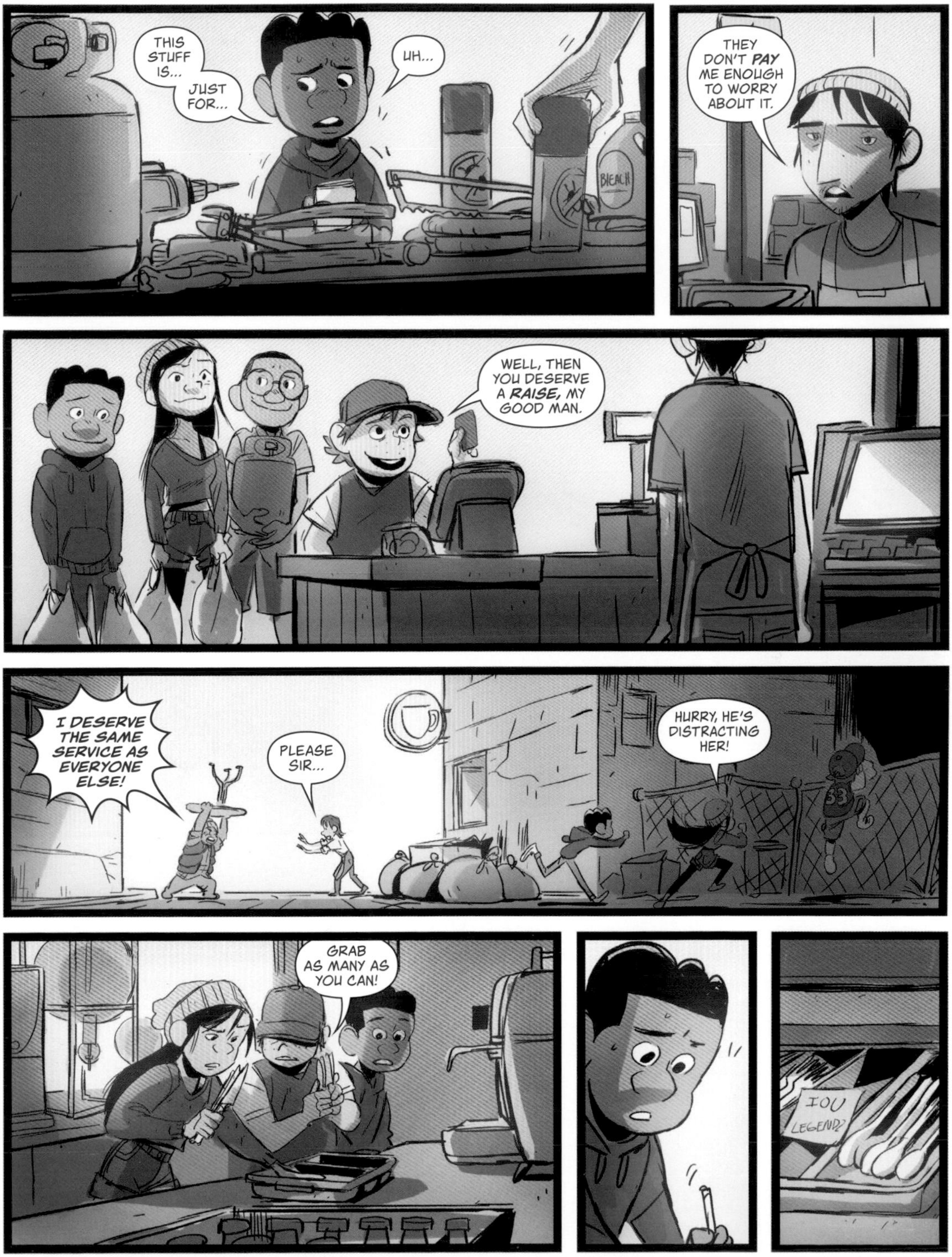

THIS STUFF IS... JUST FOR...
UH...
BLEACH
THEY DON'T PAY ME ENOUGH TO WORRY ABOUT IT.
WELL, THEN YOU DESERVE A RAISE, MY GOOD MAN.
I DESERVE THE SAME SERVICE AS EVERYONE ELSE!
PLEASE SIR...
HURRY, HE'S DISTRACTING HER!
33
GRAB AS MANY AS YOU CAN!
IOU
LEGEND?

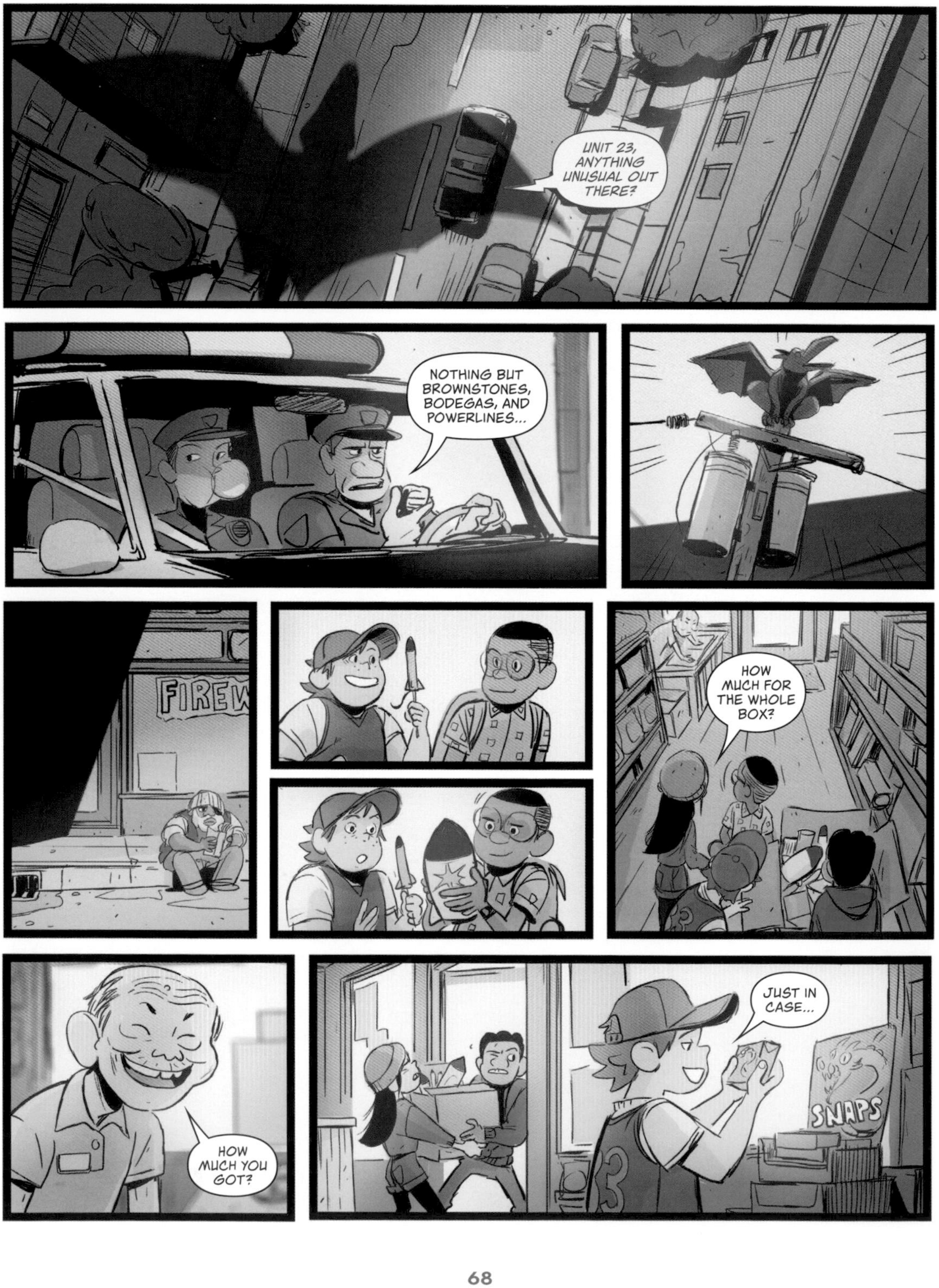
UNIT 23, ANYTHING UNUSUAL OUT THERE?
NOTHING BUT BROWNSTONES, BODEGAS, AND POWERLINES...
FIREW
HOW MUCH FOR THE WHOLE BOX?
HOW MUCH YOU GOT?
JUST IN CASE...
SNAPS

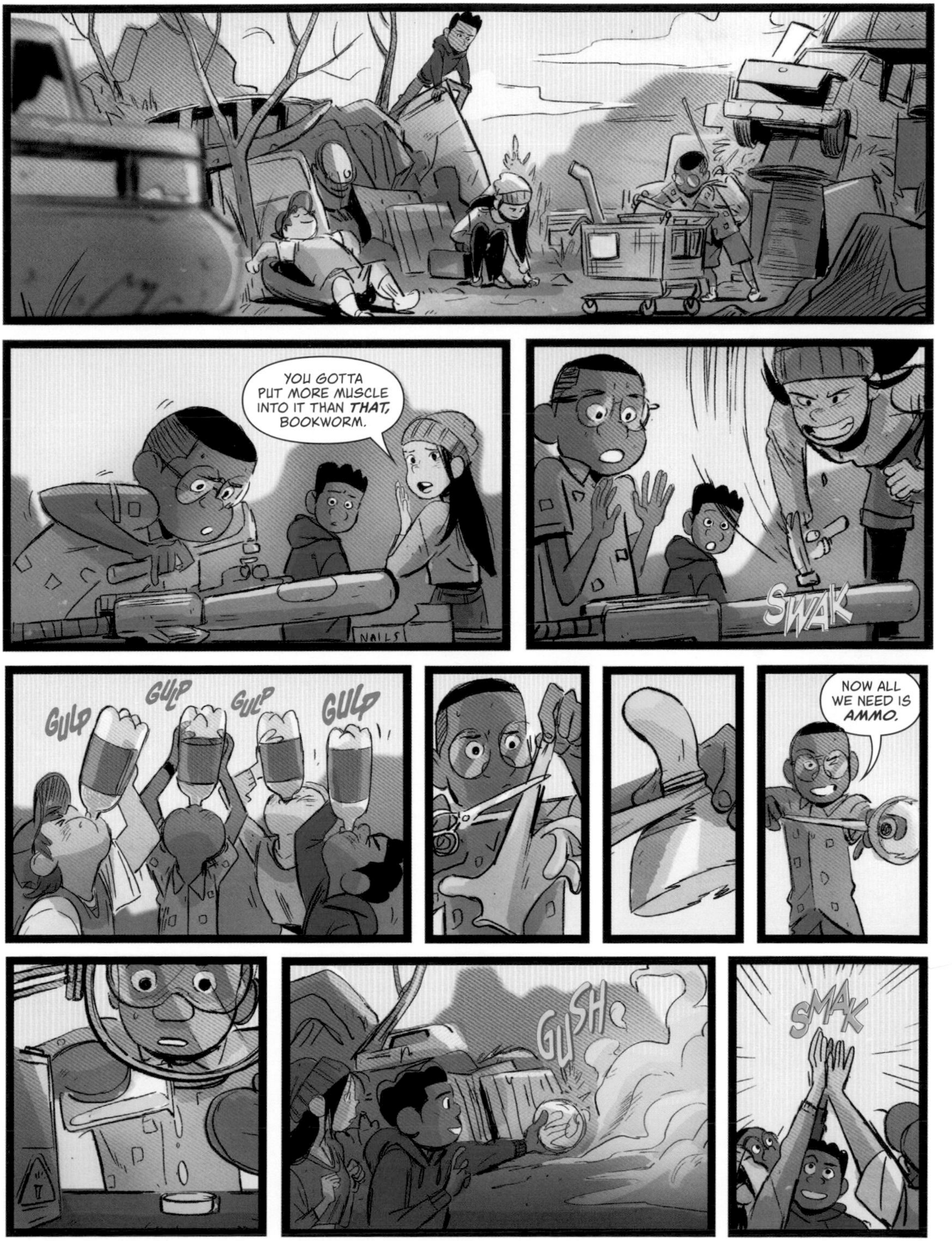
YOU GOTTA PUT MORE MUSCLE INTO IT THAN THAT, BOOKWORM.
NAILS
SWAK
GULP
GULP
GULP
GULP
NOW ALL WE NEED IS AMMO.
GUSH
SMAK

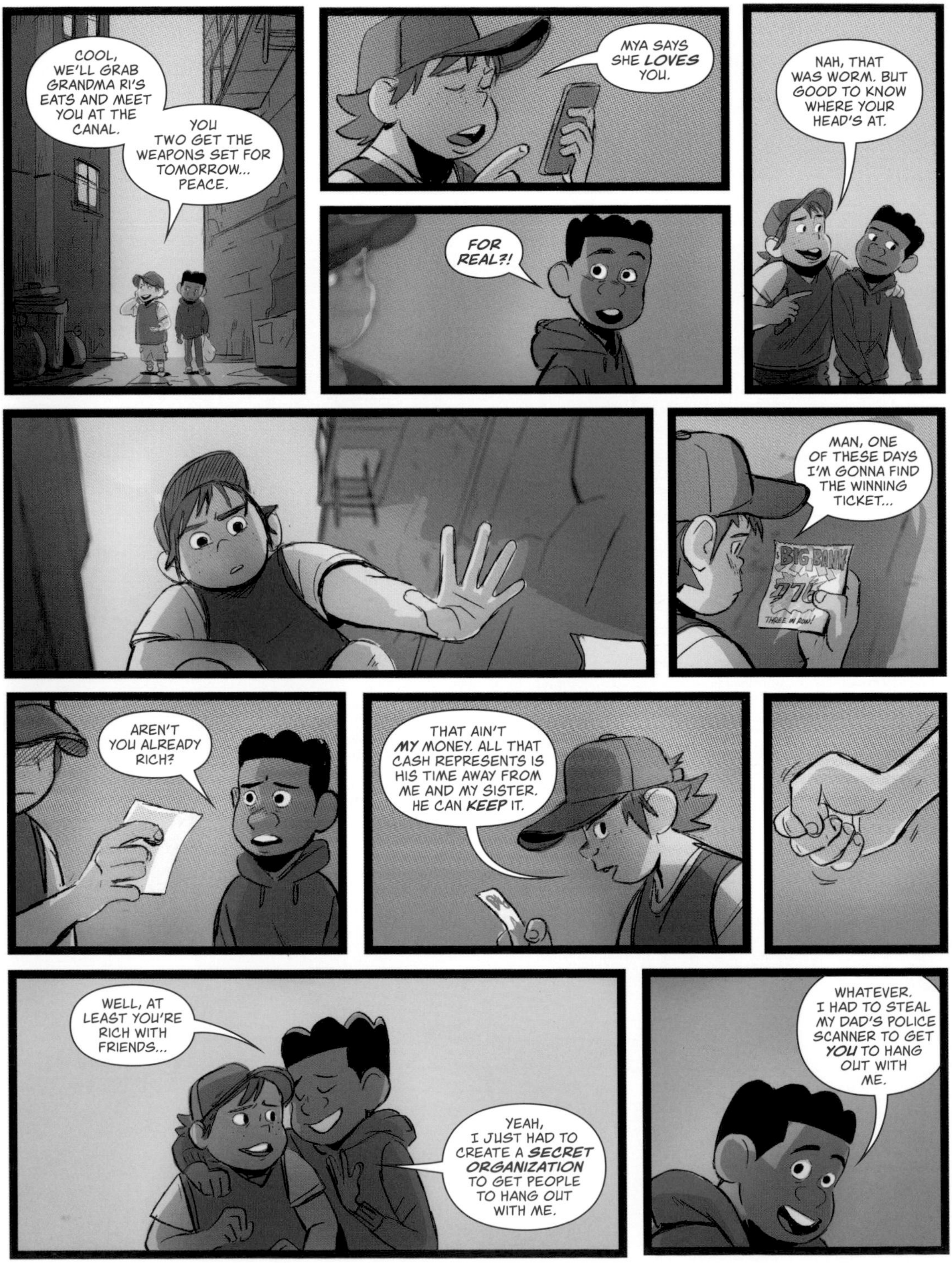
COOL, WE'LL GRAB GRANDMA RI'S EATS AND MEET YOU AT THE CANAL.
YOU TWO GET THE WEAPONS SET FOR TOMORROW... PEACE.
MYA SAYS SHE LOVES YOU.
FOR REAL?!
NAH, THAT WAS WORM. BUT GOOD TO KNOW WHERE YOUR HEAD'S AT.
MAN, ONE OF THESE DAYS I'M GONNA FIND THE WINNING TICKET...
BIG BANK
THREE IN ROW!
AREN'T YOU ALREADY RICH?
THAT AIN'T MY MONEY. ALL THAT CASH REPRESENTS IS HIS TIME AWAY FROM ME AND MY SISTER. HE CAN KEEP IT.
WELL, AT LEAST YOU'RE RICH WITH FRIENDS...
YEAH, I JUST HAD TO CREATE A SECRET ORGANIZATION TO GET PEOPLE TO HANG OUT WITH ME.
WHATEVER. I HAD TO STEAL MY DAD'S POLICE SCANNER TO GET YOU TO HANG OUT WITH ME.

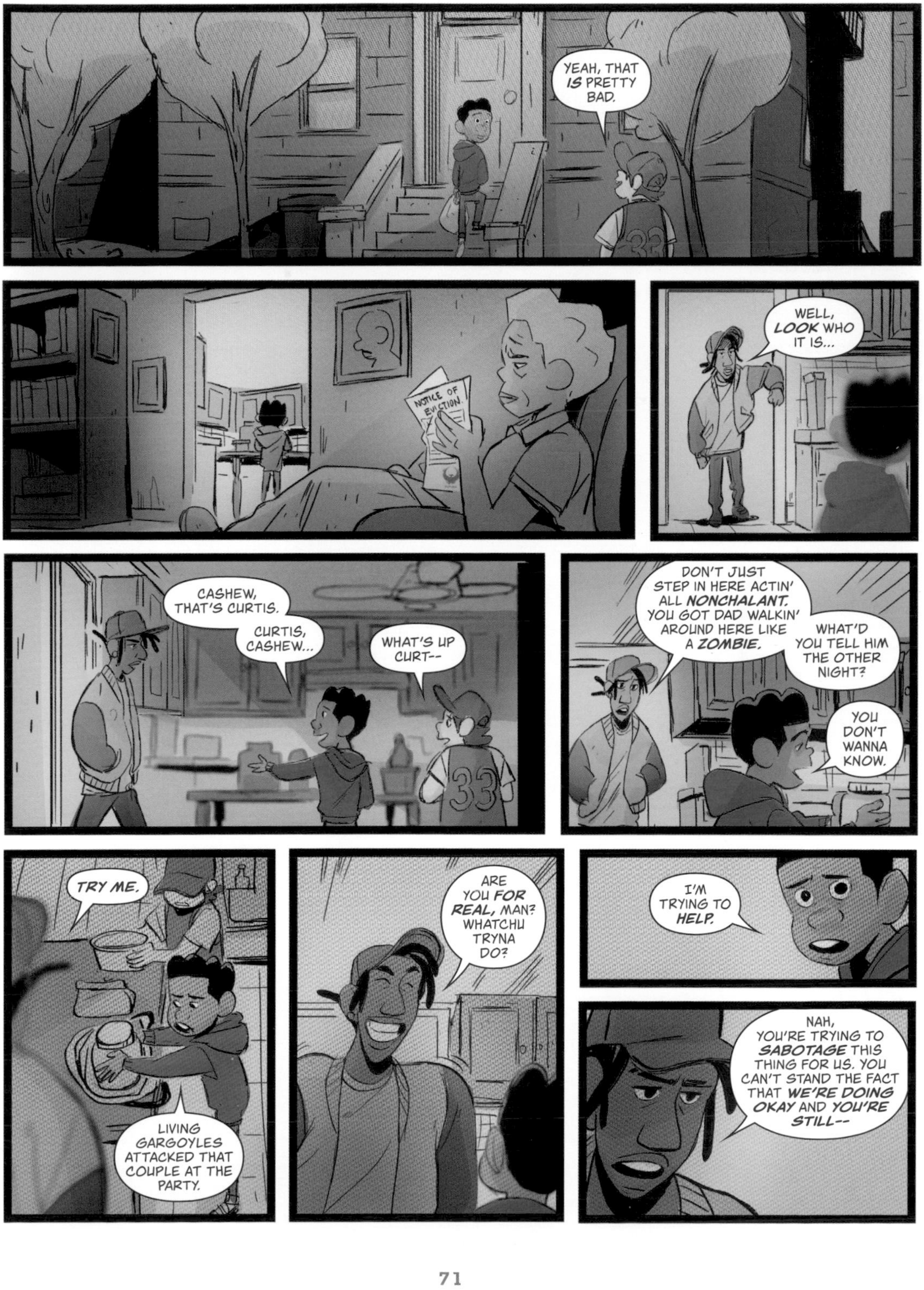

YEAH, THAT IS PRETTY BAD.
NOTICE OF EVICTION.
WELL, LOOK WHO IT IS...
CASHEW, THAT'S CURTIS.
CURTIS, CASHEW...
WHAT'S UP CURT--
DON'T JUST STEP IN HERE ACTIN' ALL NONCHALANT. YOU GOT DAD WALKIN' AROUND HERE LIKE A ZOMBIE.
WHAT'D YOU TELL HIM THE OTHER NIGHT?
YOU DON'T WANNA KNOW.
TRY ME.
LIVING GARGOYLES ATTACKED THAT COUPLE AT THE PARTY.
ARE YOU FOR REAL, MAN? WHATCHU TRYNA DO?
I'M TRYING TO HELP.
NAH, YOU'RE TRYING TO SABOTAGE THIS THING FOR US. YOU CAN'T STAND THE FACT THAT WE'RE DOING OKAY AND YOU'RE STILL--

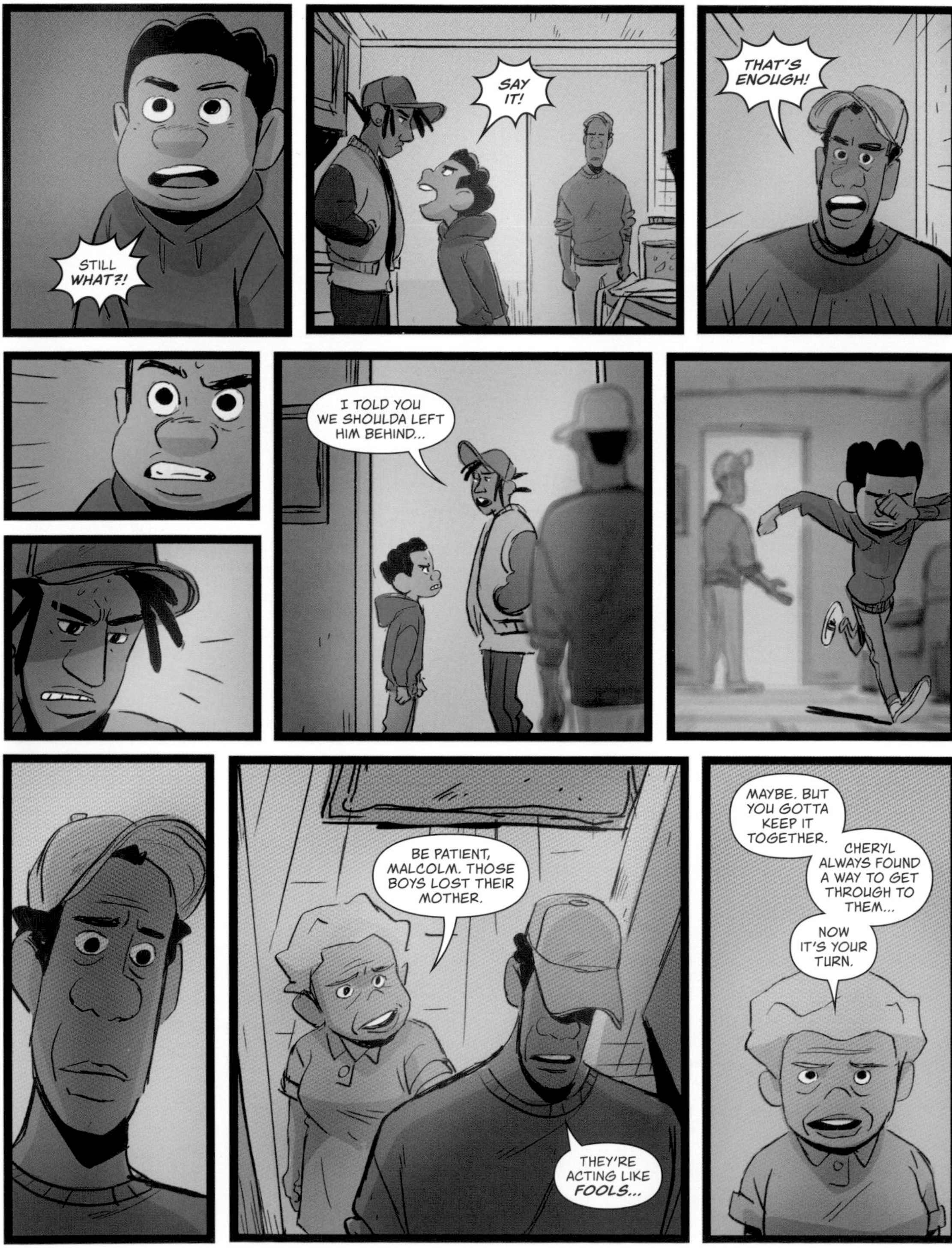
STILL WHAT?!
SAY IT!
THAT'S ENOUGH!
I TOLD YOU WE SHOULDA LEFT HIM BEHIND...
BE PATIENT, MALCOLM. THOSE BOYS LOST THEIR MOTHER.
THEY'RE ACTING LIKE FOOLS...
MAYBE. BUT YOU GOTTA KEEP IT TOGETHER.
CHERYL ALWAYS FOUND A WAY TO GET THROUGH TO THEM...
NOW IT'S YOUR TURN.

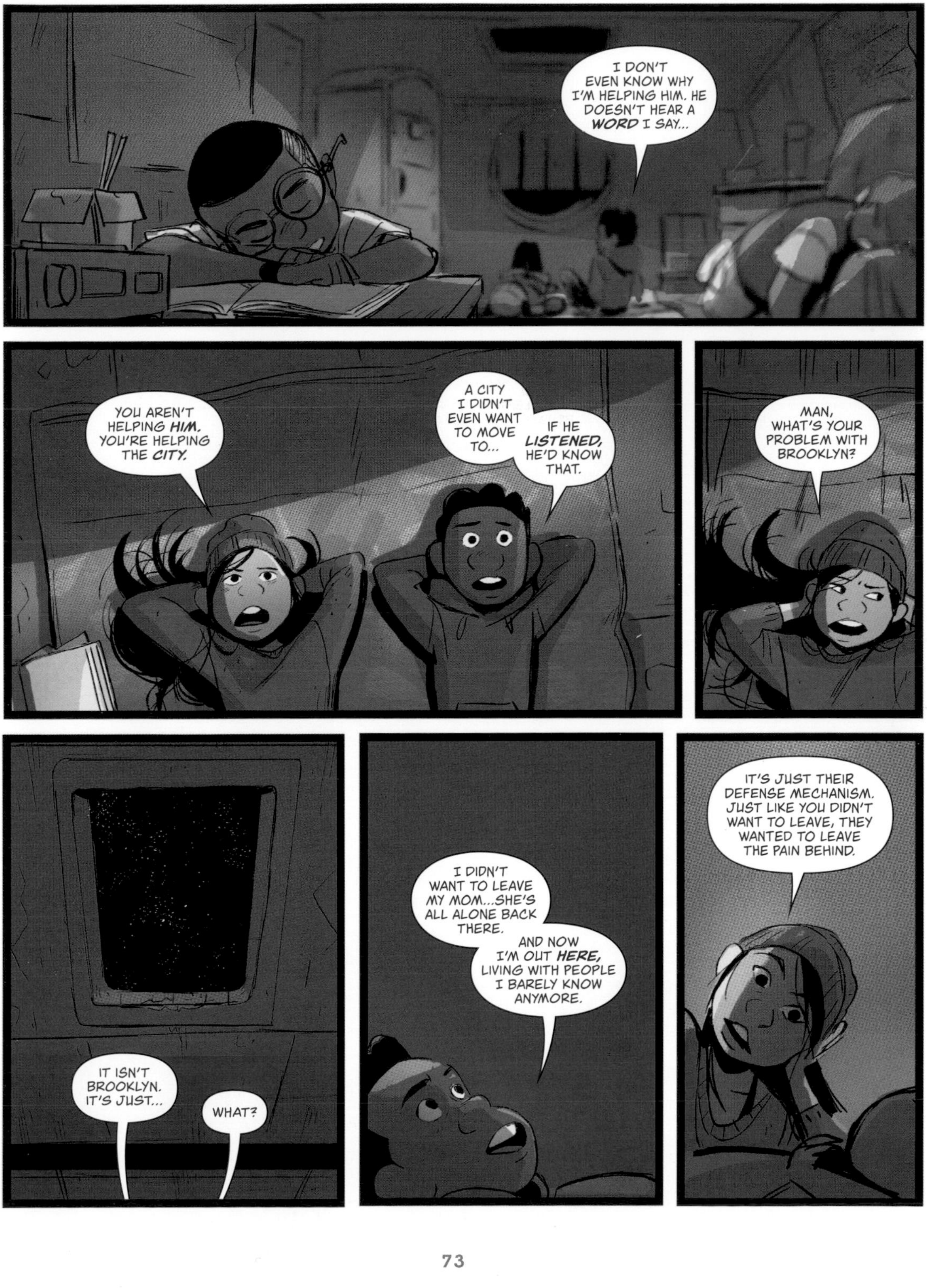
I DON'T EVEN KNOW WHY I'M HELPING HIM. HE DOESN'T HEAR A **WORD** I SAY...
YOU AREN'T HELPING ***HIM.*** YOU'RE HELPING THE ***CITY.***
A CITY I DIDN'T EVEN WANT TO MOVE TO...
IF HE ***LISTENED,*** HE'D KNOW THAT.
MAN, WHAT'S YOUR PROBLEM WITH BROOKLYN?
IT ISN'T BROOKLYN. IT'S JUST...
WHAT?
I DIDN'T WANT TO LEAVE MY MOM...SHE'S ALL ALONE BACK THERE.
AND NOW I'M OUT ***HERE,*** LIVING WITH PEOPLE I BARELY KNOW ANYMORE.
IT'S JUST THEIR DEFENSE MECHANISM. JUST LIKE YOU DIDN'T WANT TO LEAVE, THEY WANTED TO LEAVE THE PAIN BEHIND.

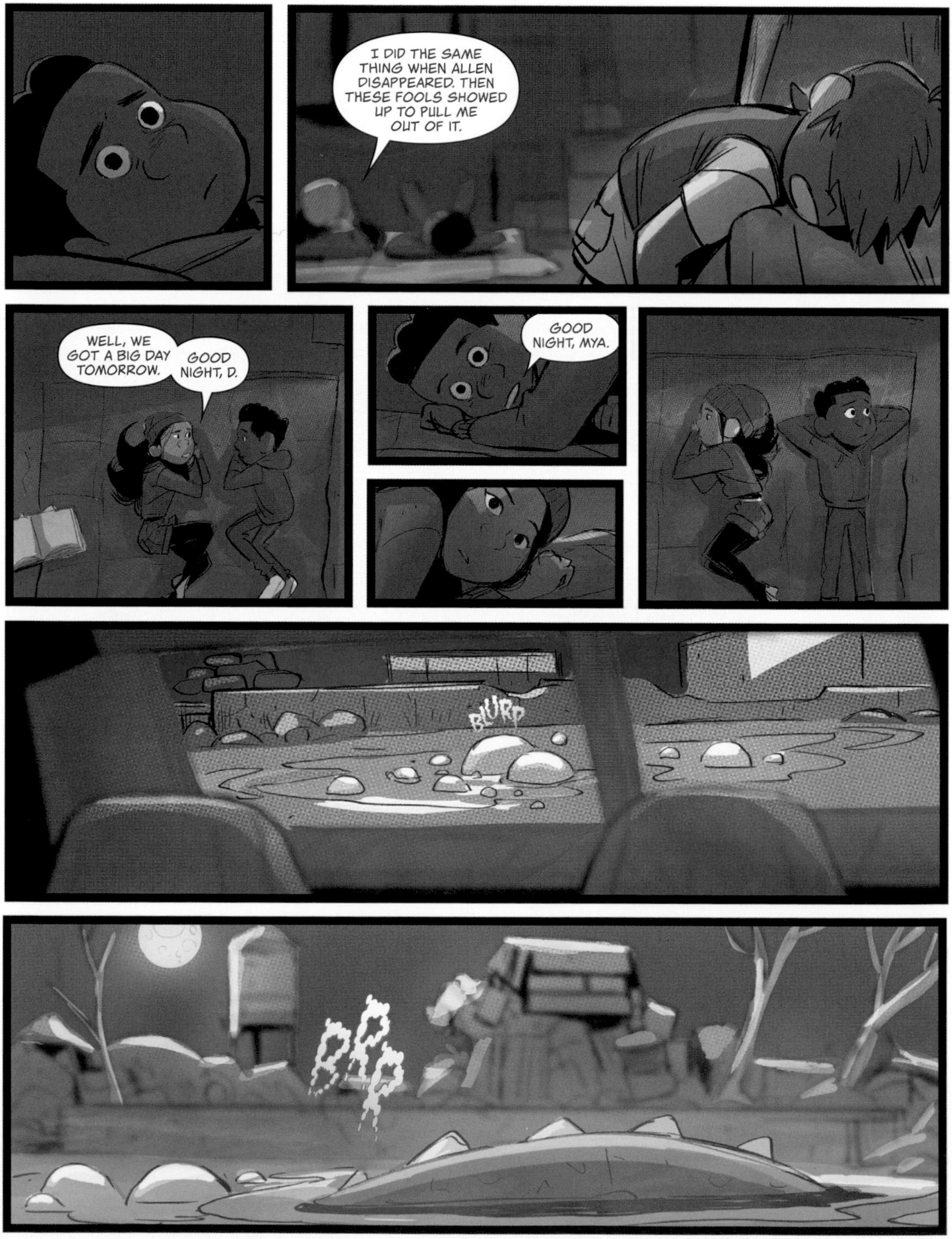
I DID THE SAME THING WHEN ALLEN DISAPPEARED. THEN THESE FOOLS SHOWED UP TO PULL ME OUT OF IT.
WELL, WE GOT A BIG DAY TOMORROW.
GOOD NIGHT, D.
GOOD NIGHT, MYA.
BLURP
BRP

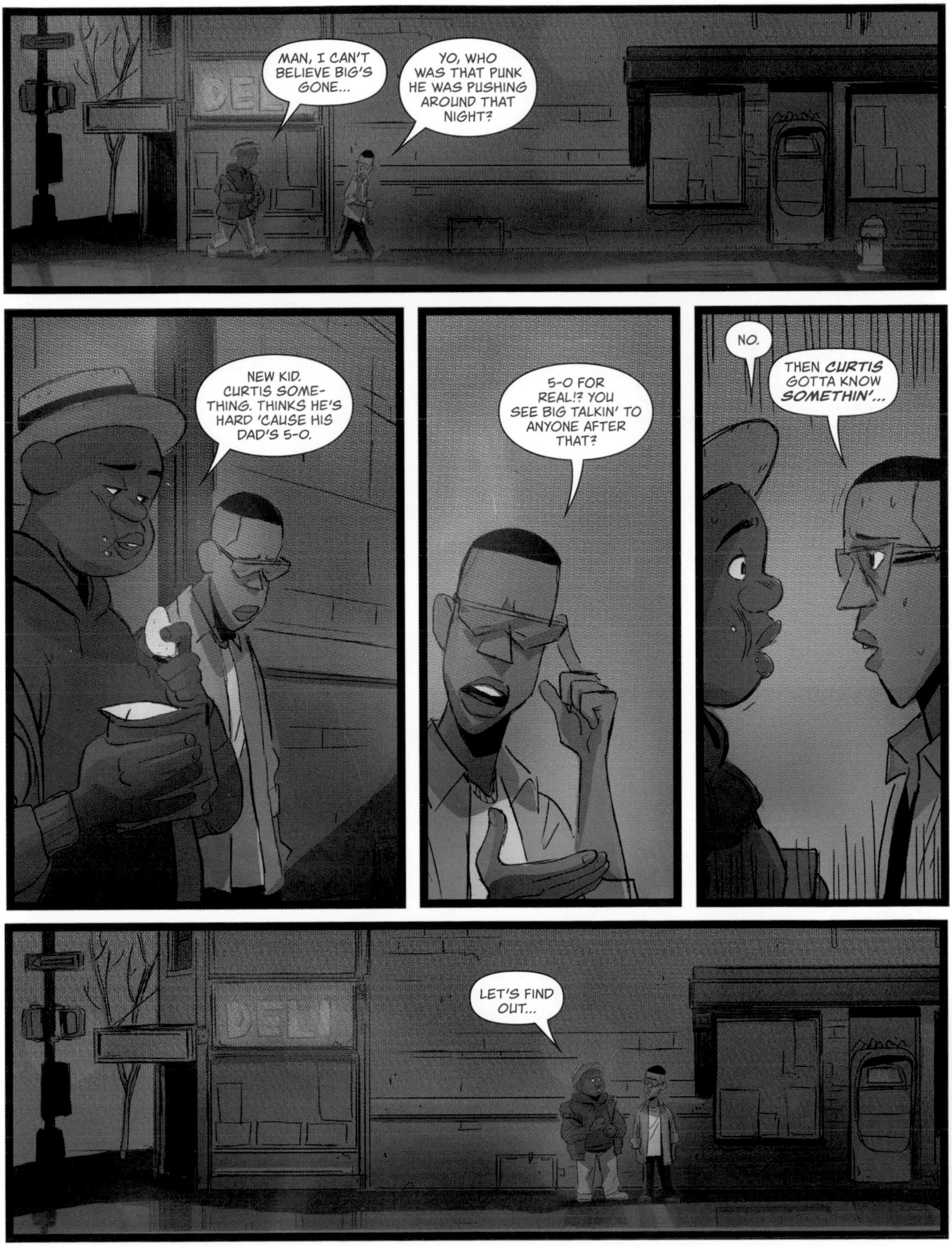
MAN, I CAN'T BELIEVE BIG'S GONE...
YO, WHO WAS THAT PUNK HE WAS PUSHING AROUND THAT NIGHT?
NEW KID. CURTIS SOMETHING. THINKS HE'S HARD 'CAUSE HIS DAD'S 5-O.
5-O FOR REAL!? YOU SEE BIG TALKIN' TO ANYONE AFTER THAT?
NO.
THEN *CURTIS* GOTTA KNOW *SOMETHIN'*...
LET'S FIND OUT...

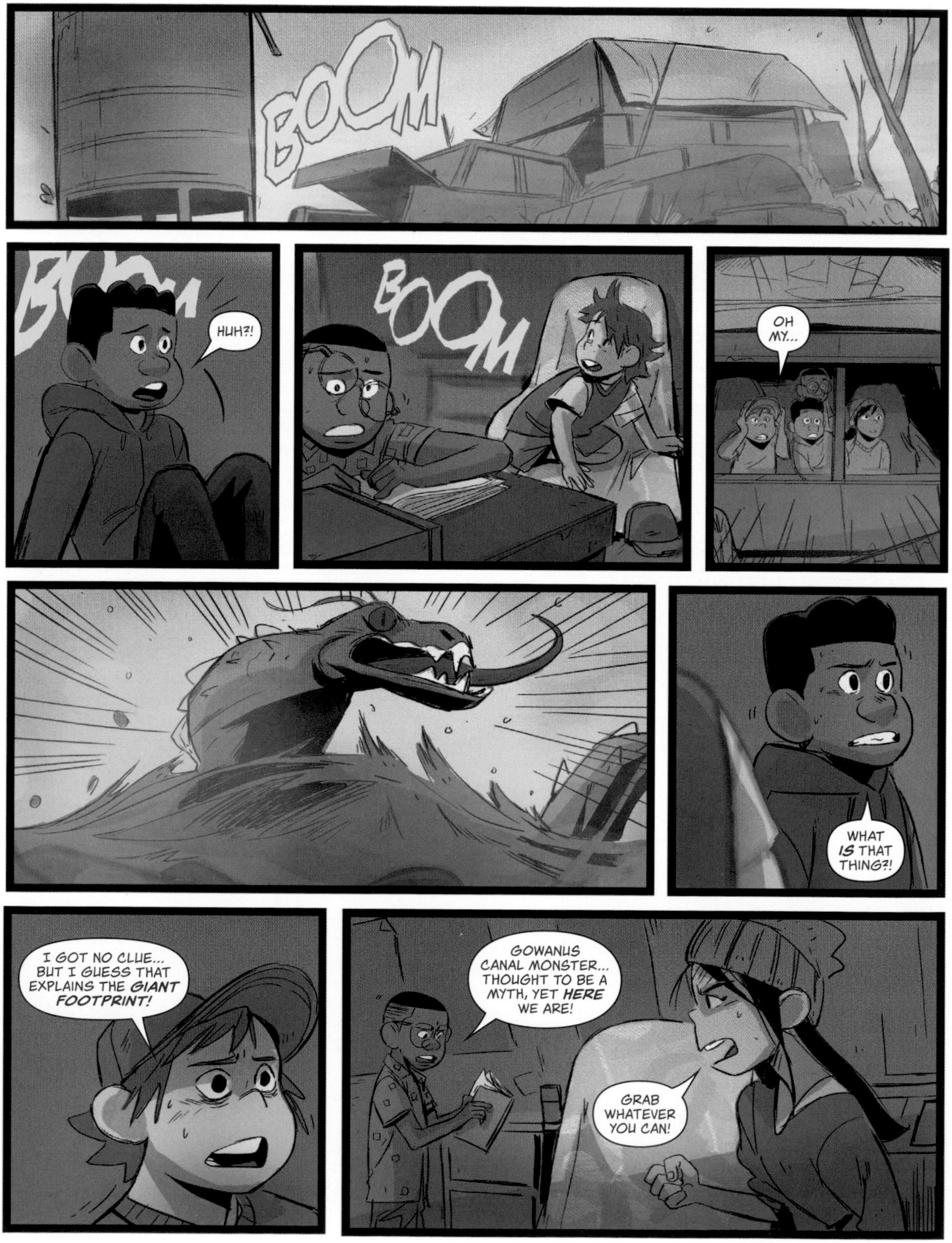
BOOM
BOOM
HUH?!
BOOM
OH MY...
WHAT IS THAT THING?!
I GOT NO CLUE... BUT I GUESS THAT EXPLAINS THE GIANT FOOTPRINT!
GOWANUS CANAL MONSTER... THOUGHT TO BE A MYTH, YET HERE WE ARE!
GRAB WHATEVER YOU CAN!

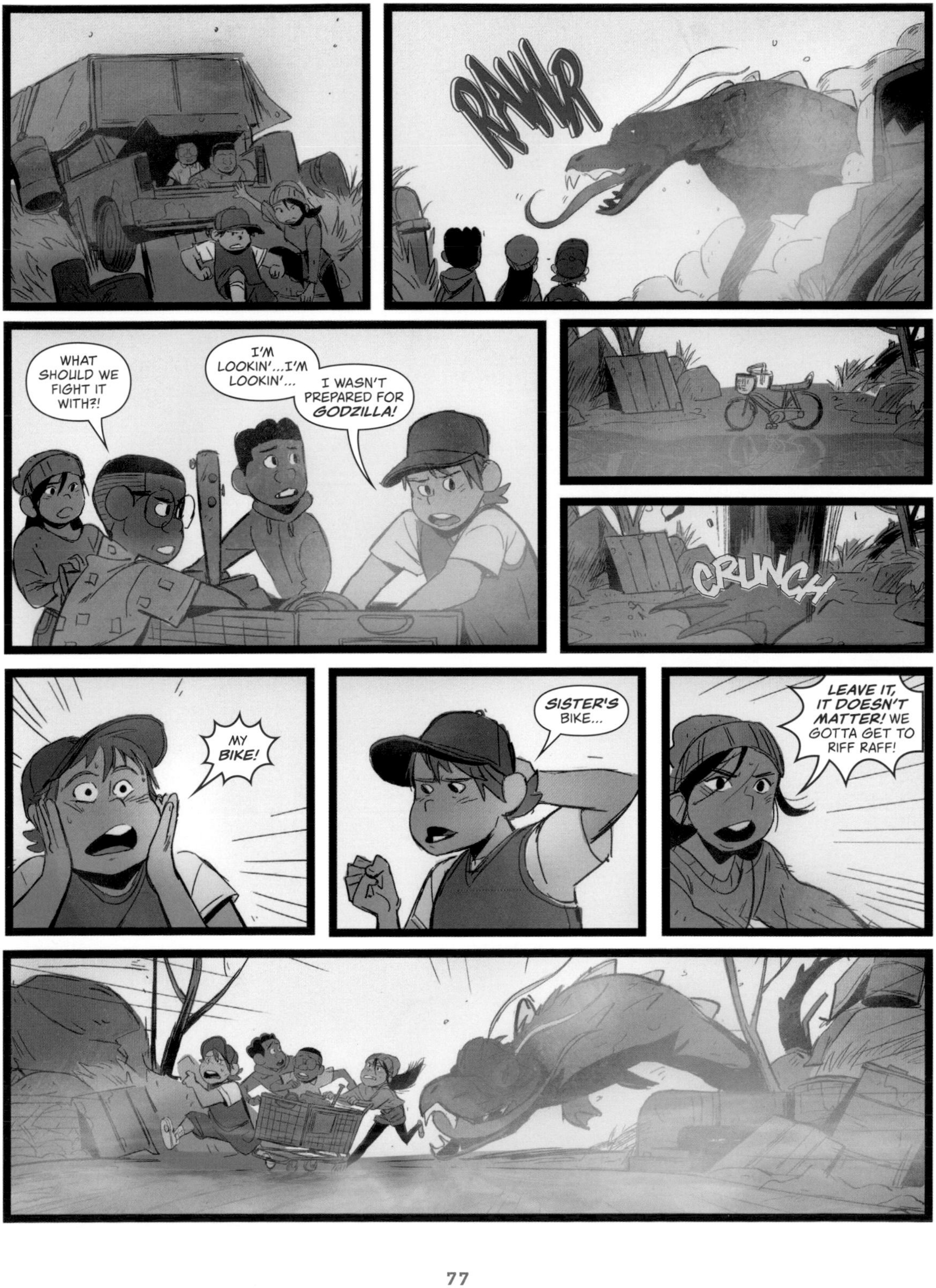
RAWR
WHAT SHOULD WE FIGHT IT WITH?!
I'M LOOKIN'...I'M LOOKIN'...
I WASN'T PREPARED FOR GODZILLA!
CRUNCH
MY BIKE!
SISTER'S BIKE...
LEAVE IT, IT DOESN'T MATTER! WE GOTTA GET TO RIFF RAFF!

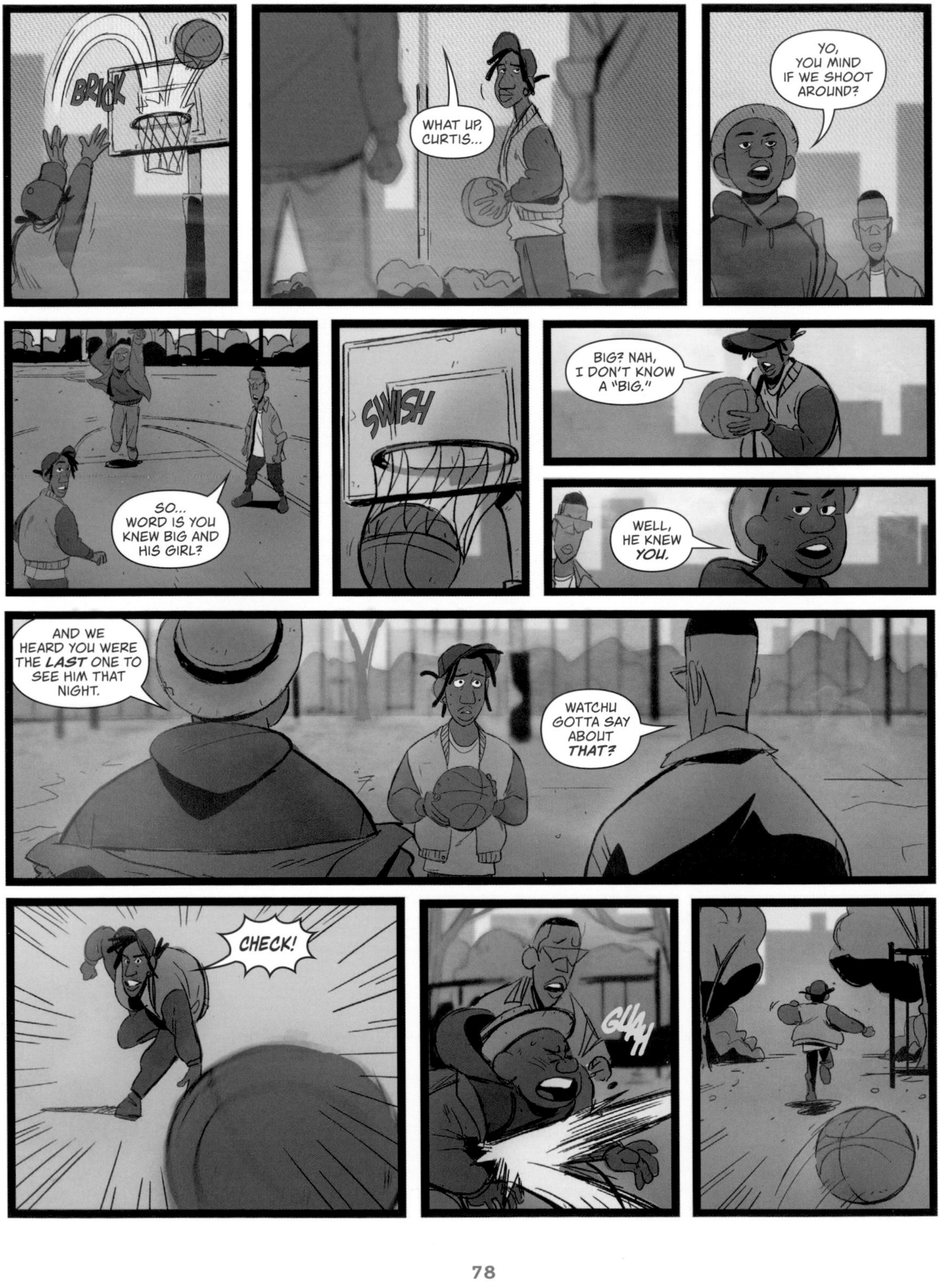
BRICK
WHAT UP, CURTIS...
YO, YOU MIND IF WE SHOOT AROUND?
SO... WORD IS YOU KNEW BIG AND HIS GIRL?
SWISH
BIG? NAH, I DON'T KNOW A "BIG."
WELL, HE KNEW *YOU.*
AND WE HEARD YOU WERE THE *LAST* ONE TO SEE HIM THAT NIGHT.
WATCHU GOTTA SAY ABOUT *THAT?*
CHECK!
GUAH

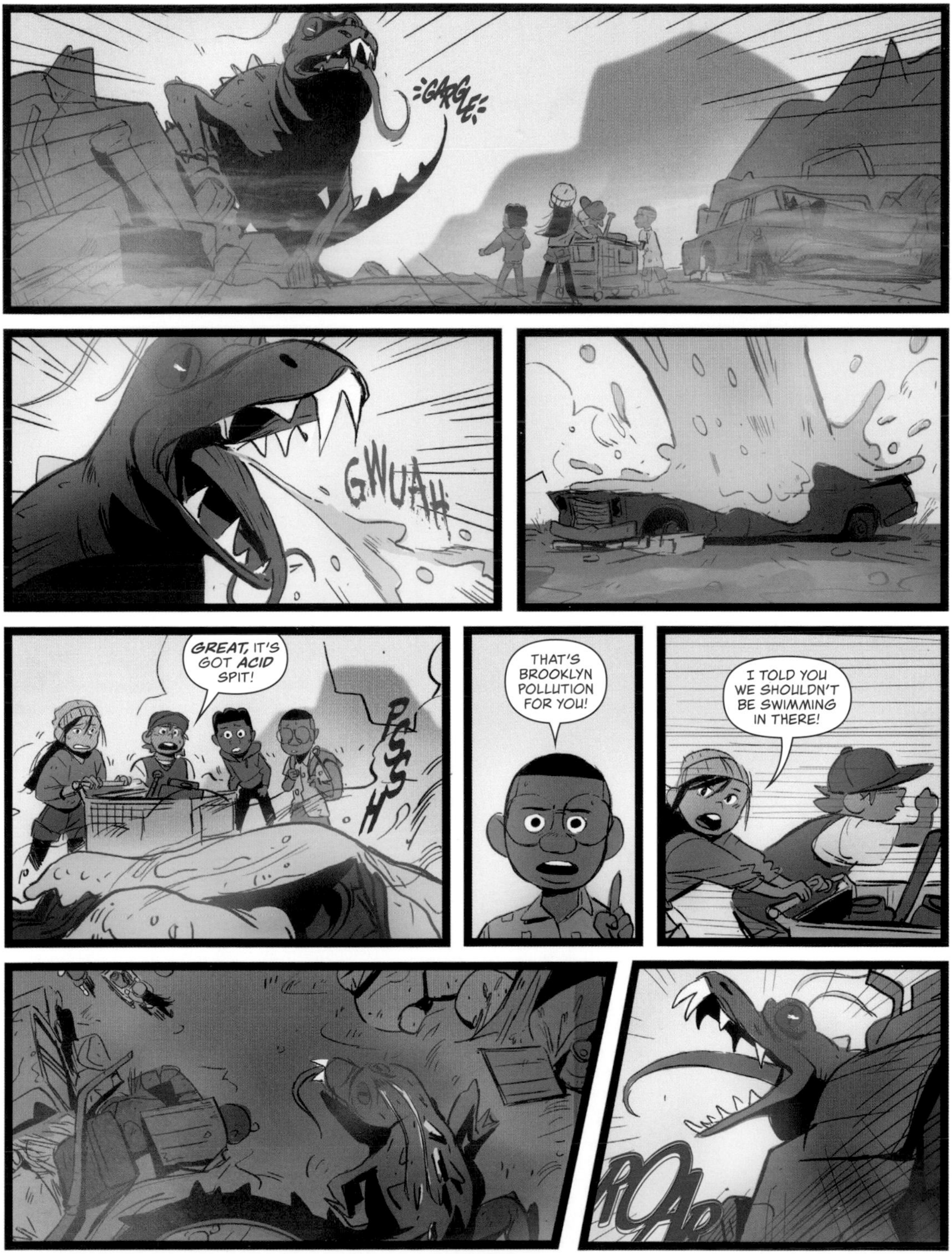

GARGLE
GWUAH
GREAT, IT'S GOT ACID SPIT!
PSSSH
THAT'S BROOKLYN POLLUTION FOR YOU!
I TOLD YOU WE SHOULDN'T BE SWIMMING IN THERE!

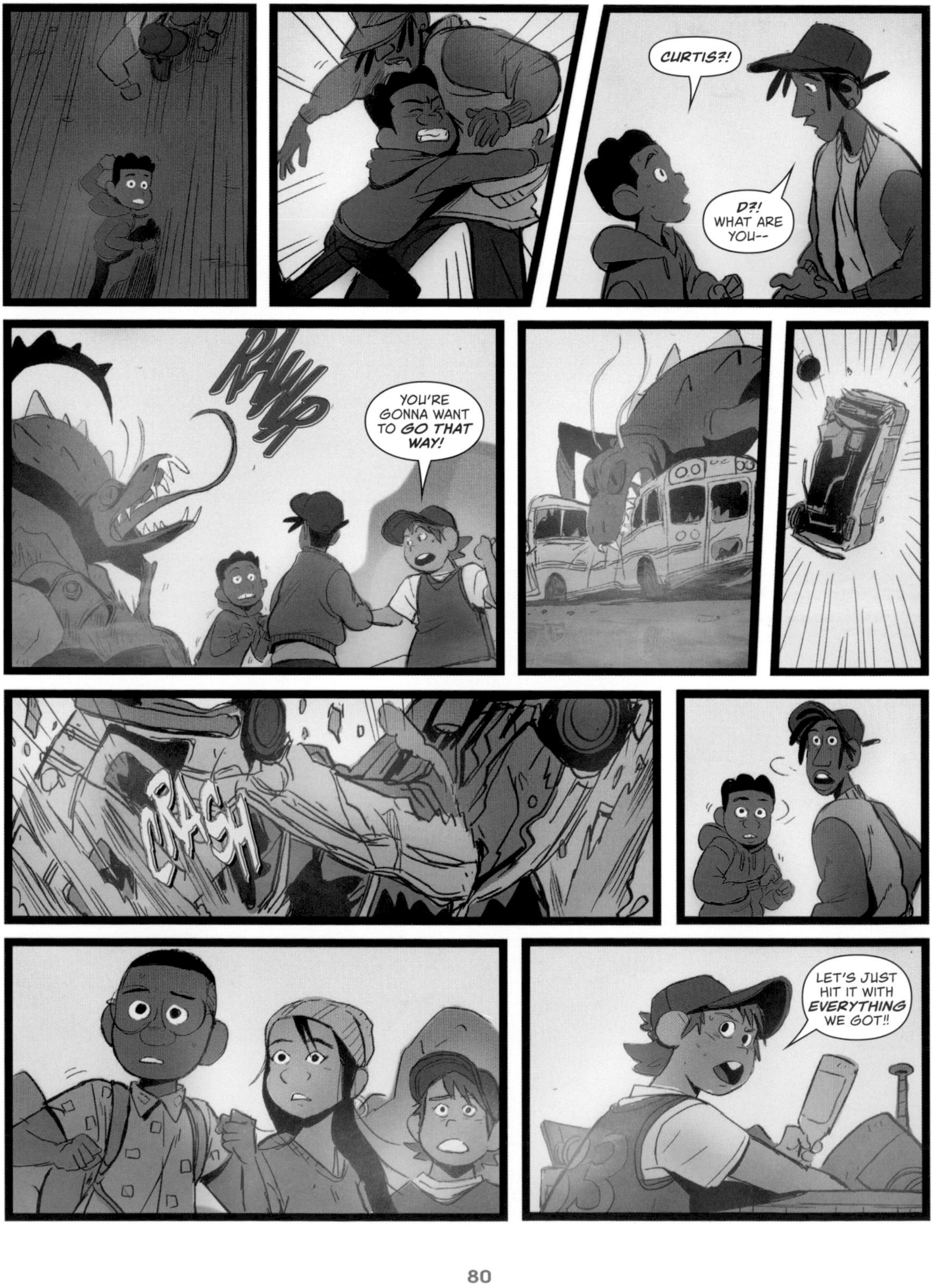
CURTIS?!
D?! WHAT ARE YOU--
RAWR
YOU'RE GONNA WANT TO **GO THAT WAY!**
CRASH
LET'S JUST HIT IT WITH **EVERYTHING** WE GOT!!

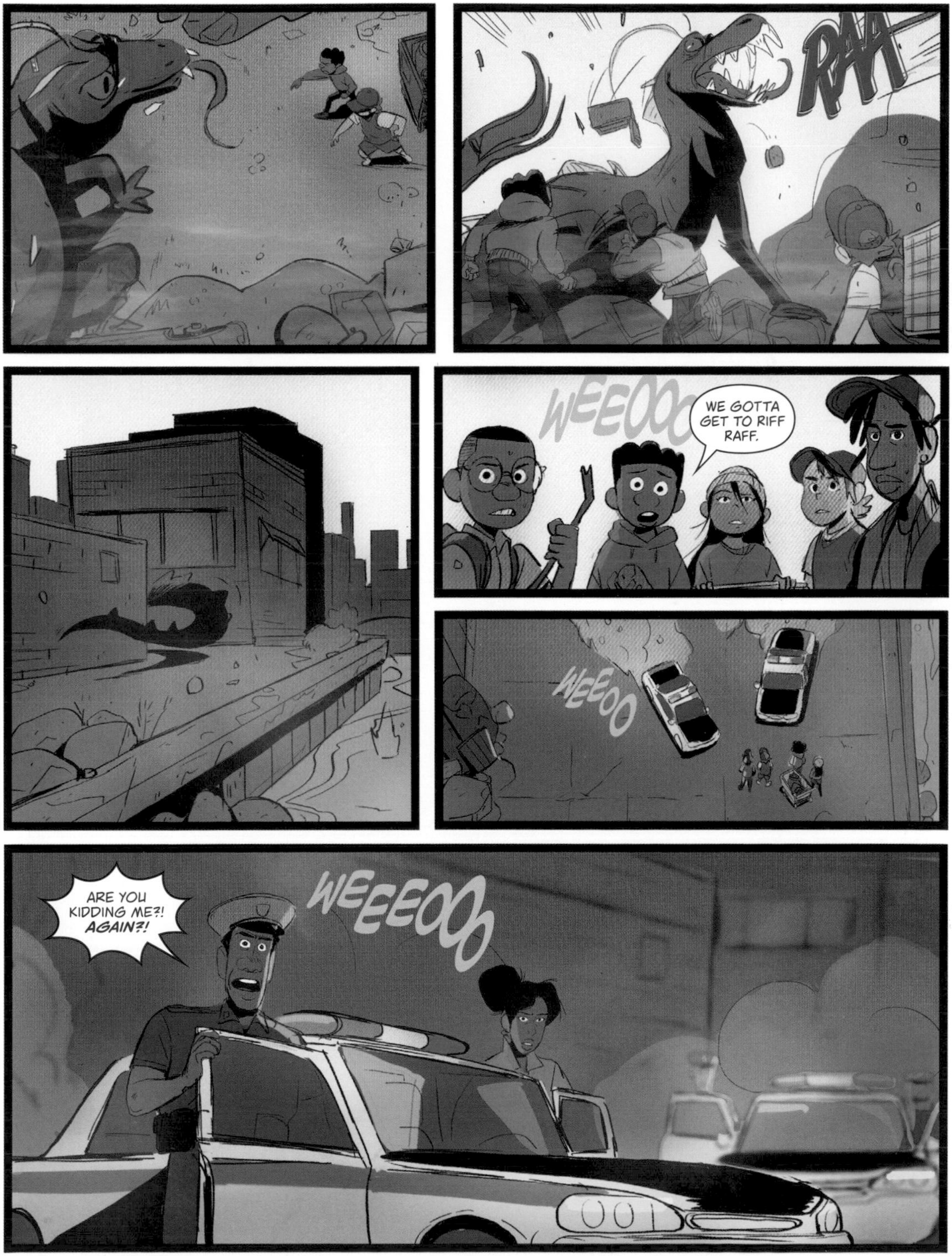
RAA
WEEOOO
WE GOTTA GET TO RIFF RAFF.
WEEOO
ARE YOU KIDDING ME?! AGAIN?!
WEEEOOO

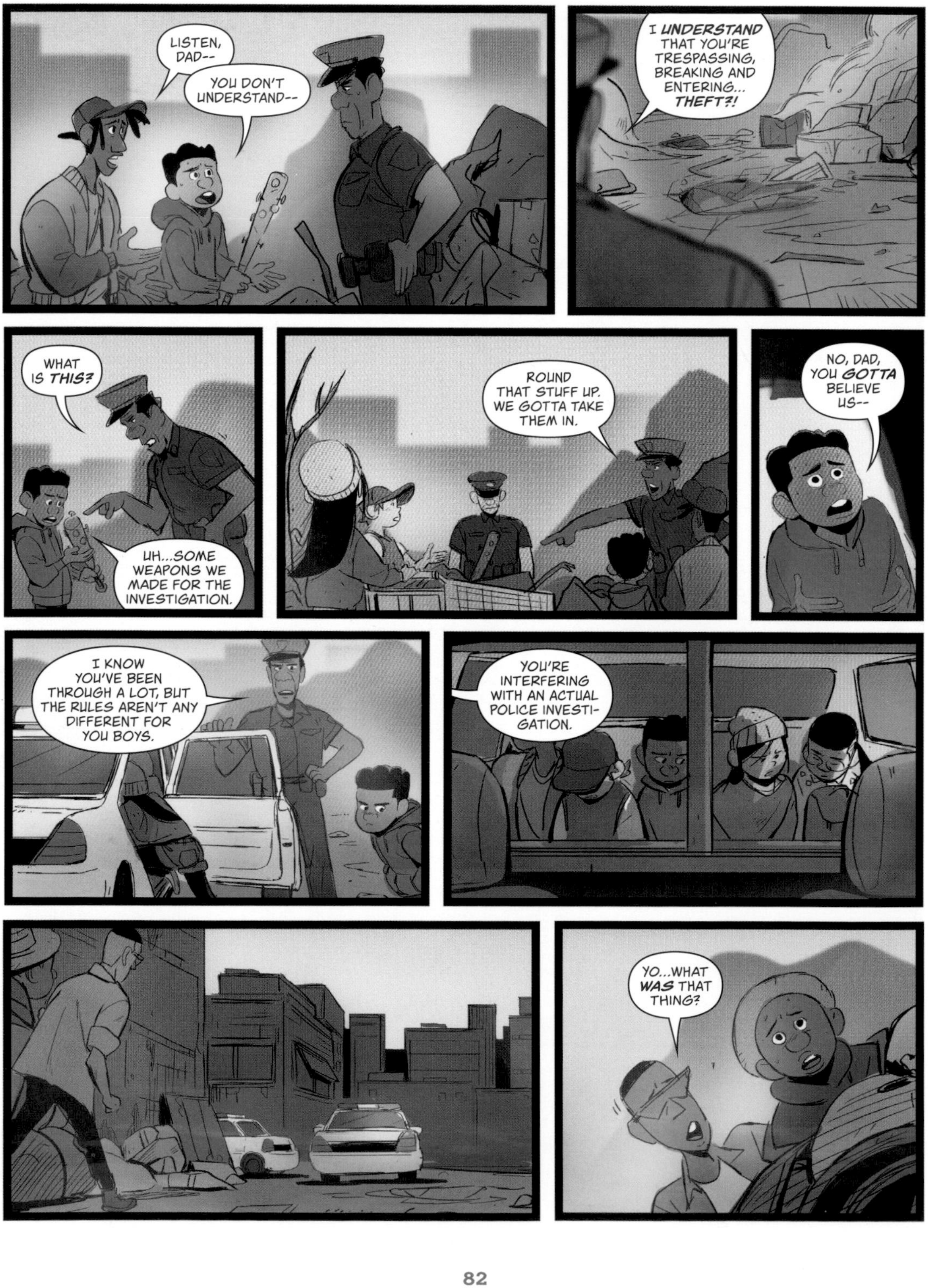
LISTEN, DAD--
YOU DON'T UNDERSTAND--
I UNDERSTAND THAT YOU'RE TRESPASSING, BREAKING AND ENTERING... THEFT?!
WHAT IS THIS?
UH...SOME WEAPONS WE MADE FOR THE INVESTIGATION.
ROUND THAT STUFF UP. WE GOTTA TAKE THEM IN.
NO, DAD, YOU GOTTA BELIEVE US--
I KNOW YOU'VE BEEN THROUGH A LOT, BUT THE RULES AREN'T ANY DIFFERENT FOR YOU BOYS.
YOU'RE INTERFERING WITH AN ACTUAL POLICE INVESTIGATION.
YO...WHAT WAS THAT THING?

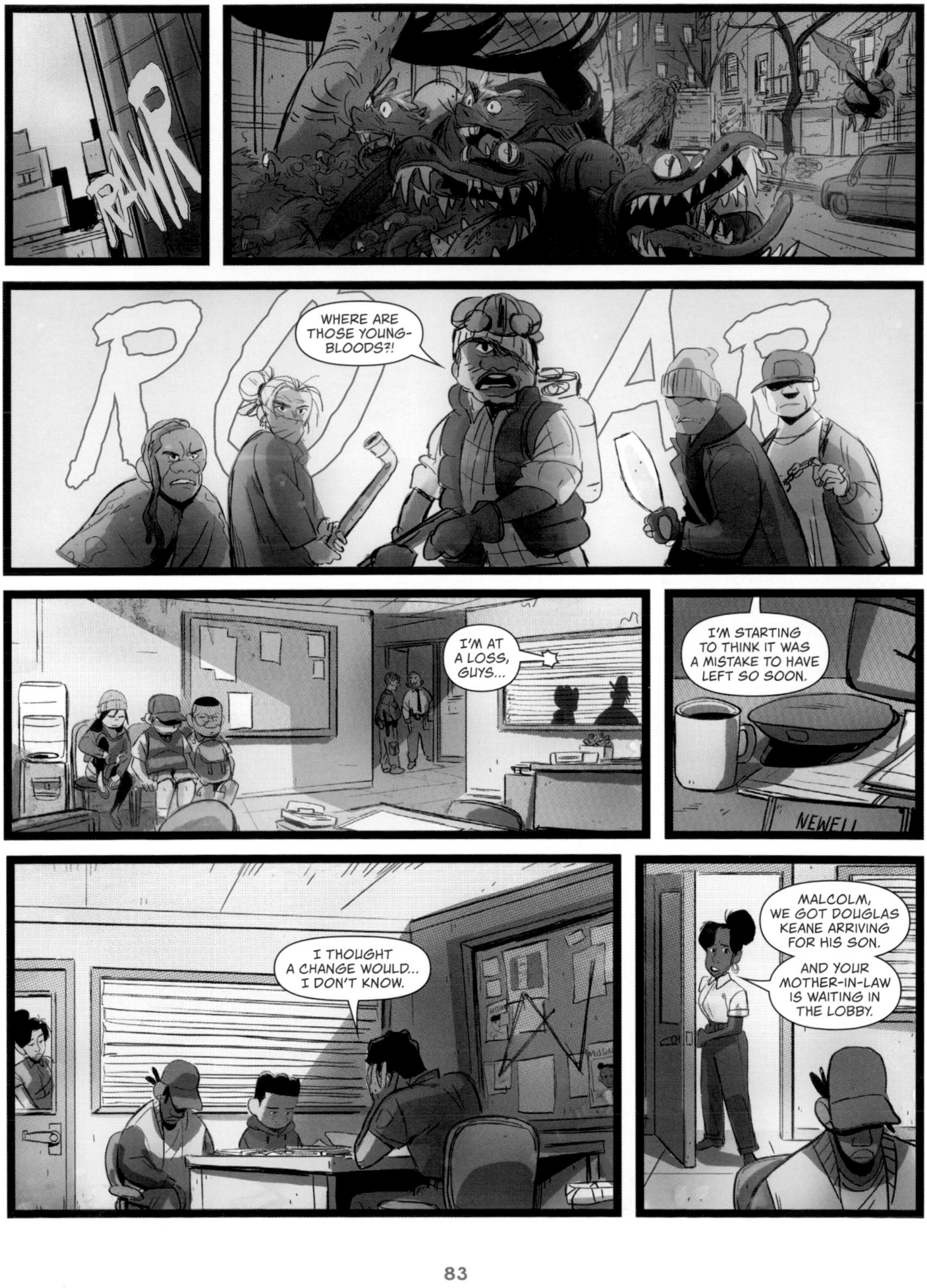
RAWR
ROAR
WHERE ARE THOSE YOUNG-BLOODS?!
I'M AT A LOSS, GUYS...
I'M STARTING TO THINK IT WAS A MISTAKE TO HAVE LEFT SO SOON.
NEWELL
I THOUGHT A CHANGE WOULD... I DON'T KNOW.
MALCOLM, WE GOT DOUGLAS KEANE ARRIVING FOR HIS SON.
AND YOUR MOTHER-IN-LAW IS WAITING IN THE LOBBY.

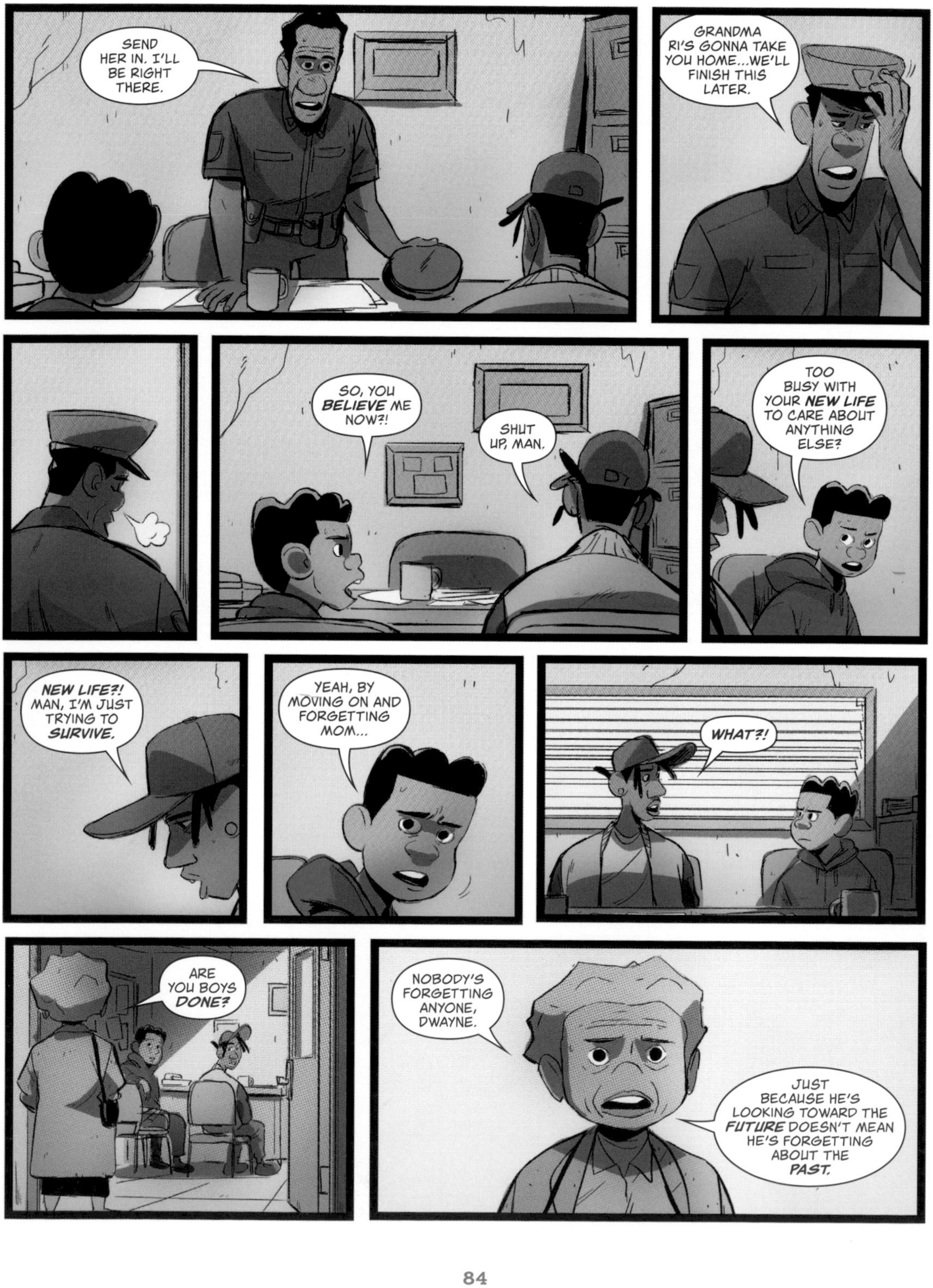
SEND HER IN. I'LL BE RIGHT THERE.
GRANDMA RI'S GONNA TAKE YOU HOME...WE'LL FINISH THIS LATER.
SO, YOU BELIEVE ME NOW?!
SHUT UP, MAN.
TOO BUSY WITH YOUR NEW LIFE TO CARE ABOUT ANYTHING ELSE?
NEW LIFE?! MAN, I'M JUST TRYING TO SURVIVE.
YEAH, BY MOVING ON AND FORGETTING MOM...
WHAT?!
ARE YOU BOYS DONE?
NOBODY'S FORGETTING ANYONE, DWAYNE.
JUST BECAUSE HE'S LOOKING TOWARD THE FUTURE DOESN'T MEAN HE'S FORGETTING ABOUT THE PAST.

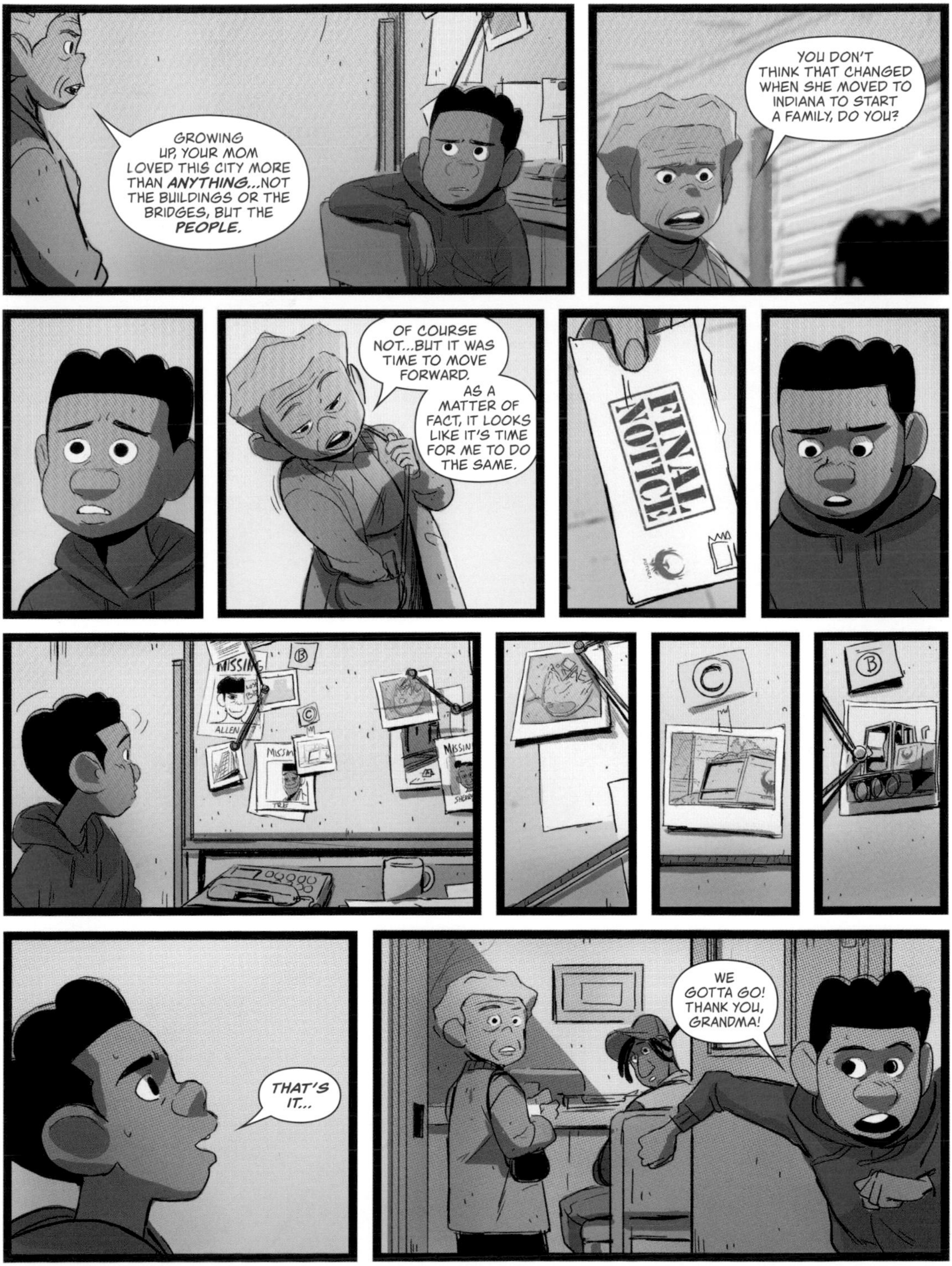
GROWING UP, YOUR MOM LOVED THIS CITY MORE THAN ANYTHING...NOT THE BUILDINGS OR THE BRIDGES, BUT THE PEOPLE.
YOU DON'T THINK THAT CHANGED WHEN SHE MOVED TO INDIANA TO START A FAMILY, DO YOU?
OF COURSE NOT...BUT IT WAS TIME TO MOVE FORWARD.
AS A MATTER OF FACT, IT LOOKS LIKE IT'S TIME FOR ME TO DO THE SAME.
FINAL NOTICE
MISSING
ALLEN
MISSING
MISSING
THAT'S IT...
WE GOTTA GO! THANK YOU, GRANDMA!

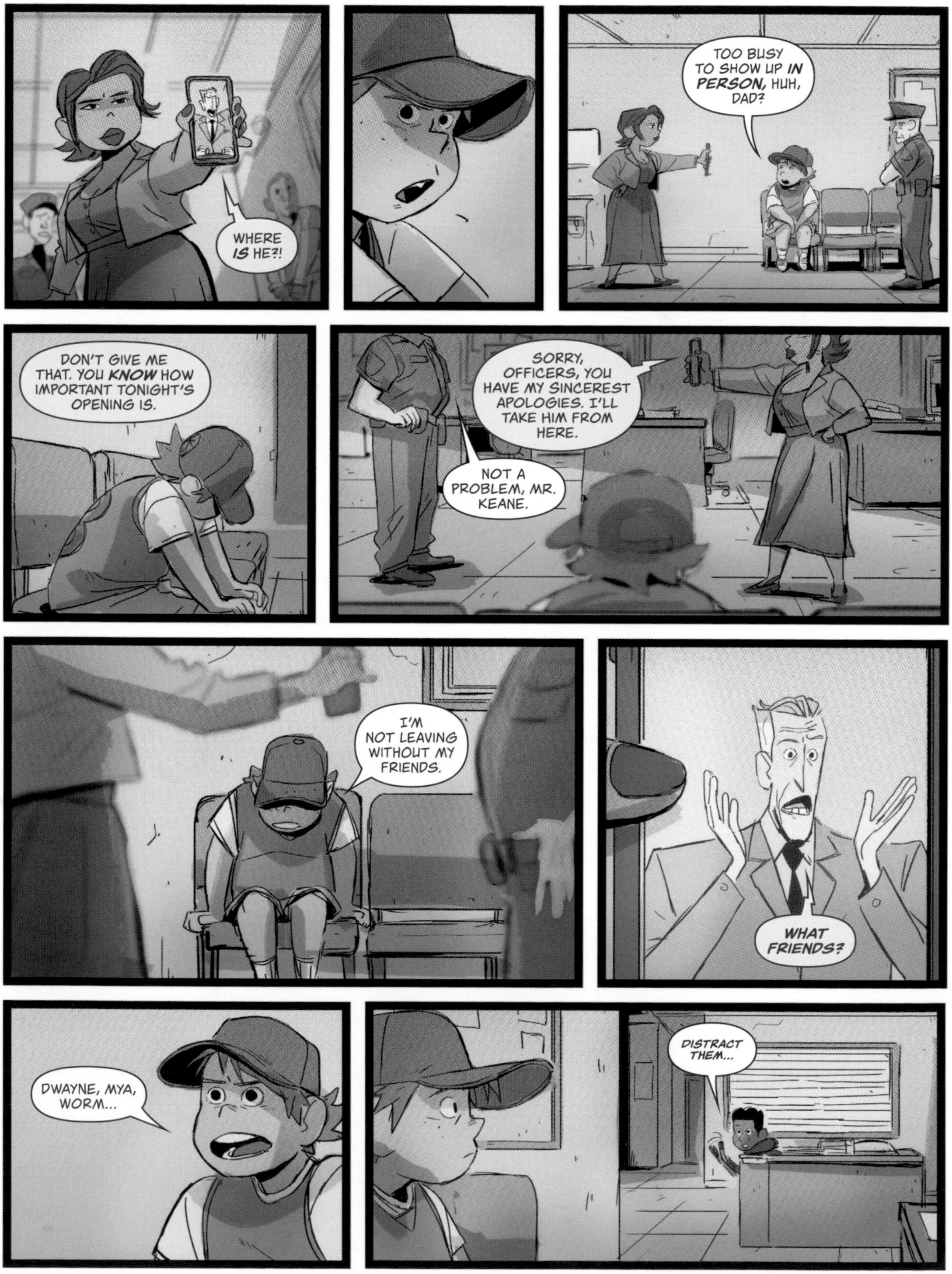
WHERE IS HE?!
TOO BUSY TO SHOW UP IN PERSON, HUH, DAD?
DON'T GIVE ME THAT. YOU KNOW HOW IMPORTANT TONIGHT'S OPENING IS.
SORRY, OFFICERS, YOU HAVE MY SINCEREST APOLOGIES. I'LL TAKE HIM FROM HERE.
NOT A PROBLEM, MR. KEANE.
I'M NOT LEAVING WITHOUT MY FRIENDS.
WHAT FRIENDS?
DWAYNE, MYA, WORM...
DISTRACT THEM...

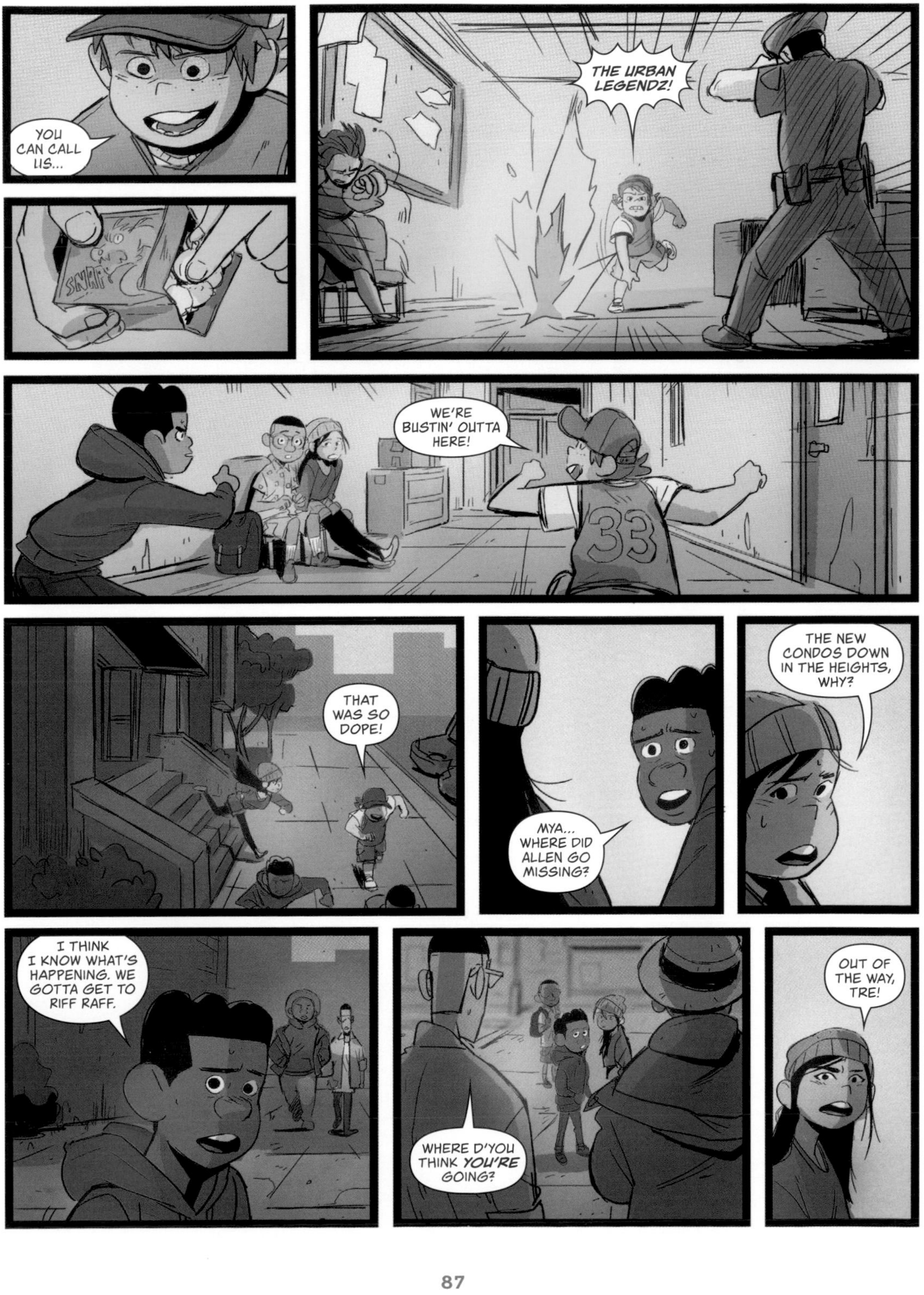
YOU CAN CALL US...
THE URBAN LEGENDZ!
WE'RE BUSTIN' OUTTA HERE!
THAT WAS SO DOPE!
MYA... WHERE DID ALLEN GO MISSING?
THE NEW CONDOS DOWN IN THE HEIGHTS, WHY?
I THINK I KNOW WHAT'S HAPPENING. WE GOTTA GET TO RIFF RAFF.
WHERE D'YOU THINK *YOU'RE* GOING?
OUT OF THE WAY, TRE!

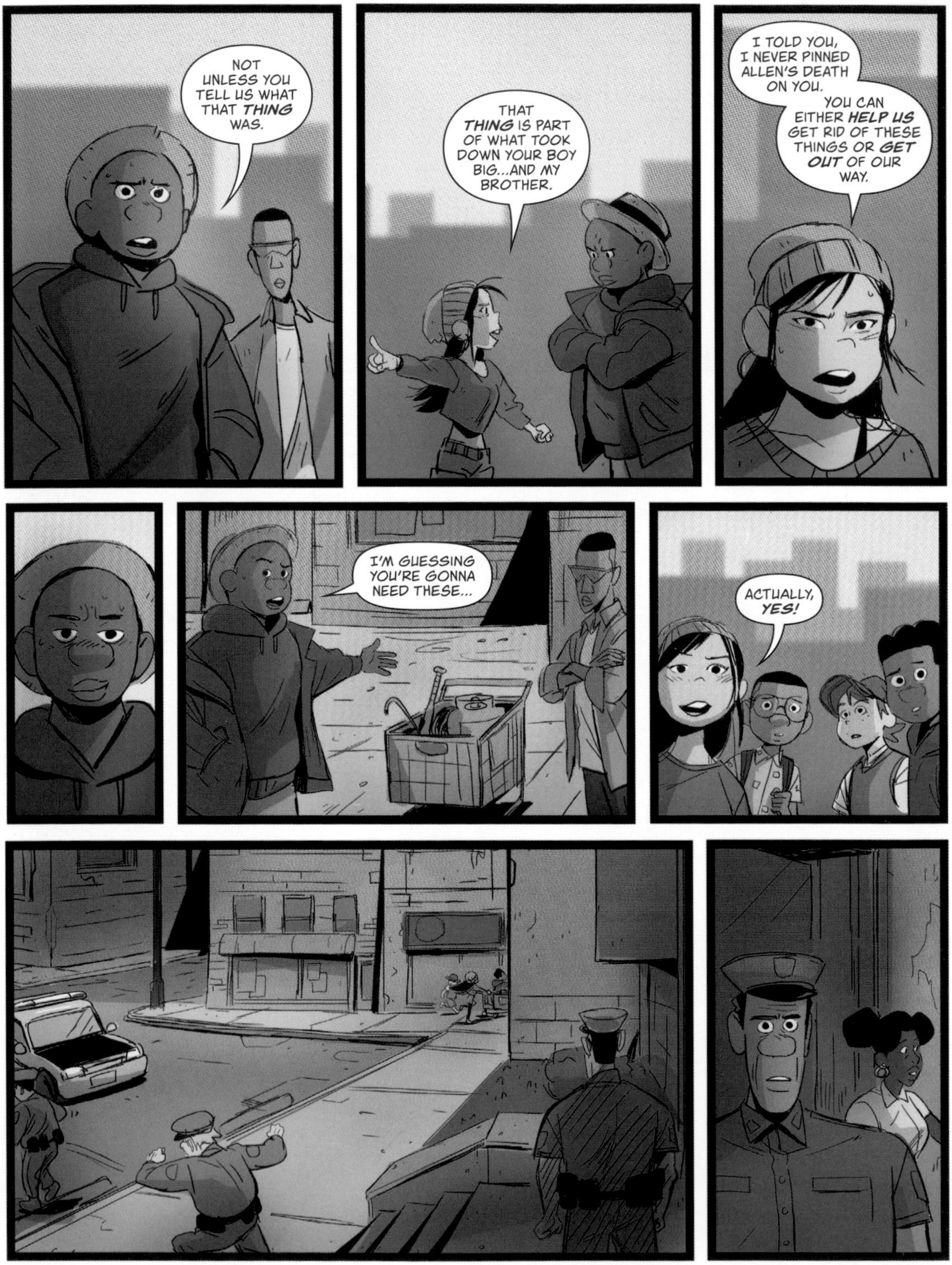
NOT UNLESS YOU TELL US WHAT THAT *THING* WAS.
THAT *THING* IS PART OF WHAT TOOK DOWN YOUR BOY BIG...AND MY BROTHER.
I TOLD YOU, I NEVER PINNED ALLEN'S DEATH ON YOU.
YOU CAN EITHER ***HELP US*** GET RID OF THESE THINGS OR ***GET OUT*** OF OUR WAY.
I'M GUESSING YOU'RE GONNA NEED THESE...
ACTUALLY, ***YES!***

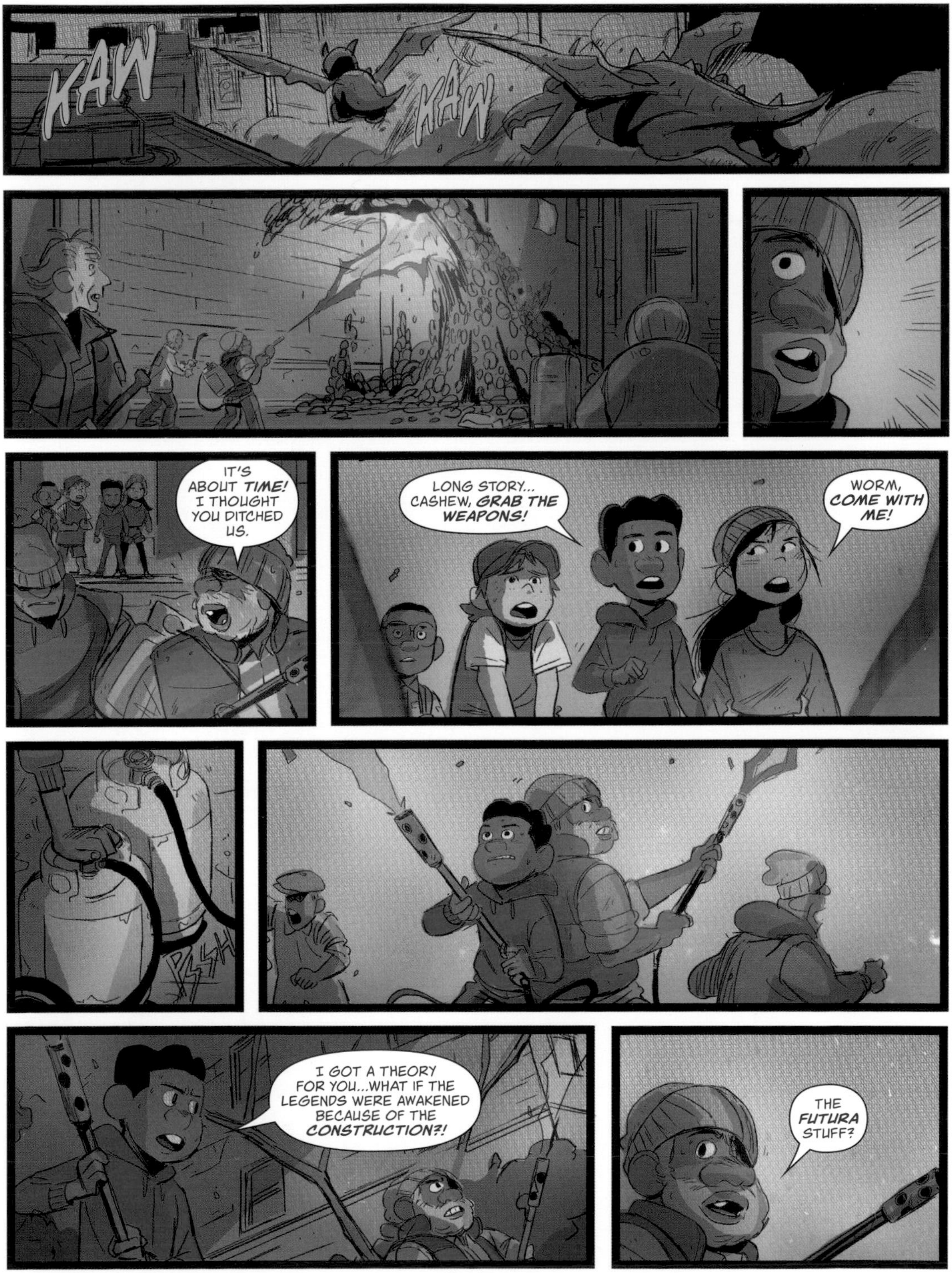
KAW
KAW
IT'S ABOUT TIME! I THOUGHT YOU DITCHED US.
LONG STORY... CASHEW, GRAB THE WEAPONS!
WORM, COME WITH ME!
PSSH
I GOT A THEORY FOR YOU...WHAT IF THE LEGENDS WERE AWAKENED BECAUSE OF THE CONSTRUCTION?!
THE FUTURA STUFF?

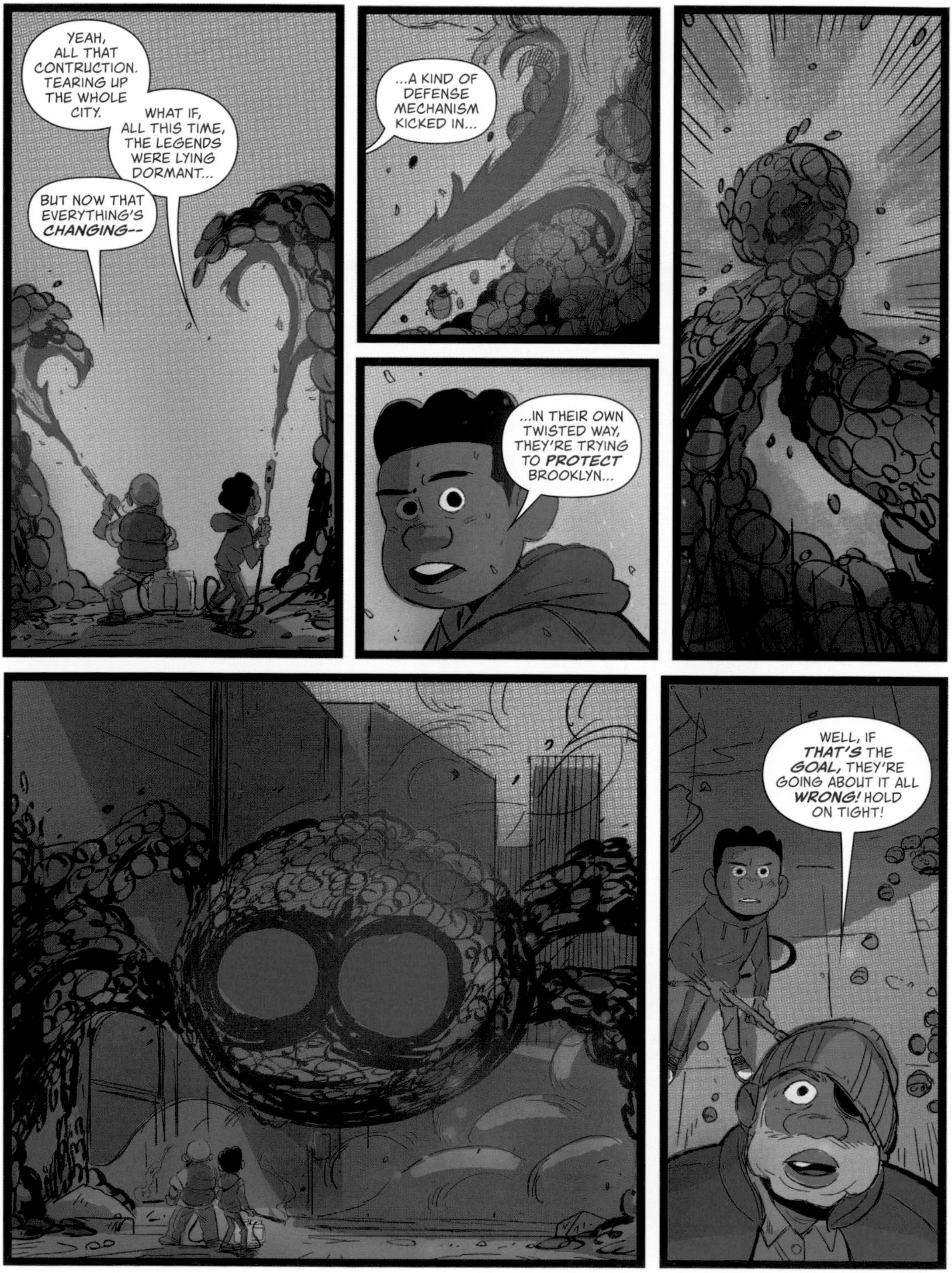
YEAH, ALL THAT CONTRUCTION. TEARING UP THE WHOLE CITY.
WHAT IF, ALL THIS TIME, THE LEGENDS WERE LYING DORMANT...
BUT NOW THAT EVERYTHING'S *CHANGING--*
...A KIND OF DEFENSE MECHANISM KICKED IN...
...IN THEIR OWN TWISTED WAY, THEY'RE TRYING TO *PROTECT* BROOKLYN...
WELL, IF *THAT'S* THE *GOAL*, THEY'RE GOING ABOUT IT ALL *WRONG!* HOLD ON TIGHT!

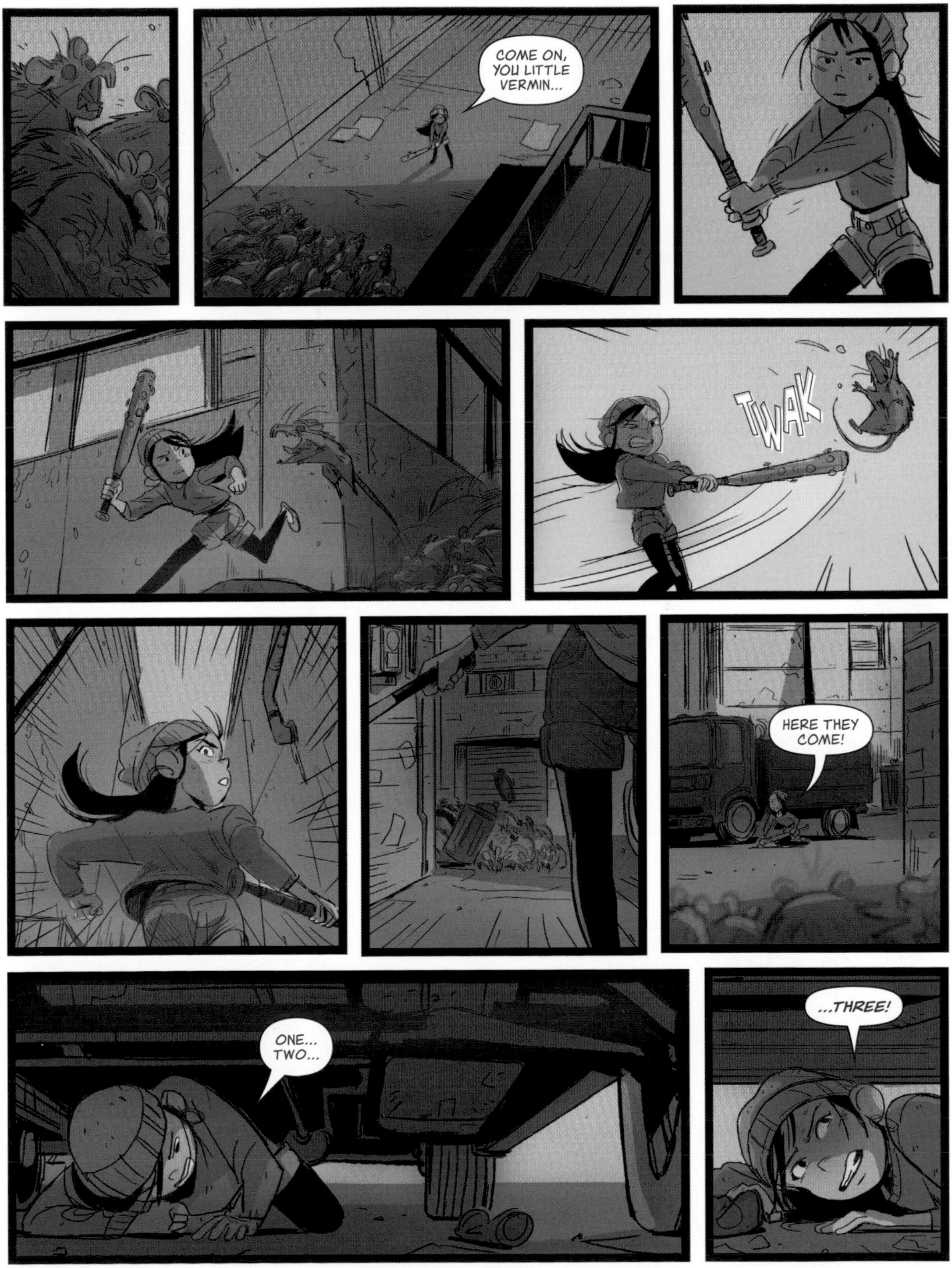
COME ON, YOU LITTLE VERMIN...
TWAK
HERE THEY COME!
ONE... TWO...
...THREE!

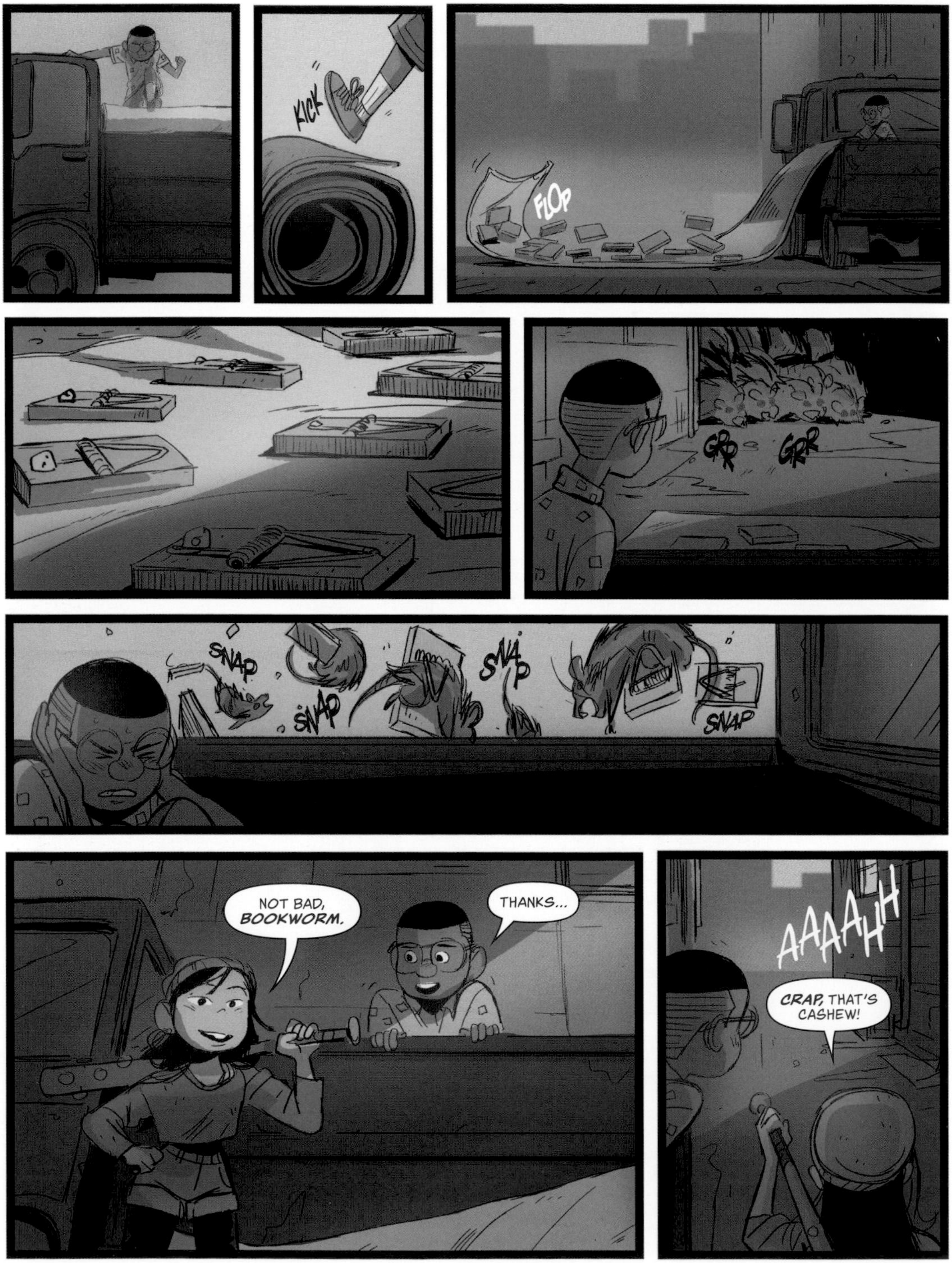
KICK
FLOP
GRR
GRR
SNAP
SNAP
SNAP
SNAP
NOT BAD, BOOKWORM.
THANKS...
AAAAHH
CRAP, THAT'S CASHEW!

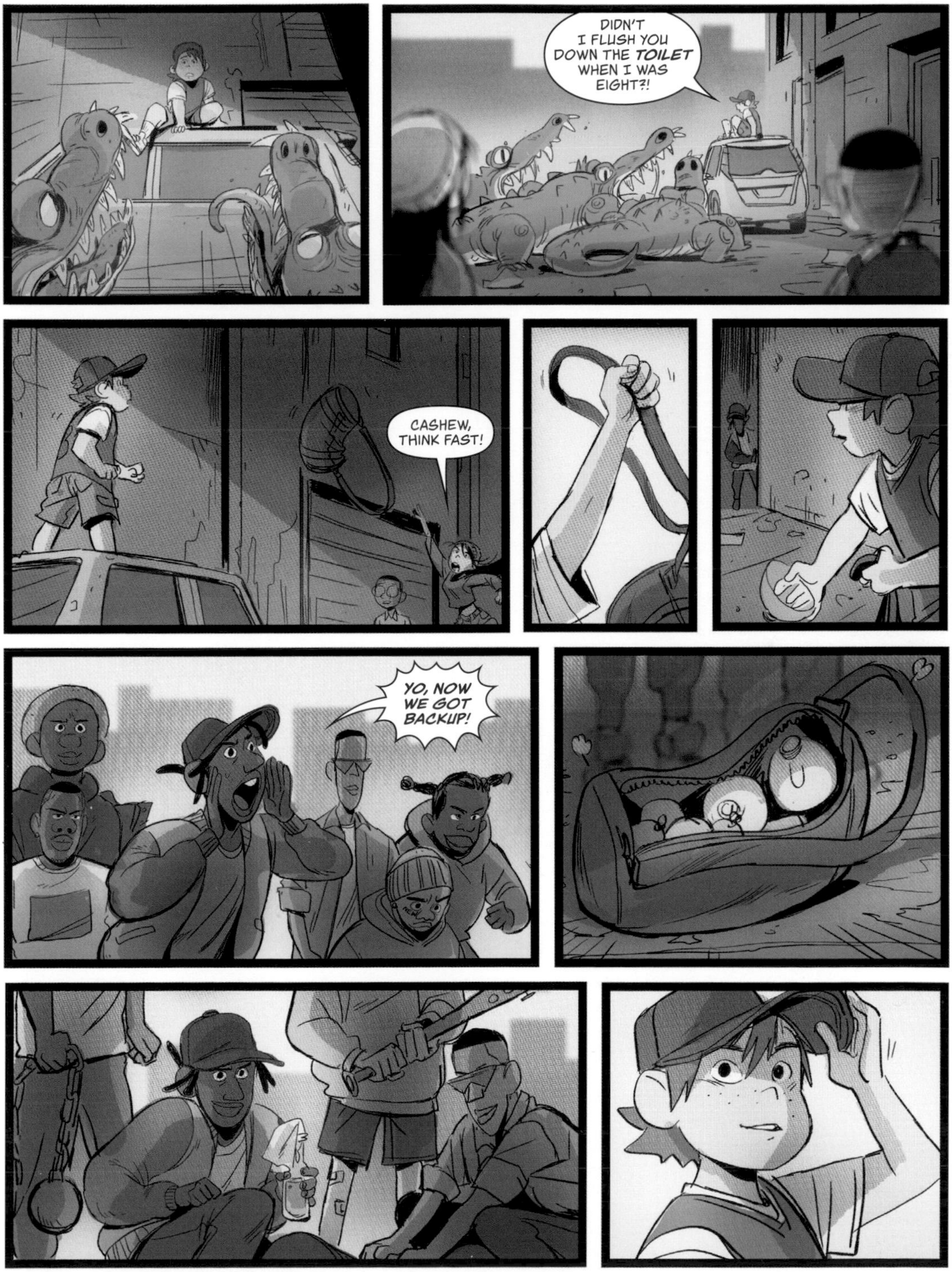
DIDN'T I FLUSH YOU DOWN THE TOILET WHEN I WAS EIGHT?!
CASHEW, THINK FAST!
YO, NOW WE GOT BACKUP!

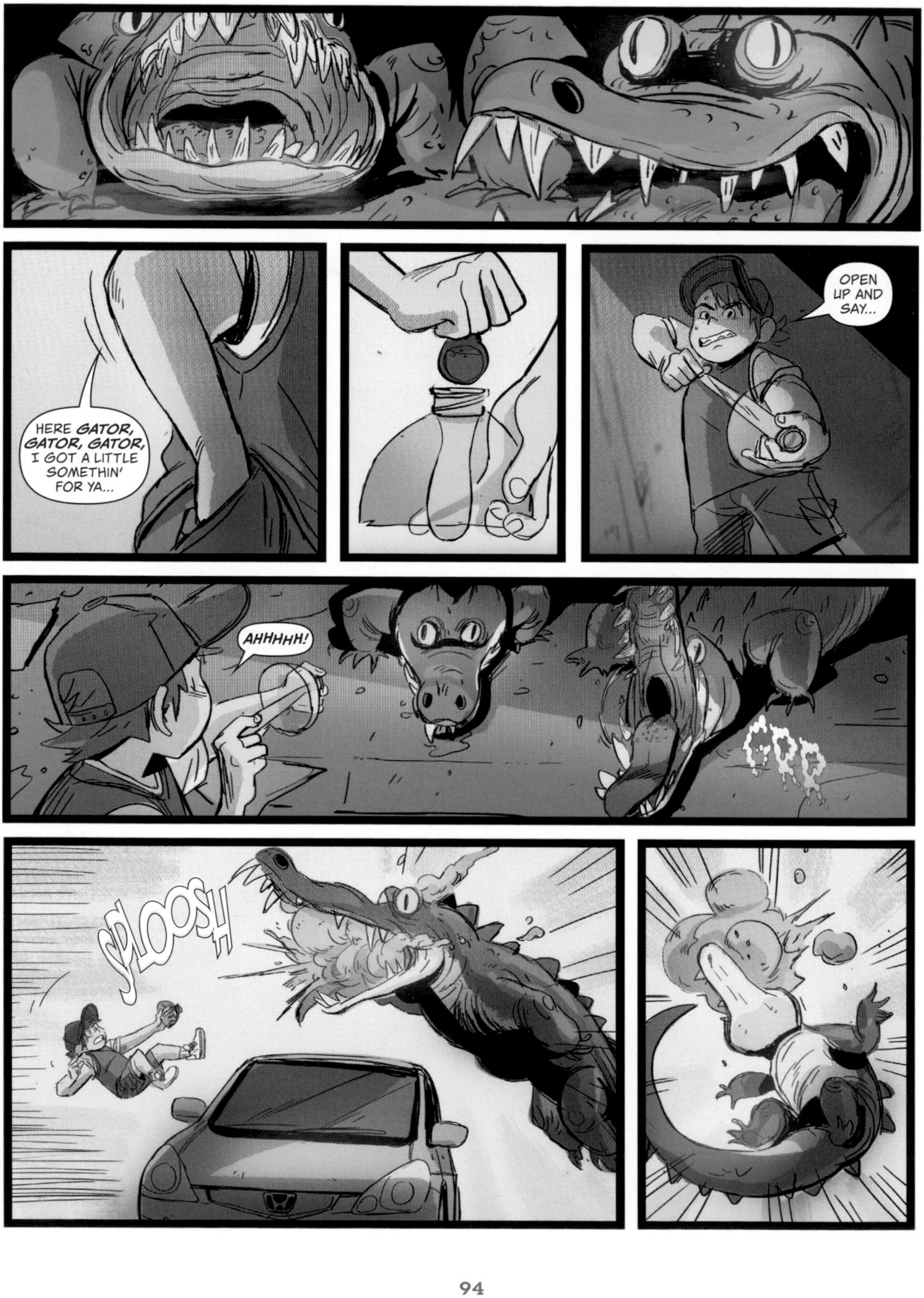
HERE GATOR, GATOR, GATOR, I GOT A LITTLE SOMETHIN' FOR YA...
OPEN UP AND SAY...
AHHHHH!
GRR
SPLOOSH

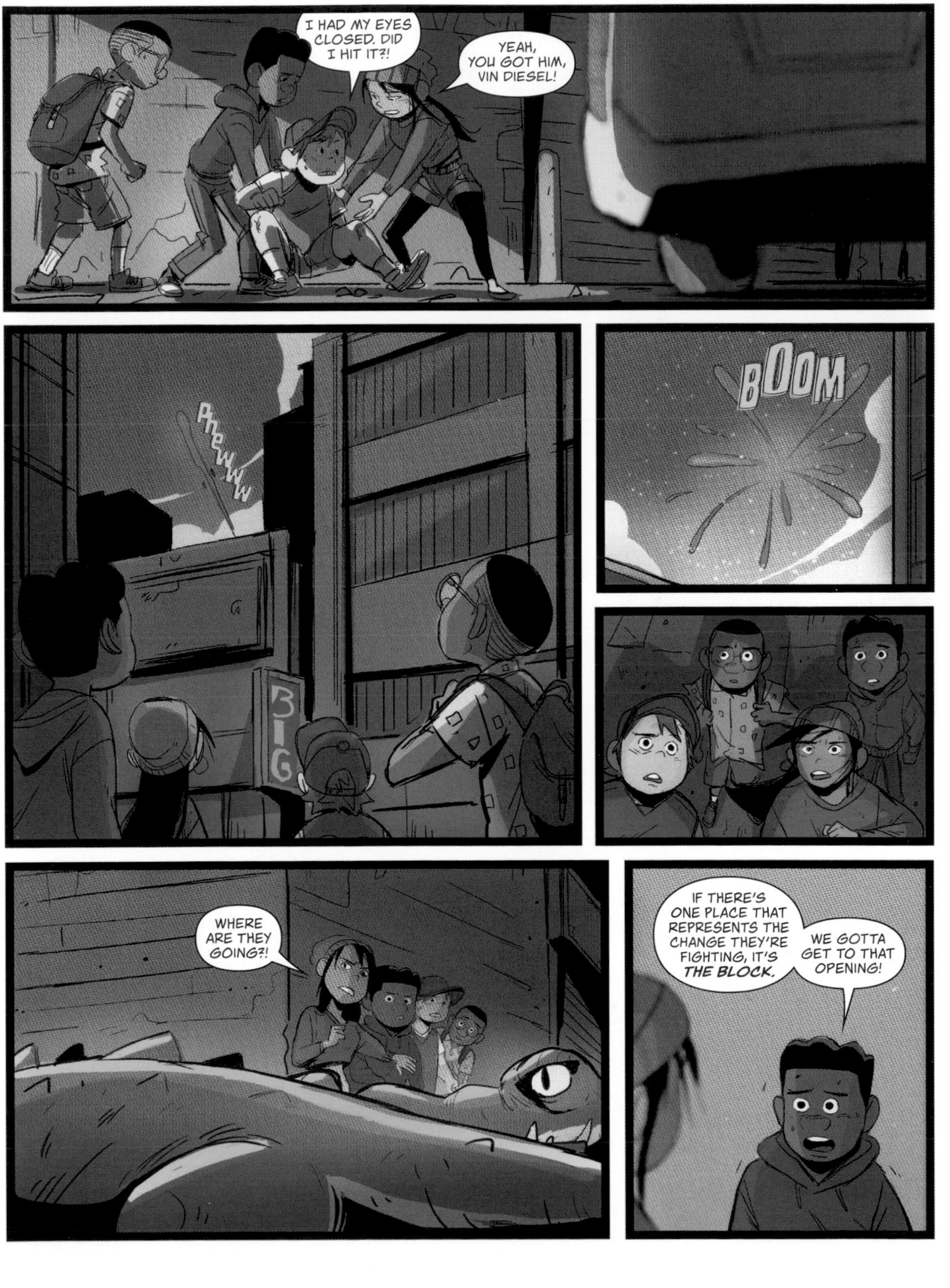
I HAD MY EYES CLOSED. DID I HIT IT?!
YEAH, YOU GOT HIM, VIN DIESEL!
PHEWWW
BOOM
BIG
WHERE ARE THEY GOING?!
IF THERE'S ONE PLACE THAT REPRESENTS THE CHANGE THEY'RE FIGHTING, IT'S *THE BLOCK.*
WE GOTTA GET TO THAT OPENING!

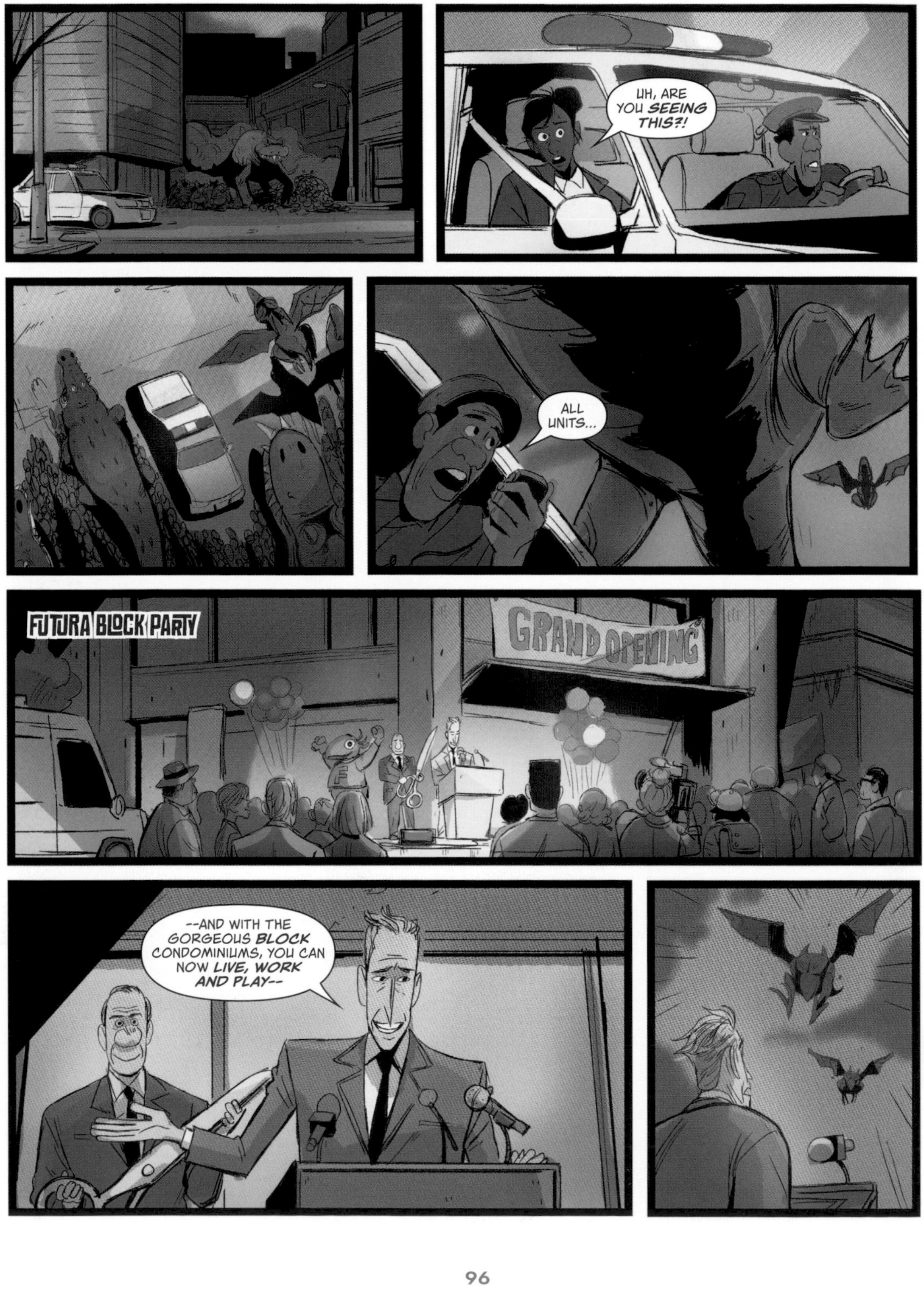
UH, ARE YOU SEEING THIS?!
ALL UNITS...
FUTURA BLOCK PARTY
GRAND OPENING
--AND WITH THE GORGEOUS BLOCK CONDOMINIUMS, YOU CAN NOW LIVE, WORK AND PLAY--

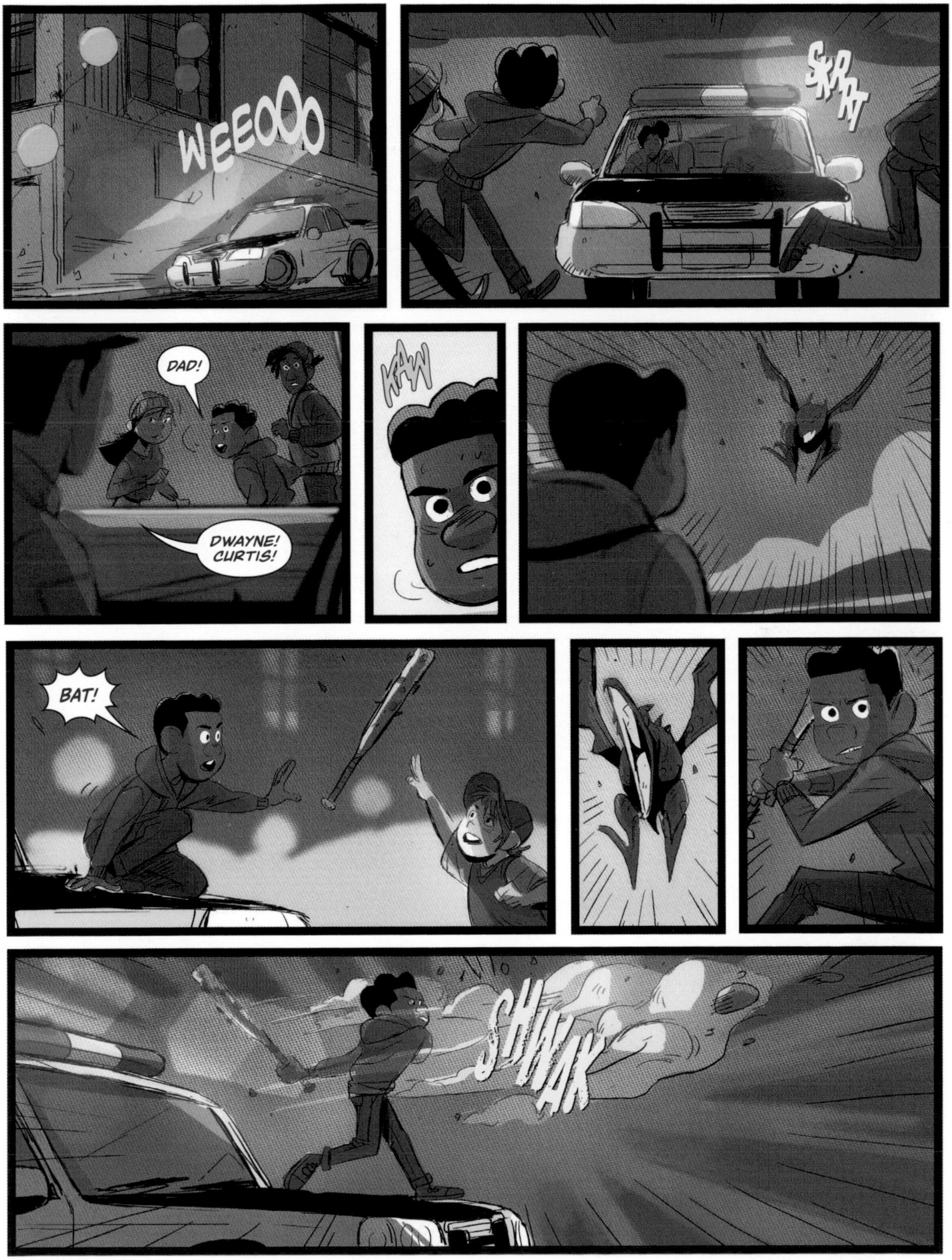
WEEOOO
SKRRT
DAD!
DWAYNE! CURTIS!
KAW
BAT!
SHWAK

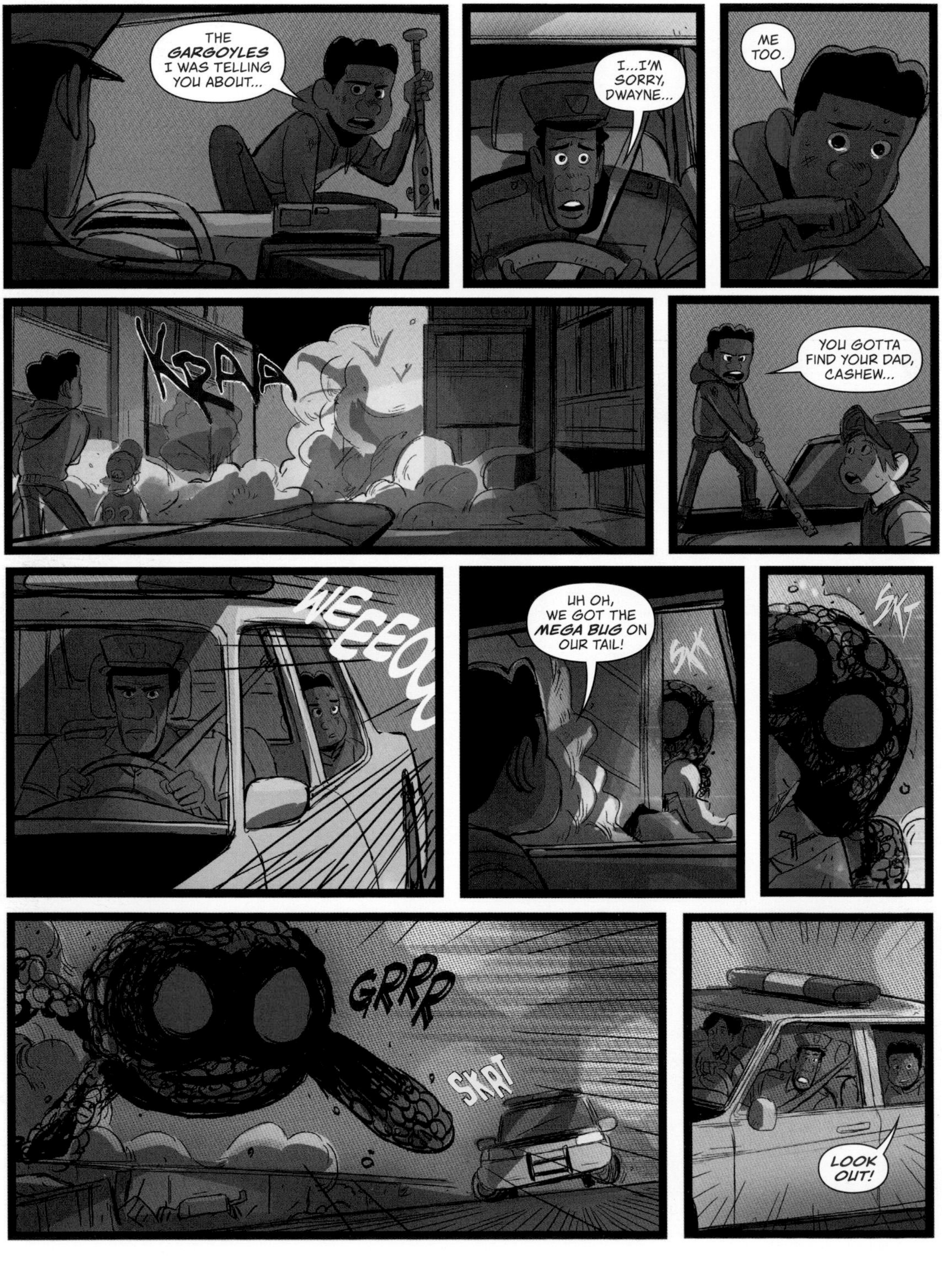
THE GARGOYLES I WAS TELLING YOU ABOUT...
I...I'M SORRY, DWAYNE...
ME TOO.
KRAA
YOU GOTTA FIND YOUR DAD, CASHEW...
WEEEOOO
UH OH, WE GOT THE MEGA BUG ON OUR TAIL!
SKK
SKT
GRRR
SKRT
LOOK OUT!

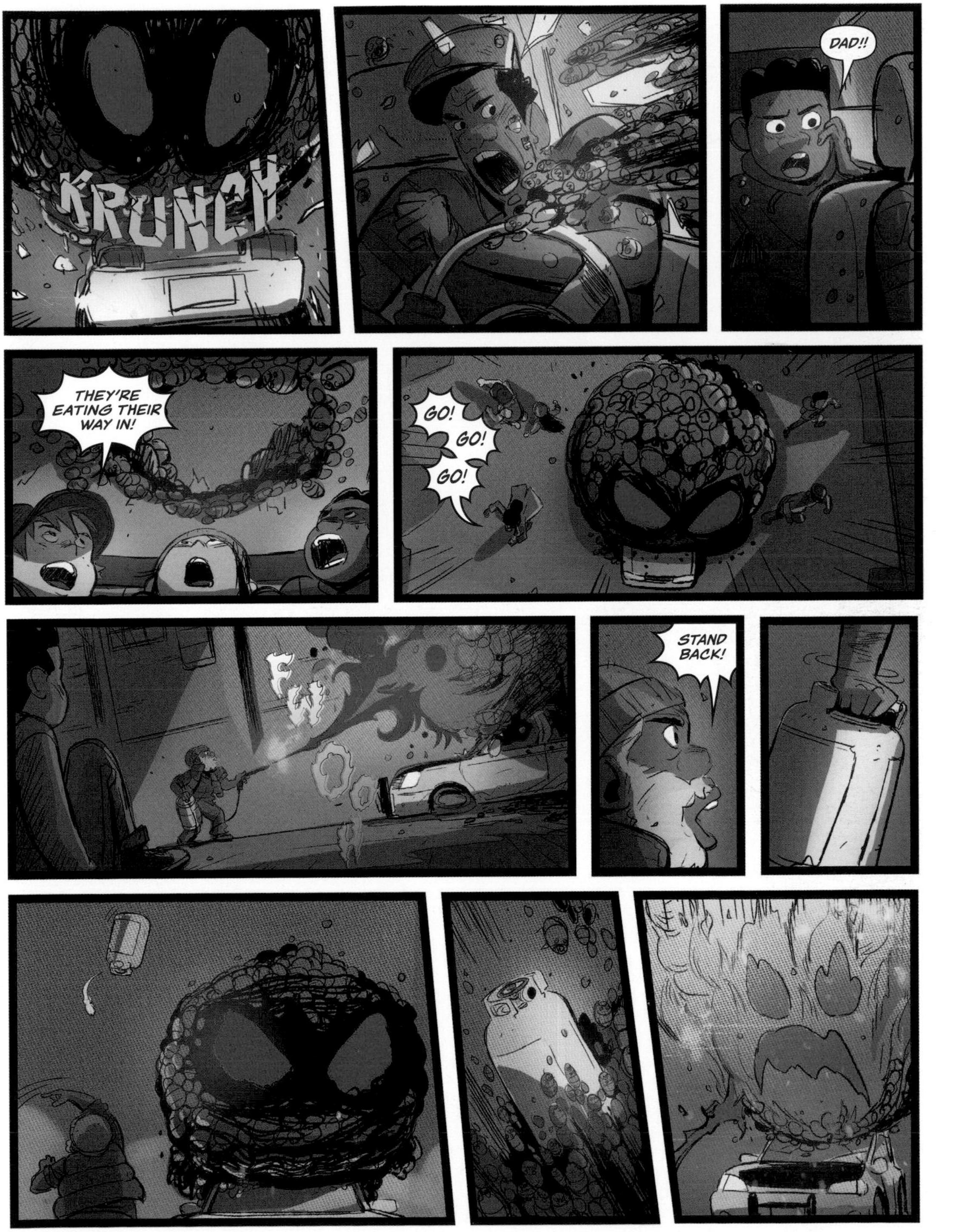
KRUNCH
DAD!!
THEY'RE EATING THEIR WAY IN!
GO!
GO!
GO!
STAND BACK!

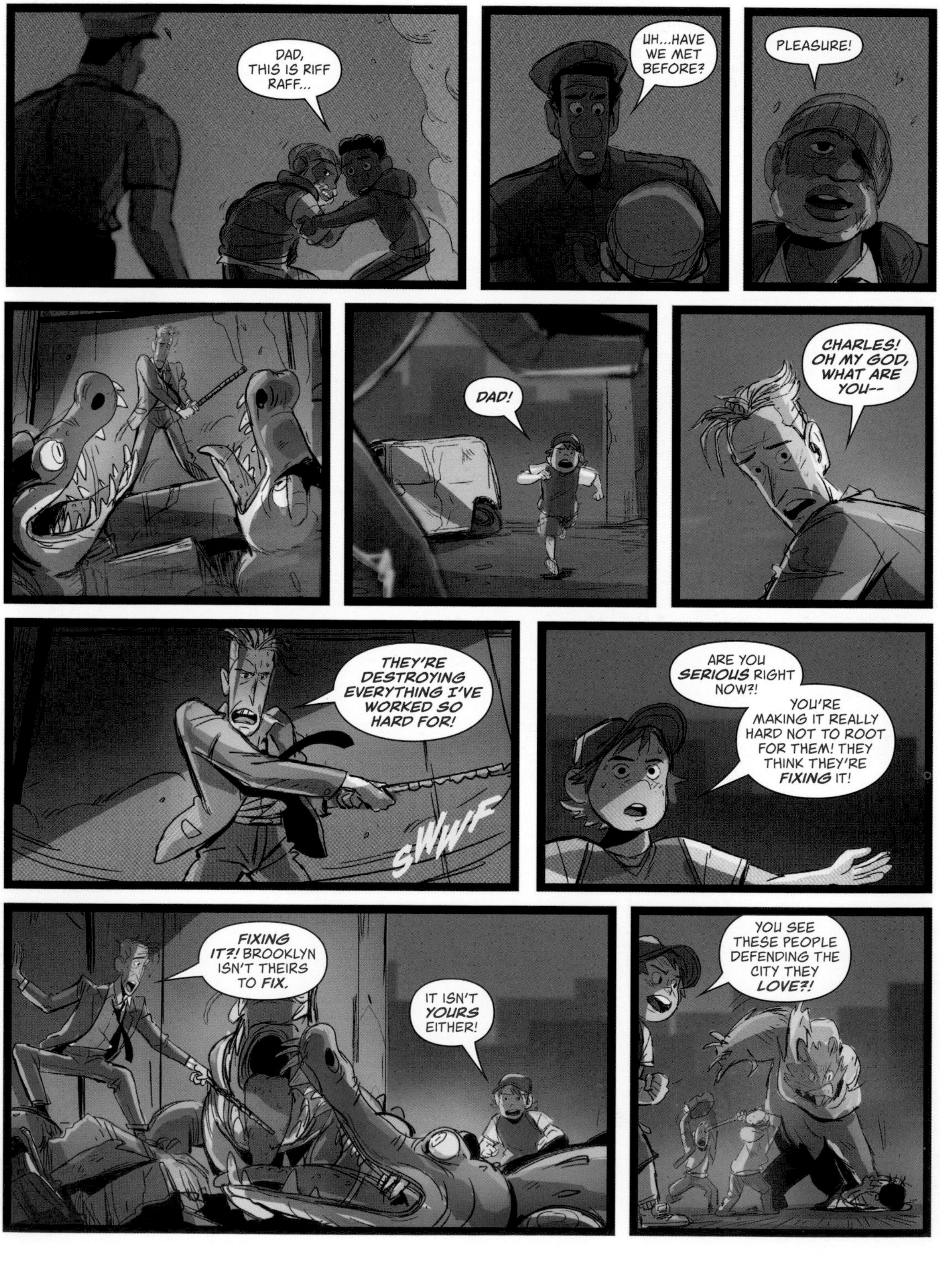
DAD, THIS IS RIFF RAFF...
UH...HAVE WE MET BEFORE?
PLEASURE!
DAD!
CHARLES! OH MY GOD, WHAT ARE YOU--
THEY'RE DESTROYING EVERYTHING I'VE WORKED SO HARD FOR!
SWWF
ARE YOU SERIOUS RIGHT NOW?!
YOU'RE MAKING IT REALLY HARD NOT TO ROOT FOR THEM! THEY THINK THEY'RE FIXING IT!
FIXING IT?! BROOKLYN ISN'T THEIRS TO FIX.
IT ISN'T YOURS EITHER!
YOU SEE THESE PEOPLE DEFENDING THE CITY THEY LOVE?!

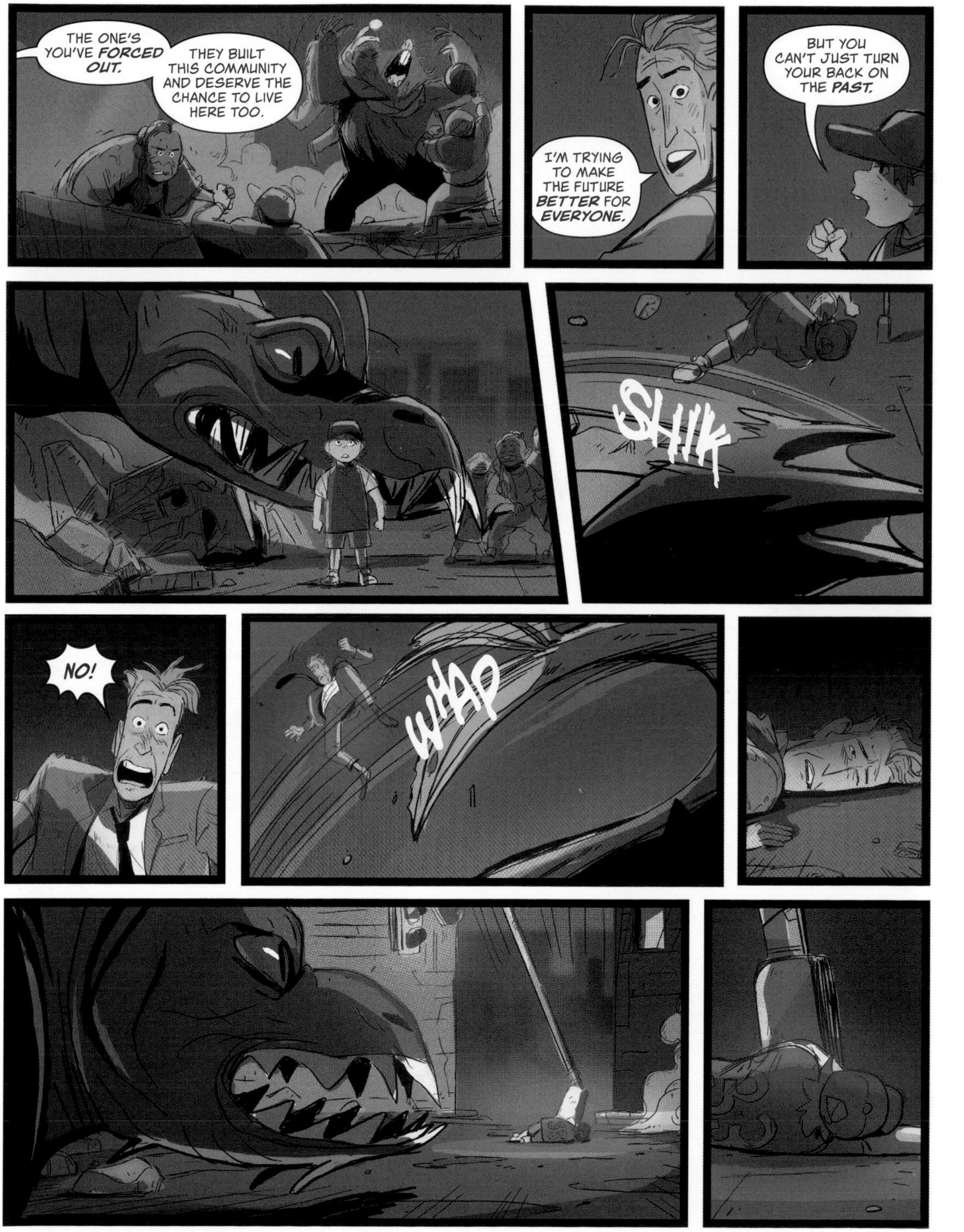
THE ONE'S YOU'VE FORCED OUT.
THEY BUILT THIS COMMUNITY AND DESERVE THE CHANCE TO LIVE HERE TOO.
I'M TRYING TO MAKE THE FUTURE BETTER FOR EVERYONE.
BUT YOU CAN'T JUST TURN YOUR BACK ON THE PAST.
SHIK
NO!
WHAP

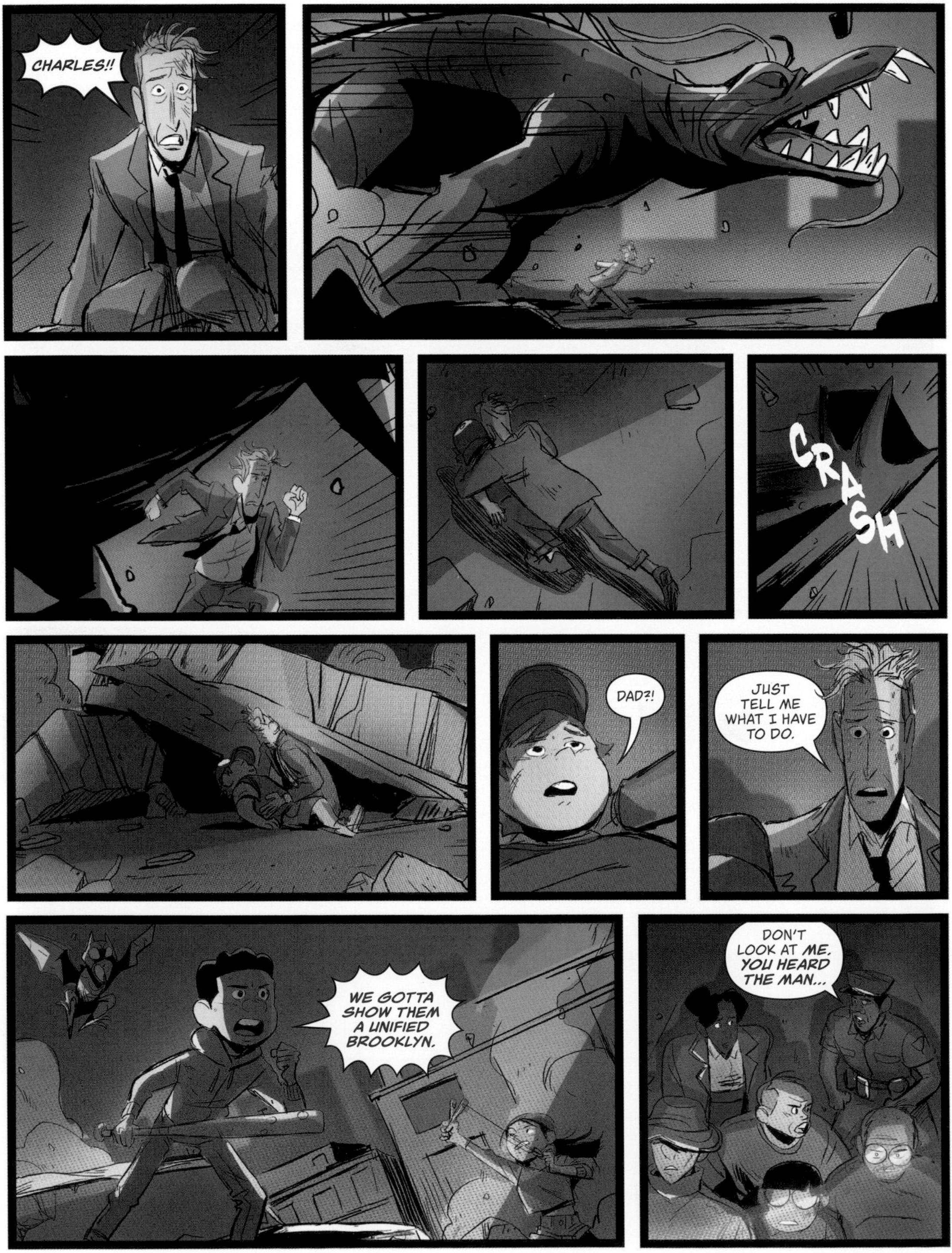
CHARLES!!
CRASH
DAD?!
JUST TELL ME WHAT I HAVE TO DO.
WE GOTTA SHOW THEM A UNIFIED BROOKLYN.
DON'T LOOK AT ME. YOU HEARD THE MAN...

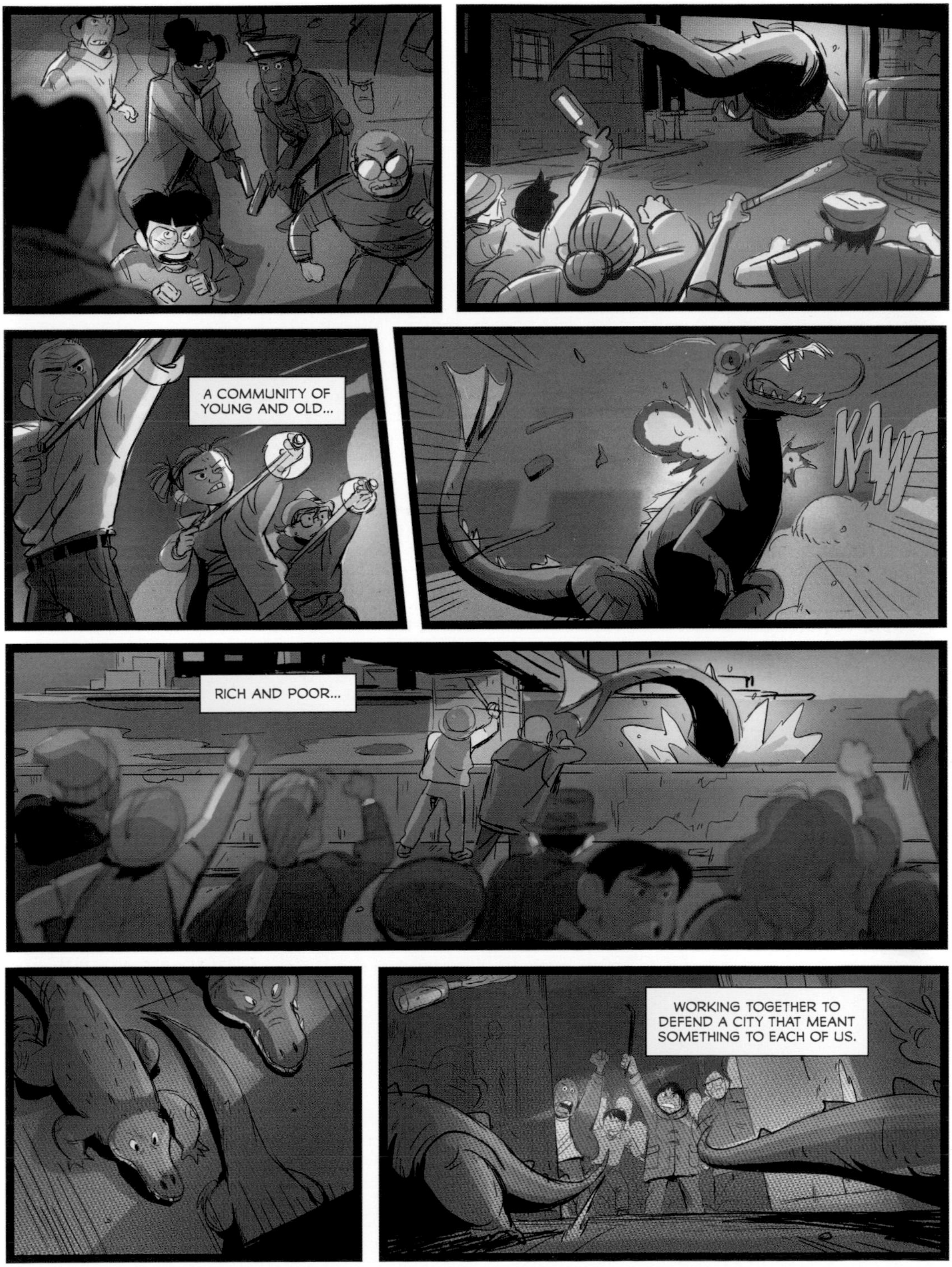
A COMMUNITY OF YOUNG AND OLD...
KAW
RICH AND POOR...
WORKING TOGETHER TO DEFEND A CITY THAT MEANT SOMETHING TO EACH OF US.

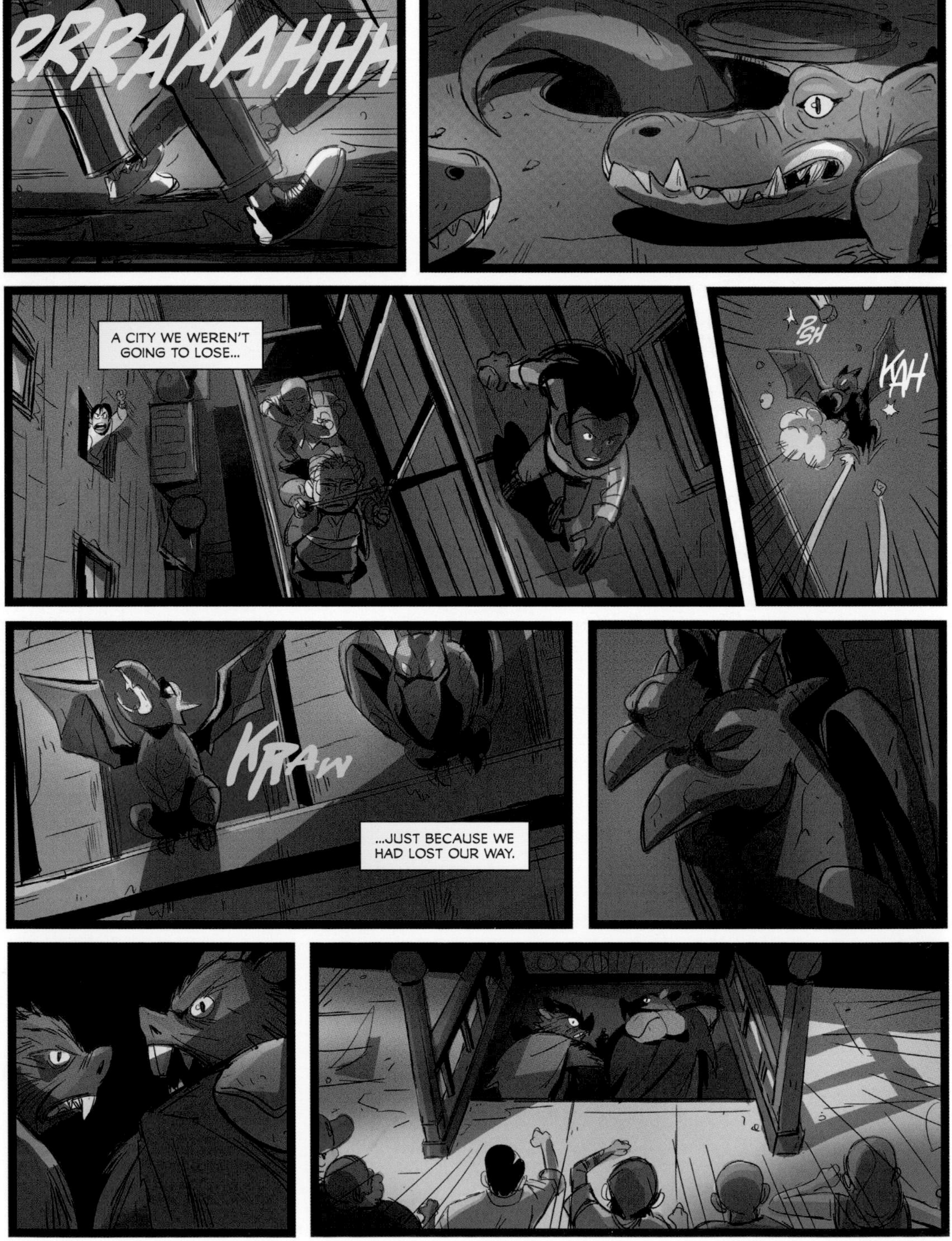
RRRAAAHHH
A CITY WE WEREN'T GOING TO LOSE...
PSH
KAH
KRAW
...JUST BECAUSE WE HAD LOST OUR WAY.

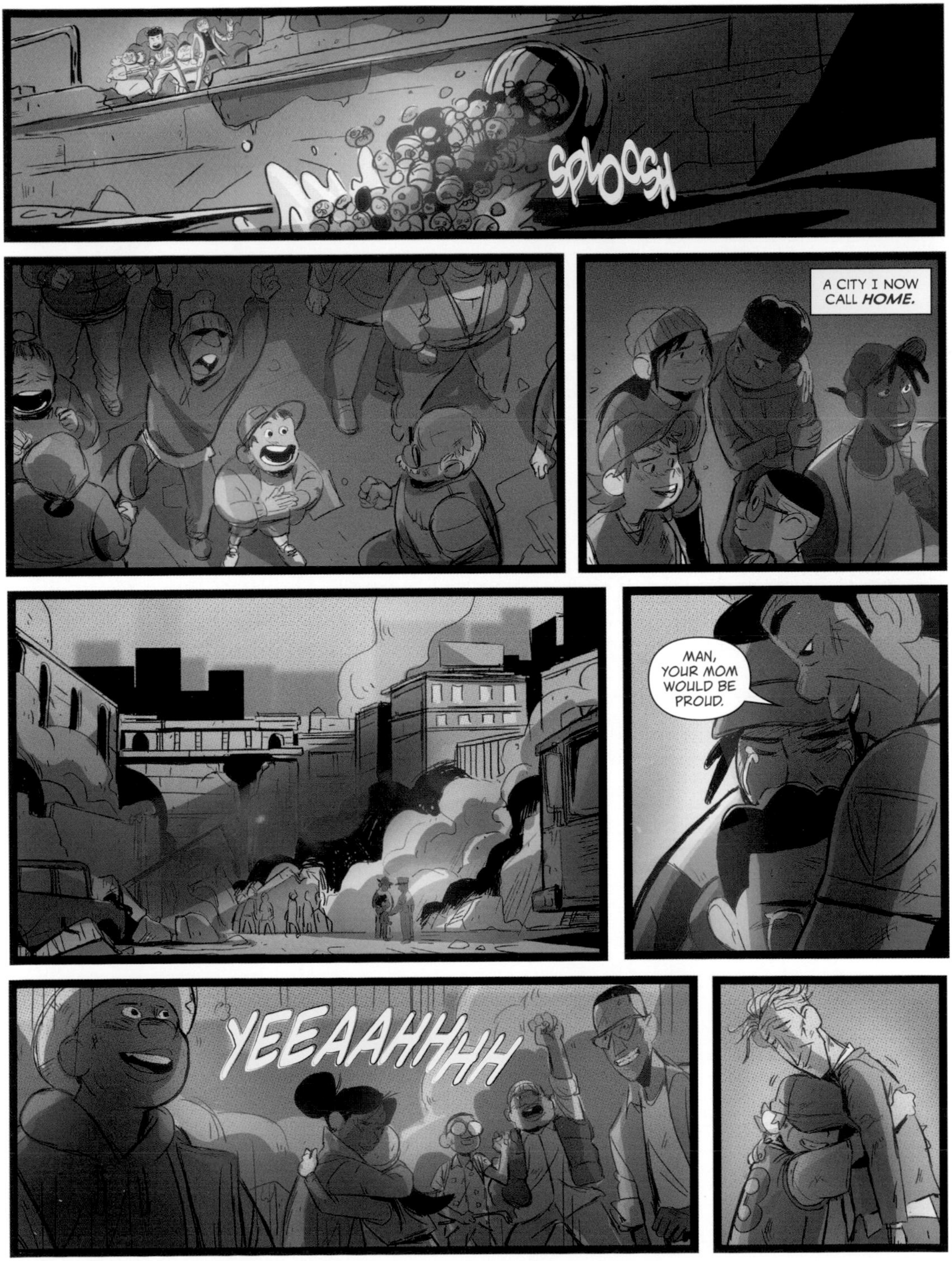
SPLOOSH
A CITY I NOW CALL *HOME.*
MAN, YOUR MOM WOULD BE PROUD.
YEEAAHHHH

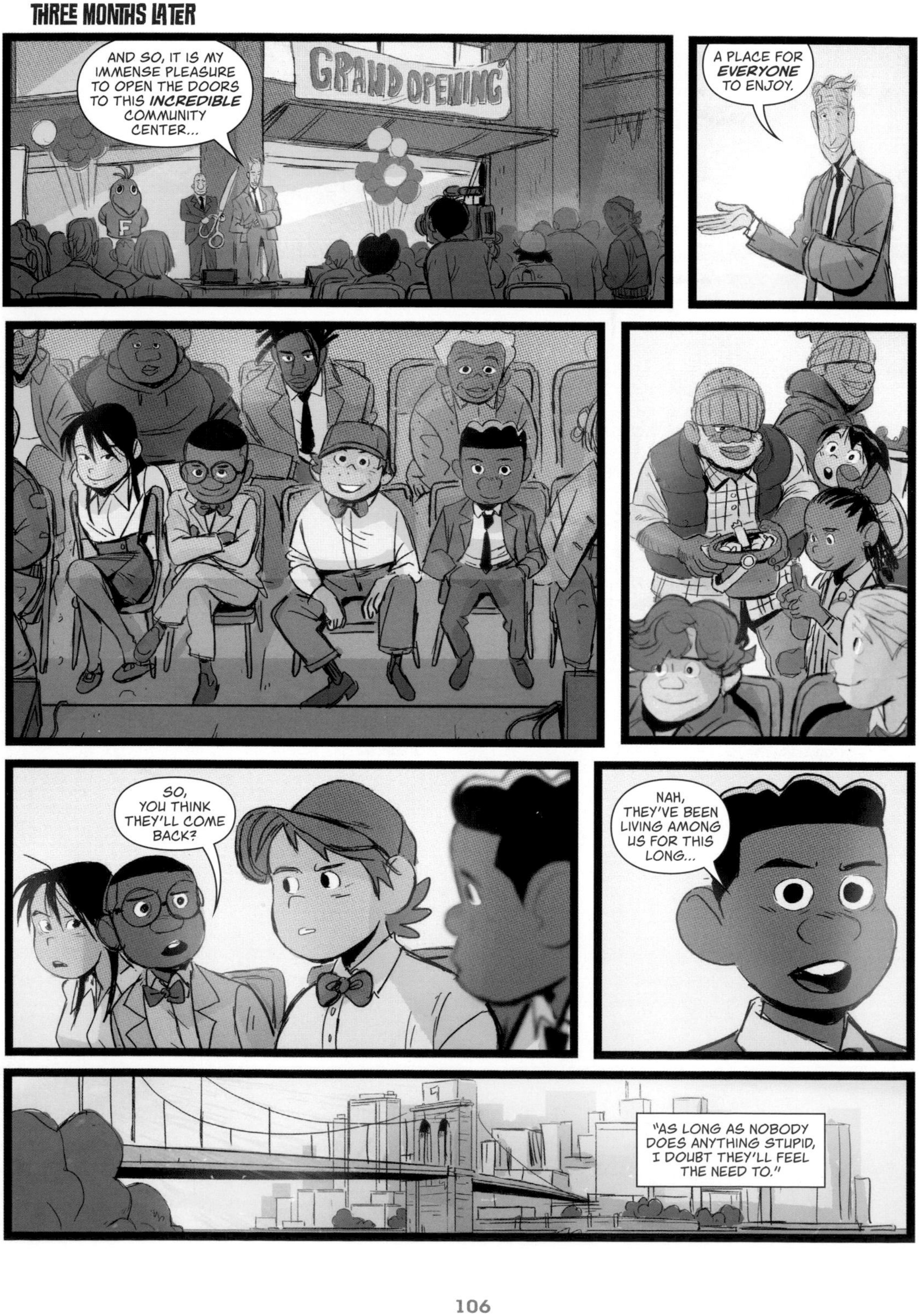
THREE MONTHS LATER
GRAND OPENING
AND SO, IT IS MY IMMENSE PLEASURE TO OPEN THE DOORS TO THIS INCREDIBLE COMMUNITY CENTER...
A PLACE FOR EVERYONE TO ENJOY.
SO, YOU THINK THEY'LL COME BACK?
NAH, THEY'VE BEEN LIVING AMONG US FOR THIS LONG...
"AS LONG AS NOBODY DOES ANYTHING STUPID, I DOUBT THEY'LL FEEL THE NEED TO."

CONEY ISLAND, NY

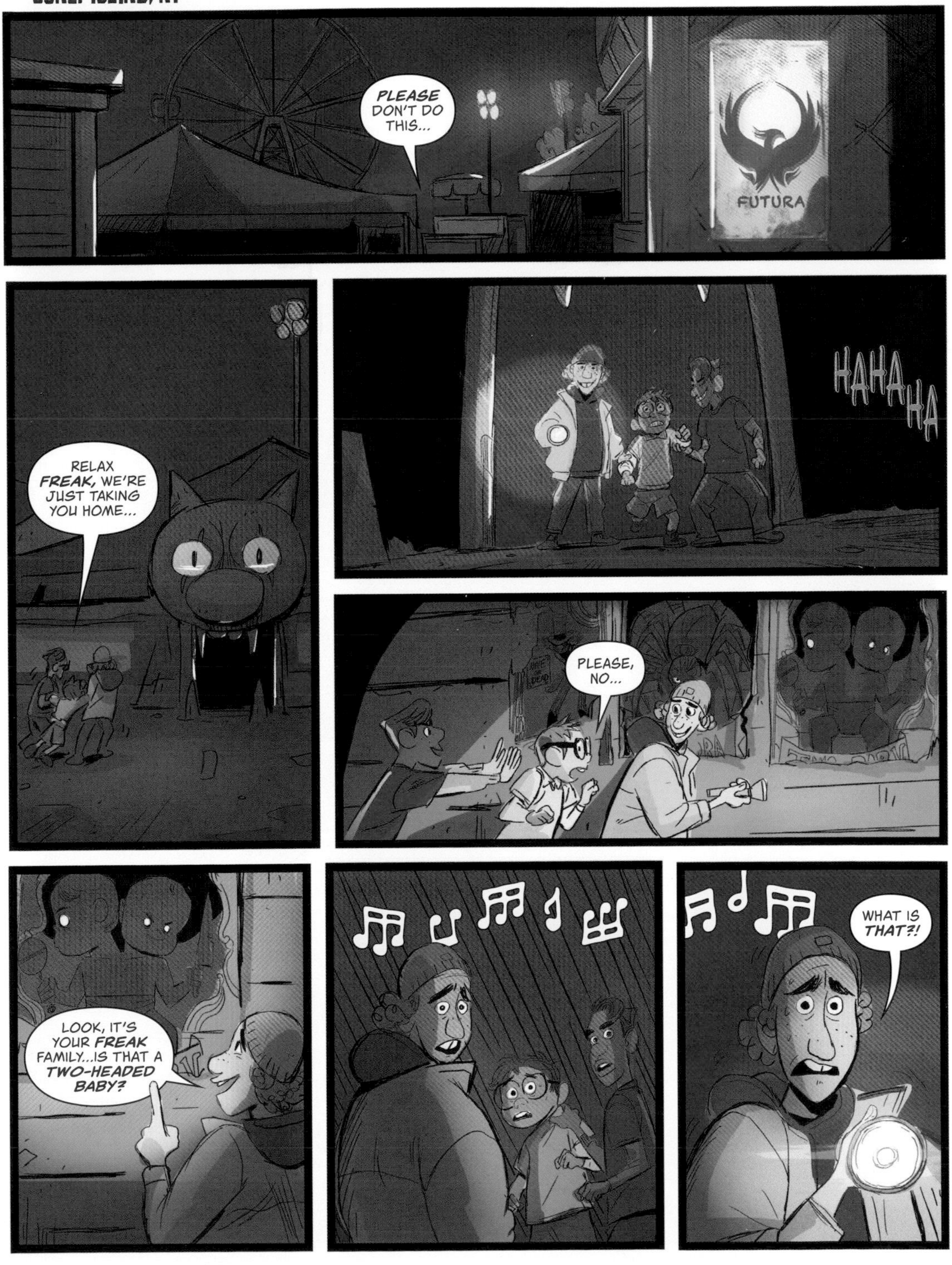
PLEASE DON'T DO THIS...
FUTURA
RELAX FREAK, WE'RE JUST TAKING YOU HOME...
HAHAHAHA
PLEASE, NO...
LOOK, IT'S YOUR FREAK FAMILY...IS THAT A TWO-HEADED BABY?
WHAT IS THAT?!

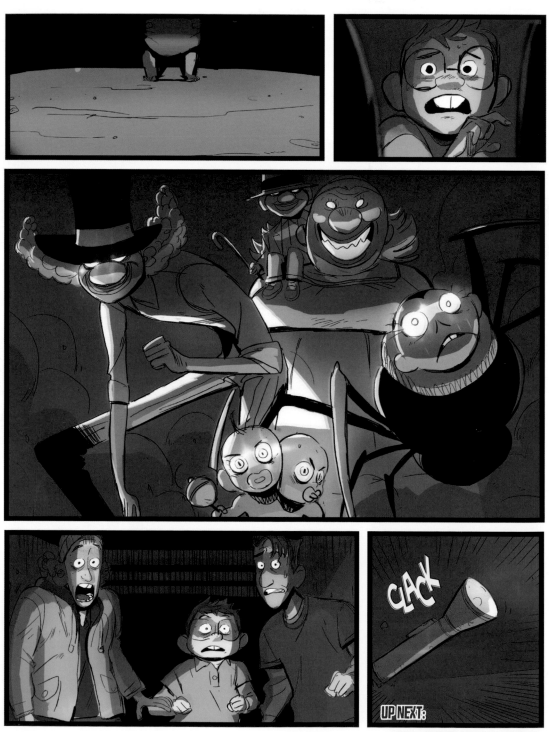

UP NEXT:

CONEY ISLAND CIRCUS FREAKS

BONUS

URBAN LEGENDZ

ASSEMBLING A CREW

When assembling your own neighborhood crew, you must first figure out everyone's strengths. Here's a snapshot of the unique qualities each of our heroes brings to the Urban Legendz crew.

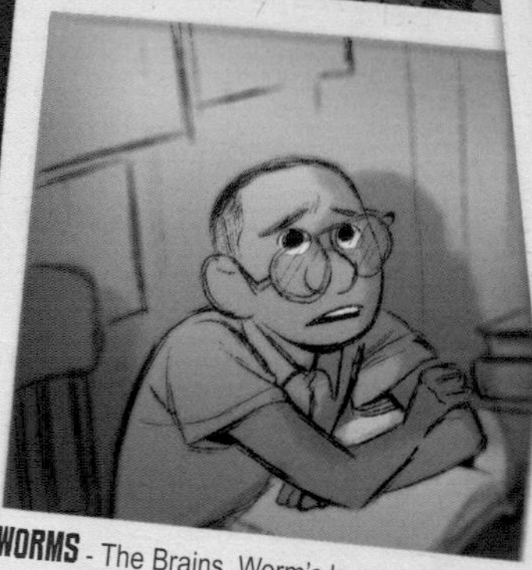

WORMS - The Brains. Worm's love of math and science, in addition to a huge collection of science fiction, make him a huge asset to the team.

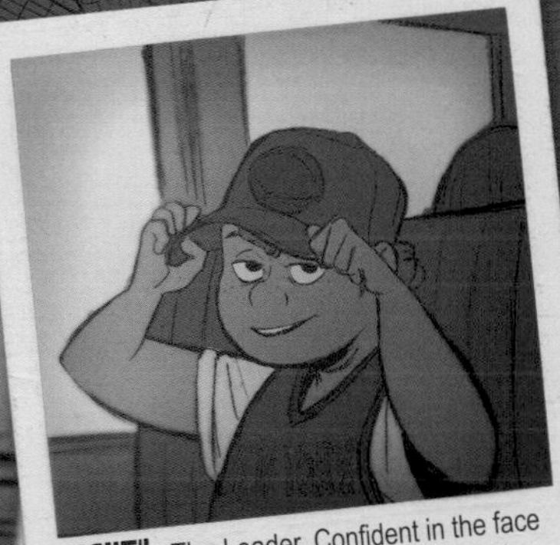

CASHEW - The Leader. Confident in the face of danger, Cashew is forever willing to step up and defend what he loves. Even if he gets hurt along the way.

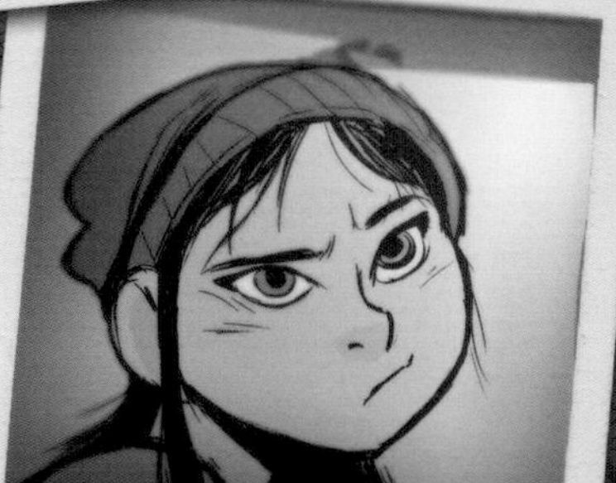

MYA - The Strength. Street smart and outspoken, Mya's knowledge of neighborhood factions, graffiti, music and breakdancing brings authenticity to the crew.

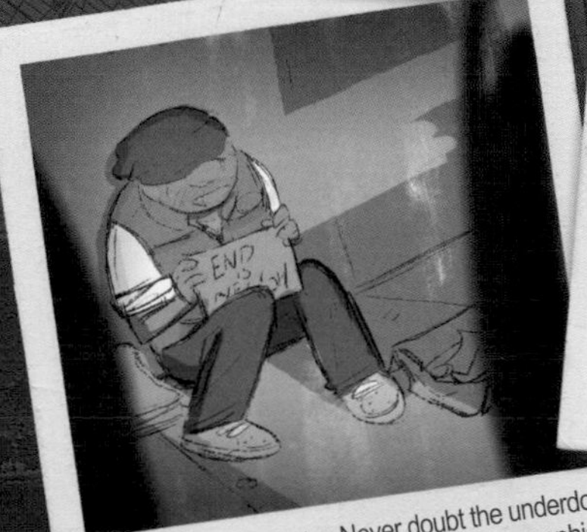

RIFF RAFF - The Mentor. Never doubt the underdog. Riff Raff's knowledge of Brooklyn, its demographic, history and future make him the perfect source of insight.

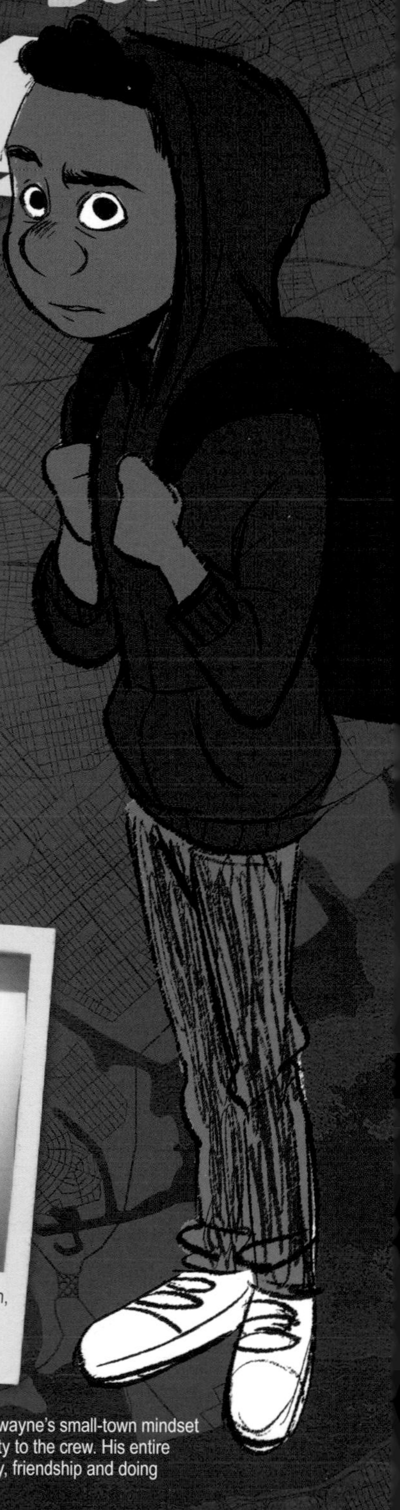

DWAYNE - The Heart. Dwayne's small-town mindset brings a level of sincerity to the crew. His entire world is driven by family, friendship and doing what's right.

WELCOME TO BROOKLYN

WILLIAMSBURG

Giant bedbugs come out at night in this quiet part of the borough, mainly known for its Orthodox Jewish population. There, Yiddish is the first language, though in recent years, more young professionals have made this area their favorite place to live in.

BROOKLYN BRIDGE PARK

The night Dwayne's dad starts his new job, he's at this location, where a giant monster footprint has been found.

CLINTON HILL

This is where Dwayne and his family live. Rapper Notorious B.I.G. was also from this neighborhood (after he died, a mural was painted at 1091 Bedford Ave as an homage).

GOWANUS CANAL

This little canal is located at the border of the Gowanus, Caroll Gardens and Red Hook areas of Brooklyn. Our heroes have set their HQ there. A former industrial neighborhood, Gowanus has morphed into a more artistic area in recent years.

CONEY ISLAND

At the very end of our book, we meet the Circus Freaks for the first time. They come from Coney Island. Originally a real island, the peninsula is located on the tail end of Brooklyn and was connected to the mainland in 1824. Since the late 19th century, it's been home to one of the oldest amusement parks in the United States!

BONUS

URBAN LEGENDZ

BEDFORD-STUYVESANT

This is the third most populated neighborhood in Brooklyn. Though historically an African-American neighborhood, other ethnic groups have begun to populate this area. This is where the alligator first comes out of the toilet in our story!

Brooklyn, home of the Urban Legendz, is one of New York City's 5 boroughs (along with Manhattan, the Bronx, Queens and Staten Island). It's also the largest, with nearly 2.7 million residents—making it the second most densely populated county in the United States!

Brooklyn is connected to Manhattan by the Manhattan Bridge (1909), the Brooklyn Bridge (1823) and the Williamsburg Bridge (1903). The Verrazzano-Narrows Bridge (1964) connects Brooklyn to Staten Island, and the Kosciuszko Bridge (1939) connects it to Queens.

DID YOU KNOW?

BROOKLYN WAS FOUNDED IN 1636 UNDER THE NAME "BREUCKELEN." IT WAS FIRST A DUTCH COLONY WITH 6 VILLAGES, WHICH HAVE SINCE TRANSFORMED INTO MORE THAN 60 NEIGHBOR-HOODS! BROOKLYN BECAME A BOROUGH OF NEW YORK CITY IN 1898.

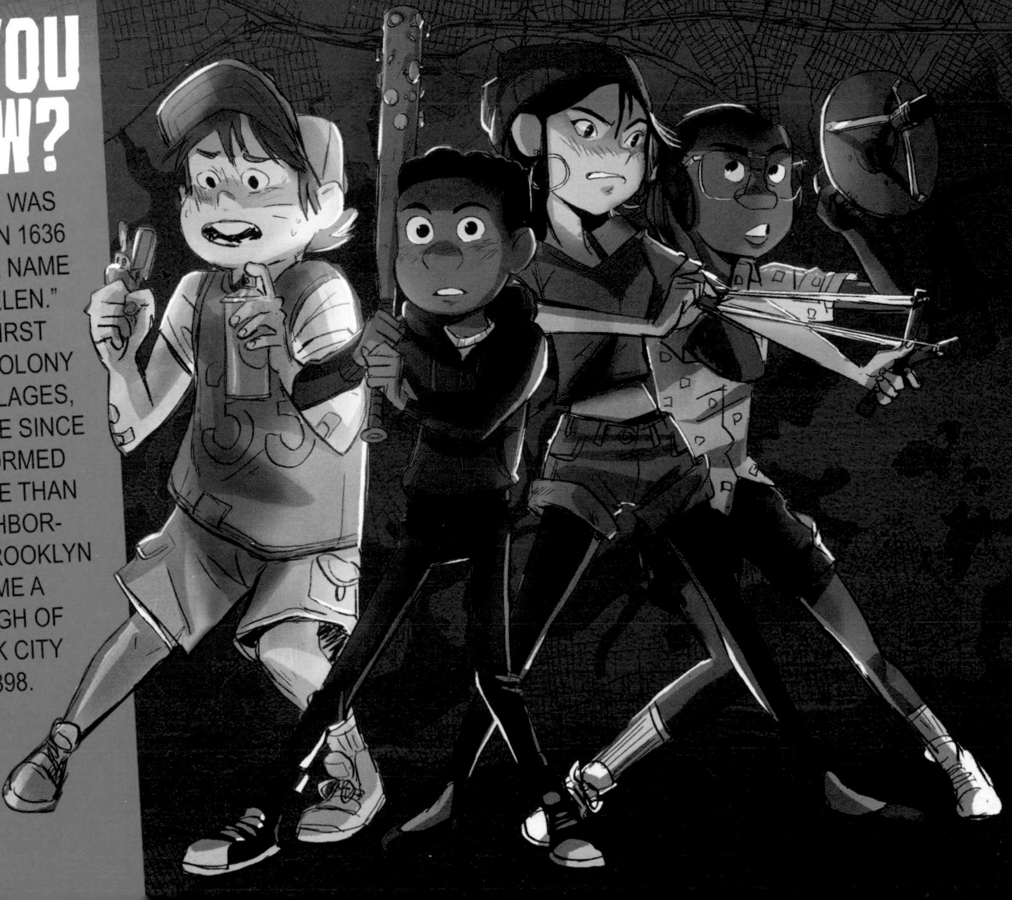

URBAN LEGENDZ

BONUS

BEHIND THE SCENES WITH THE CREATORS

In order to develop the book's visual style and communicate our vision, Michael created these *Urban Legendz* poster images. Although the art style changed a bit, these really helped set the tone for the project.

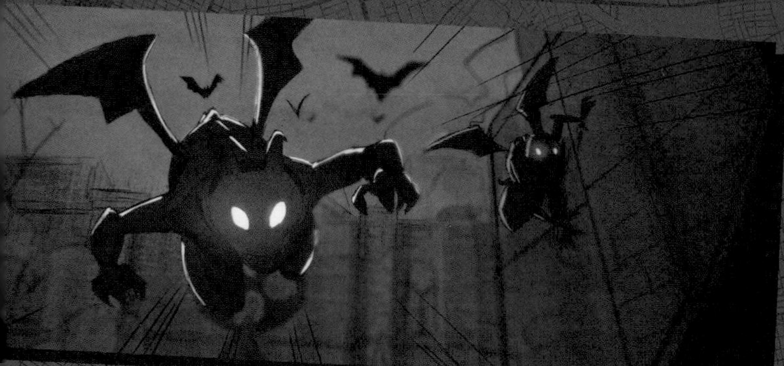

Living Gargoyles terrorizing the neighborhood!

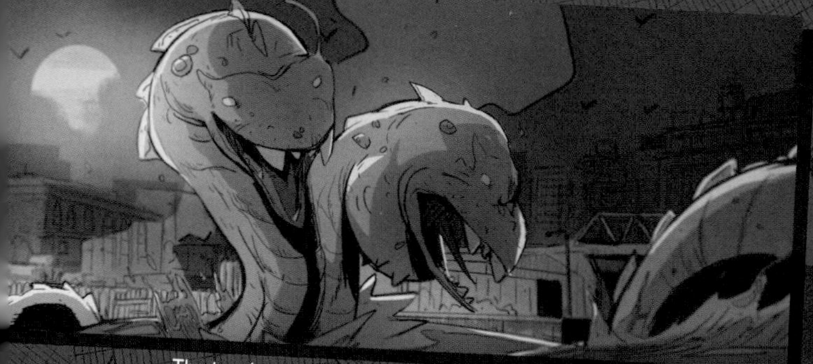

The two-headed Gowanus Canal Monster emerging from the sludge!

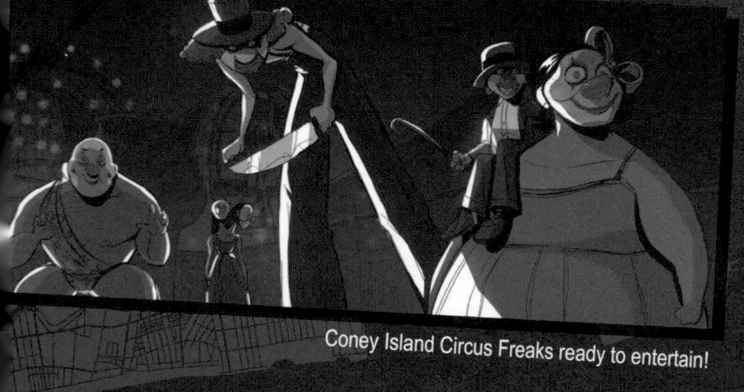

Coney Island Circus Freaks ready to entertain!

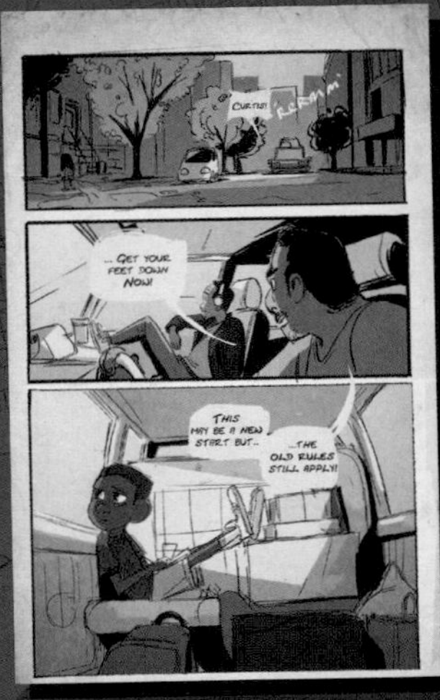
CURTIS!
... GET YOUR FEET DOWN NOW!
THIS MAY BE A NEW START BUT...
...THE OLD RULES STILL APPLY!

Immediately after reading the first *Urban Legendz* outline, Michael started to visualize. This was one of the first images he produced.

This was the first cover that Michael developed in order to sell the idea. We loved the colors and the eerie feel.

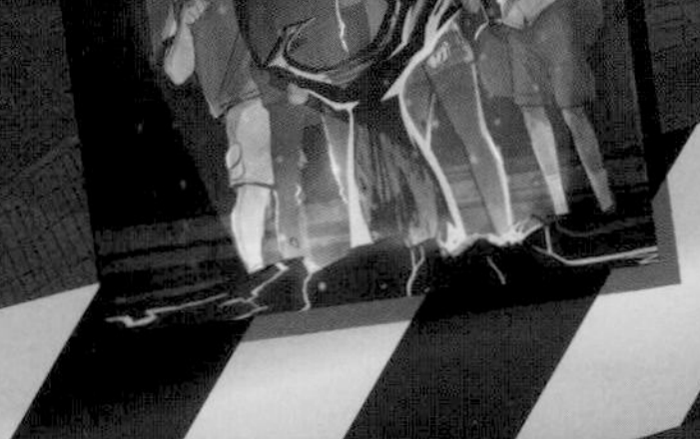
THE URBAN LEGENDZ